Josh's expression was one of incredu[illegible]d on the car fender to take the weight from his leg. "Christ! You're going to investigate on your own! What chutzpah! You have no authority here. Where the hell would you start?"

"*We* start with Emma Mosel's roommate."

Josh shook his head. "Let's be realistic. I don't know about you, but I've been out of it too long. I've . . . we've got a business to run. I'm no longer a legman." Nevertheless, despite the protestations, he felt the adrenaline flowing. He moved off the fender, unsure of what was going through his mind.

Chelsea waited until they were both seated. "Josh, do you feel old? So old that all you can do is direct men to watch monitors?"

"You want me to be frank? I say yes. It's been ten years. I don't know whether I can cope with police work again."

"And you've lost all taste for the chase? I can't believe it. What happened to Blue Jay Two? Has he retired to a lounge chair, maybe playing shuffleboard with the neighbors?"

Josh winced. "You think running my firm is a slow death? I started it from scratch and . . ." He halted, realizing he was being baited. "Christ! Joe! Don't do this to me." He banged the steering wheel, then suddenly laughed aloud. A couple walking to their car stared at him as if he were drunk. "Oh, Jesus!" he exclaimed, "God help me! Why not!"

SUNSET DETECTIVES

HERMAN WEISS

BERKLEY PRIME CRIME, NEW YORK

SUNSET DETECTIVES

A Berkley Prime Crime Book / published by arrangement with the author

PRINTING HISTORY
Berkley Prime Crime edition / October 1996

For information address: The Berkley Publishing Group, 200 Madison Avenue, New York, NY 10016.

The Putnam Berkley World Wide Web site address is
http://www.berkley.com

ISBN: 0-425-15514-5

Berkley Prime Crime Books are published
by The Berkley Publishing Group,
200 Madison Avenue, New York, NY 10016.

PRINTED IN THE UNITED STATES OF AMERICA

10 9 8 7 6 5 4 3 2 1

For Viola and Paula
Two octogenarians who continue to be young in spirit

1

DELRAY BEACH, FLORIDA
MID-OCTOBER, 1990

"What's wrong with it, Joe?"

"With the apartment? Nothing."

"So, why the face? I thought we'd decided."

The realtor, a frail man in his late fifties, eyed them knowingly. "We do have less expensive apartments but this is the last end-unit."

Joe Chelsea's gray eyes flashed briefly. "Have we discussed any financial arrangement as yet?"

Unconsciously the agent took a step backward, suddenly intimidated by this tall, barrel-chested client. "Of course not. I merely assumed . . ."

"It would be an egregious error to assume anything prematurely—if at all."

The agent fingered the too-large collar of his shirt and reminded himself this prospective client was a retired police captain of detectives. From New York no less. "Yes, you're quite right." He hesitated a moment. "Is there anything more I can show you?"

Chelsea looked at his wife. "Ellie, does the kitchen meet with your approval?"

After thirty-five years of marriage Ellen Chelsea knew her husband's moods well. A virile man, and in almost perfect health despite his sixty-six years, even after one year he had yet to adjust to retirement. The health spa, deep-sea fishing, and an occasional stab at golf did little to alleviate his moods of ennui. The move to Florida had been Ellie's idea of readjustment, although Joe's younger, former partner, Josh Novick—retired prematurely because of a medical disability—had been an added catalyst. She could tell, however, that Joe wasn't completely sold on the idea.

Ellen gave her husband a reassuring smile, then turned to the agent. "I'd like to go over the appliances once again."

Chelsea walked through the living-dining room to sliding-glass doors that opened onto a terrace. He leaned against the wrought-iron railing that overlooked the pool four stories below and the wide beach bordering the ocean beyond. The beach conjured up a vision of another time, on another shore, saturated with bodies. . . .

He shook his head, erasing those memories. Below him royal palms reached upward, their fronds waving in a slight breeze, as if informing him this wasn't Omaha Beach. Clusters of green coconuts looked like grapes ripe for picking. About a quarter of the chaise longues surrounding the kidney-shaped pool were occupied by idle sun-worshippers. Off to one side, beside a hedgerow of flowering hibiscus—*Why did he think of it as a hedgerow?*—on a well-kept lawn, card players sat at umbrellaed tables. He noted, with cynical amusement, that no one took advantage of the clear blue water rippling in the pool.

His glance centered on a table with four men—all middle-aged or older, or so it appeared from this distance—whose interests seemed to lie in directions other than cards.

Stocks? *Finances*? Or was it the slim bikini-clad woman stretched out on one of the lounges nearby? Chelsea sniffed disdainfully. *This is retirement?*

It was at this moment that he decided to rethink Josh Novick's offer. His gray eyes narrowed in thought.

Josh had said $50,000 would make Joe an equal partner in his security firm—and that he could pay it off at his own convenience, without interest. The thought brought a smile to Joe's rigid features. Josh, coming out of a wealthy household—his father had owned a chain of fast-food restaurants—had to have been the richest man on the force. Being wealthy—and Jewish—had caused him some problems, but he'd weathered them when Chelsea became his "Rabbi," his mentor. They had remained close friends for more than twenty-five years.

Fifty thousand, equal partnership, Chelsea pondered. His brows knitted. There was no way he would accept those terms, knowing full well Josh was throwing him a bone. His operation, from what the older man had heard, was worth five times that figure. In his mind he reviewed his own finances.

The house purchased in Queens twenty-five years ago had cost a mere $25,000. With the present sale pending, in today's market he and Ellie stood to clear $135,000. On top of that he had $180,000 in government securities inherited from his father. His pension, combined with judicious investment, should bring in over $50,000 annually. Added to this, there were Ellie's investments. Refusing to live on her earnings as a foreign-language teacher at Columbia, Joe had invested her income wisely—thanks largely to Josh, who was a financial wizard. Today, even in retirement, they could count on more than $70,000 a year after taxes. A smile creased the ruddy features. He was in far better shape than most retirees, cops or otherwise.

As the shadows deepened on the fourth-floor terrace, Joe looked out at the sea. To the east the horizon was darkening. He glanced at his watch: 6:30. It was time to settle with the agent. He reentered the apartment and found Ellie waiting for him.

He didn't have to ask if the five-room condo met with her approval. Her eyes glistened with that intelligence he had recognized from the moment they met, almost forty years ago. He winked at her and addressed the realtor.

"I have two questions." The agent shrugged, his body language implying, *Here comes the bargaining*. "Just ask, I'm here to help in any way."

"Is there a 'no smoking' rule in this building?"

The man's eyebrows lifted. He became aware of the tobacco pouch peeking from Chelsea's jacket pocket. "In some areas. In the shops below. In the restaurant cigarettes are permitted in a designated area. Otherwise . . ." He shrugged bony shoulders without stirring his jacket.

"Second question . . . If I write out a check for the entire amount, how soon can we take possession?"

The agent's lean face failed to camouflage his surprise. *A retired policeman paying out in full?* His eyes altered, squinting in calculation. "With no mortgage, four . . . No, five days. Please have your attorney present at the signing tomorrow morning. Will ten o'clock be all right?"

Ellen could barely contain her own surprise, but she waited until they were beneath the marquee at the building's entrance. She tugged at his arm.

"Hold it, Joe. What was that about? Since when did *we* decide on no mortgage?"

Chelsea looked at the fountain opposite the entrance—stone dolphins sprayed a steady stream of water ten feet high—and removed his jacket. He gave her a sidelong glance. "For protection. I'm sixty-six. If anything should happen to . . ."

Her eyes blinked in astonishment, and then displayed annoyance. "For Pete's sake, Joe. I'm only three years younger than you."

Chelsea grinned mischievously. "All right. So we're both protected. In any case, neither of us is stuck with an unpaid mortgage." His eyes turned from her to search the parking lot at the side of the building. "Now . . . where did we leave Josh's borrowed 'metal trap'?"

The switch in subject was obvious, but Ellen let it pass. Josh's metal trap was a white Porsche. Chelsea, with his 220-pound, six-foot-three figure, could barely get behind the wheel.

Spotlights suddenly split the twilight, illuminating the frolicking stone dolphins and the palm trees bordering the grounds. Chelsea shook his head and grimaced. "This is going to take some getting used to."

Ellie's eyes flickered with amusement. Playfully she knuckled a fist into his ribs. "Come on, Joe. It's a new plateau in our lives. Accept it. No more junkies, no homicides to contend with . . . It's time to relax and enjoy."

"Yeah, sure," he muttered.

"Want me to drive? You can stretch your legs out on the passenger side."

Squeezing into the seat, he gave her an unobtrusive glance. Five-seven, at about 130 pounds, she had kept her figure over the years. At age sixty-three she used cosmetics to advantage—it must be something intrinsic to the French female psyche—hiding the inevitable wrinkles with extreme skill. Unlike him, she didn't look more than fifty. She appeared happy—her natural inclination overriding his dour mood—and that was all that mattered, as far as he was concerned. *A new plateau?* he mused.

He nodded imperceptibly to himself. She deserved the best he could give her.

He was pushed against the back of his seat as she pulled out of the driveway onto A1A. “Christ! Take it easy! Josh’ll have my head if you put so much as a scratch on it.” His lips compressed. Ellie still wheeled a car like a teenager.

“We’re late, Joe. Josh said he’s barbecuing steaks on his patio. I promised to help Cindy with the salad.”

“All right. Then take the first crossing to Federal Highway and pull into the nearest shopping center. Our new plateau deserves a bottle of champagne.”

“Does the ‘new plateau’ include taking Josh up on his offer?”

He gave her a quick glance; her gaze was on the wide boulevard and its building traffic, searching for a liquor store. His eyes blinked; she was good, reading him like a familiar book.

“Yes,” he said, without further comment and noted her quiet, satisfied smile. He would have leaned over to kiss her, but the seat belt was too much of an encumbrance. He stretched back instead, a sense of relief overtaking him.

2

The jalousied terrace was about twenty by thirty feet, its expensive furnishings of thickly cushioned wicker modestly described as Old Key West by Josh Novick. The terrace was at the rear of the twelve-room Spanish-style villa. Joe Chelsea held a butane lighter to his Dunhill briar. A newcomer would have been surprised to learn Josh was a retired policeman. Years back, when Chelsea had first learned of Novick's wealth, he had questioned his motives in joining the force. "Just making an attempt to balance the reputations of my horse-thieving ancestors," he had replied cryptically. Eventually Chelsea learned that he was referring to a grandfather and uncle who had made a fortune in the black market during the First World War.

Joe watched the smoke from his pipe drift through the half-opened glass slats, through the screen, to dissipate in the night air. Fifty yards away, the Novicks' 54-foot Hatteras motor yacht was tied up at a private dock in a channel that was an offshoot of the Intracoastal Waterway.

With his free hand Chelsea finished his Moët. Setting the

glass aside, he gave Josh a studious glance. The five years since his friend's forced retirement had wrought little change on the surface; the same alert face and wiry build displayed a permanence, a resilience. The lone discomfort was revealed in the pronounced limp during bad weather. Two bullets in the thigh, one almost shattering the bone, was the cause of his retirement. Josh had donated all the monies he received to the policemen's fund.

"Why a security firm?" Chelsea asked, by way of opening the subject. "You certainly don't need it. You're more than capable to be a financial advisor."

"Financial advisor!" Josh snorted. "The last thing I want to do is handle someone else's funds."

"You handled mine."

Novick made a face. "C'mon, Joe, you know it's not the same thing. As for the security business, it's something I need to keep busy. What the hell would I do? Tennis is out—so is golf. I use the pool an hour a day, but that's the extent of my physical activity. We've both spent time in burglary, and know the business."

"Granted, but the firm isn't that large. What have you got? Three trucks and ten men? You don't need me."

Josh delivered an oblique look. "You trying to weasel out, Joe? Forget it. With your expertise we can expand. The men I have are good but they aren't in your class."

"I was in homicide the last ten years."

"So was I. What are you trying to say? You can't handle it?" He gave Joe a sharp glance. "What's the problem? Afraid you'll miss the action? I can guarantee you won't be bored."

Chelsea remained unconvinced. "Your trucks are well equipped. They must have set you back at least a hundred grand. Your home base operation has electronic gear—oh, I would estimate another hundred and fifty. All told, I would sum it up at better than a quarter-mil." He glanced levelly at Josh. "You're asking fifty grand for an equal partnership?"

"All right. What's the deal you want?"

"I'll go with the fifty grand you're asking—and the salary offered—but only twenty percent of the profits, if any."

Josh grinned, pleased no end. He should have known better. "You drive a hard bargain, Joe. Agreed. Want to seal it with a refill? It's a double celebration, a new business and a new home."

Chelsea shifted in his seat. "No more hard drinking for me. I'll have coffee whenever the women have it ready."

As if on cue Ellie and Cindy appeared, each carrying a tray. One held a carafe of coffee and four mugs; the other overflowed with fruit tarts and miniature Danish. Ellie was all smiles as she set her tray on a glass-topped table that seated four. Both women were in a good humor, knowing that they would soon be neighbors again.

Except in their elation, the two women were unalike. Ellie was dark, her hair frosted with silver; Cindy had been a natural blonde, but touched up her graying hair with ash-blond silver. Each woman had kept her figure but Cindy was two inches taller. Her blue eyes seemed to have a perpetual sparkle. Although she was dressed in a designer skirt and blouse, Chelsea noticed that she wore no jewelry other than a plain wedding band.

"Where's Madelaine?" Josh asked. Madelaine was their live-in housekeeper, a middle-aged heavy-set mulatto whose husband had run off some years ago with—as she put it—"a piece of younger stuff." Madelaine had been with the Novicks for almost three years.

"On the phone." Cindy said. "I told her we're not taking any business calls tonight unless it's an emergency." Joe noted the light on the console beside Josh's chair. It reminded him that he had to call his attorney to finalize the condo deal.

Ellie caught Joe's eye. He responded with a wink, signifying all had gone well.

The housekeeper appeared as Cindy was pouring coffee. "Mr. Novick . . ." She pronounced it *Noveek*. "A Lieutenant Carbolo from the sheriff's office wishes to speak with you."

Cindy made a face but continued to fill the mugs. Joe saw Josh frown as he squinted at his watch. The deepened lines emphasized his age, Joe thought morosely, knowing his own mirror didn't lie. Josh switched a button on the console and lifted the receiver.

"Josh. What's up, Rudy?" He listened for a while, his lips compressed. Briefly, his eyes met his wife's. He listened in silence for another minute, then said, "All right, Rudy. When?" Seconds later, "Tonight? I have guests here. What purpose would it serve? I met with her for only a few minutes."

The next few seconds brought another frown. Nodding, he glanced at Joe. "All right, Rudy. And I'm bringing a friend along. I assure you he won't be in the way and in fact might be of some help." He checked his Rolex. "In twenty minutes. Okay?"

Josh replaced the phone and held a palm out, forestalling questions. To Cindy he said, "Remember the woman who called on us last week? Emma Mosel? Well, her roommate found her dead in their apartment about two hours ago. Rudy came across our number in her telephone book."

Josh got to his feet. "It can't be helped. Joe and I have to go."

"That poor woman," Cindy said. "How did it happen? Despite her age she seemed to be in excellent health." She hesitated, suspicion flaring. "Has it anything to do with what she told us?"

Josh shrugged. "I doubt it. Carbolo said heart attack."

Chelsea took a quick swallow of coffee, then stood up. He delayed questions for the drive. Turning to Ellie, he said, "I hope you don't mind my going along."

She waved him away good-naturedly. The month-long sag in her husband's shoulders had straightened. Reflecting briefly, she waited for the men to leave before saying to Cindy, "The Blue Jays are at it again."

Years earlier in their careers, when the two men wore blues in their squad car, they had been dubbed Blue Jays. Joe was Jay One, Josh Jay Two.

Cindy smiled, despite the ruined evening.

"Fill me in, Josh. Where are we going?"

"Back to your complex, in the adjacent building. The sixth floor. The two women shared a leased condo—some owners buy on speculation and rent it out." Chelsea merely nodded. Speculation in Florida property wasn't a new idea.

The five-mile drive allowed Josh to fill Chelsea in. Emma Mosel had insisted on coming to his home despite the fact that she needed a PI, not a security service. She was in her early seventies, a widow with three married daughters, all living up north. Her story was that she had seen her brother—a brother she had assumed dead. Both had been inmates at Dachau and it was a painful recollection for her. When Josh questioned the long time span, she remained adamant in her belief that she had seen her brother.

"She wanted me to find him—an impossible task—a job I wouldn't even think of attempting."

"How did she describe him?"

"Tall, thin, balding—with a fringe of white hair—and

solemn, unsmiling eyes. She said his eyes still held the look of the camp."

"Where was she supposed to have seen him?"

"On the beach. Jogging, of all things. The man would have to be in his seventies."

"Was she lucid? Believable?"

"Somewhat. To placate her, I advised her to contact the police—Missing Persons. Maybe they could suggest an agency for her. She said she had, but they claimed they needed more information. Someone in the department recommended me—probably to get rid of her."

"The locals didn't bother to investigate at all?"

"No. How could they? A vague description, no address. What should they look for? A man with a solemn face?"

"She never accosted this man to speak with him?"

"Once. Two days later. She was watching for the tall jogger." Josh felt Chelsea's eyes on him. "I know this is wild. The man was annoyed, denied ever knowing her. He accused her of being an old woman with bitter memories and said he didn't know what she was talking about."

"How did she answer him?"

"She couldn't. He took off without another word. As far as I know, that was the last she saw of him."

"The lieutenant thinks it was a heart attack?"

"I said that for the benefit of the women. Carbolo is homicide. He didn't offer an opinion."

Chelsea reached for his pipe, then clamped it between his teeth without filling it. "How well do you know him? What's he like?"

"Puerto Rican. He's been in the sheriff's office for about fifteen years. He's called me in a couple of times, once when investigating an attempted burglary of one of my clients which ended up in a killing. Likable guy, seems to know his job."

* * *

They were on A1A and passing Chelsea's new building. Chelsea glanced at it without comment. When they were stopped by the security guard at the building complex, Josh identified himself. "Novick. The lieutenant is expecting us."

The apartment was three and a half rooms: bedroom, kitchen, bathroom, and living-dining room, well appointed with expensive furnishings.

In the living room the medical examiner had just finished examining the deceased. She was sitting in a fan-backed chair, facing a television set, her head leaning forward as if she had fallen asleep. Not a gray hair on her head was disturbed. Her attire was immaculate, expensive-looking. She wore a diamond wedding ring, a wristwatch on one arm, a gold bracelet on the other. A thin gold necklace hung loosely from her wrinkled throat.

Chelsea took it all in with a practiced eye. He wrinkled his nose at the fetid odor permeating the room.

He glanced around the room. Nothing looked disturbed. Appearances could be deceiving but it ruled out ordinary robbery. Plainclothesmen moved about, one dusting a desk for fingerprints. The woman who shared the apartment with Emma Mosel was nowhere to be seen. Too clean, too pat, Chelsea thought. Especially in light of the background he'd gotten from Josh.

The lieutenant wore a white jacket and slacks, and an open-necked print shirt. His hair was black, slick, his face dark, and he was handsome in a way, reminding Chelsea of old movies depicting stereotyped gigolos. Giving his man his due, he might have been called out from a party.

After being introduced, Chelsea asked, "What have you got, Lieutenant?"

Carbolo lifted dark eyes, then looked him up and down as if Chelsea were an alien just arrived from outer space.

Josh smiled. "Rudy, Joe Chelsea is from New York. Until a few months ago he was a captain of detectives in Homicide."

Carbolo fingered a thin, well-trimmed mustache. "Really! From the Big Apple? Gee!"

"Sorry, Lieutenant," Chelsea said. "It's almost automatic for me to start questioning when entering a crime scene."

Carbolo grinned good-naturedly. His teeth displayed excellent dental work. "Apology noted." He looked closely at Chelsea. "You've got questions? Let's hear some."

"The woman who shared the apartment—did she mention her friend having a heart problem?"

"The only medication the victim used was a diuretic for high blood pressure." Carbolo fingered his mustache again. "Next question." He appeared to be enjoying himself.

"May I examine the body?"

"Be my guest."

Chelsea leaned over the woman in the chair and lifted her left hand without touching the wristwatch. The hand was already stiffening and the watch moved slightly. His face remained expressionless as he studied the concentration camp number tattooed on her wrist. He concentrated on the skin, then repeated a like examination of her other wrist. "Did the ME venture an opinion on the cause of these abrasions?"

Carbolo raised an eyebrow. "He mentioned it as too-tight bracelets. The autopsy will tell him more."

"These are rope burns," Chelsea said. "Probably from thin nylon."

The lieutenant regarded him obliquely. "There was no sign of violence."

Chelsea didn't reply. He examined the nails, then went to the old woman's hair. "Her hair was combed, or brushed, after she died. It's still damp."

"What makes you so certain? She could have washed it before she sat down to watch television. The TV was still on when we arrived on the scene." Carbolo checked his digital watch. "About an hour and a half ago."

Chelsea shook his head. "If she had washed her hair, she would have used a hair dryer before sitting here wearing her jewelry and dressed in this outfit."

The lieutenant stuck his hands into his back pockets. "You're implying this nice old lady was murdered."

Chelsea straightened from his leaning position. "By a professional."

Carbolo eyed him for a solemn moment. "This is speculation, not deduction."

"Did the medical examiner mention the pinprick on one of the tattooed numbers?"

The lieutenant cocked his head; he felt as if he were being interrogated by his own superior. "No, he's assuming death by heart failure until he's through with the autopsy. Why are you attaching so much importance to a pinprick?"

"Ever hear of Evathane? A single injection induces symptoms of a heart attack. An overdose of potassium chloride accomplishes the same thing within thirty minutes. I doubt the autopsy will find any trace of it. And by the way . . ." Chelsea nodded toward the far corner. "Why the check for fingerprints on the desk?"

Carbolo bowed slightly. "Thanks for giving me some credit. The victim's roommate said her friend kept her valuables in the desk, in particular a black book, a diary of sorts. We couldn't find it. Her jewelry was intact, for whatever that's worth." He scratched his chin absently and turned to Josh. "I know about the complaint she registered two weeks ago. Your name was in her telephone book. Where do you fit in?"

Josh briefed him on what he had told Chelsea earlier.

The lieutenant blew out a deep breath. "All right, I won't detain you further."

Chelsea held back. "Are you going to continue with the investigation? The woman did give some description."

"Yeah. An old man, balding, with some white hair, jogging on the beach. Big deal. That narrows it down to a few hundred. Shit! These beaches are loaded with old men who refuse to believe their ages." He stared at Chelsea. "What would you suggest? I hold each one for questioning?"

Chelsea's eyes narrowed. "That's your problem, not mine. I'm retired, Lieutenant."

Once in the corridor, Josh said, "What was that about? You think this case will go into the dead-end files?"

"No. We got his attention. My gut says he'll be calling us again."

Josh gazed at his friend warily. Chelsea was beginning to act like his old self, like a hound dog released, with the scent in his nostrils. Struck by that train of thought, he stopped Chelsea from getting into the car. "Hold it a minute, Joe. I can hear the gears meshing in your head. That crack about old men refusing to believe their ages got to you." The statement drew a stony stare from his former partner.

"I don't deny I'm getting older, maybe slowing down, but I'm as mentally alert as I ever was. This business about accepting aging gracefully is pure horseshit!"

Josh rolled his eyes. "Shit! You're backing out of our deal!"

Chelsea rested a hand upon his friend's shoulder. "I'm not reneging. I would merely like a month's postponement of our partnership. After signing the deed to the condo tomorrow, I was scheduled to go back north to finalize the sale of my house but I've just decided to let my accountant take care of the sale in New York. Just indulge me for a few more days. At least until the condo is furnished."

Josh's expression was one of incredulity. He leaned on the car fender to take the weight from his leg. "Christ! You're going to investigate on your own! What chutzpah! You have no authority here. Where the hell would you start?"

"*We* start with Emma Mosel's roommate."

Josh shook his head. "Let's be realistic. I don't know about you, but I've been out of it too long. I've . . . we've got a business to run. I'm no longer a legman." Nevertheless, despite his protestations, he felt the adrenaline flowing. He moved off the fender, unsure of what was going through his mind.

Chelsea waited until they were both seated. "Josh, do you feel old? So old that all you can do is direct men to watch monitors?"

"You want me to be frank? I say yes. It's been ten years. I don't know whether I can cope with police work again."

"And you've lost all taste for the chase? I can't believe it. What happened to Blue Jay Two? Has he retired to a lounge chair, maybe playing shuffleboard with the neighbors?"

Josh winced. "You think running my firm is a slow death? I started it from scratch and . . ." He halted, realizing he was being baited. "Christ! Joe! Don't do this to me." He banged the steering wheel, then suddenly laughed aloud. A couple walking to their car stared at him as if he were drunk. "Oh, Jesus!" he exclaimed, "God help me! Why not! Let's call it a last fling for the Blue Jays." He hit the ignition switch. "And by the way, don't knock shuffleboard. Down here it's not a game. It's a sport the older generation take seriously."

3

ONE WEEK LATER

Joe Chelsea was on his fifth lap across the sixty-foot pool. His stroke was easy and unhurried despite the cool water; he decided ten laps would be a daily personal ritual. It was only about twenty minutes past sunrise and, as expected, he was the sole occupant of the pool and its immediate grounds.

Earlier, from his balcony terrace he had watched a predawn mist dissipate as the sun ascended from the ocean's horizon; the growing light skidded across the water, washing it in a pink glow. He had left Ellie sleeping.

It had been their first night in the condo, and they had blessed it properly in their new bedroom. As the commercial said, "Doing it less, but enjoying it more."

For many years now Chelsea had been unable to sleep more than five hours at a stretch; originally he'd believed it was a habit formed by the demands of his job, but in recent years he grudgingly acknowledged that it was part of the normal aging process.

Like hell!

He finished his ten laps and emerged from the pool.

Unlike most men his age he was almost all bone and muscle. He was a man who took pride in his physique, never allowing himself to go to fat with the years. He didn't have more than a half-inch overlap on his swimming trunks. Perhaps he was satisfying vanity because of his inability to produce even one child. Both he and Ellie were sterile. His sterility could be traced back to a case of the mumps when he was in his early teens. Ellie's condition had a less natural cause. "Our meeting must be fate," she had said. "We were meant to share only each other."

As Joe toweled himself briskly—the air was chilly after coming out of the water—he wondered why he was suddenly reminded of the cause of her alleged sterility. Perhaps it was the recollection of the tattooed number on Emma Mosel's wrist.

Ellen Berne, daughter of Parisian Jews, had been a teenager when the Nazi horde marched into the city. Her parents had placed her in the care of the Cotys, a childless Christian couple.

Raised by the Cotys, unknown to them she had fallen in love with a young man working with the French underground. When she too joined the partisans, she acted as lookout during their acts of sabotage. In doing so, she truly believed she was avenging her parents, who had been taken by the Nazis. In reality, for her and her young boyfriend it had become a time of romance and excitement in which they gave little thought to the consequences of their lovemaking or the sabotage.

In her innocence Ellen hadn't known she was two months pregnant when she lingered too long at the railroad trestle. The ill-timed explosion killed all but two of the saboteurs. Ellen, damaged internally, lost the fetus, and was told there was no possibility of her ever conceiving again.

Years later, after finishing college and armed with a

degree in languages, she was employed as an interpreter for the French delegation at the United Nations. It was there that she met a young policeman, Joe Chelsea.

Upon graduation from high school in 1941, Chelsea had lied about his age and enlisted in the Army. Three years later he was in on the invasion of Omaha Beach. Amazingly he never received a scratch during his march across France. Years later he learned that in the week of R&R he spent in Paris he had been at one time within a block of Ellie's home.

After the war, Joe took advantage of the GI Bill by enrolling in law school. He was just finishing pre-law when he lost his mother in a street mugging. Extremely angered, and against his father's wishes, he left school to join the police force. Meeting Ellie had made that the wisest decision he ever made.

Chelsea's mind dwelled on their first meeting, deeply pleased. They were so young then, both so full of life, even knowing there would be no children in their future.

Joe Chelsea loved his police work and Ellen had been accepted as a foreign-language teacher at Columbia University. Their marriage and love had grown stronger through the years. Although policemen were cautioned not to take their work home with them, Joe occasionally shared his problems with Ellie. He respected her intelligence and sought her opinion. If a difference in thought occurred, it was always solved. No matter the discussion, their feelings were never remote.

Joe's thoughts rambled, and he recalled a scene from back in New York, a week after his retirement. Disgruntled, he had cut himself shaving. "Damn!" he had yelled, loud enough to bring Ellie into the bathroom.

He saw his face in the mirror and Ellie's behind it. Scowling, he addressed his image. "Look at that corrugated face. How can a young mind possess such an old face!"

Ellie's laughter rippled across his shoulder; like a salving balm it eased the knot in his stomach. "Corrugated indeed! That's character, an image people yearn for."

"Horseshit!" He grinned, in spite of himself.

Leaning toward the mirror for a closer look, she said in mock seriousness, "I would say the face is suffering from withdrawal symptoms." She leaned back again. "Yes, I do believe that's your trouble, withdrawal from excitement. What do you intend doing about it?"

Joe shook his head to clear away the recollection. He walked over to the anchor fence—the only dry spot when he'd come down; the lounge pads were still wet with morning dew—to retrieve the white terry-cloth jacket hanging there. He donned it, then slipped into a pair of sandals. He checked a pocket, reassuring himself that his notebook was still there, then picked up a folding chair and carried it out to the beach.

The water washed up in small crests, as if reluctant to fight an ebbing tide. Joe set the chair down and settled into the vinyl seat, enjoying the view of the lonely stretch of beach. His eyes searched both directions. No one, not even a young jogger—no less an aging one. It was a long shot, he knew, but it was the only lead.

He idly watched four pelicans patrolling the shoreline, then sweep out to follow a trawler a half-mile offshore. Screeching sea gulls came out of nowhere and flew off in pursuit.

What else is new? Joe thought cynically. *No different from people—we're all scroungers of a sort, looking for handouts wherever possible*. It was pitiful in the big cities; the homeless and the poverty a reminder of what he had learned in school of the Great Depression. His voiced political opinions regarding present conditions in the city had gotten him nothing. Nothing, that is, except never getting beyond a captaincy in the department. There were men, less qualified than he, who were appointed to higher positions. Joe scowled; his eyes, darkening, became pinpoints.

Shit! Forget about it. It's over and done with!

He tugged out his notebook to review the conversation of three days ago with Nellie Bohmer, Mrs. Mosel's roommate—and sister-in-law, they had learned. She was a thin, dour woman with well-coiffed white hair. Her face was lined and taut, the eyes holding memories of suffering. Reticent at first, she had become talkative when Joe told her he was sort of a business acquaintance of her sister-in-law; that Mrs. Mosel had contacted his firm only three weeks earlier. He explained that she'd really needed a private detective and, unfortunately, it wasn't their line of business. He was seeing Mrs. Bohmer, both to offer condolences and to satisfy his own curiosity. "Had she hired an investigator?" he asked.

The woman waved a bony hand. The veins were turgid on the translucent skin. "Emma never needed one. We had numerous arguments on the subject." She raised her eyes, as if seeking consolation from a Higher Authority. "Emma was impossible at times. Having met her, you should know that."

"She met with my partner. I was away at the time." Joe paused briefly. "Why do you say 'impossible'?"

"This had happened before. In New York." She clasped her hands together and rubbed her swollen knuckles. "At least three times over the past five years she claimed to have seen her brother." Joe was seated on a sofa, Mrs. Bohmer in a straight-backed chair. She eyed him for a moment, hesitant. "I hate to say this—since we were not that far apart in age—but the family did believe she was becoming senile."

"Then, this claim of seeing her brother was a fantasy?"

"Hmpf!" Mrs. Bohmer snorted. "Her brother died in a camp many years ago."

Joe nodded compassionately. "Yes, I can understand a woman in her condition wishing him alive. For her it was more than desire to see him once again. Perhaps a sort of guilt complex for her having survived. My partner said you mentioned a diary. Could it have shed light on her thinking?"

Mrs. Bohmer grimaced. "That diary . . . It was a fetish with her. She was never without it. Every night writing in it and every day reviewing its contents. She was like a miser, hoarding it from prying eyes." Mrs. Bohmer permitted a tired sigh. "Emma hid it well. As far as I could tell, it was the only item missing from our apartment. I doubt the police even believed it existed."

A bead of water dropped from Joe's wet hair. He gently wiped it from his notebook, then closed the book and abstractedly finger-combed his damp hair. It was a futile effort; some gray strands had dried and become wiry. Even without a mirror, he knew his mop of hair, uncombed, resembled Alfred Einstein's unruly thatch.

He wrote a reminder on the back page of his notebook to bring a comb along the next time he came down. Then he sat back and closed his eyes.

In review he was certain of two things: Emma Mosel had been murdered—and by a professional. Questions followed: Why? For the missing diary? Joe believed Nellie Bohmer's story, no matter Carbolo's insouciance. Joe hadn't seen the lieutenant since that first evening, but he was unconcerned. Josh had some connections with the burglary detail because of his firm. He knew how to garner and sift information when and if it became necessary.

The sun, combined with the warm breeze, was making Joe sleepy. Dozing off—he didn't know for how long—he was awakened by loud laughter from a young couple racing along the shoreline. Raising his head, he became aware that the beach was coming alive with sound and activity. Beach umbrellas and lounges were now in evidence and, not more than three feet from him, Ellie was sitting in a chair and sipping what he assumed to be orange juice. He thought she looked good, pleased with herself. She was wearing a playsuit, and it reminded Joe of their younger days.

She handed him the plastic foam container to finish. "It's juice. Did you eat anything yet?" She smiled gently. "I also brought your comb." He took both items from her.

"You're slipping," he said. "You forgot the coffee."

She gave him her rippling laugh. "I'm retired also, Joe. Get used to it. The snack bar at poolside is open."

"If they don't make bacon and eggs, I'm selling the apartment."

"Hah! His first morning on the beach and he wants VIP treatment." Ellie's eyes sparkled in enjoyment. "I'm living like the natives. I've already met some. Bring me back a bagel and cream cheese."

Joe got to his feet and leaned down to kiss her on the forehead. "Okay, I'll bring it and then leave. I have work that can't be postponed." When she sighed, he added, "It's something I must do."

She nodded, understanding, resigned. He had discussed Emma Mosel with her the previous evening, and she realized he had committed himself. She blew him a kiss. "As long as it makes you happy."

4

The man was tall and thin, with a long straight back, narrow hips, and strong legs for someone his age. Although he was past seventy-five, he could have been taken for a healthy sixty-year-old. Wearing only a pair of blue sweat-pants and a T-shirt, he seated himself at a triple-mirrored dressing table. Staring back at him was a hard, hawklike face and clever, unsmiling eyes. At times his eyes resembled opaque stones. This was one of those times.

Spread out before him were clippings of several newspaper accounts about the death of Emma Mosel. They were already a few days old; the natural death of one of the town's aged citizens was no longer news.

He smiled for the first time, and the lines in his face deepened, hinting of cruelty underlying the tanned surface. The hard features displayed neither malice nor emotion, except for "the stupid woman!" There was a remote flash of regret in the opaque eyes, but it was so brief he wasn't aware of it. Involuntarily he glanced at the tattooed number on his wrist; his expression remained impassive.

He lifted the short-cut white hairpiece from the dresser top and fitted it in place. It was an expensive piece, and it fit well. The fringe around his pate had been trimmed to blend perfectly. More important, it appeared as natural as if it were his own hair.

His vanity satisfied, he walked over to a valet-chair and, sitting, squeezed his feet into a pair of running shoes. It was now safe to continue with his early morning beach-jogging. It was imperative he stay fit until he completed his mission.

He crossed the bedroom, walked out onto the balcony terrace, and stood there in silent reflection. Fate had taken an odd turn in bringing Emma Mosel into the picture. *His sister*! It was impossible. He was never told he had a sister; therefore he did not. She had left him no recourse. The woman was senile and living with distorted memories. She no longer had any recollection of the true events in her life. There were no options. The woman *had* to die.

True events, he thought. Why did he frame it in this way? For a moment he lost his train of thought. The pain at the back of his head had returned—and disappeared as quickly. It had been happening quite often of late.

His face remained hard, unchanging, as he walked through the recently leased one-bedroom furnished apartment. He had been wearing his new hairpiece when he rented the flat. The beachfront complex was two miles north of the original building. No one here could possibly associate him with the elderly bald gentleman who had been accosted by the late Emma Mosel. His appearance was further altered by the sweatpants that covered his scarred legs.

He glanced at the phone installed three days ago. He had made one call and had received one in return. The voice, as always, spoke in a monotone as it asked first for his identification number. The man always gave the number tattooed upon his wrist. He was told the headaches would be attended to when the mission was finished.

The tall man took one final look around the apartment before leaving for his morning jog. A puzzled frown creased the lean, hard face. *Why, after forty-plus years, would she believe him to be her brother*? He squinted, desperately trying to recall anything of the first thirty years of his life. The effort availed him nothing but the dull ache at the nape of his neck.

In the hospital in Germany, he had remembered nothing of the war which had ended three months previously. The tattoo, it had been explained to him, meant he was a survivor of a death camp. All records had been destroyed, so his identity could not be traced. His legs were bandaged, and he was told he had been caught in an air raid. His life from that time forward was in the hands of his "benefactors." He had been grateful.

Josh handed Joe a mug of hot coffee, then sat down on the corner of his desk. "The woman's mind was twisted. Let's say he was her brother. How could she recognize him after more than forty years?"

"According to Mrs. Bohmer, he was supposed to have resembled Mosel's father at a late age." Joe took a sip of coffee, then put the mug aside on the desk. Seated in an armchair, he leaned forward to retrieve his notepad from the back pocket of his slacks. "Everything I've got points to murder by a professional. Yet—if the mysterious tall, thin man was her brother—it makes no sense he would kill her."

"Speculating, I would say it's more likely she mistook an ex-Nazi for her brother. The memory plays tricks over forty years. Her roommate said Mosel had a memory problem.

But my problem is how do you envisage a man in his seventies being an assassin, hired or otherwise."

He looked up to catch Josh grinning. He put away the notepad. "I know—you don't have to tell me. I'm an old warhorse who refuses to be put out to pasture. Jesus! Don't you find it intriguing? Isn't your appetite whetted?" His friend's grin moderated to a compassionate smile.

"To be frank, Joe, I don't really need it. I've already adjusted to my situation." He tapped his thigh. "Admittedly, it took some doing. If you think I had an easy time of it, just talk to Cindy."

Joe removed the pipe and tobacco crammed into his shirt pocket. He fingered the briar in silence, gathering his thoughts. "Josh, you have money, and more important, a family. Two children—both married—and each has given you a grandchild. You have something to—"

"Stop the horseshit, Joe! Self-pity doesn't become you. It was never part of your makeup. What about Ellie? Isn't she a major share of your life? Could you ask for anything better?" He slid from the corner of the desk to seat himself in the leather swivel chair behind it.

Joe struggled inwardly, but offered no response.

Josh leaned forward on his elbows. "Joe, what the hell's bothering you? Fear of aging? C'mon, let's hear it," he prompted. "Is it the condo? Are you in over your head?"

Joe attempted a smile he didn't feel. Josh was hitting where it hurt. "The condo is part of it," he said at last. "Not the cost. I can handle it. It's a buyers' market compared to northern prices. I got it cheap enough. At least thirty percent less than I had figured."

"So . . . For Christ's sake, Joe. Spit it out!"

"The other tenants—my neighbors. Almost all retired, almost all living in the past. Most are okay, but the widows and widowers . . . Their loneliness is etched on their faces. They've lost something that can't be replaced." He paused briefly. "If anything should happen to Ellie . . ."

Josh stared at his friend in disbelief. He had never seen him like this. Joe Chelsea was always a driver, always knew the direction in which he was heading, an uncomplicated man, and now he was beginning to sound like one of the neighbors he had described. "Jesus!" he exclaimed. "You're as healthy as a horse. And so is Ellie. You've no right to complain. Shit! Life is what you make of the conditions forced on you. Aging is part of it, but you don't lie down and quit because you resent it. I know you almost as well as Ellie does—in some ways, better. You're too tough to lose incentive, and . . ." He cocked his head suddenly. "Am I getting through to you, Joe?"

Joe held the unlit briar in his teeth like a bit. "Loud and clear." He leaned forward. "Now, about *your* incentive . . . Do I get any help from you?" He removed the pipe to reveal just the hint of a smile.

Josh reacted with a stare. "What is this? A new routine?" He got a grin from Joe. "Jesus! You'd think I'd know better after all these years." In the back of his mind he wondered whether the depressing picture painted by his friend was really a put-on.

"You never answered me," Joe prodded.

"I said I would. Why the push? I haven't heard anything from Carbolo. And I doubt I will. He doesn't need us to do his job."

"Do me a favor. Give him a call. He'll speak with you. I need to know if he verified my suspicions." As an afterthought he said, "Ask about the forensic report."

Novick regarded Chelsea. The gray eyes were bright, reminding Josh of deep water. His face was now tanned, imparting an indeterminate coloring. His hair was silvering, bleached from his daily vigil on the beachfront. The wedge-shaped jaw jutted out in anticipation.

"You're asking a hell of a lot to expect him—" The telephone rang and he held up a hand.

"Novick Security," he said. A moment later his eyes lifted and his lips silently mouthed "Speak of the devil!" "What can I do for you, Lieutenant?"

Joe filled his pipe but his eyes sought to read Novick's expression. Josh was rubbing his balding pate and frowning. His eyes glinted and he shoved a pad and pencil toward Joe. He repeated an address given to him. "Twenty minutes okay? Yes, my friend will be with me." He hung up and hit a button on the intercom to let one of his men know he'd be gone for a couple of hours.

"Well?" Joe asked, studying the address. It was an apartment complex about ten miles in from the beach. He and Ellie had looked at it before making up their minds. It was less expensive than the condo they eventually purchased, but neither of them liked the idea of a catwalk fronting the apartments.

Josh moved out from behind the desk. "Let's go, Joe. It's another murder—yes, he said 'murder.' A male this time. Also with a tattooed number on his wrist."

Palms and greenery fringed the parking lot, offering only scant relief from a hot noonday October sun. Both men put on sunglasses before squeezing into the Porsche. Neither spoke until their seat belts were fastened. Joe then asked, "Why did he call for us?"

Josh grinned, displaying a perfect set of capped teeth. "His own words, 'Bring the captain, if he's available.' " The grin broadened. "He wants your expertise. Why complain? It's what you wanted." Joe said nothing until they escaped the heat that rose in waves from the pavement of the parking lot.

"What I want, is to know whether the two victims were in the same concentration camp."

Josh shrugged, his eyes on the road.

5

The tall man was sweating as he entered his apartment; he had already checked the door for any sign of an attempted break-in. Caution was an automatic watchword. He had started to pull off his T-shirt when the phone rang.

A nondescript voice asked for identification. As always, he gave the number on his wrist. The voice continued. "One of your terminations was not sanctioned. Why was it performed?" The tone of voice was unemotional, as if the caller were asking about the weather.

"The woman had become hysterical, believing I was her long-lost brother. I had no choice."

"Do you feel any remorse?" The query brought no immediate response. "Please reply."

"No, I was never told that I had a sister."

"Are your headaches severe?"

"When I have them."

"Continue with the prescribed medication until you complete your final mission." The caller gave him a name, number, and address to be committed to memory. "You have one week to complete your assignment. You will then be recalled home." The voice paused briefly before adding, "You have done well. The political picture is changing rapidly—and to our benefit. You have played a major role for us. You will be properly rewarded for services rendered." The phone went dead.

The man used his T-shirt to wipe sweat from his face. *Sister*? Was it possible one existed they didn't know about? He had to have had a family somewhere. He fingered the back of his head tentatively, half-expecting the abominable headache to reappear, as it usually did when he attempted to delve into his lost past. No. She couldn't have been his sister; he would have felt something other than a piercing migraine. The Benefactors had assured him they were his only family—and that he had no loyalty to any other.

He walked to the bureau, opened a drawer, and pulled out an amber bottle containing small pills. He popped one in his mouth and swallowed it without water. A quick glance at the clock atop the dresser told him it was noon. There was plenty of time to shower and have a bite before going out to check his next assignment.

It was a large complex, with two swimming pools and a clubhouse that served three nine-hole courses. Stately palms dotted the landscape and hibiscus flowered in abundance. Palmetto scrubs skirted the fairways and, surprisingly, no golfer took notice of them unless caught in a bad lie. As in all Florida complexes, most of the inhabitants seemed to be unaware of the surrounding beauty bestowed by man and nature alike. It was something they had become accustomed to; it was all too familiar after a while, something taken for granted. Only tourists and new tenants stopped to admire the scenery. At the moment there were few people about; it was lunchtime.

Lieutenant Carbolo was wearing a beige linen suit, an

open-necked print sport shirt, and a religious medallion that hung from a chain around his thin neck. Joe still thought he looked like an old-time gigolo, or an up-to-date pimp. They greeted each other with nods.

Carbolo said, "Want to look at the victim?" The body was already bagged, but Joe nodded. A paramedic unzipped the cover.

A man of medium height with shaggy white hair; the face muscles were loose, the skin texture dry, and an indentation on the nose gave evidence of his having worn spectacles. Chelsea thought the beaked nose gave him a predatory look, much like the lieutenant's at the moment. Chelsea straightened from his kneeling position.

"You said 'murder' over the phone. What do you base it on?" Joe was surveying the one-bedroom apartment before Carbolo could answer. The furnishings were old and inexpensive, probably brought south from the victim's previous home. Sepia pictures of family hung on all the walls, the history of the sixty-odd years of the man's life.

"He lived alone, a widower the last two years. Nothing in the apartment was touched. First appearances said heart failure, but the coroner found a puncture mark at the base of his skull." Carbolo shook his head, frowning. "Can't even imagine the motive. Since you were so observant on the woman, I thought you might have some ideas."

Chelsea was silent a moment. He didn't want to seem pushy, even thought he'd been asked for an opinion. "Concentrate on the background of both victims. See if there's a parallel."

Carbolo eyed him speculatively. "What would I look for especially?"

"Find out whether they were in the same concentration camp."

Carbolo's eyes widened. "You're not suggesting a serial killer targeting survivors of the Holocaust?"

Chelsea shrugged. "You're the man in charge. You have the wherewithal to investigate."

"Have you any idea how many of those survivors live down here?"

"You asked for my opinion on a course of action. I gave you a starting point."

Carbolo seemed amused. Obviously relishing the situation, he said, "The Mosel woman was at Dachau in 1944. I got that from her family when they arrived to claim her body." He nodded toward the body that was being removed. "Sonnenberg's son in Chicago was notified and he'll be here tomorrow."

Chelsea's lips held a tight smile. "Don't be coy with me, Lieutenant. Why bother to ask me for direction when you have the answers?"

"Curiosity," he replied tersely. "I checked with NYPD. I wanted to know how good you were."

Chelsea pulled out his tobacco pouch. He spoke quietly. "And how good was I?"

"I spoke with a Commander Gallagher. He had nothing but high praise for you. Your last five years in homicide you had better than a ninety percent arrest and conviction rate." His eyes squinted with question marks. "It made me wonder. That much praise and you only retired with a captaincy."

Chelsea filled his pipe without bothering to reply. Josh intervened. "You need us for anything else, Rudy?"

The lieutenant appeared uncertain for the first time. Whatever the motives behind the two crimes, he was at a loss as to how to handle it. It smacked of something more insidious than the usual homicides he had encountered. This was assassination, but totally unlike the modus operandi of the hit men who worked in the drug trade. There was nothing on record resembling the sophisticated expertise of the killer. In the second killing, a wild guess suggested that the assassin was an ex-Nazi hiding his past, but, logically, how would the Mosel woman claiming she saw her brother, an old man, trigger the killings?"

"No. That'll be all," he said finally. He caught Chelsea lighting his pipe. "Stay available."

Chelsea peered over a haze of tobacco. His face remained impassive, but his eyes smiled. "I'll be around. I'm still settling in." He felt the detective's eyes on his back as he left.

Josh stopped him on the catwalk that bordered all the apartments. "What was that about between you two?"

"Carbolo's out of his league with these killings, and he knows it. He's pretty smart—I'll give him that—but his cute act belongs in an old B movie. He's torn between asking me for help or looking to the FBI for information."

"Interesting," Josh remarked. "And may I ask what you intend doing about it?" He had recognized familiar signs in his friend, in particular the deep puffs from his pipe.

"Dave Ward," Chelsea replied laconically.

"Ward?"

"You might remember him. We worked on a case together, about ten years ago. I believe it was his final case before retiring from the FBI. Sheer coincidence, but I think he lives somewhere around West Palm Beach. It shouldn't be too much trouble for you to locate him."

"Man, you're really into it. The name doesn't ring a bell. How old would he be?"

"I doubt he was fifty when he quit."

"What makes you think he would get involved? You don't even know whether he's alive."

"Ward was too energetic, and too smart, to become a

prisoner of aging—" He was about to add, "like most," but was interrupted by an elderly woman standing beside the elevator door. Without speaking, she pointed to a No Smoking sign. Joe smiled deferentially and removed the pipe from his mouth.

"You said he retired at fifty," Josh remarked. "How did he accomplish that?"

"The man was a fishing nut. I got a Christmas card from him once. He bought a Sport Fisherman and charters it out."

Josh still had doubts. "No family?"

"A widower. I think he had a son." Reflecting, he added, "Yeah, I remember. His son was going for a Navy career. Father and son both must have sea water flowing in their veins."

"You're assuming he'd make himself available."

"If he's alive and well, I'm willing to bet on it."

Josh shrugged, a helpless gesture, but a cheerful smile played on his lips. "Okay, I'll go along with it. Now, tell me how we're going to explain this escapade to the women."

"No problem, Ellie understands."

"You're a fortunate man, Joe. It's about time you realized it."

Chelsea gave him an oblique glance. "You're not going maudlin on me?"

"No, but I think it's time I became *your* Rabbi. And to switch subjects, how about spending the rest of the day at *our* office? You have to get started sometime."

"All right. You have telephone directories covering all counties?"

Josh held out his hands, palms up. "I give up. Let's go."

It was a day of bright sunshine and almost no movement of air. The humidity hung over the men, beading their faces with sweat as they traversed a long concrete walk leading to the parking area. Chelsea looked up at the palm trees bordering the walk; not a frond stirred. He grimaced. "Is it like this every day?"

"It's got snow and ice beat. C'mon, cheer up. We can go out on the *Ark* tonight and have dinner aboard."

"Why not? I imagine Ellie would welcome the change from shopping for the new apartment."

Checking the Yellow Pages under "Yacht-charters," Chelsea finally located Ward's office number in West Palm Beach. A pleasant-voiced woman answered the phone. "Mr. Ward is on his boat. Can I help you?"

"I'm Joe Chelsea, an old friend of his. Can you tell me when he'll be back?" Aware of the woman's hesitation, he repeated hastily, "I *am* an old friend and would like the chance to see him again."

"Does your visit have anything to do with his former occupation?"

"I'm retired, Miss . . ." She hadn't offered her name. "I assure you it's merely to discuss old times."

Josh tugged his shoulder, and whispered, "Ask if she can contact him ship-to-shore." Chelsea gave her the suggestion.

"Let me have your number. I'll get back to you."

"Well?" Josh asked.

"She's going to call back. Odd—she didn't give her name. She had a British accent, and now I wonder if Ward remarried." He weighed a thought. "I also wonder whether Ward might still be working for the government."

"Why would you think that?"

"She was too wary, too suspicious." Chelsea gestured carelessly. "In any case, we can only wait it out. I suspect she's checking me out with Ward right now."

Chelsea refilled his pipe and lit it. He stared abstractedly at the blue-gray smoke swirling into the window air-conditioner. He knew he was trying Josh's patience by postponing his formal entry into their partnership.

After a brief silence he said, "Bear with me, Josh. I asked for a month, which means another three weeks. I fully intend sticking to my promise, no matter how this turns out."

"Okay, I'll take you at your word. Just don't disappoint me." He looked up at Chelsea from behind the immaculate desk. "You don't honestly believe you're going to solve two murders in that—"

The phone rang, interrupting him. "Novick Security," he said, and he listened a moment. "He's right here." He handed the phone to Chelsea.

The British accent came through, apologizing. "Sorry if I seemed rude earlier. When you said 'old friend,' I had to be certain. I'm sure you understand."

"It's quite all right."

"You inquired earlier if Mr. Ward had ship-to-shore. Yes, he has. He said he would be happy to speak with you." In an efficient manner she gave him the code.

"Thank you. And how is Dave? In good health, I hope."

"His health is excellent." Her voice lost some of its stiffness. "By the way, I'm Mae Warren, Dave's girl Friday, as you Americans would say it. May I ask a personal question?"

"Go ahead." Chelsea smiled; she was warming up.

"Your name—Chelsea—is British. You don't sound it."

"My grandfather was a barrister in prewar London. We never met; he passed away before I was born. I saw my paternal grandmother once, when I was six. Here in America." He grinned. "How else can I help you?" This drew a small but pleasant laugh. She was unwinding.

"Just out of curiosity I have to ask whether you ever returned to the land of your ancestors."

"Just once. For two months. It preceded the landing at Omaha Beach. You wouldn't by any chance remember D-Day?" This brought heartier laughter.

"Hardly. *That* war was finished before I was born. In any case, I won't keep you. Dave is anxious to hear from you. Thank you for calling."

"Who was the woman?" Josh asked, taking the phone from Chelsea.

"Mae *Warren*—not Ward." He handed Josh the radio code for Ward's boat. "Do you call from here or your boat?"

"Here. It'll save time." A smile brightened the lean face. "Ask where his marina is, and if they'll have an open berth this evening. We can take the women along and make an evening of it."

In less than fifteen minutes Ward was on the radio-phone. His voice whipped through elatedly. "Joey Chelsea—of all people—it's great to hear from you." His speech was effusive, without slackening. "Are you free tonight? Can we get together? I should be in port in another two hours."

Chelsea explained that he was with an old friend and that they'd like Dave to join them and their wives for dinner aboard Josh's boat that evening. "Bring your girl Friday along," he added. Loud laughter undulated across the wire.

"My girl Friday! That's terrific. Joey, my boy, Mae is my secretary, housekeeper, and lover. Terrific at all three. She's been with me for four years and I couldn't exist without her. You still married to Ellen?"

"Like you, I couldn't exist without her." Chelsea felt Josh's impatience. "Where is your marina, and can you get us a berth for a fifty-four-foot Hatteras?"

"No problem. The season's early yet." He gave Joe the address. "When can I expect you?"

Chelsea looked at Josh questioningly. "Eight?" Josh nodded.

"Perfect. Casual dress, Joey. Don't go formal on me. I've become an old seadog. All right, I have to sign off now. Got the marina? Okay, I'll be watching for your Hatteras."

"Phew!" Chelsea shook his head. "The man is still a whirlwind. Asks a question and answers it himself." He could see Josh making mental calculations. "Something amiss?"

"Is Ellie a good sailor? Taking the ocean shoreline would be faster than the Intracoastal, but a little rougher. The ocean route could save us a half-hour."

"Make it the ocean. Ellie would love it."

6

Dave Ward at five-ten and a hundred and eighty-five pounds was squarely built, broad in the shoulders and chest. Despite the imposing figure, he had a remarkably innocent face for a man in his former line of work. A contributing factor was perhaps the silver-streaked black beard and small mustache he sported, not to mention his outgoing nature. He'd turned sixty on his last birthday and, in his shorts, displayed well-muscled legs that would have been impressive on a man ten years his junior. He had just caught up with the harbormaster.

"They call in yet?" he asked, in a deep baritone.

The harbormaster, a tall, slightly plump man in his fifties, nodded. "Just got off the radio. The *Novick's Ark* is coming through the channel now. Want to lend a hand tying her up?"

"That's why I'm here, Luke."

Leaving his young assistant in charge, Luke led Ward out to the dock. "The ship has power and water if they want it," he said over his shoulder.

Ward nodded and then waved to a statuesque blonde, who

was standing on the terrace of the posh yacht club, to join him. She waved back and moved quickly, catching up to them by the time they reached the reserved slip.

Mae Warren was almost as tall as Ward. Longish hair lapped the collar of her striped linen shirt. An oval face displayed sensitive, alert blue-green eyes, which Ward had described as resembling the shallow waters of the Gulf Stream. The twenty-year difference in their ages had no effect on their relationship. They had met four years earlier on a cruise, and she had come ashore and stayed with him. Watching *Novick's Ark* entering on its own inertia, Mae's eyes glistened with anticipation.

Although both had outgoing natures, the couple rarely entertained in their small, Spartan apartment; Dave still had another year to pay off his boat. They enjoyed some privileges in the yacht club, but were not members.

"Your friends must have money," Mae whispered.

Ward laughed softly, amused. "Not Joey. He has some, but not like Novick. I never met Novick. He was in the hospital when I worked with Joey. I learned later he was the wealthiest man on the force."

Following the harbormaster's directions, Josh expertly maneuvered the yacht into its slip, prow forward. From the forward deck Cindy threw down a line for Ward. Chelsea waited for instructions on the open afterdeck. In minutes the yacht was tied up.

The *Ark* was elegant in its fittings; there was a large lounge on the bridge deck and a spacious salon below it. A lower deck had four staterooms, three of which had queen-size beds and access to private heads.

"Well done," Ward remarked warmly as he and Mae were invited aboard, Mae, being the youngest, wasn't quite sure what to expect, but was pleasantly surprised by the exuberant welcome from Cindy and Ellie. Ward greeted Chelsea with a bear hug, as if meeting a long-lost brother.

"I'll be damned, Joey. You really stayed fit." Without giving Chelsea a chance to respond, he turned to Josh. "So, you're the one I never got to meet. I see you came out of it in one piece."

"Well, almost," Josh replied cheerfully. "C'mon, let's get off the deck and into the salon. You guys must be hungry. I hope you like lobster tails."

"Anything you have will be okay," Ward replied. "We're starving. We usually eat earlier." Mae gave him a deprecating look. "It's okay, Mae honey. Joey knows me."

Cindy tugged at Ellie's arm. "We may as well get started. "Would you like to help?" she asked Mae.

"Yes, of course. Please excuse Dave. There are times when his outspokenness gets out of hand."

Ellie laughed. "Welcome to the family."

In the salon Ward dropped onto a leather sofa, one of two flanking a low table that could be raised to dining height. Josh asked, "What are you drinking?"

"A Scotch and soda, some ice." He grinned. "I'm not driving." Chelsea settled into a leather chair at one end of the table. He blew out a deep breath. "Man, you never slow down."

"Can't, Joey. You never know who's chasing you." He leaned forward and rubbed his knees. "Okay, let's get down to it. You said 'retired.' What brings you here? It's how many years now? About ten?" Josh, at the well-stocked bar, took ice cubes from the icemaker and smiled. The man might not look it, but he was quick on the draw.

Chelsea, shaking his head, reached for his pipe and tobacco. The man was still a dynamo; there was no other way to describe him. Before he could speak, Ward said, "Josh, I see you allow smoking aboard."

"In the salon, with the doors opened, yes." With that, Ward reached into a shirt pocket for a pack of cigarettes.

"Go ahead, Joey. I'm waiting."

Chelsea barely contained a laugh. "You retired from the service and still nurse suspicions. What makes you think I'm about to call in an old marker?"

"Quit stalling, Joey. I just turned sixty, and getting older by the minute. How can I help you?"

Chelsea nodded. You can't fool an old pro.

"I served my time on the force—so they told me—and came down south to join Josh's security firm. A few days later I was brought in by chance to look at a murder victim. The circumstances surrounding the case were too tempting not to investigate on my own." Ward leaned forward, his eyes displaying interest. He understood the circumstances behind enforced retirement.

"The victim was a survivor of Dachau, and . . ." Ward stiffened in his seat, and his eyes narrowed.

"Do you know the cause of death?"

Josh set Ward's Scotch on the mahogany table and pushed an ashtray in front of him. Ward hadn't lit up as yet.

Chelsea continued. "There was a needle puncture on one of the tattooed numbers." He lit his pipe and eyed the ex-FBI man over the lighter. "Want to speculate on it?"

Ward's expression wasn't one of idle curiosity. He pulled out a cigarette, lit it, puffed thoughtfully, then lifted his glass to take a deep swallow. "I'll withhold speculation until I hear more. And I'd like Mae to hear it."

Chelsea and Josh exchanged glances. *Why was it important that Mae Warren listen in*? Chelsea's thoughts rambled, settling on: *They know something*. "Okay, Dave, I'll just add one more thing. There was another murder—early this morning—similar MO."

Ward downed his drink. "Jesus! It's still going on." He

waved Chelsea's hand aside. "Wait for Mae." As an afterthought he asked, "Are your wives privy to this?"

Both men nodded, and Chelsea said, "I always share with Ellie." He knew, in this instance, that Josh had discussed it with Cindy. Having met the Mosel woman, she had been too inquisitive to be excluded.

In the silence that followed, Chelsea got up to make himself a drink. He waved Josh back into his seat. "You want something?" Josh shook his head.

The bar was in the far corner of the salon, to the right of the doors leading to the afterdeck. Chelsea stood there, surveying the labels, undecided. He didn't really want a drink; he was merely marking time. The case, or at least the MO, was familiar to Ward. That was obvious. Joe speculated. *Was Ward still active—despite his innocent appearance? And how did Mae Warren fit in?*

He finally settled on straight vodka, with an ice cube, and waited.

As if orchestrated, the women returned from the forward galley. Cindy was carrying a platter of broiled lobster tails. Mae had a huge bowl of tossed salad. Ellie followed with a tablecloth and place settings.

Cindy made a face. "Josh, the table . . ."

"Sorry, I'm sleeping." He pushed a button beneath the mahogany top and the table rose from a brass column. Next he lifted the leaves underneath and the coffee table was now a dining table accommodating up to eight people.

Midway through the lobster, Chelsea became impatient. "Dave, we're all here. It's time we continued our earlier discussion." Ellie and Cindy didn't seem surprised, having known beforehand what their husbands were pursuing. At Chelsea's nod, Ward centered his attention on Mae Warren.

"Joey and Josh have come across two concentration-camp survivor assassinations." Mae's eyes darkened as she turned to Chelsea. "I thought you said you were retired."

"I was—er, I am."

"Then, why—"

He interrupted her, and filled her in on what he'd told Dave. "We have nothing to do with the police. It's mere curiosity on our part to know more."

Her eyes didn't believe him; Joe wondered why. Did he detect uneasiness in her?

At Ward's reassuring nod, she took a sip of the wine that had been served. Reflecting, she put her glass aside and spoke quietly.

"Did you ever hear of the Benefactor Alliance?"

Amidst the puzzled looks, Chelsea pursed his lips, suspecting they had opened a can of international worms. Mae was British, and somehow connected. He glanced at Ward, who busied himself lighting a cigarette. "No, please continue," Joe said softly.

She spoke tentatively, hesitating, seemingly measuring and censoring her thoughts. "I left MI5 about seven years ago." She appeared to gain courage once she'd begun. "I was a secretary to one of the superintendents and was privy to many of the cases in progress. I don't believe the events dealing with the survivors of the concentration camps would fall in the classified files." She caught Ward's encouraging nod. "The first assassination was in London about 1982, the second, a week later, in Canterbury."

Cindy and Ellie listened in breathless silence, astonished by her revelations. Then gazed in awe at Mae Warren. MI5 didn't need explanation; they knew about such things from their husbands. Chelsea chewed on his lip, wondering where Mae's disclosures would lead.

"The assassin was careless in the commission of the second murder. A neighbor of the victim caught him coming out of the flat. Thinking him a burglar, she chased him, screaming bloody murder, not knowing he was an assassin. Believe it or not, the people in the street caught him in a wild foot chase." She paused, gathering her thoughts. "In any case, by the time the constable arrived on the scene, the killer was half-beaten to death. The man was unconscious until he was placed in an ambulance. There, he came to and took in his surroundings, then looked up at the inspector accompanying him. According to the inspector's report, the battered man smiled and said, 'You can't stop the Benefactor Alliance,' and then stopped breathing."

When Mae paused, Chelsea asked, "Did the man have a tattoo on his wrist?"

"Yes. His fingerprints were later checked, but they weren't on file anywhere, not even at Interpol. From Interpol it was learned that there were fifteen other similar assassinations, in different countries, over a period of twenty-five years."

Chelsea's eyes narrowed in thought. Although it didn't make sense as yet, they had a definite lead. For whatever it was worth, *certain survivors of the death camps had become assassins of other survivors.* All from Dachau?

The others around the table nibbled at their food, utterly fascinated by Mae's story. Chelsea asked, "The two victims you know of—were they former inmates of Dachau?"

Mae nodded, seemingly talked-out. She reached for her wineglass again. Ward leaned forward and took her hand from across the table. "I'm retired, Mae. It's out of my province. All they want from me is information." She nodded, forcing a smile she didn't feel. Her father had been among the war correspondents entering Dachau. Years later she had come across the pictures he had taken of the obscene camp.

Ward turned to Chelsea. "I can recall only one similar

case while I was with the Bureau. On a train, the Chicago–New York run. I came aboard at Cleveland because the body had crossed state lines."

"You knew nothing about the Benefactor Alliance?" Josh asked.

Ward fingered his beard. "Until meeting Mae I never heard of it. I've been out of it for ten years. Her account—as old as it is—is more up-to-date." Turning, he directed a shrewd look at Chelsea. "Okay, Joey, what did you *really* expect from me?"

"Nothing," Cindy interjected. "At least not before we finish eating. For dessert, Key Lime pie will be served on the afterdeck." She stood up, as if terminating any disagreement before it began. The discussion had taken on an ominous overtone, which left her wishing the Blue Jays wouldn't pursue this matter so diligently.

While the women were preparing dessert and coffee, the men left the air-conditioned salon for the rear deck. Since the evening was balmy, the mica windows had been rolled up, permitting a gentle breeze to waft under the fiberglass canopy. Another bar, complete with icemaker and fridge, stood against a bulkhead. A curved table followed a padded bench, which could seat ten people comfortably.

Chelsea's eyes roamed the marina; yawls, sloops, boats of various sizes, occupied most of the slips. At a dock beyond, aboard a megayacht at least 150 feet long a party was in progress.

"Some people know how to live," he remarked without envy.

"That ship is old money," Ward offered. "It's a normal way of life for them that has it. Now, you take my Viking. Another year of payments and it's all mine. I don't need *anything* else."

Chelsea gave him a close look. "You still owe me a

marker, Dave." Ward casually lifted his lighter to a fresh cigarette. "I was afraid you were going to call it in." He flicked off the lighter, and his expression turned somber. "If it's info—okay. I have some friends. Other than that, no involvement."

Chelsea nodded. "That's all I want."

Ward looked at him intently. "Tell me, Joey. Why do you want it? You're retired; you don't need it."

"Interesting," Josh interjected. "The two of us thinking alike, with the same questions. Yeah—Joey, my boy—tell me again why you need it."

Chelsea grimaced. "Retirement was something forced on me. I wasn't prepared for it. I can't resign myself to it overnight. You two guys are something. I don't know how you stand the lazy life."

"Horeshit!" Ward exploded. "Christ! You're afraid of getting old! I've seen others suffering the same complaint. You're built like a brick shithouse! You should take a good look at some of the specimens down here, and then thank God you in no way resemble them." When Chelsea kept stoically silent he added, "Okay, I owe you. Let's have it."

"First," Chelsea said, "let's do some summing up."

Josh interrupted by handing both men bottles of beer, then settled down on the bench. "Shoot," he said, "you've got our attention."

"To begin, let's make some assumptions—if only temporarily. We can assume *all* the victims came out of Dachau. Question: Why Dachau, and not some other camp? Answer: Something happened there—or in the vicinity—that all were witness to." He waved aside Ward's attempted interruption. "Yes, I know, plenty happened there. I'm referring to something additional—an occurrence, or possibly an activity—that was never brought to light."

Josh stared glassy-eyed, listening to his friend. In his

mind's eye he was transported back in time, to the squad room, listening to the morning briefing before going out on the line. The picture lasted mere seconds, but it was then that he understood Joe's dilemma. Joe wasn't out of it long enough to adjust. The man was in his element now, just as he was then, with his computerlike mind busily processing every detail. Within himself, Josh felt the old, almost forgotten, response to duty. He glanced at his former partner, wondering whether it was an atavistic trait in both of them, a basic characteristic that couldn't be denied with age. ". . . Are you with me," cut into his wandering thoughts.

"All the way." He sipped his drink.

"All right. To move ahead, another question: How do you turn an elderly survivor into a murderer of other survivors?" Ward cocked his head, finally comprehending where Chelsea was leading. He licked his lips as if he had tasted something sour.

"Christ!" he burst out. "You're assuming they were brainwashed!" He winced at the thought. "Joey, you missed your calling. You should be writing fiction." He waved a deprecating hand. "As far as I know, the liberating forces found no evidence that would correspond with your suspicions. Whatever brainwashing techniques the Nazis used, they weren't that sophisticated during those years." He took a swig of his beer, then peered at Chelsea. "Jesus! That's what you want me to look into, isn't it?"

Chelsea remained unruffled. "I'm sure you still have contacts in the Miami agency. Unless you've lost your touch, I'm certain you can make discreet inquiries."

"Into what? New brainwashing techniques?"

A barely perceptible smile softened Chelsea's features. "No, I'd like to know more about the Benefactor Alliance. You might try digging into old government files, try checking into Emma Mosel's background. I believe she might have been a pretended survivor."

"You know something I don't?" Josh asked, more than a bit puzzled.

With all eyes upon him, Chelsea became hesitant. "Well, I know it sounds farfetched . . ."

"You said you 'believe.' "

"All right, strike 'believe.' It's only guesswork. Carbolo honored my request to investigate Mrs. Mosel's background. She came out of a DP camp around 1949. A year after her arrival in the States she married Gunther Mosel." He hesitated again. "Well, this is where it gets hairy. In checking with Emma's in-laws I learned that Gunther Mosel, although a native American, was a prewar Bund member in New York."

A stunned silence lasted only seconds. Josh broke it. "I saw a menorah in her apartment. Are you telling us it was all sham, window-dressing to hide a sinister past?"

Chelsea chewed on the stem of his pipe but kept silent.

"It could explain her death," Ward said. "Someone recognized her from the old country, whoever she was."

Chelsea snorted derisively. "You saying the Alliance is an avenging organization? For more than three decades? And on more than one continent? I can't go along with that. There has to be more to this—and we can't solve anything with wild speculation." He turned to Ward. "Can you help us?"

Josh almost laughed at Ward's pained astonishment. "I heard you used to be a computer whiz. My outfit owns all the equipment you'll ever need."

Ward's eyes were those of a man in turmoil. "Have you any idea what you're asking? You're not talking FBI files. This is CIA territory." He looked challengingly at Chelsea. The man who had saved his life in a terrorist shootout in

Manhattan was smiling. Eventually Ward answered his own question. "Yeah," he said. "You do know what you're asking."

They could hear the women coming with dessert, and Ward needed some answers. "Why are you chasing this case? What's the point of it?" With a look of disdain he said, "Please don't give me any more of that 'I can't retire' shit! No matter the information gathered, we're no longer equipped—not to mention authorized—to do a damn thing about it. Where can you go with it? I have to know the heading."

Chelsea shrugged his big shoulders disarmingly, unconcerned. "Let's just take it one step at a time, and see what develops."

7

From the air the forty-acre island appeared as a green jewel planted in the Gulf Stream. Terraced lawns led up from the water to a massive U-shaped building cresting the top of a hundred-foot rise on the island. Although of contemporary design, the architecture suggested something of the Mediterranean. Situated ten miles south of Nassau, the island was known to Bahamians only as a private retreat for retired executives of an international combine. Deplaning at Nassau, the visitors went from there to the island estate by launch or by helicopter, both privately owned.

Two immense generators supplied electrical power for all amenities, including a 5000-gallon-a-day desalinization plant for the imposing beige brick-and-stucco structure. Fronting the building a staircase led down to a docking facility that on certain occasions was used by a 250-foot yacht.

At the moment there was one tying up.

The island had no bathing beach. The owners assumed the absence of one would discourage inquisitive sailors from coming ashore. An oval swimming pool was located at the rear of the property, in a courtyard protected on three sides by the mansion; the remaining side had a row of whispering Australian pines that kept a constant breeze from intruding.

Six men disembarked from the megayacht; they were the last of a dozen expected. All six were clad in Western dress, but one wore a kaffiyeh head-covering. None used the staircase. Instead, they walked to one side of it, to enter a tram-car which resembled the funiculars of Italy. When all were seated, a male attendant pressed a switch and the car slowly rode up the incline.

The men knew where to go; a waiting attendant motioned them through the marble foyer. The ecru stone walls were bare, devoid of any feminine touch. Although housemaids were on the premises, no other women had ever been on the property, not even the wives of the men who made infrequent appearances; in fact, they knew nothing of its existence.

The six men joined six others, at a long conference table in a windowless room. With the exception of two men, all were in their mid-fifties or sixties. The eldest, the chairman, sat at the head. He was strange-looking, almost feminine, with translucent skin stretched across tiny facial bones. His expression was like that of a predatory bird, with deep-set, teary eyes watching the others as they took their places at the table. He was old, and appeared ancient as he gave a slight nod—as if it were too tiring to speak—to the youngest member, seated at his right hand.

The younger man, in his forties, was the son of the elderly chairman, and had been presiding for the past five years. Six-two, slim and wiry, with a thatch of sandy hair, he scanned the length of the table. A pitcher of water and a glass were set at each man's place. There were no ashtrays. He spoke softly, with a slight edge to his voice.

"Gentlemen, we've encountered a problem." All remained silent. His voice carried above the slight hum from an air duct. "Someone has attempted to obtain information about the Benefactor Alliance." This brought a gasp from one man, but he made no interruption.

The speaker eyed him a moment, then resumed. "Factor number 111 was forced into an unanticipated termination." All eyes were trained on the speaker. "A woman, a mentally disturbed survivor of the camp, claimed he was her brother." A harsh look was directed at one man who raised his hand. The hand was withdrawn.

"Please reserve all questions until I have finished." He adjusted wire-rimmed spectacles and continued. "Our original Factors are wearing down. With one more termination they themselves—having become obsolete—will be eliminated. The present system is working well. The newly designed microchips installed on younger replacements have exceeded expectations. A majority have successfully established themselves in particular government positions, which bodes well for the future. European countries are in flux now, as you well know. Our younger Factors have been prepared and are slowly, but surely, gaining entrance to the positions that will create the future we intended." He paused briefly. "That returns us to the one problem remaining. We have to remove an Achilles' heel, the Factor who precipitated an investigation into the Benefactor Alliance. As yet, we do not know why this occurred, except that this particular Factor had a flaw—headaches, which if allowed to continue, could possibly cause an exchange of memory. He is the last of the brainwashed 'originals' and—as such—won't be replaced. All others are too young to use his memory bank. Once finished with his final termination, he will be recalled for total extinction."

He glanced down the length of the table, at no one in particular. "This meeting is now open for discussion."

A gray-haired, well-known industrial figure raised a finger. "You mentioned a problem. You said that someone attempted to obtain information about the Benefactor Alliance, but you neglected to furnish any details."

The man chairing the meeting looked to the wasting figure beside him. He received a nod. "We thought it prudent to withhold the details, since it is in *our* province to deal with a problem of this nature. However, with the Doctor's permission . . . A man, Joseph Chelsea, a recently retired homicide police officer, has—for some unknown reason—taken it upon himself as a personal duty to investigate the death of the unanticipated termination mentioned earlier. Chelsea also has involved two other men; one, namely Joshua Novick, is a former lieutenant of police; the other, David Ward, is a former member of the Federal Bureau of Investigation." The speaker's brows knit in concentration; he spoke without benefit of notes. "Our sources advise us that Ward is also a computer expert and that he was the individual attempting to access the Alliance code. Nevertheless, there is no doubt in our minds that this search was instigated by Chelsea. We are on top of everything and will treat the matter with extreme care.

"The single disturbing note in this is how they learned of the Benefactor Alliance. However, I can assure you they will never access the code."

A well-known international financier signaled for permission to speak. "As always, we leave it in your capable hands." He hesitated briefly. "The headaches that Factor number 111 has complained of . . . Are others having a like problem?"

"No. It was a flaw confined to the originals, of which he is the last. Our methods have greatly improved over the years. There is no fear of it occurring in the Factors in place now."

Another figure, a shipping magnate in his fifties, raised his hand. "At this stage, can anything go wrong?"

The ancient, silent chairman, known as the Doctor, spoke for the first time. In a reedy voice he said, "You are a fool to think it possible. Within the present decade you will control the chessboard of governments. You will accomplish this without the decimating consequences of military juntas. This planet will be yours. Your only problem will be seeking other worlds to conquer."

The younger, presiding chairman lifted his head imperiously. "Gentlemen, on that note we will conclude the meeting." He got to his feet. "Your usual rooms are in readiness if you wish to stay overnight. Both the launch and helicopter are at your disposal should you decide to leave now. For those staying, dinner will be served promptly at seven. Please notify the staff of your intentions."

The speaker waited for all to file out, then pressed a button beneath the tabletop. A muscled attendant, clad in white jacket and dark trousers, appeared with a wheelchair. At a nod, he lifted the Doctor and settled him into the chair.

The Doctor looked up at his son. "You will tend to this Chelsea?"

"Need you ask?"

The old man grunted. "It will be in your hands."

The son watched the attendant wheel out his father, the man whose brilliant scientific mind had conceived the Benefactor Alliance more than four decades earlier. Unlike Hitler, his vision was to conquer without the sense of subjugating the foe. Except for the arms industry, war was useless. War wrought only hatred and dissension. With Factors already in position—five European countries had a combined total of twenty in elected office, with more expected—the Alliance would own the world. It was no longer a dream. There would be another fifty Factors in high places—including the Americas—in the next few years.

He smiled suddenly, but his eyes were humorless. There remained only a single witness to the original experiments—and he would soon be dealt with. Chelsea, and his fumbling cohorts, would be watched carefully to ensure they were no threat.

He fingered an onyx-and-gold ring, in concentrated thought. It would be interesting to see how close these meddling retired policemen could come. Never one to be indecisive, he resolved to cancel his earlier decision to terminate them. The challenge of the three elderly detectives was too much to resist. He understood the risk, but he was unworried about being discovered by the elite members of the Alliance. Their greed made them simple to manipulate, easy prey for the new Factors secretly established in their corporations and conglomerates. Unknown to the aging members, a new variety of Factors was in preparation to assume command from them. Another five years, he estimated, for total takeover.

His ruminations should have created a sense of elation, but he realized that unless his father received a new host body soon, he might not live to see the completion of the plan. Beset with morbid thoughts—one in particular—he wondered why ten years ago his father decided to take up residence in a high-rise condominium located in Palm Beach County. Conscience? To live out his life among so many of the survivors of the death camps? A postmortem study of live bodies was the way the Doctor explained it to his son. But Jon Seltzmann didn't believe it; aging had created a guilt complex.

Except for one weekend each month spent at the island, the Doctor was known as a retired chemist. His circle of friends at the condo understood his absence to be a monthly visit to his physician somewhere up north. A middle-aged nurse, masquerading as his wife, attended to all his needs.

So be it, Jon Seltzmann thought. *Let him flagellate himself. It changes nothing.*

8

It was almost noon when Chelsea got back to Josh's office. He had just purchased a new, white Oldsmobile Ciera. Earlier he had phoned his lawyer-accountant in New York and had instructed him to sell his old Buick. He and Ellie couldn't go on borrowing Josh's Porche or Cindy's station wagon. The Ciera had been available on the lot, and at the moment bore temporary plates.

"Jesus!" he remarked dryly. "I walked right in. When are you going to hire a receptionist?"

Josh pointed to a monitor overhead. "There's my receptionist. It's dependable. Never fails me, rain or shine." He was sitting behind his desk, studying résumés. "Talk about hiring, you can do me a favor, Joe. There are three applicants coming in this afternoon. I'd like you to interview them." He looked up to catch his friend's mind elsewhere. "Is that too much to ask?"

"Josh, I've had two men tailing me ever since I left the apartment this morning." Chelsea tossed a small card on the desk, a license number and make of car written on it. "See what you can find out. It's possible that I—or we—have struck a responsive chord. Dave warned us that even though he hasn't broken their code, they would know someone was making the attempt."

"He'll be back tonight. Despite his original protests he apparently finds it too challenging to give up." Josh made a sour face. "I'm not sure I want him to continue." He hit a button on the console at the corner of his desk. The picture on the overhead monitor changed scene, and was scanning the firm's parking lot.

Chelsea watched the screen for a few seconds. "Across the street, the black Toyota. Two men in it."

"Shit!" Josh exploded. "Joe, I've been out of it too long. I don't like what's happening."

Chelsea stirred impatiently. "You sit tight and keep an eye on the monitor. I'm going out the back door."

Josh's lips tightened, with full comprehension of Chelsea's intention. It recalled incidents he'd sooner have forgotten. He opened a drawer and withdrew an S&W police special. "You better take this," he said soberly.

"Won't need it. Just keep an eye on the monitor." Chelsea disappeared before Josh could protest. Josh worked the console until the monitor showed the Toyota in close-up.

Chelsea left by the back door and cut through spongy undergrowth to the next property, to the rear of a window-blind warehouse. Continuing past, he pushed through wild vegetation until he came out at the end of the block. Striding to the corner, he found himself about thirty yards behind the car.

Few people were about, the area occupied mostly by small factories, some in dire need of repair. He approached the car unhurriedly. Two men sat in the front, smoking cigarettes and occasionally looking across to the security firm. Both men appeared startled when Chelsea, smiling, leaned toward the open passenger-side window.

"I'm new here," Chelsea said casually. "Can either of you direct me to the Benefactor Alliance?"

The man in the passenger seat dropped his cigarette. He made an unsuccessful swipe to protect his slacks. The driver, at first bewildered, then retorted aggressively. "No, we can't help you, Mac. We're new here also." His face reddening, he switched on the ignition and assumed a diffident manner. "Sorry, we've got places to go." The effort to control his temper was lost as the Toyota took off with rubber burning.

Chelsea adjusted his sunglasses, grimacing in disgust. "Rank amateurs!" he spit out, crossing the street to rejoin Josh.

"It doesn't make sense," Chelsea said. "I can't see them working for an assassination bureau. What we're seeking should be more sophisticated. Those guys are small-time hoods, slow-witted and totally inept."

"So, why are they tailing you?"

"Good question," Chelsea said, in deep concentration. Josh watched him standing at the window of the small office, staring out abstractedly at the quiet street. He recognized the easy calm behind the ill-concealed introspection; Joe was separating speculation from fact. In due time he would find a working solution. More often than not, his speculation, added to known facts, proved to be on the mark.

Chelsea turned from the window. "Someone is testing us," he said quietly. He pulled out his tobacco pouch and pipe. Josh patiently withheld any interruption. "What does 'Alliance' mean? Simply stated, it's an amalgam of organizations or people. We do know this alliance is international, and that it's been in existence for years. It has to be vast, and yet no one knows of it. As a matter of fact, not even the two mugs in the Toyota. Both seemed more puzzled than embarrassed. Why? Again, simply stated, the Benefactor Alliance doesn't exist except in the minds of those who control it." He stopped to fill the Dunhill briar. Josh leaned back in his swivel chair and marveled at the workings of his friend's mind.

Without lighting up, Chelsea resumed. "Dave won't find anything. The Alliance exists only as a front for an amalgam of other organizations."

Josh clapped his hands together softly. It was time he conveyed his own thoughts.

"Terrific! Your speculation is beautiful. So now all we have to do—just the three of us—is to discover the identity of a worldwide organization supplied with assassins. Just great! In all due respect, Joe, this is one time you've gone too far out in your thinking." He straightened in his chair, now more fearful than ever of where Chelsea was headed.

Chelsea held his gold lighter to the briar. Clouds of gray smoke drifted lazily across the room until finally dispersed by the air duct. "Granted, they're unproven opinions, but my gut tells me I'm on track. Those two idiots don't belong in any international organization. I repeat, someone is testing us. As far as we know, they only kill certain survivors of Dachau. Why send dodos to watch *us*? They want to see how far we can, or will, go."

Josh shook his head, greatly disturbed. "How far are we going?"

There was no hesitation from Chelsea. "We get Dave to go into the computer files, in search of an ex-Nazi formerly stationed in Dachau. Someone of prominence—perhaps an industrialist—or possibly a scientist. All the Allies grabbed them at war's end for their own use."

"Then what? Even if Dave agrees—and I'm not sure he will, or can, for that matter—where do we go from there? What can we possibly do with the information?"

Chelsea smiled tolerantly. "Dave still has some warm contacts. And he's a man of discretion. As to what we can do, the watchwords remain 'one step at a time.'"

Josh regarded his friend with trepidation. "More than instinct tells me we're playing with our lives." He shifted uneasily. "By mentioning Benefactor Alliance to those hoods, you've addressed the so-called testing blatantly. Where is it written that they stop at killing camp survivors?"

Chelsea's craggy face creased in contemplation. "*My* instinct says someone is playing a game with us." He tapped his nose. "It's never been wrong. He—or they—will play us out. Perhaps they're waiting to find out how their security has been breached. They might be checking for heretofore unknown loopholes."

"After four decades! C'mon, Joe. Let's be logical."

Chelsea took a seat opposite the desk. Except for the résumés lying there undisturbed, everything was in its proper place. No one could accuse Josh of being sloppy. Nevertheless, Josh's attitude had become ambivalent—that, or he was playing devil's advocate.

Chelsea's own detached tranquillity was deceptive. Inwardly, he felt a growing excitement. It was this particular case, he told himself, hinting of international intrigue; a case resembling nothing they had ever encountered before. He found it difficult to understand how Josh could reject the challenge. He looked up to find his friend eyeing him.

"Joe, I know what's going through your mind. You're thinking, 'My friend is getting old, he's lost the will.'" He gave a tentative laugh. "You want the truth? Age has nothing to do with it. Oh, sure, there might be some atrophy—it's not surprising, with my leg . . . To be candid, Joe, it's confidence I lack, not will. I simply don't have the energy or dedication to match yours. I would be kidding myself to say otherwise."

Chelsea shrugged resignedly, his disappointment keen. "Okay, I'll accept that, Josh. Can you at least check out the license number I gave you?"

"I don't have to. The plate tells me it's a rental. And the driver's name will most likely be fictitious. Fingerprints might tell us more, but there's no way I can pursue it without questions being asked."

Chelsea nodded, remarking, "Your mind hasn't atrophied." He leaned forward in his chair. "You were forced to leave the department with an unfinished career. Wouldn't you like to go out in a blaze of glory?"

"Or just a blaze!" Josh wore a saturnine expression. "I left ten years ago, Joe. I'm not the same guy." He gave Chelsea a harsh stare. "Christ! Don't start pulling my one good leg. We're supposed to be running a business together. When will you drop this to join me?"

"I still have better than two weeks on the month I promised you."

"I hate to keep harping on it, Joe. Whether or not you come up with something?"

"I've given my word." Chelsea glanced at his watch. "Can you call Carbolo without making waves?"

Josh rubbed his forehead. "How do you segue so matter-of-factly?" He reached for his Rolodex. "You owe me lunch for this." The lieutenant wasn't in. Josh left a message saying he'd call back.

Chelsea got to his feet. "Dave won't arrive until tonight. Meanwhile, to show good faith, I'll meet with your present crew on tap and go over your operation. After lunch I can take on the interviews with the new applicants."

Josh stood up and mock-saluted. "I can only marvel at the captain's ability to adapt."

Chelsea's eyes sparkled. "Let's go eat."

The tall wiry figure patiently wiped his glasses as he waited for the fax machine to stop. The information was sent out of South Florida to an office in Chicago that had been rented only to receive the fax and then relay it to another, similar "office" in Bimini. From Bimini it went to its final destination, the private isle ten miles from Nassau. Once relays of the current message were completed, the office would be emptied and abandoned. No trace of the tenant would remain.

The slim figure, clad in a white terry-cloth jacket and swim trunks, had just returned from the outdoor pool to his command post on the first floor of the mansion. His pale blue eyes squinted in amusement as he scanned the message and the accompanying photos.

In one picture Joseph Chelsea, the former NYPD homicide captain, was leaning toward the side door of a black Toyota. The image was exceptionally sharp. Other photos showed him as a large man in nondescript clothing; his sport shirt resembled those usually worn by tourists. One photo, apparently an enlargement of the original, showed his face in complete detail. His lips were grim, his eyes wary. In a second, later shot, he seemed amused. Had he detected the photographer?

The man ran a hand through his damp, sand-colored hair as he reread the data on the torn-off sheets. It was a complete readout of Chelsea's history, dating from the time of his birth. It was quite extensive, arousing the reader's interest. He found a wicker chair and sat down to better study the biography.

A half-hour later he returned to the photos. He regarded

the exterior of Novick Security's nondescript building with clouded eyes. Its appearance belied the equipment used by the firm. The attempt to break into the Alliance code employed sophisticated computers—not to mention an accomplished computer expert. Chelsea? No. Nothing in his bio suggested it. Joshua Novick? Possibly. An employee? No. Chelsea wouldn't trust it to an outsider. It had to be Dave Ward, the ex–FBI man.

He put the sheets aside and switched on the fax machine. A message went out to an office in Atlanta, from where it would be relayed to a member of a federal agency in Miami. The Alliance director wanted photos and detailed reports of everyone entering and leaving the Novick Security firm. And he also wanted experts to follow Joseph Chelsea's moves twenty-four hours a day. He stressed *experts*; no others would do. Should anything go amiss, they would be held accountable.

The director leaned back, a grim smile tightening his lips. This man Chelsea intrigued him no end. How had he tumbled onto the Alliance? He had retired from police work and consequently wielded no authority. The encounter with the operatives in the Toyota proved, if nothing else, that Joe Chelsea was not one to shy away from confrontations. *The man was either a fool or extremely clever.* The director's eyes narrowed with some concern. If a leak in the foolproof system had occurred, he had no choice but to pursue it to its source.

"Let's see how clever you really are, Chelsea. As the great Sherlock was wont to say, 'The game's afoot.' "

He smiled languidly, his confidence and self-esteem once again intact. Dismissing Chelsea from his mind, he left the command post, crossed the marble foyer, and ran up the winding, stone staircase two steps at a time. A young housemaid, much more entertaining than his wife in Nassau, was waiting to share a shower with him.

The youngest member of the Alliance had reached the second-floor landing when he halted abruptly. His face contorted, struck by a painful recollection. Chelsea had arrived in Florida a mere two or three weeks ago.

The leak could be no other than Factor number 111!

9

The sun seemed to be playing hide-and-seek with the clouds. It was the sort of morning that tested the mettle of meteorologists. Early-morning overcast had been predicted, clearing before noon. The clouds overhead now were dark and, when blocking the sun, cast a gray pall upon the deserted beach. Deserted except for Chelsea and Ellie, who, despite the cool breeze, had decided to join him in his daily ritual.

Ellie had been lying on a pad, eyeing an ominous dark cloud, waiting for it to cross the horizon. She twisted onto an elbow. "Joe, what are we doing down here?"

Chelsea, seated in a deck chair, lifted his head. "I don't get it. What do you mean, 'down here'?"

She made a face. "I mean the beach, not Florida."

Chelsea didn't respond, listening to the sound of running footsteps. Coming into view not a hundred yards from them was a tall, elderly man, treading heavily along the wet shoreline. Chelsea quietly observed the blue sweatpants and matching sweatshirt, and the full head of white hair atop a strained face. He saw the man look back over his shoulder. Another jogger was trailing him, about fifty yards to the rear.

"We're not the only nitwits out today," Ellie remarked dryly.

Chelsea remained silent, his eyes busy, scanning the younger, well-muscled jogger, who was gaining on the elderly man. *Was he chasing him*?—*or just running hard*?

Another slow thirty seconds and he had his answer. The younger man, thirtyish, with a shock of unruly red hair, caught up, and as he started to pass, suddenly lurched into the gray-haired man. *Intentional*? The elderly runner slumped to his knees.

Chelsea leaped from his chair with a shout. Unruly Red Hair spun around, stared at the source of the shout, and instantly took off at a dead run. A single glance told Chelsea he couldn't catch him.

Ellie sat there horrified, unable to find her voice. She vaguely heard her husband's "Stay put, Ellie!" as he darted toward the stricken man.

The man was on his back, his legs doubled beneath him, his cracked lips moving but saying nothing intelligible. The eyes held a stark, terrified look, as if he recognized death approaching. Chelsea lifted his head, and none too gently yelled, "Who was he?"

The man stretched an arm and caught hold of Chelsea's terry-cloth sleeve. His lips were flecked with foam and the words came out haltingly and rasping. "Why . . . why are they eliminating me? I—" He coughed up a glob of bloody phlegm.

Chelsea knew the man wouldn't last long, the pall of death hung over him. "Who are 'they'?" he shouted unkindly.

The eyes stared, attempting to focus on the source of the

voice. "I haven't fulfilled the final termination . . . Why are they doing this?"

Sweat poured out of Chelsea. "Dammit! Tell me who 'they' are!"

"Joe!" Ellie had reached them unnoticed. She tugged at Chelsea's arm. "What are you doing to this poor man!"

"Be calm, Ellie. A doctor can't help. Call the police. Ask for Lieutenant Carbolo. This man is another victim." He turned back to the man, knowing time was running out.

" 'Victim'?" the limp figure mumbled, appearing lost, struggling. His eyes dilated. "Yes, we're all victims." His chest heaved and he coughed up blood.

Chelsea took the damp towel from his own neck and wiped the man's mouth. The stricken man spoke before Chelsea could ask another question. "Yes . . . I see now . . . It's true. We're all victims of Dr. Seltzmann . . . He . . ." His hand tightened on Chelsea's sleeve, then loosened and fell away.

Chelsea placed the towel behind the dead man's head before releasing him. He felt for the carotid artery, knowing it was a useless gesture. Removing his hand, he noticed the uneven hairline. He tugged at it and pulled away the white hairpiece. After an interval he discovered the numbered tattoo upon the wrist. A long, deep sigh escaped the former policeman.

The alleged brother of Emma Mosel!

And now he was a victim as well, thought Chelsea somberly. His mind flashed back to the dead man's words: *I haven't fulfilled the final termination . . . we're all victims . . . Dr. Seltzmann.*

Fulfilled a termination! What a horrible euphemism for outright murder. If Chelsea had ever given any thought to backing off from the search for the Alliance—as his friends were urging him to do—that was now out of the question.

Dr. Seltzmann! Chelsea smiled grimly. Now, there was a name to ponder. German? Formerly from Dachau? It smelled of dirty dealing. Had the OSS, the forerunner of the CIA, pulled Seltzmann out for their own ends? Good God! What purpose would be served by killing those who had survived the death camps! Chelsea shook his head, aghast at the thought Americans could be behind it. Yet . . . He twisted his head, hearing sirens.

Three four-by-fours tore up the sand, racing down the beach. Lieutenant Carbolo was in one of them.

After a brief examination of the body Carbolo straightened up and turned to Chelsea. "Jesus Christ, Captain, why didn't you pick somewhere else to retire?" Chelsea shrugged.

"I did. I used to live in New York. Now I live in Florida. That's 'somewhere else.'"

A mirthless smile played on the lieutenant's lips. "Okay, let's have it. I didn't get much from your wife." Ellie was nowhere in sight. Chelsea assumed she had remained in the apartment after calling the police.

Chelsea regarded Carbolo's *I Love Florida* T-shirt, then gave him an account of the killing.

Carbolo's eyes lifted. "That's it? The victim didn't say anything?"

Let him stew, Chelsea thought. Carbolo had been much too cutesy when Chelsea had been seeking information. He decided to give an inch to see what Carbolo would do. "I got 'failed to fulfill a termination' before he went out. Make whatever you can of it."

His eyes hooded, the lieutenant nodded reflectively. "You're intimating he was the alleged killer of the Mosel woman." He cocked his head. "Could be you're right. He fits the description. So, why was he knocked off if his quota is unfinished? An avenging angel?" When Chelsea remained noncommittal, he said, "Give me the description again of the red-haired man. He could be heading for the airport."

By this time a crowd had gathered. Carbolo instructed two of his men to question the onlookers for possible identification of the victim. A man came forward voluntarily. "I know that man," he said in a reedy voice, pointing to the body being examined by the coroner. The witness was elderly, bald, and slightly stooped. Flowery shorts displayed bony knees. He adjusted his metal-rimmed spectacles, as if to better focus disbelieving eyes.

At Carbolo's prompting, he said, "I don't really know him, but I do remember him jogging along the beach. He didn't wear a wig then." He shivered slightly, unable to remove his myopic eyes from the corpse. "No, I don't really know him, I just remember him jogging and thinking he was *meshuga*. A man of his age running . . ." He clucked his tongue disconsolately.

Chelsea looked up at the gray sky. The weather prophets had miscalculated. Lightning flashed on the horizon, a harbinger of what could be expected. The crowd that had been attracted by the beach patrol sirens started to disperse.

He turned and left, knowing he would find Ellie more than a little disturbed.

She was seated in a straight-backed chair, holding the morning paper stiffly; her face was drawn, her lips tight.

"Don't reproach me for seeming callous, Ellie. That nice elderly gentleman was a cold-blooded killer." The paper slid to her lap. Skeptical eyes searched his.

"How can you be so cocksure?"

"The man's eyes, nose, and mouth were a perfect replica of Mrs. Mosel's." Her shoulders sagged; he leaned toward her. "Yes, I know. As incredible as it sounds, I'm telling you it's possible he killed his own sister. And for what it's worth, I doubt he knew it."

Her eyes were querulous, as she tried to reconcile her feelings with her husband's reasoning. "Ellie, listen to me carefully. You saw the red-haired man . . . Did he see you?"

Her eyes lifted, suddenly alert, recognizing danger signals in his voice. "Yes . . . When he turned at your shout I was only a few feet away from you. He must have seen me."

Chelsea took her hands and brought her to her feet. "Ellie, call Cindy and ask if you can stay with her for a few days." He waited a moment, hesitating. "Never mind, I have to contact Josh anyway. Get dressed while I make the call.

Her eyes blinked with full comprehension. A forced smile followed but she was in command of herself. "Some retirement! Who said 'relax in the land of perpetual sunshine'?" Chelsea nodded, pleased that her sense of humor hadn't deserted her.

After giving Josh an account of the morning's events, Chelsea asked him to get in touch with Dave Ward ASAP. Dave was to use all his ingenuity in a computer search for a Dr. Seltzmann. "Have him check old CIA files, if possible. Then try the industrial field, in particular all companies dealing with biological experimentation."

"Why biological?" Josh's voice registered strained credulity.

"A strong hunch, Josh. I'm convinced that the elderly assassin represented a progression far beyond ordinary brainwashing."

"And you think the CIA might be involved?"

"Not necessarily, but anything is possible."

Silence greeted the flat statement. "You there, Josh?"

A disgruntled "Yeah, I'm here," came over the wire. "Joe,

do you realize where all this could land us? You want to make waves. Who says they—whoever *they* are—will sit around—"

"Are you telling me you won't take Ellie for a few days?"

"Don't be a schmo. Of course we will."

"Sorry, Josh, I should know better. Okay, get crackin' with Dave. And, Josh, remind him to ask Mae if she was privy to the forensics report on the London assassin she told us about."

Chelsea heard a deep sigh at the other end; he could almost see the rueful expression on Josh's face.

"What are you looking for?" Josh asked. "That happened seven or eight years ago."

"The John Doe victim had a surgical scar at the base of his skull, noticeable only with the hairpiece removed."

"Man, what are we getting into!" Abruptly switching the subject, Josh asked, "Didn't Carbolo ask you to work with a police artist?"

Chelsea relaxed; the former police lieutenant had returned to duty. "I expect he'll be calling me back any minute."

10

TWO DAYS LATER

Dave Ward's 45-foot Sport Fisherman looked more like a cruiser than the usual charter fishing boat. The salon was compactly furnished with a soft J-shaped leather sofa, a navigator's desk, and, just forward, a galley. Below, three cabins could accommodate six comfortably.

At the moment, Ward was seated behind the desk glumly tugging at his ear lobe. Morning sun splashed light on his right cheek, but it did nothing to alter his mood. He looked over at Chelsea and Novick, who were seated on the sofa, leaning their arms on the mahogany table that held two mugs of coffee.

"We got trouble," he stated somberly. "I'm being watched." Chelsea nodded, not altogether surprised. Josh gave him an I-told-you-so look, but kept silent.

"By Red?" Chelsea asked. Ward grimaced as if tasting something tart.

"Forget Red. He's probably long gone. We're messing with an organization. It's of little consequence, but I don't believe it's any government agency. I've checked thoroughly and nothing's come up."

Chelsea stirred impatiently. Ward was holding back. "Get to the point. What did you come up with?"

"A Dr. Emil Seltzer was conscripted—conscripted in quotes, that is—by an American agency at war's end. Very hush-hush, a scientist, but in what field I have no idea. Whether this Dr. Seltzer is now Dr. Seltzmann would be pure conjecture. I can't find a trace of him anywhere." He twisted his mouth reflectively, then looked with shadowed eyes at his two visitors. "I had an old buddy do some checking for me . . . Twenty minutes before your arrival I learned he was killed by a hit-and-run."

Josh gaped at him, then pulled a pack of cigarettes from his sport shirt. Chelsea spoke gently, and cautiously. "A minute ago you said no government agency was involved."

Ward constrained a rising temper. "Christ! I worked for the Bureau. I can't believe they would take out one of their own."

"Times have changed, Dave," Chelsea said. "Over the years they've acquired some strange bedfellows."

"Maybe so," Ward conceded. "But if you want an educated guess, I say it's a private organization, one strong enough to infiltrate even government agencies." Chelsea sat back, mulling this over, not altogether in disagreement.

"Okay," he said shortly. "So to follow up . . . Since the death of your friend has anyone from the Bureau tried to contact you?"

"No . . . Look, Joe, if they thought I was involved in any way, they would have picked me up last night, minutes after the alleged hit-and-run."

"But there *is* surveillance on you! How can you dismiss that?"

Ward snorted derisively. "That's why I'm certain it's a

private organization, not the Bureau. Shit! Joe! Why would I be under surveillance instead of having my ass hauled in for questioning?"

"He's got a point," Josh interjected.

"A strong point," Ward added. "My friend would never have involved me."

"Okay, tell me about your shadow," Chelsea said.

Ward regarded him beneath hooded eyes. Chelsea was in charge. In earlier days, Ward's FBI standing would have preempted Chelsea's leadership. But now, with a sense of relief, he realized that he preferred Chelsea to handle the situation.

"I saw this Taurus parking in the marina lot last night, not more than five minutes after I got back from working on Josh's computers. I believe it was the same Taurus I saw parked in the warehouse lot next to Novick Security." His eyes sparked. "My old talents haven't completely deserted me. In any case, it left the marina about midnight. But not until another car, a blue Chrysler Le Baron, pulled in to take the spot it vacated. This morning the Taurus reappeared. A man sat in it for a while, positioned to observe my boat. After a few minutes of waiting he left the car to enter the yacht club." Ward paused, waiting for expected interruptions. He didn't get any. "The man was about thirty, at least six-foot, tanned with a healthy head of dark hair. He was well-dressed in casual summerwear but definitely not yachting clothes."

"Not much to go on," Chelsea commented. "It could be coincidence."

Ward shook his head. "Sorry, I should have said this fellow entered the yacht club's dining room—which I remind you—is open only to members. By members, I mean old money, nothing less. This guy flashed an ID—or possibly a badge—and walked right in for breakfast. If he's a member, he was installed overnight. Which means, if he's not old money, he's got connections."

Josh finished his cigarette and reached for another.

Chelsea had no reason to discount Ward's observations; he was too good at it. "Any license numbers?" he asked.

Ward opened a drawer in the desk and pulled out a sheet of paper. He leaned toward Josh and handed it to him. "Your job," he said. He noticed Chelsea looking at the small computer set on a shelf beside the desk. "What's on your mind, Joe?"

"How good is it?"

"Good! It set me back six grand. I don't have all Josh's hardware but it serves my purpose."

"Can it access CIA files?"

"Christ! You're not asking much! There's no way I can do that without arousing suspicion. When you attempt entry of any data center, it's recorded. That's how companies protect themselves from abuses. For CIA entry, I would have to enter my name, grade, and whatever. You tell me how it could be done."

"You could use your late friend's name. The chances are his death hasn't been filed yet."

Ward's eyes narrowed. "Sure, I could use his name, but it would avail me nothing without his access code."

"C'mon, Dave. You're the expert. There's a way of gathering information by cross-reference once you're in."

Ward blew out a puff of air. "Joey, you've got guts." He swiveled around in his chair and switched on the computer.

He typed in : LANGER, GEOFFREY.

The machine clicked almost inaudibly, then provided a menu. Ward chose BIOG. He breathed easier when he saw there was no notation of Langer's death. His fingers darted over the keys. When he stopped, GIVE ACCESS FILE NUMBER appeared on the screen. He shook his head and called back the main menu, then typed in GIVE LATEST ENTRY.

Chelsea and Josh were leaning forward, trying to read the diminutive screen.

QUERY INTO DR. SELTZMANN.

Ward typed in the name, and asked for his bio.

ACCESS DENIED.

"Damn!" Chelsea said. "It doesn't deny his existence. Dave, try for Dr. Emil Seltzer."

DR. EMIL SELTZER WORKED UNDER THE SPONSORSHIP OF THE FEDERAL GOVERNMENT FROM 1945 UNTIL HIS DEATH IN 1953. HIS DEATH PROMPTED ABANDONMENT OF THE PROJECT.

"Ask what the project was." Chelsea said.

CLEARANCE NEEDED: ACCESS DENIED.

Ward spun around to Chelsea. "Every time it says 'Access Denied,' it records Langer's identification. They'll know someone's been prying after his death." He shut down the machine, and the screen went dark. "I just pray their system isn't sophisticated enough to put a trace on the source of this entry."

Chelsea's face was study in concentration. "If so, the alleged Seltzmann organization will be privy to it also. They have been, so far." He turned to Josh. "We need an ID on those plates. My sixth sense tells me they won't be stolen vehicles."

A brief silence followed. Josh and Ward were weighing the consequences of their actions. Chelsea knew that Josh already had a two-man detail guarding his estate.

Chelsea broke the silence. His eyes held a strange light. "Dave, is the Taurus still here?"

"Yeah. As a matter of fact, the car's parked directly opposite the rear end of yours. The driver's in the club, most likely sipping his third cup of coffee. Positioned at a window table, he can keep an eye on my boat."

Josh eyed Chelsea, recognizing almost-forgotten symptoms. The "captain" was formulating a devious plan. Josh was seized with trepidations. "Joe, what do you intend doing?"

Chelsea was mentally constructing a scene. "If my car is in reverse," he said, "and my foot slips from the brake, I back into his rear fender."

"Your new car!" Josh appeared genuinely shocked. Chelsea waved his reaction aside.

"A minor dent—just enough to bring out the driver." He grinned, seemingly enjoying himself. "We have to exchange driver's licenses and registrations . . ."

Ward held up a hand, doubts clouding his eyes. "Joey, you won't be conning him. He knows you and Josh are here."

"It won't matter. There's bound to be rubberneckers. He can't afford to resist my lawful request."

"Then what?" asked Josh carefully.

"I'll have his identity, and proof of ownership. If it's a company car, we'll also know who he's working for."

"So what!" Ward exclaimed. "He could be a freelancer, working for someone else."

Chelsea's eyebrows lifted. "No. If he's freelancing he would be an utter fool to be driving a company car."

"What if the car is registered in his own name?" Ward asked, quieting down, somehow suspecting the reply.

"Simple. You go into the club's computer and seek out his sponsor. A club of this type doesn't accept a new member without one." Chelsea looked from one gray face to the other. "What can we lose?" he added.

Ward said, "I've been thinking of Mae. You have security patrolling Novick's estate."

Josh intervened. "I hired two new men yesterday. You can have them. Both have excellent résumés."

Ward eyed him warily. "I prefer two of your old crew to stand watch."

Josh shrugged. "No problem."

"And it's at your expense. You guys got me into this."

"Again, no problem."

Chelsea put on his dark glasses. "You ready, Josh?"

A crowd congregated seconds after the crash; the noise was louder than warranted by the damage—a slight dent and cracked tail lights on both cars. The ages of the onlookers ranged from late teens to middle age; most were clad in shorts and stood around appraising the damage. A youngster in a T-shirt that said *I Love Sailing* remarked, "It ain't too bad." Chelsea asked if he knew the owner. An elderly gentleman, leaning to plump but not quite fat, said, "I believe the owner is in the club." Chelsea offered the youngster a dollar to find out. Accepting it eagerly, he took off on a run for the club.

The owner was wearing a blue blazer, sport shirt, and dark trousers. Not exactly morning wear. His shoes were polished to a degree that would satisfy the most exacting sergeant. He stiffened slightly, aware of Chelsea and Josh beside his car.

Chelsea started the charade with a contrite "Sorry, it couldn't be helped. My foot slipped from the brake." He pulled out his wallet and dug for his license. The man in the blazer remained silent, his lips twisted in uncertainty.

"Here's my license and registration," Chelsea said, and digging deeper fished out his insurance identity card. "May I see yours?"

The man hesitated; then conscious of the small crowd—some had already dispersed, no longer interested in a minor accident—he reached into his jacket for his own identification. Wordlessly, he exchanged it for Chelsea's.

Josh, peering over Chelsea's shoulder, remarked with undue expression, "Wellington Security! Whaddaya know. We're in the same line of business." He knew the firm very well. They were national, located in all major cities, and, as of late, were gobbling up the competition.

The driver, George Estry, said with a hint of a smile, "Yes, I know your firm. I was looking at your property only yesterday. We were thinking you might be open for an offer."

"Really!" Chelsea said. "A nice thought, but we're not on the market."

George Estry took back his papers, and offered a business card in exchange. "In case you should change your mind." Chelsea noted the address in Atlanta, Georgia.

Five minutes after George Estry's departure, Chelsea was still studying his business card. Josh was examining the damage to the Ciera. His expression was one of admiration; Joe had achieved his objective and come out with nothing more than minor damage. He straightened to find Chelsea gazing out over the marina. An unlit pipe was clamped in his lips. Josh recognized the posture.

"Okay, Joe, you concocting our next move?" He asked, knowing beforehand it was unnecessary. Chelsea, once started, no matter the pressure, never vacillated on a course of action.

Chelsea glanced at his watch; it was almost noon. "We call the girls and let them know we'll be busy until dinnertime. We have more work for Dave and his computer."

Josh clicked his heels together and executed a comic salute. *"Oui, mon Capitaine."*

Chelsea didn't respond. Although Josh had accepted the situation forced upon him, he wished he could be that certain of Ward.

"Neither the CEO nor the president of Wellington Security is Seltzmann," Dave said. "What now?"

Chelsea tapped his teeth with the bit of his pipe. "Wellington most likely is a conglomerate. Find the parent company."

Two different corporations were named as majority stockholders. Once again Dave looked for Seltzmann, but to no avail. "See who owns both those corporations," Chelsea ordered.

This went on for six hours, the search going deeper and deeper, until it appeared hopeless. Each corporation was a conglomerate or holding company of one, two, or three others. It required a squad of skilled attorneys to keep track. No two were in the same city and some were multinational; and although they dealt in a variety of products and services, none resembled anything that tied in with biology.

Josh had stretched out on the leather sofa, his eyes tired from looking at the small screen for so long. Chelsea, seated in a deck chair at Ward's side, went over the list already compiled by Ward's computer service; except for the tedium it wasn't too difficult to summon the prospectus of each corporation.

The printout was forty feet long, containing more than fifty corporations and their directorships. Chelsea, showing no signs of frustration, studied the names as if reading them for the first time. Ward leaned on an elbow, waiting, and stifling a yawn.

At length Chelsea said, "Get back Resources Unlimited, Dave."

Ward's face displayed tired lines. "Joey, my boy. I thank

God I didn't work under you in my younger days." He stifled another yawn. "I'll give this another hour—I've got an early charter tomorrow morning. I don't know how you guys manage, but I've got a business to run."

Chelsea winced. Without Ward and the computer all trails would be dead ends. His back ached and he too was about ready to pack it in. "All right, let's try a new tack. List all the CEOs and find out whether any of them share directorships in common on any board."

Ward shrugged resignedly, but as he turned back to the keyboard he heard someone coming aboard.

Mae Warren knocked at the salon door and slid it open. She noted their surprised faces. She also noticed the monitor. "You're wasting your time if you're searching for the Benefactor Alliance. I don't believe it exists. At least not under that name."

Ward looked up at Chelsea. "Let's table it for another time." He started to switch off the computer, but Chelsea motioned for him to wait. He turned to Mae Warren. "Where did you get that information?"

"Reflecting back, from Interpol. For what it's worth, it was their opinion." She caught the men exchanging unhappy looks. "What's the trouble? Did I interrupt a stag party?"

Chelsea threw his hands up in defeat. "Okay, okay. The truth is we just didn't want any of the women involved."

Mae gave him a harsh stare. "You didn't want us involved! You're joking, surely. Since your first call to Dave we've all been involved. What's happened to alter the situation?"

"Nothing's happened. It's just that . . ."

Josh intervened. "It's done, Joe. Forget it. Let's call it a day, shall we?"

When Chelsea appeared undecided, Mae said, "Stop protecting me. My presence shouldn't put you off."

"That goes for me too," Ellie said, countering a negative response. She had entered the salon unnoticed with Cindy at her heels. "Please continue with whatever you were doing before our arrival." Her look said "no foolishness."

Josh said, "Well, Joe, we were going to see if any CEOs shared directorships on the same board."

Chelsea's gaze lingered on Ellie. He had an odd feeling about this. He noted her determined expression daring him to shut her out. He shrugged, shaking off misgivings. "Go ahead, Dave. The ball's in your court."

Ten minutes later Ward leaned back and exclaimed, "Bingo!" He looked at Chelsea, wonderingly. "Resources Unlimited has twelve CEOs of other firms on their board." He hit the keys again, and then squinted in disbelief. "Resources doesn't list a CEO of their own."

Chelsea's blood stirred. He stared at the screen. "Where are they located?" he asked.

"Bimini!" Ward snapped, his eyes narrowing in disappointment. "You know what that probably means."

Josh, leaning back on the sofa, sat up abruptly. "It means it'll be a room with an answering machine, in a nondescript building. I'll give odds you won't find it in any directory. Most likely it's nothing more than a cover for syndicate money."

Ward nodded agreement. "The corporation heads we've listed have merged to become a separate international combine. There's no way anything that large could set up shop in Bimini."

Chelsea knew better than to dispute either man. Dave, in his former position with the FBI, knew all about money laundering; and Josh's financial acuity was unquestionable.

"You said 'answering machine' . . ."

Ward's eyes blazed. "Sweet Jesus! Get the idea out of your head. I owed you a favor, Joey, but it's time I drew the line. You wanted a friend of mine to check out Seltzmann, and now he's dead. This combine, for whatever purpose, has been killing survivors of a death camp, wiping them out over a number of years. I don't know what the hell is driving you, but as far as I'm concerned I've had it. I have a nice easy life here with Mae and my boat. I prefer it to remain that way. My bones are too old and fragile to rattle."

The sound of applause made everyone turn to Mae. Chelsea's gaze included Ellie. She was biting her lip. Frightened?

Chelsea broke his silence. "All right, Dave. Thanks for all you've done. Just let me have the number. I'll take it from here."

Josh got to his feet, his expression pained. "Hold it, Joe. Where can you expect to go with this?"

"Nowhere," Ward interjected as he scanned the monitor's latest data. "Resources Unlimited is listed as an investment counseling firm. It doesn't even have a fax number. If you dial the telephone number, it will in all probability be relayed to another. The Bureau's encountered the system before. It's untraceable."

Chelsea remained implacable. "Why is it listed at all?" In the background, unnoticed, Ellie smiled. She fully understood her husband's gentle maneuvering.

Ward eyed Chelsea dolefully. *Persistent old cop*! "Oh, they'll accept a call. If the party calling doesn't ring true, both the so-called office and phone will be removed. You'll note there is no address, other than Bimini, for the so-called firm."

"And suppose a phone call rings true?"

Ward didn't hesitate. It was old hat for him. "They will suggest a private meeting, at a location of their own choosing and time. The *time* is their protection. It allows them a period of investigation into the caller."

Josh saw that Ward's appeal wasn't affecting Chelsea's devotion to the so-called case. Chelsea was slowly filling his pipe, his analytical brain seeking answers to Ward's astute summary. Josh grew impatient and decided to make his own appeal.

"Joe, it's obvious, after these readouts, that the Alliance is a conspiracy. Just look at the names we uncovered. They deal with oil, power facilities, airlines, chemicals, shipping, and—above all—they kill people to protect whatever it is they're hiding." He eyed him briefly and saw he was getting nowhere. Chelsea was pulling at the stem of his pipe as if he hadn't a care in the world. He watched a cloud of smoke drift lazily across the salon. "Oh crap! Joe, what are you trying to accomplish?"

"All I want to do is shake them up."

Ward exploded. "Shake *them* up! You're shaking *me* up." He snapped off the computer switch. "Just what we need—a macho ex-cop." He waved his arms in a helpless gesture. "Christ! Doesn't any of this scare you!"

Chelsea's eyes sparked. "Of course it does, but it doesn't stop me. My mother lost her life in a senseless street killing almost forty years ago. Apart from law and order, it was the principal reason behind my getting into blues. The Mosel woman, we've discovered, was a link in a chain of ongoing senseless killings. By an 'alleged' outfit spanning continents—a *killing combine* that no one suspects but our little group. I think about those who have been killed and the one remaining to be 'terminated.' Even though we're groping in the dark, we've come closer than anyone to date. Whatever else we can discover will be just an added benefit. If I accomplish nothing else, then yes, I want to spook them. Before I become rusty with age I want them brought to light. We get enough, the feds can take over."

Josh and Ward stared in amazement. The timbre of Chelsea's voice was strong, although he had not spoken above a whisper. It was like a call to arms; it would be unpatriotic not to enlist.

Mae glanced at Ellie. Did she understand what her husband was doing? One look told it all; her expression was one of unqualified admiration. Yes, Ellie was aware of her husband's talents.

Ward was the first to break the heavy silence following Chelsea's oratory. He cleared his throat.

"Can you believe this guy?" he said lightly, speaking to no one in particular, as if debating with himself. "Spook them?" He stopped abruptly, reminded of something said earlier. He turned to Josh. "Anyone in your organization know anything about demolition?"

Josh arched his eyebrows. "I have one . . . No, wait. The two new men Joe interviewed spent time in Vietnam."

"Good. I want one of them to check out my boat every morning. Our friend Joey can pay for their time."

Josh stared in shock. "You serious? You expecting . . ."

He caught Chelsea carefully relighting his pipe. Novick was acutely aware that his friend, subtly and in his own quiet way, was expertly maneuvering the others in a direction of his own choosing. Josh never understood whether it was a natural gift or a practiced discipline—whichever, curiously, no one seemed to recognize, or mind, that they were being manipulated. Looking back, Josh remembered that the old squad accepted Chelsea's leadership without question. How could one doubt the best tactical mind in the department?

Chelsea scanned his audience from over the bowl of his pipe, then nodded to Ward. "Where's your phone?"

Without a dissenting word, Ward obediently pulled down a speaker-phone from the shelf above the navigator's desk and plugged it into a jack on the bulkhead. "It's hooked up to a line on the dock." He hit the speaker switch so everyone could listen.

With the dial tone buzzing, Chelsea paused to address Josh. "When I finish, try squeezing Carbolo for the forensic report on the beach victim." Josh, acquiescent, understood all systems were now "go." Nevertheless, behind his back, he crossed his fingers.

The phone continued to buzz. Chelsea looked at Ward. "Neither of the two new men hired have ever worked for any of the firms we uncovered in our computer search. Neither do they have scars at the nape of their necks." He smiled artlessly. "That's in case you were wondering." His mind free of those two matters, he punched in a telephone number.

After a brief interval, an answering machine responded. The voice was female, with a refined British accent:

"Resources Unlimited, Financial Investment Counseling. After you hear the beep, please state your name, address, and business affiliation. Please be advised before you do so, that we do not manage accounts under seven figures." The beep followed five seconds later.

Chelsea noted the grim faces watching him. He winked and leaned toward the speaker. "My name for the moment is unimportant, as is my address. If you should wish to contact me, I'm certain you will have no trouble doing so. As for the purpose of this call, I would like to know whether I can invest in the Benefactor Alliance." He paused briefly. "Thank you."

The "you" never made it; the phone had gone dead at the other end, returning the dial tone.

Ward muttered an oath, his fingers working the keyboard furiously. "You did it, Joey," he said dryly. "You knocked out Resources Unlimited. It no longer exists—on any sheet." He lifted his head. "You know what I'm saying?"

Chelsea nodded. "Benefactor Alliance was the code phrase. The mere mention of the name programmed a vast erasure system to take effect." He shrugged; it wasn't more than he had expected. "More important, it also means we'll be hearing from *them*, whoever *them* is."

"Then what?" Josh interposed.

Chelsea's smile was one of contentment. He was truly enjoying himself. His career had come to an end abruptly, but in retirement he was relishing the adventure of a lifetime. He was a man who suddenly believed in fate, that the opportunity thrust in his path couldn't be ignored. The Alliance had been extending its tentacles like a huge octopus, growing ever larger—and amazingly undetected—over the years. Unlike the embryonic syndicates laundering drug money and other ill-gotten gains through diversified, legitimate industrial ventures, the names associated with the computer readout read like a Who's Who of the industrial world, past and present.

Chelsea harbored no macho illusions of breaking the combine. Not by himself. So far he couldn't even begin to prove that these famous names were involved in any clandestine operation. All he wanted was to scratch their veneer, disturb them to a degree, where . . .

Josh's voice penetrated his ruminations. "Joe, where do we go from here?"

Ward, thinking of his friend allegedly killed by a hit-and-run, remarked dryly, "Yeah—and whom do we trust?"

Chelsea was thinking Carbolo was only local, but that he could be trusted, and that his appetite might be whetted once he was apprised of the circumstances behind the private investigation. It was imperative that someone with authority be part of their group. Whether the lieutenant would go along . . .

He put the question to Josh, adding, "Or do you think he'll claim we're obstructing justice by withholding information? Not to mention intrusion in his case."

Ellie played with an unlit cigarette, her eyes never leaving her husband. He was like a dedicated architect, disclosing plans to an engrossed, captive audience who, no matter their qualms, couldn't refuse to listen.

Josh looked askance. "Why would you expect him to work with us? He's got the authority to use as he sees fit. He doesn't need us."

"You will have to convince him that we just might be the only ones he could trust in this investigation. For openers, give him the hit-and-run, with Dave's suspicions. If that doesn't do it, we'll have to come up with something else. We simply can't afford anyone who refuses to adapt to the obvious."

Josh smiled mournfully. Their investigation had certainly graduated from an intellectual exercise. Fret lines deepened around his eyes and mouth. "Okay, just what can I reveal without abusing his feelings? I remind you—he's not our flunky. And *we* are the outsiders."

"Use your judgment, Josh. Feel him out. Convince him it's vital we work undercover. And even though it's an imposition on our part, we do need his cooperation. Somehow I think he'll go for it."

"Why not convince me to go for it?" Mae interjected, her eyes narrowing as she caught Ward's attention.

After a heavy moment, he said, "Mae, It's not just eloquence. I can't leave it unfinished. Not after what happened to Geoffrey." Mae looked up, as if seeking guidance.

"All right, I'll accept it, but"—she turned to Chelsea—"I hope you know what you're doing."

11

It was obvious from the outset that Lieutenant Carbolo thought he was being used, possibly looked down upon in the process. "You guys are somethin' else," he muttered. He addressed no one in particular but pointed his black cheroot at Chelsea. "You know, I could pull all of you in for withholding evidence. Not to mention obstructing justice."

Chelsea silently reprimanded himself; he had misjudged the lieutenant badly. *I'm retired from the force. I no longer have the right to impose authority. Here, or anywhere else.* He mentally groped for a way to appease Carbolo.

"Lieutenant, if our positions were reversed I would ordinarily agree with you. But in the present instance . . ."

Carbolo coolly examined his cheroot. "What instance are we discussing? The matter of those survivors killed recently or others you're hinting about? Without proof, I might add."

Chelsea leaned forward, his sense of purpose strengthened. "You can easily check with Interpol. But we prefer you didn't."

Carbolo displayed annoyance. *Why had they called him*

in? "And why shouldn't we check? You don't think me—or any of my squad—capable of handling a widespread investigation?"

"Suppose I told you you could be putting your life on the line if your pursued this investigation too openly."

Silence followed, the lone sound being the slight hum of the bilge pump working aboard *Novick's Ark.* The four men were in the boat's main salon; the women were in the house. Carbolo pressed out the cheroot and reached for his unfinished Scotch and soda. He spoke quietly, and carefully.

"Okay, let's have it. I've been patient so far. What haven't you told me?"

Chelsea nodded to Ward. "Tell him, Dave."

Ward told him of the hit-and-run death of his FBI friend. And his suspicions regarding it.

Carbolo set his drink aside and glanced at his wristwatch. He looked as if he had had it. His face registered disgust. "So, that's it. You called me in because you need someone to act in an official capacity." He leaned forward; angry flecks appeared in the dark eyes. "Let's get something straight. I'm neither your subordinate nor your informant." He got to his feet.

"Please sit, Lieutenant," Chelsea said calmly. "You're mistaking our intentions. We don't need or want you as a subordinate. What we need is your expertise."

"Don't butter me up, Chelsea. I'm not some spic from the Bronx you can push around, and—"

"Why don't you hear us out? You've nothing to lose."

Carbolo regarded Chelsea warily. He chewed on his lip, attempting to assess the former police captain. Grudgingly he had to admit that the man's soft-spoken manner was not overbearing. "Can I get a refill on the Scotch?" he asked, slipping back into the director's chair. As Josh poured, Carbolo said, "Okay, shoot. But it better be good."

Chelsea played the game confidently, knowing he had aroused more than a little curiosity. Carbolo's gesture of leaving was a put-on, letting them know that he was the only one present with authority. Chelsea read him well, with complete understanding. It was a need to assert himself. Chelsea glanced at him solemnly and measured his speech carefully.

"To begin with, Lieutenant, I will confess the three of us have been operating undercover on our own." He held up a restraining hand when Carbolo stiffened. "Hear me out. When I'm finished you'll understand why, and why it now requires your expertise—and above all, your cooperation. Certain incidents have ballooned beyond our wildest speculation. And I must now warn—no—caution you that our discussion must not go beyond this room."

Chelsea paused for a signal from Carbolo. He was aware of the inner battle shaking the Hispanic detective.

Carbolo's stomach was hollow with excitement. *Three retired officers from police and government employ were operating on their own? What the hell? Should he believe them?*

He straightened; a decision had to be made. "What you're asking involves a code of ethics. You have no official status." He cocked his head. "Or are you guys conning me?" The bland expressions of the other two men told him nothing.

"There's no con. We wouldn't be in this if you hadn't started the ball rolling by calling us in on the Mosel case. Before I continue it is essential that I have the forensic report on the beach victim."

Carbolo's curiosity reached a straining point. "And if I offer it, will I get a straight story from you?"

"You have my word."

The lieutenant took a tentative sip of his drink. "The John

Doe was in excellent health—better than most in their seventies. The scar at the nape of his neck was old, the reason for it unknown. The ME could only conjecture that something of a gelatinous nature had been implanted beneath the scar. For what purpose, he couldn't even begin to guess. In any case, he said, and I quote, 'the location had to affect the man's brain in some way.' The surgical procedure was expert, he also noted. The cause of death was a needle puncture at the hip. A poison, as yet unknown, caused almost instant hemorrhaging." Carbolo fell silent a moment and then said, "I can't furnish you with anything else unless you share what you've got."

Chelsea sensed a small triumph. The man's appetite had been whetted. A new confederate had joined the group.

Fifteen minutes later everything was out, including the computer readouts which Josh had brought to the table. Carbolo, aghast at what the data revealed, asked numerous questions. His stomach churned as he realized the enormity of what was developing from an "ordinary" murder case.

He sat back finally, his mind reeling from its implications. He now understood why secrecy was so essential.

He pulled a fresh cigar from his shirt pocket and as he held a match to it, his hand was shaking.

"What do you want from me?" he asked, his voice suddenly thick.

"We would like to have your full cooperation," Chelsea replied.

Carbolo had a sudden distaste for the cheroot. He set it into a weighted ceramic ashtray, his usual forceful manner subdued. Discomfited he said, "I still have a superior to contend with. I can't suppress . . ." He looked up, feeling all eyes upon him. A reserve energy asserted itself. "It depends on what you expect from me."

Chelsea pointed to a name on the computer sheet. The

man was titular head of a corporation that supplied equipment for NASA. "This man," he said, "lives in Palm Beach. Without making waves, can you put a twenty-four-hour tail on him?"

Carbolo's eyes lifted expressively. "From my department? No way." He shook his head. "Even if it was possible, how would I explain taking such action?"

Chelsea's face remained impassive. "I meant someone like a trusted snitch. Or, better yet, a closemouthed PI. Two at least, on twelve-hour shifts. In your position you must have some reliables. I know of a couple up north but I'd rather not call them down." He noted Carbolo's frown. "Surely there's someone . . ."

The lieutenant rubbed a twitching eyelid, hiding his chagrin. He should have realized Chelsea didn't want anyone from his own department. Somewhat flustered, he gestured foolishly. "Sorry, let me think," he said at length.

He lifted a finger and caught Novick's eye. "Do you know Aaron and Noah Brenner?" Ward stirred before Josh could reply, and a smile played on his lips.

"I know of them," Ward offered quietly. "They're brothers. They work out of Miami. Both are in their early forties and do very well, occasionally working security for wealthy clients." His smile broadened. "And they're good at what they do."

Chelsea tossed him an inquiring glance. It was obvious Dave thought them an excellent choice. "Let's hear the rest of it. You know them personally?"

Ward lit a cigarette as he dredged up old memories. He chuckled. "We never met. I know of them from FBI files. They came to Miami from Israel a few years ago. Both were decorated in the Yom Kippur War. Not for soldiering per se, but for their work in the Mossad."

Chelsea was uncertain. *Would it be wise to involve them?*

After a brief pause he said, "Disregarding availability, are they trustworthy in this instance?"

Ward chuckled again, fully enjoying himself. "Trustworthy? You can bet on it." He leaned forward and slid his fingers down the computer sheet. He stopped at Suliman ben-Hussad, a well-known figure in the Mideast oil cartel. "You show them that name and you can bet they'll also be available."

Chelsea still displayed a reluctance. "Would you advise bringing them up to date on all information? We can't have the FBI or the CIA watching their every movement."

"They were listed as friendlies a couple of years after their arrival. I doubt there would be any trouble." He gave Chelsea a meaningful look. "Unless *we* make waves."

Carbolo, in a more genial mood, said, "These guys don't work for nothing." All eyes turned to Josh.

"Christ! There goes my profit for the year. If my accountant won't deduct this as a business expense, it's going to cost you, Joe."

"It'll be worth it," Chelsea said. "This will be the greatest undertaking of our lives." He turned to Carbolo. "We bust this, you could go down as one of America's greatest sleuths."

The lieutenant winced. "Or martyr." He looked from one face to the other, puzzled. "Why are you doing it? You guys must be—what? In your sixties? Doesn't it scare you? I'm only thirty-five and it scares the shit out of me. You should be on the beach, drinking piña coladas and basking in old memories."

Chelsea wrinkled his nose. "In our line of business, regardless of age, you always knew death was a reality. Until I had to retire I never dwelled upon it. It might be considered irrational reasoning, but I find it comforting to still be of use in this world. My life has been governed by fighting wrong and, no matter my age, I have to continue until it is no longer feasible to do so!"

Ward applauded silently. "A great epitaph, Joey. I can't help wondering what Ellie would say about it."

Chelsea contemplated replying, but decided to keep it private. No matter what the fates had in store for him, Ellie would be provided for. He grimaced suddenly. It wasn't a thought to dwell upon. "Enough morbidity," he said abruptly. "It's a cold war, nothing more. All we have to do is open a can of worms. The proper authorities can take it from there. I say, let's get started. Well, Lieutenant, can you make the call to the Brenner brothers?"

Josh held up a delaying hand, his features somber. "Hold it a minute. You've said your piece, Joe. Right now we're approaching the point of no return. Are we all agreed that we continue? To be truthful, I've already been on the brink of death and I can tell you I didn't find it fascinating. This so-called can of worms could erupt like an intercontinental missile, and we'll be riding it." He caught Ward's eye. "Last chance for all of us."

Ward fingered his beard. "In the beginning, I intended offering nothing more than information. Now, every cell in my body says, 'Go for it.' Don't ask me why. Perhaps it's Joey's inner fire feeding me, or it could merely be a sense of patriotic duty instilled by my former employers. In any case, I now feel obliged to continue. Life is short anyway. Why let that stop me?"

"Sweet Jesus!" Josh exclaimed. "I think we're all nuts. If the Alliance doesn't get me, Cindy will." He turned to Carbolo. "You've got the ball, Rudy. Call your play."

The lieutenant wondered whether they could see the blood coursing through his arteries. Too tense to light up again, he stubbed out his cigar. "You guys are something else," he said in awe. "You leave me no alternative. Like the admiral said: 'Damn the torpedoes, full speed ahead!' Before I start thinking rationally, get me the telephone directory."

Chelsea sat back, relieved. An elation swept through him like nothing he had ever experienced. They were all eager, excited as rookies on their first assignment. He searched their faces, Josh's and Dave's in particular. Observing their tight smiles, he experienced a nebulous guilt. Was it bravado they displayed in the undertaking of a dangerous venture? Or were they simply yielding to his own personal vanity because of old ties? An uncompromising chord said: *They are reconciled to satisfying the human ego, no matter their age*. He had merely been the catalyst making them responsive to it.

He watched Carbolo, the youngest, and now the most avid of all. The man's dark eyes gleamed as he searched through the directory for the Brenners. His dreams were not of valor or the inherent dangers but of enhanced stature—the Hispanic who had possibly come out of the slums of Puerto Rico to become a police lieutenant and now a partner in the exposure of a treasonous cartel. "I've got it," Carbolo's voice cut into his ruminations.

A humid breeze crossed the afterdeck of the *Ark* tied up at the concrete seawall bordering the Novick property. Chelsea twisted as if hearing an intruder. The verdant lawn, its lawn chairs, lounges and table, wet with night dampness, glistened with reflected light from the dock area and the large house. He looked at Carbolo, already punching numbers on the phone.

At peace, Chelsea refilled his pipe.

Noah Brenner put the phone down and stood in silent contemplation, his expression curious. The six-foot figure had a rugged face featuring a strong jaw and firm mouth; the eyes under dark eyebrows were gray and alert. His hair was dark and thick, graying only at the temples.

His wife, Yetta, came into the Florida room, wiping her hands on her apron. Her hair was a rich brown piled loosely above a tanned face. Smoke-gray eyes under dark eyebrows observed him intently. "Something wrong, Noah?"

"No." He smiled easily, disarmingly. "Someone calling about a job." He checked his wristwatch: almost 10 P.M. "I'll have to speak with Aaron."

His brother Aaron was forty-two, two years younger than Noah. The two families lived in detached houses located in Fort Lauderdale, in a middle-class neighborhood.

Yetta regarded him warily, with intelligent eyes. "You don't like the job."

"They want surveillance."

"So?"

"It means we might have to be away for a few days." Changing the subject, he said, "The kids asleep?"

She hesitated, her eyes becoming pinpoints. "Noah, you're not going to tell me what it entails?"

His eyebrows arched. "Such a suspicious woman," he answered lightly. He kissed her on the cheek. "We left the Mossad years ago. This is just a job. Stop worrying." He started for the back door. "I'll be back in an hour."

Why did he feel he had to mention the Mossad?

She watched him leave, then shrugged and removed her apron. It was foolish of her to worry. They were in America, finished with the old ways. She returned to the kitchen to empty the dishwasher.

Aaron was sitting in the Florida room, a duplicate of Noah's. He was alone, watching television. Noah tapped at a jalousied window and when his brother spun around, he motioned for him to come out.

Aaron Brenner did not resemble his brother. He was as tall as Noah, but leaner, with a kinder face. There was an aura of intelligence about him although he was not an intellectual. His bright brown eyes softened a deep, powerful voice. His sun-streaked thinning brown hair was carefully combed to hide a high forehead.

He glanced questioningly at Noah in the darkness; his brother rarely used the yard, day or night. Noah motioned him toward the bench-swing, which was usually shared by their children.

"Why the secrecy?" asked Aaron. "Hold your voice down," was the reply. Sounds carried in the night. Aaron lit a cigarette before seating himself.

Noah said, "I just got a phone call, asking for a surveillance job." Aaron's eyes didn't sparkle; they narrowed.

Noah told him about Lieutenant Carbolo's call. "Do we want it?"

Aaron studied his bother in silence for a moment. "Why do you ask me? What have you omitted?"

"The subject—unnamed—is the head of an aeronautical corporation. It smacks of international intrigue. Carbolo wouldn't give details over the phone, other than to say it pays well."

Aaron looked up at the night sky and observed the stars. Not as clear as the sky over the Negev, he thought nostalgically. "Why doesn't this police lieutenant use his own men?"

"Good question. I also asked it. All I got was: 'An explanation will follow when we meet.' With three other gentlemen, by the way." Noah twisted to face Aaron. "Do we meet? He gave an address in Boca Raton."

Aaron stubbed out his cigarette against the iron pole support. "He never mentioned industrial espionage?" He waved his own query aside. "Sorry, he wouldn't say anything before a meet." He shrugged suddenly. "It won't do any harm looking into it. As a matter of fact it sounds intriguing. And it's a change from what we've been doing." He caught Noah's reluctance. "Look, we talk, we listen—then make up our minds. It's not like the days when we were committed." He stood up. "What time is the appointment?"

Noah didn't stir, and he didn't immediately respond. Finally he said, "I have a feeling about this. Why did the cop single *us* out for this particular assignment?"

Aaron smiled gently. The thought had occurred to him too. "We'll know tomorrow," he said, shrugging philosophically. "What time?"

"Ten in the morning." Noah stood and regarded his brother levelly. "If I don't like it, don't try talking me into it."

"This lieutenant didn't give the name of the three men we're to meet?"

"No. That's what bothers me. Why admit someone high in aeronautics is involved, then tell us nothing else?"

"This Carbolo . . . How well do you know him? He doesn't stir any memories for me."

"Another mystery. I never heard of him. And yet he calls us." He tapped Aaron's arm. "Any ideas, *chuchim?*"

"To me it's obvious. Somehow he knows of our past history." Aaron reached into his shirt pocket for another cigarette, then changed his mind. His wife, Eva, was at the window, squinting through the glass panes.

"Hmm. And needs us for a special job? I now like it even less."

Aaron prodded his arm. "Leave it for tomorrow."

12

The Brenner brothers arrived in an inconspicuous gray van. The street was a dead end, a road barrier preventing anyone from driving into the canal. The address given them was the last property on the long block. Noah entered the circular driveway and parked ahead of a white Ciera and beige Saab Turbo.

Walking toward the front door of the cream-color stuccoed mansion, Aaron remarked, "It can't belong to the policeman." Noah didn't disagree.

The brothers exchanged surprised glances, noting the mezuzah on the doorjamb. Aaron touched a finger to it, then brought it to his lips. He gave Noah a look and he did likewise, somewhat condescendingly. He punched a button which set off chimes within the huge house.

The housemaid opened the door and looked at them questioningly. "Yes, can I help you?"

"We're the Brenners. I believe we're expected."

The door opened wider. "Yes. Mr. Novick *is* expecting you. They're on the courtyard terrace, Please follow me."

Although the name wasn't familiar, neither man registered surprise.

They followed the maid through a wide hallway that bisected the mansion and led out at the end into a courtyard where three men sat, sipping coffee from mugs, at an umbrellaed table.

Josh got up and came forward eagerly, extending a hand. After introductions were made, Noah's eyes surveyed the courtyard. "What happened to Lieutenant Carbolo?" he asked.

"He couldn't make it. Departmental business came up. Unavoidable. You'll meet later." Chelsea observed the brothers silently. Both fit and intelligent-looking. He noticed Noah Brenner's eyes flicker, seemingly interested in something beyond them. Unobtrusively as possible, he turned to scan the canal. Other than the *Ark*, there were two sailing vessels, both tied up at the opposite sea wall of the waterway. He could detect nothing of any interest.

Noah walked around the table, and with his back to the canal, held a finger to his lips. His meaning was unmistakable: Silence. He fished a ballpoint and small pad from a shirt pocket, scribbled something on the pad and laid it on the table.

THE 40-FOOT SLOOP ACROSS THE CANAL IS USING A MICROPHONIC EAR!

Chelsea's lips compressed, then eased into a smile. Ward was right. *These men were good!* "You have any trouble finding us?" he asked, making light conversation.

"Not at all," Aaron Brenner said, while adding something to the note: LET'S ALL GO OUT FRONT.

Going out, past the mezuzah, Aaron whispered to Josh. "We didn't expect a landsman." Josh merely smiled. "There's a number of us down here."

Noah pointed to the two vehicles. "Both cars unlocked?" he asked.

"You don't really think—" Josh began, but Noah was walking away, toward his van.

Unlocking a side door, he slid it open and went inside. Ward, who hadn't spoken as yet, nodded knowingly and appreciatively. *They not only had been professionals, they still were.*

Noah Brenner returned carrying a small box with a red bulb on top. He approached the Ciera first. His rapt audience watched in silence as he pressed a switch on the box. The tiny bulb remained unlit until it went under the steering post. It was now flickering.

Chelsea chided himself for his carelessness. Ward was also chagrined. Neither man had thought to check his vehicle. They should have anticipated something like this.

Aaron removed the bug and Noah went to examine the Saab, which five minutes later was determined to be clean. Aaron took a flat half-inch square of metal and placed it in a birdbath on the lawn. "Any other cars?" he asked.

"No," Josh said. "My Porsche is being serviced at the dealer and I know the wagon in the garage has been swept."

"Well, these are safe now," Aaron said confidently and looked to Noah for further instructions. He could tell that Noah was already in the job, even though they still hadn't heard what the job entailed. *Surveillance? Indeed! Microphonic ear!*

"Well, gentlemen," Noah said, "I believe it's confession time. I was told it involved surveillance." He jerked his thumb toward the unseen boat in the canal. "That says something else. I have to know what you expect from us."

Chelsea responded. "We can't make a full confession without a guarantee of silence from you."

Noah took in the imposing figure, obviously the trio's

spokesman. He held his hands out, palms up. "You have to give me something."

Chelsea, quickly deciding he liked the Brenners, revealed the full details of the group's backgrounds. "Do we meet with your approval?" he asked coyly.

"I don't know. All you've told me is that you're all former law officers, now retired."

Josh opened his mouth, but Chelsea interrupted. "Suppose I told you of a secret society that for the past four decades had been killing certain survivors of Dachau. Would that affect your decision?"

The brothers exchanged sober glances. This was something they hadn't anticipated. Noah broke out in a cold sweat and his mouth tightened. Now he understood why they had been singled out. Aaron felt as if he'd been punched in the gut.

"We'll work for expenses only," Aaron said.

Noah nodded solemnly. He'd been born in a Viennese wine cellar where a Christian family hid his parents from the Nazis for almost three years. Aaron had been born in Cyprus, in an internment camp set up by the British.

"Replace the bug," Noah told his brother. "We don't want them alerted." To the others he said, "I'll expect to hear the entire story later. Meanwhile, be careful what is said in that vehicle." He addressed himself to Josh. "You own the Hatteras tied up at the dock?"

"Yes, I do. Why? You think the *Ark* . . ."

"First things first. Take the black bag," he ordered Aaron. To Josh he said, "How many phones are inside the house?"

Josh eyed him sideways. "Give me some credit. One of my own men has swept all the rooms thoroughly. The house is clean. Other than the gardener, no one outside the household has been on the property in days."

Noah eyed him candidly, calculating. "Your Hatteras, does it do better than twenty knots?"

"Twenty-four, maximum. Why? Is it important?"

"The sloop has only a single engine. I'd guess ten to twelve knots tops. Let's see if we can stir it into action."

Chelsea checked his watch. "Josh, leave a discreet message for Cindy and Ellie, and also one for Carbolo. I want him to check ownership of that sloop."

They had taken the Waterway north. It was Chelsea's decision; traveling in that direction there would be enough traffic and sounds to keep the sloop's electronic ear busy.

"It's actually a microwave transmitter-receiver," Aaron informed them. "It's similar to what the Russians used to monitor the American Embassy in Moscow."

They were passing Spanish River Park when Noah asked Josh to find docking space at any one of the piers opposite. "There's no point continuing farther. We're definitely under surveillance by the *Sea Mist*."

Aaron reached for the bag he'd taken aboard and pulled out a white box about a foot square and three inches high. To the top of it he attached a concave dish with a cone-shaped object in the center. "It could be a jammer," Ward whispered to Chelsea. "I've been out of it for a while."

Chelsea had observed the Brenner brothers long enough to recognize that they were an extremely efficient team. He couldn't even begin to guess what their formal training had consisted of. Most of the time the brothers were silent, not taciturn, but speaking only when they deemed it necessary. Their movements were methodical, and Chelsea didn't think it necessary to question them. He watched Aaron set the jammer atop the shelf in the wheelhouse, facing the *Sea Mist*. Noah switched the battery-operated device on and turned to address his audience.

"Now we can talk. They will get nothing but static from us. It is time we hear something more of the 'secret society' you mentioned earlier."

While Josh brought out the computer sheets, Ward spoke to Aaron. "The jammer . . . Is it a new type?"

"A couple of years old, but it could already be obsolete. It's especially good in jamming microwave transmitters." He jerked a thumb backward, indicating the galley just behind the pilothouse. "The jamming could also have been accomplished with the microwave oven in the galley, so they won't get too suspicious."

Chelsea explained how they were drawn in by the survivor murders, then nodded to Ward, giving him the floor. Dave filled them in on everything leading up to the printing of the data sheets, and the follow-up phone call to Resources Unlimited.

When the Brenners finished scanning the readouts, Noah was the first to speak. "More than ninety percent of the names on those sheets are probably nothing better than John Does." He lifted his head. "As for the rest . . . I simply don't know." The gray eyes darkened, reflecting on the number of killings the group had mentioned. "As a matter of fact, all the names could be aliases."

"Yes, except for Resources Unlimited," Chelsea countered. "Which, by the way, no longer exists in the computer. That alone should suggest something to you."

A slight tension was building. Aaron Brenner sighed audibly. "Look, gentlemen, someone has to play devil's advocate. This has to be examined carefully. To accept these heads of international corporations as being a secret cartel is one thing . . . to suspect them of being a malevolent society of assassins is another."

Chelsea bit his lip. They weren't operating on his wavelength. Why? Had they lost their former incentives?

He said finally, "It's your privilege not to join forces with us. But I tell you now, in no uncertain terms, we intend to continue with our investigation. The assassination bureau is a side issue. I want to know the reasons for the existence of this Alliance."

Noah's eyes flared. "Who said we're dropping out? I'm merely trying to tell you we would need a team of operatives to break up this alleged cartel. Young and experienced . . ."

Chelsea stiffened. "You mean, as opposed to old and decrepit retired men of the law?"

Noah muttered an oath in Hebrew, then calmed himself. "Perhaps I was too hasty. My apologies. I fully realize you've uncovered a plot that no one in their wildest dreams would ever have suspected. My sole contention is that we can't do a damn thing about it. Where would we start? By keeping surveillance on a wealthy industrialist making parts for a space agency? The name could be phony, or he could be an innocent dupe. Just the thought makes me feel like an utter fool."

Chelsea restrained a growing impatience and sought a vulnerable spot in the former Israeli's argument.

"Look, Noah, I was never a secret agent working undercover. I was always a plodding policeman, using time-proven methods to solve problems. It has never failed me. Nothing was ever accomplished overnight." He paused briefly, but held their attention. "The man we want kept under surveillance is our first lead. There are other names, but this one is in our territory. The Alliance has to have an occasional meeting and it is imperative that we be ready to follow him. It may sound trite to you, but I still take one step at a time."

Aaron interjected. "Suppose they meet monthly. Can we wait?"

"We don't have a force to investigate all the John Does. Even if we did, I wouldn't know whom to trust." Chelsea glared at the brothers. "It's up to us old *codgers* to do the trick. Our job is to discover the meeting place of the Benefactor Alliance. Nothing more." He spun on Dave Ward as if terminating further discussion on that subject. "I want you to input all the facts of our investigation onto a disk. It has to be a matter of record." He turned back to look at the Brenners, anticipating possible disapproval, but none was forthcoming. He nodded with a no-nonsense look. "So be it. We begin."

As if observing Chelsea for the first time, Noah took in his profile; the skin tight on a strong jaw, the look of a determined man. Chelsea appeared physically fit; he wasn't going to seed. His eyes moved to Ward. The FBI man's gray hair and streaked beard were misleading. The wiry build in cut-off shorts displayed muscled calves; he was also fit. As for Novick, he appeared quite capable despite a pronounced limp. *Acquired in performance of duty? Well*, Noah thought philosophically, *some of us carry invisible scars.*

Noah finally decided that these men deserved more respect from him. Their backgrounds alone warranted it. "All right . . . To be perfectly frank I haven't a clue where we're headed, but we'll go all the way possible." He caught Chelsea's eye. "There also must be an understanding. Leadership must be shared. There will be areas where one of us might be more experienced than the other."

Chelsea relaxed, and a trace of a smile appeared. "Agreed. Operation Search begins with each of us being addressed by our first name." He turned to the younger brother. "Aaron, can your device reverse itself to listen in?"

Aaron looked to his brother and got a positive nod, "As you said, Joe, we begin." He moved to the microwave transmitter. "Once it's activated we don't speak. We don't want to chance feedback. Understood?"

"And there's no turning back," Noah added solemnly. "It won't take long to discover we're listening in on them." To Aaron he said, "Never mind the headphone. Keep the speaker volume low. Who knows what equipment they're carrying."

A wave of suppressed excitement pervaded the *Ark*. Josh and Ward sat back and lit up cigarettes. Chelsea played with the stem of his pipe. Noah observed them silently. Though not a religious man, he prayed they weren't fools.

Ward eyed Noah with unobtrusive interest, his emotions masked, his mind playing with an idle thought. *Were the Brenners still connected to the Mossad?* That would be an involvement he wouldn't welcome. He glanced at Chelsea, and caught a reassuring wink from him.

Good Lord! They were reading each other's minds.

The speaker crackled softly and he turned his head.

Cindy and Ellie, carrying packages, walked unhurriedly from the Royal Palm Plaza and through the parking lot to Cindy's station wagon. The sun glared down on the hard surface and shimmering heat waves gleamed at their feet. Both women were uncomfortable and beginning to perspire.

Cindy struggled to find the tailgate key and almost dropped her packages with the effort. A weary sigh escaped her, and she said, "I suggest we get into our new bathing suits and jump into the pool before lunch."

"You won't get an argument from me. Just get this thing open." Ellie looked at the traffic crawling on Route One and made a face. "From now on we're doing all our shopping earlier."

Dumping everything inside finally, each woman moved to opposite sides of the car. Ellie glanced back at the flamingo-colored tower of the Boca Raton Hotel and, reminded of its busy golf course, shook her head in dismay. "How can they play in this heat?"

"They've got their problems, we have ours. Let's get out of this heat." Cindy unlocked the door on the driver's side—and froze.

A man had come out of nowhere and stuck a hard object against her hip. At the same instant, as if coordinated, another man came up behind Ellie. Turning her head, she saw that he was tall and dressed in a beige linen suit. "What is this?" she exclaimed, more angry than frightened; then, thinking: *Oh, God! No! A mugging in broad daylight!*

Ellie's voice cracked as she spoke. "Take what you want. We won't make a fuss." Joe had always cautioned her never to fight back.

The man behind Cindy, similarly attired in a beige linen suit, whispered, "Do as you're told and you will not be harmed. Get into the back seat." She had no choice but to follow his orders. She didn't have to guess what he was prodding into her side. Ellie was told to sit up front. The other man slipped into the back seat to sit beside Cindy. Ellie recognized the S&W police special in his hand. When she gasped, the man ordered her to be silent.

The man's look-alike partner slid into the driver's seat. Despite the heat and tense atmosphere, Ellie was struck by an amusing thought: The men must have gone together to a fire sale.

The station wagon left the parking lot and turned north on the Federal Highway, and reaching Glades Road, made a left turn. Ellie glanced at the driver furtively. She had to be able to describe him to her husband. In his middle thirties, she judged, close-cropped reddish-blond hair. Not a man one would suspect of being a mugger, or even worse, but looks were deceiving. She had been a policeman's wife too long not to know that. Although she and Cindy were as yet unharmed, she could not dismiss the hard, unfriendly eyes of the driver. All she could remember of the man beside Cindy was a full head of dark hair and icy-blue eyes. *Watch the eyes. It can mark the most sensitive of men as a cold-blooded killer.* Joe had told her that.

She clasped her hands together, stilling a tremor. She didn't want to think about it, didn't dare turn to observe how Cindy was faring. Her heart beat faster as the car crossed I-95. For the first time "kidnapping" registered.

Unable to contain herself, she blurted out, "Where are we go—"

Reddish-blond hair raised a hand, a finger waving a deprecating no-no. "A few moments more, please."

The car slowed, passed the Glades W Plaza, then moved into the left lane to enter the larger Town Center Shopping Mall. Ellie recognized the seafood restaurant on her left where she and Cindy had had lunch two days earlier.

The driver maneuvered through the busy parking lot and found an empty space at the far end. Turning off the ignition, he opened his door and started to slide out from his seat. His colleague, in the rear, followed suit. Half-out, the driver turned to address the two women.

"A word of warning, ladies," he murmured. "*Tell your husbands to remain retired.* Have a good day," he added, and left them.

Stunned by the bizarre, abrupt departure, Cindy and Ellie remained frozen in their seats, staring numbly at each other. Seconds later, aroused from their stupor, both spun around to observe the linen suits entering another car, a white Riviera, its engine running, a driver waiting behind the wheel.

"My God!" Cindy sputtered, her voice choking with rage.

"The utter gall," she ranted, "to kidnap us in broad daylight! The nerve of them! Who do they think they are?"

Ellie took a deep breath, regaining control of herself. "Calm down, Cindy. You want me to drive?"

Cindy settled finally, but found herself on shaky legs when squeezing out of the rear seat. "You'd better," she said, leaning against the car.

Ellie got behind the wheel, thinking: *It sure* was *gall. A white Riviera, no less. It shouldn't be too difficult to trace.* Keenly observant she had caught the license number. She kept repeating it, committing it to memory. Her heart pounding with constrained anger, she muttered under her breath: "So brazenly confident. Did those men believe for one moment we couldn't—or wouldn't—identify them?"

As Ellie drove back onto Glades Road, Cindy leaned toward her. Her lips were quivering in anguish. "Ellie, this is too much. It's gone too far. We can't allow Josh and Joe to continue with this."

Ellie remained tight-lipped for a few seconds. She knew her husband well. He would never let go—especially now, with this latest incident. Vengeance was not in his character but, with or without Josh, he would devote all his time and energy to this. The secret society had threatened family and friends; he wouldn't allow it to go unchallenged. It was no longer a revolt against the aging process—it was personal.

Ellie fingered the antique Star of David on the chain around her neck. It had been years since she had sought guidance from it. She had been so young and reckless in a terrifying time, left with scars in mind and body that couldn't be forgotten. Her knuckles whitened on the steering wheel, and she could feel her pulse rate climbing with each beat of her heart.

At length, taking a deep breath and exhaling slowly, she

spoke gently with a forced composure. “We’ll have a serious talk with them.”

In her heart she knew it would avail them nothing. For Joe—and even Josh—the determination to continue would merely be reinforced.

13

Josh got off the phone, grinning expansively. “We got the contract, Joe.” When there was no response, he added hastily, “You know, the twenty-four-hour security for the new high-tech on Congress Avenue.”

There was still no response. Chelsea stood at the window that overlooked the plant next door. His mind wasn’t on new accounts. The plates on the white Riviera were stolen from another vehicle. In all likelihood the Riviera was now being driven with genuine out-of-state plates, impossible to trace.

He sighed heavily, thinking how close they had come to losing their wives. Josh, at first enraged, had cooled down when Carbolo had put out descriptions of the men involved, though knowing it would be of little use. It didn’t take much guesswork to recognize this much more effective threat as the work of the Alliance. Their supply of manpower was probably unlimited. Both the men and the car would be out of the state by now.

Josh got up and stood beside Chelsea. “There’s no answer

out there, Joe. We can take their advice and concede the investigation is too big for us."

Chelsea spoke sharply. "Not on your life! Not now!"

Josh held out his hands defensively. "Okay, okay. We can't do a damn thing until we hear from the Brenners. In the meantime we've got a business to run. I've been working on this contract for a month. You know what it entails. We've got a month to get three new security cars and the crew to handle them."

Josh's manner defeated Chelsea, so calmly discussing contracts as if nothing else mattered. "Christ!" he muttered. "Doesn't it bother you?"

"Sure it bothers me. But it's what you wanted. 'Stir them up' you said a couple of days ago. We've got someone escorting the women whenever they leave the house. What more can we do? Shit! Do you have any idea what all this is costing us? Wake up, Joe. We need the contract."

Chelsea knew Josh's assets were in eight figures. He could well afford the expense, but it didn't diminish the fact that their extra-curricular activity was causing the firm to operate at a loss.

Suddenly contrite, he said, "I wish I was in a position to help, but . . ."

"You want to help? You know the equipment needed in a security vehicle. Stop behaving like a lost retiree and haul yourself down to the Ford agency and make a deal for three cars."

"A lost retiree?" Joe asked. "Is that how you picture me?" Inwardly he knew he deserved the caustic comment.

"Damn right! You've done nothing but mope around all morning. We're no longer working with snitches, and our plodding-the-streets days are over. We can't do a damn thing until the Brenners come up with something in their bird-dogging. So, in the meantime, while we're waiting, we do the job at hand. Life goes on, we make the best of it." He paused briefly, then asked in a softer tone, "Well, do I get cooperation from you?"

Chelsea forced a smile he didn't feel. "Okay, give me the agency address." Josh had it written down; he had purchased his vans there.

Chelsea examined the piece of paper. "Souped-up engines?"

"Why not. Might as well go whole hog."

"I'd like to order one unmarked, no company logo. I'll foot the cost of the repaint job afterward."

Josh made a face, then gestured resignedly. "Forget the expense. Do whatever you think is necessary. Just make certain we get them in four weeks. Use your own judgment. Throw in a bonus if it'll help."

Chelsea's Ciera moved from the right-turn lane and merged into the traffic on the boulevard, heading for the Federal Highway, otherwise known as Route One. He got into the through lane and, from an old habit reborn, studied his rearview mirror. Over the years he had been on shadow detail countless times, but to be targeted himself was a new experience.

His eyes caught a black van coming out of a pizza parlor parking lot. He watched it for a while, two cars back, then wary, thought: Let's see what happens.

He crossed under Route 95, then jumped into the right lane, as if to enter the highway. He slowed, waiting to see whether the van followed. When it matched his lane change, he swung back onto the boulevard. Blasting horns and screeching tires followed his abrupt switch in lanes. "Shithead!" one driver screamed at him, wheeling past. Chelsea gave him the finger and, smiling, continued on his way.

* * *

The white Jaguar came off the Florida Turnpike and turned east onto West Atlantic Avenue. Once off the pike, Jon Seltzmann drove at a leisurely pace, his mind preoccupied, content to let other cars pass him. He wasn't interested in Delray's new condos and shopping centers all along Atlantic Avenue and its side streets. His sole interest was in two men, both semiretired, who were the first in forty years to ever investigate the Alliance.

It was a nagging curiosity that caused him to deviate from proper procedure. He knew it was wrong—certainly reckless—to do so. And yet he had to know for himself if it was pure luck or skill that guided them. He had to see for himself how they lived and how they comported themselves. Admitting it grudgingly, he felt an absurd fascination, bordering on admiration, that he couldn't suppress. He idly wondered what ingredients comprised the makeup of these sunset-years detectives. Men of their ages, particularly in their former line of work, should have been looking forward to a life of leisure. Where did they find the energy and enthusiasm to engage in such a dangerous pursuit? Why couldn't they recognize they were in a no-win situation?

He adjusted his sunglasses absently. On A1A the 35-m.p.h. speed limit allowed him to study Joe Chelsea's high-rise condominium for a few seconds. The background check on Chelsea had been completed, and he knew the man's assets were honestly acquired. The man was aboveboard, an ex-policeman with clean hands, a rarity in Seltzmann's experience.

The Jaguar continued south on Ocean Boulevard, past the high-rises of Highland Park and into Boca Raton. Approaching Spanish River Park he noted the public beach. On impulse he entered the parking area opposite, paying the eight-dollar fee to a gatekeeper who gazed admiringly at the luxury car.

The road circled and twisted beneath bowers of trees. There was an abundance of benches and barbecue grills set out for picnickers. A tunnel conveniently crossed under Ocean Boulevard for access to the beach.

Seltzmann had no interest in the beach or his surroundings, other than to observe the Intracoastal Waterway at the far end of the parking area.

He eased out of the car and, carrying binoculars, walked a short distance to the sea wall. As yet, there were no other cars in the immediate vicinity.

He stood there, unobserved, clad in white slacks and jacket. Tan loafers and an open-necked beige silk shirt provided the only touch of color. His face was expressionless as he peered across the Waterway, seeking Novick's estate.

As his gaze swept the opposite waterfront he found *Novick's Ark.* His lips twisted, marring the somewhat handsome face. An ex-policeman now living in better than upper-middle-class luxury . . . Chelsea's cohort. Seltzmann removed the glasses, a frown forming. Why did Novick find it necessary to join with Chelsea? And for that matter why was Ward, the retired FBI agent, involved?

Seltzmann stood there for a few minutes, then abruptly about-faced and returned to his car. He had seen their lifestyle, for whatever it was worth.

He left the park and back on Ocean Boulevard continued south. Crossing over the Waterway onto Camino Real, he found the entrance to the Boca Raton Country Club, where a reserved suite awaited him.

Noah Brenner, using a penlight, glanced at his watch. A quarter-hour till midnight. His brother Aaron would soon relieve him. He yawned uncontrollably. Surveillance was a tedious job, especially in the late hours.

The van was parked off the road, squeezed in amidst a cluster of pines. The van's green color blended like a chameleon with the verdant background, invisible unless someone came upon it with a flashlight. A security car passed every thirty minutes, but without stopping. Noah had made sure his van had left no tracks on the coarse turf.

Five minutes later, about to finish the final drops of coffee in his Thermos, he straightened. Putting the Thermos aside, he held a starscope to his eyes. A Mercedes limo had emerged from a four-car garage and was pulling up to the front of the pink granite mansion. He recognized Nestor Hobbs, supplier to the space agency, approaching the car.

Noah sensed something out of the ordinary. It was the first time in the two days of surveillance that the elderly man had left his estate after eight in the evening. Noah faced the electronic mike toward the limo.

Other than the sound of the Mercedes' engine, he could hear nothing. He cursed under his breath; the timing was wrong. Aaron was most likely parked in a lot and was even now creeping on foot through the pine trees to reach the van. They both had walkie-talkies, but they didn't dare use them now; the night air enhanced sound.

The chauffeured limo left the estate and headed south on Ocean Boulevard. There was no conversation between Hobbs and his driver. Noah waited thirty seconds before moving back onto the road. The van had a phone and he tried calling Aaron's car phone. But, as he'd suspected, Aaron wasn't in his car.

The limo drove unhurriedly, within the speed limits, whatever its destination, Noah trailing a hundred yards back. He tried the phone again.

He got Aaron, back in his car.

"They're heading south, in a gray Mercedes limo," Noah said. "Hold on . . . They're turning onto Route 80."

"Got it," Aaron responded. "I just got back in my car. I'm about a half-mile behind you. Keep me posted."

Five minutes passed before Noah spoke again. "They're crossing 95. The airport's on the right . . . Hold on. The limo is taking the perimeter road."

"Okay, I've got you in sight. Drop back as soon as I pass you."

There were few vehicles on the road, and even less air traffic. Aaron could see one plane coming in, with no other following its flight path.

It took him only minutes to realize the limo wasn't heading for the main terminal. It slowed at a security gate, then went on without stopping.

Aaron continued along the perimeter road until he came to the first of many car rental agencies. An attendant accosted him before he could park his Suburu off to one side.

"My car's borrowed." Aaron spoke casually. "Okay to park it here for a few minutes? Just until I can arrange a rental for tomorrow."

"Take your time," the female attendant said congenially. "This is a slow shift."

Aaron walked through the rental office and went out the opposite entrance. A shuttle bus was waiting for prospective passengers, but none were present. Aaron walked past, down the road, toward the entrance taken by the limo.

It was a good ten minutes before he saw the Mercedes. It was parked close to a hangar. A twin-engined Lear jet stood awaiting a signal to taxi out. Aaron could do nothing but watch.

Moments later the jet taxied across the tarmac and circled the hangar. Aaron waited to see the plane in flight, then walked hurriedly toward the hangar. Catching a security guard he gasped, “Was that Mr. Hobbs’s plane taking off?”

The man was slender and not very tall, but his eyes were penetrating. “Who wants to know?”

Aaron held a hand to his chest, feigning breathlessness. “I had a message to be delivered verbally. Damn! This could cost me my job.” The guard eyed him warily.

“If it’s important, I suggest you radio it aboard.”

Aaron’s expression became pained. “Can’t do. It’s too private.” He shook his head, as if lost. “Is there another flight? It’s imperative I give him the message.”

The guard pursed his lips and regarded the stranger speculatively. *Oh, well,* he thought. *Far be it from me to cost this guy his job.* “Try Eastern,” he said wearily. He consulted his wristwatch. “You might try the 0600 flight to Nassau.”

Aaron grasped the man’s shoulders, displaying unbounded elation. “Thanks, you’re a lifesaver. If ever I can return the favor . . .”

“If you want to be sure of a seat, you better get going.”

Back in his car, he got Noah on the phone. “Our man is on a Lear jet heading for Nassau. What now? I can make a six A.M. flight. Is it worth a try?” Noah paused for a moment before replying.

“No,” he said finally. “Let’s get to Ward’s boat and wake him up.”

“Why not Chelsea? He’s the one in charge.”

“I don’t want to use the phone, and Ward’s closer. Let’s go. They’re paying expenses. It’s their decision.”

“We could do it on our own, Noah. It’s worth the effort.” A growl hit Aaron’s eardrum.

“Forget it. This is a team effort.”

* * *

Ten minutes later the guard, continuing his rounds, suddenly halted. Something nagged at his thoughts. *The fellow never identified himself!*

He strode quickly to the nearest phone. His call was answered on the second ring. He identified himself and related the story of the stranger who had accosted him. When asked if the intruder knew the Lear's destination, the guard began to sweat. "No," he lied, hoping he sounded reasonably assuring. The party at the other end thanked him and told him to proceed on his rounds.

14

"Mr. Hobbs knows no one fitting the description. Nor does the description tally with that of anyone in local employment."

Jon Seltzmann's gaze held momentarily on the three bikini-clad women stretched out on the lounges adjacent to the swimming pool.

Three days! he raged inwardly. *Those retirees couldn't even give me three days to relax! Who else have they conscripted?* He adjusted his Dior sunglasses and returned his attention to the phone.

His eyes shone with a cruel intensity. He had allowed them too much leeway. That would end now. He spoke quietly, but with an icy harshness.

"Double the surveillance on them. I want to know their every move. And I mean their *every* move. Check on anyone they contact. I'll charter a plane for Nassau immediately." He broke the connection, then called the front desk.

"My suite is booked for two more days. Please see that I

am not disturbed with any calls or messages in the time remaining."

He hung up the phone and sat there for a few seconds in contemplation. The morning sun slanted across the table, but the umbrella-top kept him in shadow. He gazed wistfully at the lean feminine figures, then let his eyes scan everyone else around the pool before coming back to them. He never thought it would reach a point where he would suspect any—or every—one. Had two of the women in the past few minutes given him the glad eye—or was he becoming paranoid? One in particular held his gaze, an inviting smile on her lips. She lowered designer sunglasses to peer over them. His head barely moved, his mouth forming a silent "Later, perhaps." Her red lips circled into a disappointed O.

He finished his whiskey and soda and stood up. *Let them—and anyone else—believe he was staying on.*

He left the pool area. In the lounge he used a public phone to make a call. After taking care of his charter he made another call. He gave his whereabouts, then asked to have his Jaguar picked up in two days.

Chelsea called Ellie from the security firm. "How would a cruise to Nassau suit you?" he asked with some joviality.

Ellie, at first elated, felt suspicious doubts creep in soon after. "Isn't this a bit sudden?"

"Yeah, well. We thought it would be a good idea for all of us to get away for a while."

"Joe, are we running away?"

Damn! The woman was smart.

"Ellie, when did you ever know me to run from anything? It'll be a change. I thought you'd welcome it."

"Who do you think you're kidding?" She rolled her eyes.

"All right, Joe. Have it your way. What ship? And when do we leave?"

"*Novick's Ark.* And we leave tomorrow morning." Silence greeted his pronouncement. "Ellie . . ."

"The boat is small, and the ocean is a vast—" His laughter interrupted. He sounded genuinely amused, she thought.

"Josh says to tell you it's seaworthy, and that it's no more than a six-hour cruise. Cindy can hold your hand."

Ellie bit her lip, not quite satisfied. "Will Dave and Mae be aboard?"

"Yes, and so will two others. The Brenner brothers. They have experience with boats of any size. That should put your mind at ease."

It somehow didn't sound right to her, despite Joe's jovial manner. It sounded like a pitch. Eight people aboard the *Ark*? "Won't it be a bit crowded?" she asked, refusing to let him off the hook.

"The Brenner brothers will be going ashore in Nassau. They'll be back for the return trip. Just pack casual clothes. Maybe one dress in case we decide to take in a show at one of the hotels. What do you say?"

Ellie's mind groped for answers. He wasn't fooling her for one moment. She had noted his tired eyes that morning, the dogged look after Josh had phoned him.

"All right," she said finally. "If the others are willing . . ."

"Okay, get packing. Not too much stuff. Just one jacket for me. We might try gambling at the casinos."

Gambling, huh. Have it your way, Joe. "What time will we be leaving?"

"Seven. From the Novicks' dock. The weather forecast is good and it shouldn't pose a problem."

Ellie hung up, still beset by little fears. Nassau? What were they up to? What were they pursuing? She twisted her lips in a rueful expression. She was getting too old for this—even if Joe wasn't. She had hoped that here in Florida he would put his police work behind him, but now he had immersed himself in an investigation that far exceeded anything he, or possibly anyone else, had ever encountered. And for what purpose?

She shook her head. What a way to enjoy one's "golden years." She smiled wistfully. A cruise to Nassau wasn't such a bad idea at that. It *would* be a welcome change from . . .

And yet, as it had first struck her, she was certain that he *was* using the excursion for a hidden purpose. Her antennae said he was sailing toward, rather than away from, a confrontation. The smile was extinguished abruptly.

Damn! Why was he doing this! Filling their lives with uncertainty.

She felt her body trembling and clasped her arms across her breasts. Her breathing became irregular as troubling thoughts surfaced. There had been times over the years when she had survived much that upset her, but the feelings now stirring within left her weak and uncertain about her ability to cope.

Then, in an abrupt turnabout, she tossed her head defiantly, shaking off any feelings of unease. Joe was always an achiever; she had accepted him—and his work—when she married him. The ability to adapt to each other was the sole reason they hadn't ended up in a divorce court like most police couples. And this wasn't the time to criticize or alter the life style they had always shared. The search for the Fountain of Youth be damned! If Joe was content in what he was doing, he had discovered it already.

Ellie went into the bedroom, into the walk-in closet, and selected the 26-inch suitcase standing against the far wall.

The one bag should do it, she decided. Reaching for it, she hesitated, vacillating.

"No! Dammit! Not until I wash my hair!"

Joe Chelsea stood beside the desk, reproaching himself, wondering whether he was tempting fate. Was it an atavistic trait driving him? Why was he leading his family and friends to a point of no return? Was it an aberration in character that caused him to . . .

Josh came in, forcing the unpleasant thoughts to take a back seat. "It's all settled," Josh announced. "Jack will take charge for the four days we'll be gone." He regarded his friend's brooding expression. "Having second thoughts?"

Chelsea pulled out his tobacco pouch—his crutch—from his polo shirt pocket. "Somewhat," he murmured softly. "We never involved our families before."

"I thought we agreed they were safer staying with us."

Chelsea smiled, the transition forced. "You're right. I won't worry anymore. You hear anything from Dave yet?"

"No, but I think that's his car parking outside." Josh stood at the window, peering through the slats of the blind.

Dave Ward strode in, clad in sport shirt, shorts, and sneakers; his uniform, as Chelsea called it.

Dispensing with greetings, Dave said, "Hobbs is not registered in any hotel. It's possible he has an estate on Nassau. We can't know until we get there."

"Mae question the trip?" Chelsea asked. Ward's expression turned sour.

"What would you expect? It's costing us business. She agreed only after I told her your wives would be on board."

"I told you not to fret about it," Josh interjected. "Let's get down to essentials. You bringing your computer along? Or do I have to purchase one?"

Ward wore a pained expression. Although Novick could

well afford it, the affair was costing the former policeman a pretty penny. "You've contributed enough. I have my outfit already packed for delivery aboard your boat. How about the Brenners? They bringing the necessary 'supplies'?" He directed a meaningful glance at Chelsea. Chelsea nodded, his pipe sending a cloud of smoke across the room.

"Holly cow, Joey," Ward exclaimed. He waved a hand to clear the air. "You're living dangerously."

"Yeah, tell me about it."

Ward addressed Josh. "Speaking of supplies . . . Is the *Ark* ready?"

"The water and gas tanks have been topped off. In the next couple of hours the freezer will be filled. We're all set. Everyone in agreement, we cast off at seven A.M."

Ward made a move to depart. "Okay, then. To expedite matters Mae and I will come aboard this evening—if it's all right with you." There was no objection. At the door he hesitated again.

"One more important item. The Brenners' supplies . . . How will you keep them from customs?"

Josh smiled. "Trust me." Chelsea looked at him, but said nothing.

Nestor Hobbs glared at Jon Seltzmann, his dislike of the younger man ill-concealed. Hobbs, despite his seventy-odd years, was six feet of disciplined muscle and flesh, a man who took pride in keeping fit. The mane of white hair was deceptive to those who didn't know him. Those who did, knew that within that aging body lived a keen intelligence and an occasionally over-ebullient manner.

Hobbs's dislike of the younger man started with the elder Seltzmann's choice of his son, Jon, to take over the chairmanship of the Benefactor Alliance. No one on the council ever voted against the Doctor's decisions, and so the younger man took a position Hobbs felt he did not deserve.

Now Hobbs spoke in a sibilant whisper. "I didn't foul up—you did. I have twenty-four security. Some of my men are former members of the CIA."

Jon Seltzmann calmly eyed the older man. "You—not I—were under surveillance. Can you deny it? Where was your talented security?"

Hobbs surveyed the smugness, the arrogance. "My security will be checked upon my return. My interest lies in your computer. Why was my identity in it?"

There was no immediate reply. Seltzmann leaned back in the chair behind the immaculate mahogany desk. The small, private office located off the conference room was quiet. No outside sounds could penetrate the stone walls. A double window provided light and a glimpse of the Caribbean. A barely perceptible smile made a slight curve in Hobbs's lips at Seltzmann's delay. So, he had struck home. It *was* the computer. He waited for the younger man to climb out of his costly dilemma.

Seltzmann weighed a reply. Hobbs, despite his age, had to be dealt with firmly. "I must remind you that it was your own decision to be listed as an officer with Resources Unlimited."

"It still does not explain why I was singled out for observation above all others, including yourself." Hobbs eyed the younger man with suspicion. "Or was your identity omitted?"

Seltzmann waved the query away. "That's neither here nor there. The problem is what to do about your situation. I suggest stay away from meetings for a while. You'll receive minutes of each session by special courier."

Hobbs's composure was forced; he knew he had no other choice. His tracks had to be covered.

"Very well," he said finally, but unable to let the chairman off the hook, he added, "What about Resources Unlimited? Is it still listed in your computer?"

"The title has been terminated. Another name will be selected at the next meeting."

"And you have no knowledge of the party or parties involved in breaking the code? This isn't something you can keep to yourself. A point has been reached where each member has to insulate himself from—"

"It is being attended to." Seltzmann leaned forward, his eyes darkening. "You've been told their identities. The sole reason for keeping them alive is because we must find out how they happened upon the Alliance. I can assure you there will be no more leaks." He stood up, the meeting over.

With Hobbs's departure, Seltzmann opened the center drawer of his desk and pulled out a sheaf of faxes. He read them carefully, as he had done twice before. The information they contained came out of Wellington Security's Atlanta office. It mentioned an inquiry into George Estry, an employee of Wellington Security, who was involved in an auto accident with Joe Chelsea.

Seltzmann put the sheets aside, his eyes smoldering.

15

The 54-foot cruiser was tied up at the Nassau Yacht Haven by one in the afternoon. The almost-hundred-mile crossing had been accomplished without incident, the relatively calm swells in the Gulf Stream causing no undue discomfort. Applying caution, Josh had been in contact with the Coast Guard every thirty minutes.

The black customs inspector spoke with a British accent. What were they carrying and was it a holiday and how long a stay were they contemplating? He studied their passports—all American issued—then eyed the passengers and smiled affably after giving the yacht a cursory examination.

Cindy watched the Brenners finish connecting water and power lines, then turned to Josh. "I expect you and the boys will be busy. I'm taking the girls ashore for lunch. I trust you won't do anything foolish in our absence."

Josh hunched his shoulders. "You kidding? You heard the man say 'Have a nice holiday.' "

"Of course," Ellie intervened. Before she could add anything more, Chelsea took her arm.

"Need any cash?" he whispered. "Nassau has some good buys."

"Beautiful segue, Joe. We have our charge cards." In good humor she called for Mae, who stood beside Ward as he checked out the computer at the navigator's desk.

The women walked down the portside step-ramp to the dock and headed for the straw market just off Rawson Square. Chelsea waited for their departure before speaking to Ward.

"Dave, what did you make of the helicopter? It was the same chopper both times, you know."

"Yeah, I know, Joey. They—whoever *they* are—know we're here."

They were discussing a helicopter that flew over their craft after an hour at sea. It had hovered over them just a bit too long—as if making identification. It had appeared again a half-hour before the *Ark* made port.

"It was a warning," Chelsea said simply, almost too casually.

Ward stood up. "Yup—you noticed that, did you," he retorted cynically. "What were you expecting? Did you believe for one moment we'd slip in unnoticed by the Alliance? This isn't a street gang we're dealing with. It's about time you realized we're playing in the big league."

Chelsea appeared unperturbed. "Yes, and now it's our turn at bat. Let's see how observant the Brenners were."

The Brenner brothers didn't take it so casually. "They took pictures of us," Noah said. "We're no longer working undercover."

"It doesn't alter a thing," Chelsea stated flatly. "We still have to do what we came for: discover Nestor Hobbs's destination. I suggest we start at the airport. We use two cabs, one for you and Aaron, we three will take the other. Each will watch for a tail. We'll have lunch there, at separate tables while Dave speaks with an engineer friend who works in the hangar. If either cab is being tailed, it means they're really worried."

"Correction. It means *I'm* worried," Noah offered sarcastically. "I don't like playing target."

"Give me another idea," Chelsea said. "I'm open to suggestions."

Aaron nudged his brother. "Noah, Joe is forcing their hand. We have nowhere to go without them leading."

"You go first," Ward said to the Brenners. "If you're being tailed, we'll soon know. We'll only be a few minutes behind you."

Noah shrugged, resigned but not too happy. "Are you carrying anything?" he asked carefully. It brought a sharp look from Chelsea.

"No, and you shouldn't either. When and if it's called for, I'll let you know."

"I've never known a time when it wasn't called for. Do you know another way to survive this operation? If it heats up . . ."

Chelsea fought a rising anger. "Noah—" he began but Aaron intervened.

"Forget it, Joe. We're not carrying anything." He prodded his brother.

As they started to leave, Chelsea said, "Should I say *mazel tov* or *shalom*?"

Noah winced. "Better you should say a prayer." Chelsea waved them on, his eyes dark in thought.

"Should I believe them?" he asked Ward.

"I think so. You have to understand their mindset, Joey. Their people are still fighting for survival."

Josh joined them. He had been speaking with the harbormaster, regarding security in the marina. Watching the Brenners depart, he asked, "Disagreement?"

"Not exactly," Chelsea said, checking his wristwatch. "Two more minutes, then—for better or worse—we go."

The straw market was busy; two cruise ships had docked earlier and the square was crowded. Everything that could possibly be made from rattan was being offered for sale to the tourists.

Mae Warren crooked her arm in Cindy's but addressed Ellie. "I suggest we go to Bay Street and have lunch before tackling this mob. If anything here interests you, we can stop on the way back."

Ellie shot her an inquisitive look. "Mae, are you rushing us for any particular reason?"

Mae bit her lip. She was following Dave's orders to keep a wary eye, and it had paid off. She spoke in a hushed voice. "Don't turn around, but I think we're being followed."

"Oh, God! No!" Cindy sputtered. "Not again."

"Are you certain?" Ellie asked, her eyes squinting.

"We'll soon find out, won't we?" Mae urged them forward, steering them away from the market. "Keep smiling. We're tourists on holiday."

"Shouldn't we return to the yacht?" Cindy said, her face paling beneath her tan.

"No, the street's safer."

Ellie started to turn her head, but Mae warned her again not to. The younger woman prodded them none too gently, pushing through hordes of sweating humanity. Tourists fronted each stall, making purchases of items that would eventually wind up in northern attics. Basketry of all sizes and shapes took up space on the walks and the women almost stumbled over them in their effort to escape the area. Dirty looks and disgruntled remarks followed them as they elbowed through the congregation of shoppers.

They reached Bay Street, the main thoroughfare, then

Rawson Square, where the government's legislative and administrative buildings were located. Here, with a number of blue-and-white uniformed men in the area, the tension was relieved. Perspiring, they stopped to catch their breath and wipe their faces. Passers-by directed inquisitive glances in their direction, wondering why anyone would want to rush about in this heat.

Ellie asked, "Is our shadow still with us?" Mae looked at her in astonishment. Shadow? Of course. She was married to a policeman. Cindy leaned against a pole, catching her breath and dabbing Kleenex against her cheeks. "Damn! I've had it. I'm not running another step. Where is he? What does he look like?"

Mae's eyes darted in both directions. "He's gone. A man in a beige linen suit."

Ellie made a face. "Are you certain we really were being followed? Perhaps we're becoming paranoid."

"I'm certain. The body language was easily recognizable. In any case, we can now relax and have lunch."

Ellie was thinking: Beige linen suit? Just like the would-be kidnappers. Was it really a fire sale—or some sort of innocuous uniform? She noted the black traffic policeman, his blue jacket and white helmet, his white-gloved hands directing the flow of cars. So pleasant and calm, his back ramrod stiff as a military man. It was beyond imagination that anything dire could occur here.

Mae pushed aside a stray lock of hair. "Shall we? There's a restaurant across the street."

Cindy rolled her eyes. "God help us. Let's start with a drink. We'll need the strength for the return trip."

Ellie, when upset, either washed her hair or went shopping. She noted the number of shops on the street. "After lunch, we're not going back without making at least one purchase." The remark somehow relieved the tension.

Holding each other's hands, the three women crossed the busy thoroughfare.

As she entered the crowded restaurant the cumulative effects of the investigation caught up with Ellie. She shivered despite the warmth.

"You all right?" Mae asked, not missing a thing. Ellie's eyes were bright though pensive. All were taking it well, but . . .

"I'm okay. I just don't know where our men are heading with this thing. Doesn't it bother you?"

"Bother me? I've been waiting two years for Dave to pro—" She hesitated as a waiter addressed them. A table was ready.

When they were seated, Ellie prompted her to continue. Mae shook her head. "It's nothing important." She opened the menu. "Let's eat and forgo serious discussion."

Cindy said, "I don't know what thoughts you're harboring, but I do wish Josh had taken up shuffleboard."

Ellie's thoughts turned inward. "Why were we running?" she asked. "We number three, and he was only one man. What could possibly happen with all these people about?" Mae looked up from the menu.

"I caught just one; there could have been others." She hesitated. "And I don't like their idea of needlepoint."

"But why would they target us? We're not survivors of death camps."

"Don't press it," Cindy interjected sourly. "Because of our husbands we're in the same situation. You can't dismiss what happened only two days ago."

"No, I can't. All the same . . . If I were a man . . ."

"My God!" Cindy exclaimed. "How old are you, anyway! Don't you and Joe know when to call it quits!"

Ellie tilted her head. "Golden years were not meant to be rusting years. I admit I'm not happy about what Joe is involved with. Nevertheless, I don't enjoy being intimidated. I lived through a bad time many years ago, and I fought back then." She disregarded her companions' stares. "I'm beginning to understand Joe. Age shouldn't be a deterrent." She thought she noted an admiring, if cautious, smile from Mae. Cindy's mouth was agape in disbelief.

Mae extended a hand and touched Ellie's. "Let's not be foolish. This isn't a game."

"I know it isn't, but it doesn't change anything I've said. If I catch sight of that man, I intend to speak with him. As Joe would say, 'force his hand.'"

Cindy pushed her chair back and looked about the bustling restaurant. "Good Lord! Where's the waiter? I need a drink."

16

The airport restaurant had a varied menu, but the service resembled a fast-food chain. Most tables were taken with people biding their time, munching sandwiches with friends or relatives. Public speakers announced flight arrivals and departures.

The Brenner brothers sat at a table in a corner of the room, no more than four tables from Chelsea and Novick. The noise level was high—they were positioned close to the kitchen door—and the clattering of dishes added to the exuberant exchanges between old friends almost precluded conversation between the brothers.

Aaron was eating a vegetable salad. Kosher at home, he didn't dare chance anything else in a restaurant. Noah, on the other hand, had finished his hamburger, and was munching French fries between sips of black coffee. Dark sunglasses permitted them to observe everyone in the vicinity without attracting attention.

Noah studied Chelsea chewing on a cheese-steak sandwich. Facing him, Noah could see Chelsea's eyes, his expression. The American detective's eyes were bright and intelligent, with no sense of imminent danger. One cool man, he thought: good Mossad timber—in his youth, anyway—if he had been Jewish. Noah lifted his coffee mug as Chelsea looked at him for a brief moment. The man has good intuition also, he decided.

"That man is giving me the willies," Chelsea murmured to Josh. "I think he doubts our talents."

"Now you've really become paranoid. If he was in his sixties and you in your forties, what would you think?"

"Shit! What has age to do with it? You either have it or you don't." He looked up at a wall clock. "Dave is taking his time. I hope it's not for nothing."

"And if it is, where do we go from here?"

"We continue surveillance on Hobbs in Palm Beach. A man in his position must have visitors. Perhaps another name on the list."

Josh finished his tuna on rye. "We can't continue indefinitely, Joe." His brows knitted. "You leave any word with Carbolo? We can't leave him totally in the dark."

"We'll bring him up to date when we get back. Too much personal involvement could cause him trouble on his job." Chelsea raised his eyes. "Dave's in the doorway. He's signaling us. Let's go." The Brenners were already leaving some money on the table.

They walked through the terminal in separate groups, each on the alert for prying eyes. Everyone seemed to be on the move, either coming or going, some carrying luggage. No one idled, not even the porters who solicited anyone with bags.

They met just beyond a taxi stand, where they could speak without being overheard. From a distance the blasts of a ship's horn warned passengers to return. They would be at another island in the early morning hours.

In the next ten minutes the four men learned all Ward had discovered from his friend. Hobbs had arrived in a company plane—his own company—and then had taken a waiting helicopter to an outer island. It wasn't unusual; he was a frequent visitor. The island belonged to a foundation that operated a health spa and clinic for wealthy, aging clients seeking the Fountain of Youth. Ward's friend laughingly called it a retirement home for the rich and famous.

"The foundation have a name?" Chelsea asked, his eyes on the taxi drivers chewing the fat while waiting for fares.

"Surprisingly, no. He said everyone just called it the foundation. It's been around for years."

Chelsea was interested in the word "clinic." Could it be the home base for implanting something of a "gelatinous nature" at the nape of the neck? He looked at the Brenners to see how they were accepting it. Noah took it to mean "Got any ideas?"

"Where is this island located?" he asked.

"Ten, fifteen miles northeast. You can't miss it, according to my informant. The building on it is immense." He described it for everyone's benefit.

Chelsea's gaze remained on Noah. "Well, any ideas?" Noah smiled behind his dark glasses, knowing he was being tested.

"I think your women would enjoy a moonlight cruise tonight."

Chelsea nodded. "Okay, it's settled. We start after an early dinner." He searched each face, realizing he was forcing a decision upon the group. "Are we in agreement?"

Ward said, "You know we'll be observed. Why play with fire?"

"It's the only way to find out whether there's a live volcano out there." As reassurance, he added, "They won't start anything on their home base. The last thing they'd want would be an investigation on their turf. Besides, we notify the harbormaster beforehand of the short cruise we're contemplating."

Aaron Brenner shook his head, then lit a cigarette. "Something bothering you?" asked Chelsea.

Aaron shrugged. "I'm still working on why you didn't make commander with the New York police."

"It's a long story. Perhaps we can discuss it on a later cruise. The in-house politics of the NYPD is no better or worse than your Knesset."

"I also find the reason for your heroic pursuance of the Alliance obscure. What would motivate a retired policeman to do this?"

Chelsea's eyes flickered. "My wife is Jewish and she lost her parents in a concentration camp."

"We knew your wife was of Jewish heritage, but had no details on her background."

Chelsea raised an eyebrow at that statement. *They had done some checking on him.* "The Israeli consulate in New York must be a wellspring of information. You use them regularly?" Grudgingly, he admired their thoroughness.

"When the occasion demands it."

Josh, silent till now, and wanting to shift the dialogue, said, "Do we tell the women the true purpose behind the cruise tonight?"

"What purpose? As Noah said, it's a moonlight cruise. How can they resist? They can take in the casinos tomorrow evening."

"Okay, Joe. I'll remind you of that. We merely *look* at the island tonight. Without making waves," he added.

"Amen to that," Ward chimed in. This drew smiles and, relaxing somewhat, they headed for the cab stand.

In the cab, Chelsea placed a mental note in his memory

bank. *The foundation had to have a name—and a board of trustees.*

The harbormaster caught Josh about to pass his watch station and handed him a radio message. "This came in about an hour ago, Mr. Novick." Josh thanked him and shoved it into the back pocket of his jeans. He didn't open it until after he boarded the *Ark*. It read simply:

WHY ARE YOU GUYS TAKING A VACATION? CALL ME AT HOME.

AFTER FOUR. I'VE GOT SOMETHING INTERESTING HERE. R.C.

"Smart cookie," Chelsea said. "Saw your Hatteras missing and contacted the Coast Guard." He checked his wristwatch: 4:10. "Wait another five minutes."

Noah sat down in a soft chair. "Anything you say on the radio-phone won't be private, you know."

Ward snorted. "Jeez! Stop preaching. We've paid our dues." Noah shrugged, then looked at the wet bar. Josh said, "Help yourself." Aaron observed them, pleased. They were getting on well.

Chelsea stood on the afterdeck, squinting, studying each boat within sight. No one gave him a second glance; all were busy with personal chores, some furling sails, others washing down decks with fresh-water hoses. His eyes caught the stern of a 120-foot yacht on which a white-jacketed steward was serving cocktails. Dinner and the casinos would follow, Chelsea assumed. What else was there for them? The thought struck him that these people were indulging in something he had never had time for. Play. He had lived in another world where play was always out of reach. The dregs of society wouldn't allow him the time and peace of mind required for enjoyment. Between sick leave and vacations, six months of free time had been owed him when he left the force.

A screeching sea gull swooped past to settle atop a wooden piling no more than ten feet away. The bird stared at Chelsea as if he were intruding on its space.

Sighing deeply, with a curious sense of loss, Chelsea turned to watch Josh light a cigarette. "Josh, it's time for Rudy."

They got him on ship-to-shore. Carbolo came through sounding annoyed.

"You guys playing games with me?" Josh looked at Chelsea ruefully. The lieutenant should have been told.

"Relax, Rudy. Wouldn't you agree our wives deserved a short vacation? What have you got?" There was some static on the connection. "Are you getting me, Rudy?"

"I got you—I got you. There was a break-in in the apartment of a sixty-eight-year-old widower. The man was injured and is now resting comfortably in the hospital." Carbolo paused for effect. "His background matched that of the previous victims. We'll have twenty-four-hour security on him for a couple of days. When are you getting back? I suggest you don't wait. You have to follow up on the information we got. I have too much of a caseload to stay with this one. I'll keep the details for your return."

Josh nodded at the two fingers Chelsea was holding up. Their cruise would be shortened.

Joe was worried. *Was Carbolo drawing fire from his superiors?*

The women, only slightly disappointed at not taking in a casino, were more or less satisfied to relax after the events of the afternoon. Since nothing had really happened, they had decided to postpone mentioning their "shadow." The men had enough to contend with as it was.

Salads and steaks were on the menu for all but Aaron. His appetite was appeased, to some degree, with broiled snapper served on a paper plate with plastic utensils.

It was almost 8:30 P.M. when *Novick's Ark* pushed off from the dock. The sun had long disappeared below the horizon and the sky was dark in the east. The stars in the heavens were beginning to appear one by one, getting brighter with each passing minute.

Ellie caught Chelsea seated on the rear deck. "Moonlight cruise, indeed," she said. "We were at sea for six hours this morning. I'm not as young as you presume me to be. I would have preferred a good night's sleep. Truthfully, where are we going?"

He gave her a smile and pulled her down to sit beside him. He pointed toward the water and skyline. "It's only a half-moon. So it's a half-moonlight cruise. What happened to your romantic soul?"

She settled against him, but gave him a sidelong glance. "Cut the blarney, Joe. Where are we going, and how long will we be out?"

"Smart girl, thinks she knows everything," he said good-naturedly. He turned to search her face, noting the tired lines, lines that no amount of cosmetics could hide forever. Too much worrying, fretting . . . Worrying over him, he thought somberly.

"Joe . . ."

"All we're going to do is cruise past a particular island. We should be back in less than three hours."

"Checking the lay of the land?"

"Hmpf. I doubt there's a woman on that island."

She straightened. "Joe, stop giving me the business. We're all involved. The girls and I were followed today—at least we thought we were." Seeing his jaw drop, she wasted no time in telling him the full story.

Chelsea felt a knot forming in his stomach; it moved up to his throat, carrying a bitter taste. An odor of fear attacked his nostrils, recognizable from past experience. But this time it was for Ellie, not himself.

His eyes, dilated at first, were now angry pinpoints. He sat up to better face her.

"Tomorrow, Ellie, as promised we all go to the casino on Paradise Island. The following morning the Brenners will accompany you, Cindy, and Mae on a flight home to Florida. Dave and I will help Josh sail his boat back."

Ellie regarded him solemnly. She knew better than to argue. *At least he had called Florida "home."* Nevertheless, she still felt an appeal was necessary.

"You're not going to give up on this crazy venture, are you, Joe?"

His expression was a mixture of pain and frustration. "I can't. I wish to God I could. This investigation has got under my skin and is gnawing at my bones. Damn! They're killing people who survived the death camps. Your own parents could have been there." He saw her eyes misting. "I promise you, Ellie, this is my final investi—"

She placed a finger on his lips.

"Joe, don't make any promises. Just finish with it and come home."

"I intend to do just that. We'll be leaving on the *Ark* minutes after your plane." He eyed her, deeply affected. He kissed her gently, tenderly. "I also don't intend to leave you an early widow. You know I've always been careful."

"Yes, and you have the scars to prove it."

Yes, he thought, *and some scars are not visible to the naked eye.* Ellie was living proof, more than he.

Ellie fell silent, resigned to Joe's inflexible attitude. It was a fever, testing his conditioned reflexes. He had to have one more shot at being his own man. Especially after not succumbing to the department politicos, his *bête noire* for his last ten years on the force. Both she and Joe knew that his inability to adapt had cost him a possible commandership.

Chelsea's inner honesty was being tried, seeking rationalizations for illogical behavior. How could he hope to more than dent an invisible cartel?

The strains of "Lady Be Good" broke into their ruminations, drifting in from the salon and surrounding the enclosed deck. Ellie tossed Chelsea a wistful look. "I'll try, Joe."

Deeply affected again—she did that to him—he could think of no reply that would make sense. He touched her cheek and on impulse got to his feet and walked to the port rail where a single mica panel had been rolled up. The sea breeze whipped at his face, somehow easing the tension in his jaw muscles.

Chelsea gazed at the stars filling the clear night sky, surrounding the yacht in all directions out to the horizon. He gazed at the starry sky in awe, and called Ellie over to witness the glorious vastness of it all. She came to his side and slipped an arm around his waist. Her free hand reached out as if to grab a star; it seemed possible.

"You want one?" said Chelsea. "Just ask."

She gave him a quick look. "Would you give it to me? Or do I have to make a wish first?"

"If it's within my power . . ." He considered it for a moment; she was trapping him. "That is, with certain reservations."

She laughed softly, amused by his not unexpected response. Whatever else she had in mind was canceled by Cindy and Mae's entrance.

"For the young at heart," Cindy said, offering them brandy snifters.

"It's Rémy Martin," said Mae. "Dave recalled it used to be your favorite brandy."

"It still is," Chelsea said. In truth, he had cut down on his drinking since leaving the department. He took a sip, held it in his mouth for a moment, savoring it, then swallowed. A pleased smile followed. "With that, ladies, I shall leave you to see how our seamen are faring."

Ellie watched him head through the salon, then said, "I told Joe what happened this afternoon."

Cindy searched her face. "Whatever for? I thought we had agreed—" Ellie waved a hand dismissively. Mae kept silent. She set her glass down on the immovable table and settled onto the cushioned seat.

"Joe and I never kept secrets from each other, and I didn't think this was the time to start."

"Did it change anything?" asked Mae, clasping her hands together in her lap.

"Yes. We're to fly back to Florida the day after tomorrow. The Brenner brothers will accompany us."

"And the others . . . ?"

"Joe promised he would sail back with Josh and Dave, immediately following our flight."

"You believe him?"

"I have no reason not to. Joe has never lied to me." Ellie eyed Mae over the rim of her glass. "You have doubts?"

Mae shrugged. She reached for the snifter again, took a swallow, and waited for its warmth to offer refuge. She considered the question, then peered up at Ellie.

"It's Dave. I've never seen him so immersed in anything as he is in this. It was only because of his retirement from the Bureau that I agreed to stay with him. Now . . ."

A false quiet lingered. Ellie was thinking: How many times have I entertained similar thoughts. Most policemen's wives did, especially during the first three years of marriage.

"Why now?" Cindy asked. "Previously you were our strongest bulwark."

Mae gazed at her blankly, as though she wasn't listening. Ellie sat down beside her, took her glass away, and faced her. She repeated Cindy's question.

"Why now, Mae? Do you know something we don't?"

"No, not really. It's just a feeling that's gradually building within me. It isn't anything I can explain."

Cindy raised an eyebrow. She sat down abruptly, on Mae's other side. "You're not psychic, are you?" Her query was so serious it sounded comical.

"Oh, Lord! No!" Mae exclaimed, smiling in spite of herself.

Ellie took her hand. "One thing you can be sure of, Mae. We're in this together. We're all in the same boat."

The women were silent for a moment or two, then it struck them simultaneously: "In the same boat." The cliché brought tentative smiles followed by unrestrained laughter.

Later, when the laughter had subsided, Ellie asked herself: Why am I consoling *her?*

In the pilothouse Aaron sat at the helm while Josh and the others studied the navigational charts of the surrounding waters.

Josh pointed to a dot on the chart. "This is the Founding Fathers Resort." He had learned the name of the resort and its location from the harbormaster, telling him that he merely wanted to use it as a guide in starting his return run.

When they finished with the charts, Chelsea told them of the latest predicament, and his recommended change of plans.

Noah peered at him, his brow creasing. "Why should the

women being under surveillance change anything? We all knew in advance we would be watched all the way." His eyes darkened. "Or are we just playing around down here?"

Chelsea wondered whether they had erred in recruiting the Brenners. Noah, in particular. Perhaps the Mossad had thrown him out, believing him too headstrong to take orders.

"Our purpose was information-gathering," Chelsea said with a quiet calm. "We don't even know that this foundation is what we're seeking. It could be they're nothing more than what we've heard—a private health spa for wealthy patrons."

"You can't really believe that," Noah argued. "If you did, we wouldn't be here."

Chelsea's calm exterior remained unchanged. "Noah, this isn't Lebanon."

Noah realized he was pressing unduly but his obdurate nature prevented him from conceding anything. "So then, what do you recommend we do on this moonlight cruise?"

Dave interceded, trying to ease the tension. "We assume you brought night-glasses. We'll use them to observe. It wasn't our intention to do anything else . . . At least at this time."

Noah Brenner's face softened for the first time. It was a noticeable effort. "Perhaps you're right." He looked at the chart spread out on the table and nodded. "The island should be in sight in minutes. I'll have to get into my bag." He looked up at Chelsea and smiled. "Just to retrieve my glasses."

Jon Seltzmann sat in an overstuffed chair in the upper lounge. Sipping a whiskey and soda, his mind dwelt on Nestor Hobbs. *The stupid fool! They had traced him to Nassau.*

The vast room was deserted but for him. There were only three "guests" at the moment, and they had all retired for the night. Somewhere a clock chimed the half-hour, and in the nocturnal stillness it sounded mournful. Seltzmann shrugged his shoulders as if to shake off threatening hands. Finishing his drink, he set it down on a marble-topped table, then got to his feet and wove his way past a number of sofas to the rear of the lounge. There he opened a sliding glass door and went out onto the tiled terrace overlooking the lighted swimming pool. Removing a gold case from his pocket, he extracted a cigarette and noted his hand was steady. He gazed at it, satisfied. He was in control.

He felt the presence of someone behind him, and turned to see his aide approaching. He was a large man with a round face, fiftyish, but with a younger manner. When disturbed, his eyes would become opaque and discomfiting to look into. This was one of those times, Seltzmann noted.

"Yes, what is it?" he asked, with some misgivings.

The man's voice was deep, and his gaze direct. "In the past half-hour our island has been circled twice. By a better than fifty-foot Hatteras."

Seltzmann immediately made the connection. A muscle twitched in his face, and he considered the possible consequences of the yacht's appearance. "Contact Franco," he said. "I have a job for him."

17

The street below was busy with late traffic; the Fiats jumped lanes with horns beeping. It was a game all Italian drivers seemed to relish. Why should Napoli be any different than Roma? The cars stampeded around the plaza like the charioteers of ancient Rome.

She folded her arms in deep concentration and reflected on the phone call.

The man's voice was deep, resonant; he offered no name. When told she was Emilio Franco's daughter, Francesca, and that her father was not available at the moment (she omitted mentioning his illness), he left a telephone number. She recognized it as being on a Swiss exchange. The man had continued: *If the call is not returned within twelve hours, I will assume his age—or possibly his health—prevents him from accepting a new assignment.* Francesca considered the cryptic message, her dark eyebrows knitting in memory. Over the past ten years—the period of time she had managed the books for her father's salvage company—he had accepted at least five such "assignments." How many more there might have been previously, she had no idea. He would never discuss the nature of the assignments. She knew only that the monies earned were deposited in a private Swiss bank account. Whatever the assignment involved, it was performed in a foreign country within a period of a week or less.

Emilio Franco had been a young frogman in the Italian navy during World War Two. After the war he had had no trouble finding a job with an underwater salvage company, especially since the war in the Mediterranean had left countless treasures to be reclaimed. In due time he formed his own company. Although he fared better in business than most, he was not so fortunate in choosing a healthy woman for his wife. Francesca was born minutes before the death of her mother.

She gazed at him now, knowing Father Time and illness had prevailed. The substance was gone, leaving in its stead a ghostly figure of the father she knew. Six months at most, the doctor had told her. Her eyes misted, but she refused to allow tears. Early on, her father had taught her: "Tears are for the weak."

She turned away from him, an inner turmoil threatening to devour her.

Oh, Papa. Was it the assignments that brought you to this end!

She saw him stir, but his eyes remained closed. The well-loved face was drawn in exhaustion. *What was he thinking now?* She heard a bell in a church tower sound the hour, reminding her that only three hours were left of the twelve the caller allowed.

Again she turned to the window and, in the backdrop of dusk settling upon the city, she regarded her image clearly etched in the glass. It was a model's face, sculpted with high cheekbones. The green eyes that usually radiated warmth were now dark pools of resentment. She tossed her head arrogantly; the shoulder-length raven tresses swayed slightly in response. She had never quite believed it, but others thought her beautiful. Her figure was tall, lithe, and that of an athlete, due to her father's teaching her his craft.

Reflecting on the past, she suddenly knew what she had to do. She would accept the assignment in her father's place. At twenty-five she was almost as efficient as he had been at that age, and would do his name proud. She pressed a buzzer for the nurse.

In less than two hours she was back in her apartment, where she made the call.

It was a different voice this time, less baritone. Francesca introduced herself and told him of her father's illness, and that she would accept the position in his place.

At first there was a silence, as if he was contemplating a reply. "Do you have any idea what this could entail?" he asked eventually.

"Not quite." (A white lie, but she suspected it concerned underwater demolition, of which she had some experience.) "But, if need be, I can supply references as to my ability. I've worked with my father for a number of years."

Again, silence. She thought he might have been speaking with someone else at his side. He came back on the line thirty seconds later. "Be at home, alone, tomorrow afternoon. At two-thirty an interviewer will present himself to determine whether you are suitable for employment." The voice was like that of a robot, reciting programmed instructions. Before she could summon a reply the phone went dead.

Francesca stared at it, feeling slighted, yet wondering where it would lead. Interview? With whom? No name, no company, was given.

Francesca was curious, but she felt no trepidation. Why should she? From the age of ten she had attended private schools in England and France. She had left the Sorbonne only five years ago to return home because of her father's ill health. Gifted with figures, she gave up friendships to apply herself to learning the salvage business. The underwater swimming and diving was a dividend. She knew her father was proud of her, although he never expressed it openly.

She picked up the mail she had carried into the four-room apartment. Only one letter seemed worthwhile opening. A letter from her father's attorney.

Principally, it said that Emilio had added a codicil to his will. Francesca must make a choice, prior to her father's death, either to sell the salvage company after his demise or continue with the operation of it herself. She was to call for an appointment.

Francesca stared at the letter. *So coldly efficient—so emotionless: a piece of paper abandoning a man's life.* The tears welled in her eyes despite her father's training. She wrapped her arms about herself, a loneliness settling upon her like a cloud of doom. Who was there to console her? She had no friends other than her father's work crew, and their friendships never extended beyond a business relationship. It struck her suddenly that she had not bedded anyone in more than five years.

A frown marred the smooth skin. *Is that what I crave in time of stress?* Seconds passed and she shifted from unprofitable thoughts to the company. Twenty men in her father's crew, ten of them expert divers. Two ships, plus the equipment and docking facilities . . . And there was Antonio, her father's cousin, who wanted to buy the firm.

She dwelled on it for another minute. How could she make such a decision on the spur of the moment? Unable to stand still, she moved past the beige-leather sofa, pacing until she caught herself in the mirror above the wet bar. She made a face and forced a change of attitude.

All business now, she headed for the bedroom to undress and run her bath. Then she would decide which clothes to wear for tomorrow's interview.

It was a quarter past two. Francesca tamped out her third cigarette since finishing the salad she'd lunched on, then took the ashtray away to empty it in the kitchen wastebasket. Then she washed and dried it. Anything to keep busy, to keep from biting her nails. She peered furtively through the curtains of the fourth-floor kitchen window.

She had noticed the car earlier, a silver Mercedes, parked with two wheels on the sidewalk, just behind her own Alfa Romeo. The driver had been reading a newspaper. Now, after glancing at his wristwatch, he folded the paper and put it aside. She watched him get out of the car, lock it, and then observe passers-by with seeming interest. Tall, hatless, clad in a well-tailored banker's-gray suit, and carrying a briefcase, he crossed the narrow street and was lost to sight beneath her window.

She dropped the curtain, realizing it would be her interviewer. Punctual. She knew her buzzer would go off at exactly 2:30.

Thirty minutes later the interview was concluded. But it took only the first five minutes for Francesca to realize his queries were just a formality, that she had been fully investigated beforehand. The entire interview had been for another purpose, possibly to size her up firsthand, to assess and judge her reactions to his questions. Occasionally, after a particular query, he would study a file resting in his lap.

Lester Horvath spoke Italian with a slight accent, and when he asked whether she spoke English—she smiled to herself; he knew in advance she was fluent in several languages—she nodded. The conversation continued in English.

Although he smiled every so often, his eyes didn't reflect any humor. Francesca found him disconcerting. His gaze was too direct, as if she were under suspicion. His clothing was immaculate, his nails manicured, and he had about him an air of knowledgeable experience, the perfect diplomatic servant of the corporate world. He wasn't someone she would trust with her life, she thought idly, then wondered why the thought had entered her mind.

When he returned the file to his briefcase, Francesca couldn't resist asking, "Do I meet with your approval?" He gave her a brief glance and smiled his humorless smile, then pulled out a packet from his case and set it on the coffee table.

"With the preliminaries, yes." He observed her with a careful eye. "Do you know the nature of Emilio's—your father's—previous duties with us?"

Francesca realized it was a loaded question. A lie—even a white lie—wouldn't work with this man.

"Not entirely. I know it dealt with underwater demolition, but other than that . . . " He gestured dismissively, as if her reply was not unexpected.

"Are you prepared to leave for America within twenty-four hours?—possibly for a week's stay?"

She lowered her eyes, pondering. A week! There was nothing more she could do for her father, and she had only to speak with Antonio, her father's second in command. A curious, tantalizing excitement grew within her. America! She had traveled all through Europe, but had never seen America. The nature of the work required there was momentarily forgotten.

"It can be arranged," she said, as calmly as she could manage. "What must I bring with me?"

"Just clothing. You still must be accredited by the home office."

"I don't understand. You're sending me to America for another interview?"

"Please indulge me, Miss Franco," he said in a condescending manner. "I wouldn't even be here if you weren't the daughter of Signor Franco. Your qualifications are still in question." She bit her lip, silencing the retort on the tip of her tongue. Horvath watched her quietly, calmly, and said, "That's better."

Indicating the packet he'd set on the coffee table, he said, "These are airline tickets reserved for Fran Fargo—you—for a flight on Alitalia to Washington, D.C. From there you will fly to Atlanta, Georgia. All particulars are in the envelope, where to go, whom to meet." From his wallet he extracted ten hundred-dollar bills. "This should suffice for any unexpected expense. Additional payment will depend on future negotiations."

Francesca masked the intensity of her excitement. "Why Fran Fargo?"

Horvath gave her an oblique look, as though wondering if he was wasting valuable time with her.

"Don't be naive, signorina. A fictitious identity is compulsory." He showed her a passport, correct in every detail, and lacking only a photograph. "A man will be here"—he consulted a Lucien Picard watch—"in an hour to take your photograph. He will identify himself, and don't bother to ply him with questions."

Horvath left the material for her on the table and closed his case. Rising he said, "You are to say nothing of your destination to anyone." He eyed her wearily. "For your own sake, Miss Fargo." He left as quietly as he had arrived.

Francesca sat unmoving on the sofa, her thoughts rambling in all directions. She thought of the Swiss bank account: almost 250,000 U.S. dollars. Her mind's eye focused on Lester Horvath again. Who and what did he represent? She fingered the passport. Everything prepared in advance. *Why didn't they hire an American?*

Her eyes flickered in self-doubt. Could she take her father's place? *Should she?* Consternation beset her.

Papa, what did you have to do to earn it?

18

Fran Fargo, formerly Francesca Franco, was in a jumbo jet soaring at 30,000 feet above the Atlantic when Joe Chelsea parked his car in the hospital lot.

The hospital was off Linton Boulevard in Delray Beach. Rudy Carbolo was waiting for Chelsea outside the front entrance.

"The patient's under sedation," Carbolo said gruffly. "Forget him for a minute. I have a bone to pick with you. I want to know what the hell's going on with you and your crew." His dark eyes glowered. "Vacation! Shit! I want the lowdown or I call off all deals with you."

Chelsea took a small breath. "Okay, okay, Rudy. Let's calm down. I do owe you an explanation." He pulled at his arm and steered him away from the entrance toward the shade of a palm tree bordering the driveway.

"Quit stalling, Chelsea. Let's have it."

"Okay, it was an on-the-spot decision. I couldn't reach you without calling the station." Carbolo continued to glower. Chelsea gave him a fast rundown of all that had taken place in Nassau.

The lieutenant listened, eventually reaching a stage of acceptance. "The Founding Fathers Resort . . ." he murmured. "Okay, I can look into it, but I'd like to have an opinion from you."

"Legitimate or not, it's a fortress. Our night-glasses picked out armed sentries patrolling the rooftop. God only knows what security they have on the grounds. We were under surveillance the entire time."

"Why all the security for a health spa?" Carbolo's eyes squinted in the glare of the sun on the driveway. Heat waves shimmered just above its paved surface.

"Good question. That's where you come in. I hope I don't have to caution you. We don't want another hit-and-run victim."

Carbolo gave him an oblique glance. "Jeez, you are somethin', Captain." Chelsea held up his hands in mock defense. "You know . . . old habits. Don't take offense."

The lieutenant loosened up and grinned, displaying his perfect caps.

"All right. Now, about the latest victim, Izzy Gorham." In anticipation he waved an impatient hand. "Yeah, I know . . . the name . . . It probably was Gormansky at one time. Anyway, the intended victim was lucky this time. Izzy is seventy-four, and one of his daily rituals—as he explains it—is to take a nap every afternoon so's he can stay awake to watch the old movies on the late show." Carbolo paused to shake his head in wonder. "In any case, the perp doesn't know Izzy's awake, watching the late show. He walks into the apartment, sees the TV set turned on, and—the apartment is dark—assumes that Izzy's fallen asleep with the set playing." Carbolo's eyes sparked with humor. "The old geezer sees him instantly, and what does he do . . . ? He leaps from his chair and charges him head-on, knocking the intruder off his feet. Can you imagine the guts of this guy! Well, anyway, for his chutzpah—I think that's the right word—the younger man whips a gun across the old man's scalp, stunning him for a few seconds, but not keeping him from screaming for help. Needless to say, the culprit took off before he could finish the job. He left Izzy with a slight concussion."

"Okay, what's the connection with the previous attacks?"

Carbolo eyed him triumphantly. "Izzy was in Dachau, and his assailant was a redhead. Want to make bets?"

"What else? There has to be more. You can't assume . . ."

"I've got it on tape, but I'd rather you hear it live from the horse's mouth. Let's go in. He should be awake by now."

Izzy Gorham was sitting propped up in bed, his scalp covered in bandages. Nevertheless, with half-glasses perched upon his nose, he was studying a racing form. A ruff of silver hair peeked out from below the heavy bandage. His face was pale but his eyes were bright as he peered over the glasses to better see Carbolo and Chelsea. He addressed Carbolo vociferously.

"Damn the help here! They won't let me call my bookie. How the hell can they expect me to pay for this room? Medicare only pays for semiprivate."

Carbolo waved a conciliatory hand. "Relax, Izzy. It won't cost you a penny extra. I want you to meet Joe Chelsea, a landsman of yours. He's a former police captain from your home town up north." Izzy looked Joe up and down and shook his head.

"Chelsea? What kind of name is that for a landsman?" He waved a deprecatory hand. "Stop trying to humor me. I never knew any Jews on the force."

"My wife is Jewish," Chelsea said.

Izzy shrugged. "So, you're a lucky man."

"Mr. Gorham, about your assailant. Can you describe him?"

"The name is Izzy. My father was Mister." He removed his glasses.

Chelsea stifled a laugh. "Izzy . . ."

Again the old man waved a hand. "Hold on. The man was a redhead. The room was dark. I couldn't tell you more. I pulled off his cap, so I know he had red hair." He gave Chelsea a searching look. "Where were you when I was mugged in New York? Twice—once in my own shop. It's the reason I came to Florida with my wife, she should rest in peace."

"Izzy, did you know the man? Have you ever seen him before?"

Izzy shrugged. "All muggers are alike. Can you tell one from another? All I can say is if I was ten years younger, that *momzer* wouldn't have got away." And Chelsea believed him. Izzy Gorham had the thick cheeks and flat nose of an ex-boxer. "Let me tell you something, Captain. Growing old gracefully is for the birds. The Grim Reaper's not taking me without a struggle."

Chelsea tried again: "You were in Dachau?"

Izzy Gorham pinched his nose as if to block a bad odor. "Must I go through this again? What has Dachau to do with the *momzer?*"

"Bear with us, Izzy. It could be vital to the investigation, no matter how unconnected it may seem."

The old man held a hand to his forehead and looked up. "When will you let me forget? You want to know about Dr. Emil Seltzer? The man was evil, a devil."

"Yes, I understand. What can you tell us about him?"

In the next few minutes Chelsea learned about the laboratory outside the grounds of the camp. Izzy Gorham told of prisoners going in—and coming out, changed.

"How changed?" asked Chelsea.

"Not everyone that went in came out," Izzy amplified. "The ones that did all suffered amnesia."

"Hypnosis?"

"Hypnosis! *Gevalt!* No!" His eyes flashed angrily. "They were programmed all right, but not by such a simple process as hypnosis. The good *Dr. Seltzer* was both a scientist and a surgeon. Hypnosis was too mundane for him. He first emptied minds, then gave them new memories."

"How could you know this?"

Izzy Gorham stared at Chelsea as if observing a fool. Angry flecks appeared in the tired gray eyes. "Do you think I could forget! I was there! I worked in the hospital, on the clean-up crew. Which, in itself, meant I was in line to be brainwashed. In the beginning we thought working there meant safety. I learned different later. I would see the men—and some women—eventually leave the prison compound with total memory recall of events in their lives that never happened to them."

"These people—the inmates that were changed—you were allowed to speak with them?" Chelsea could feel a pressing on his heart.

"Of course. How could I not see and speak with them? The hospital staff didn't worry about me. It would be my turn eventually to join the educated zombies."

Chelsea lifted an eyebrow. "Educated?"

Izzy laughed sardonically. "A man from my barracks was a tailor before he met Seltzer. Three days later he was a mathematical genius and had no knowledge of tailoring."

Beads of sweat had formed on Chelsea's face, although the room wasn't warm. He wiped his forehead with the back of his hand.

"How did you escape the laboratory?"

"The Allies were coming. We could hear the guns getting closer. The Nazi doctor, before abandoning the hospital, issued orders to shoot all inmates working there. I was one of the lucky ones. I was shot in the chest and was left for dead."

Carbolo, although he'd heard it all the day before, was still obviously appalled. He looked at Chelsea, but allowed him to continue with the questioning.

"How many others were left alive that knew of the experiments?"

Izzy screwed up his face, then shrugged. "Maybe a hundred—maybe more, maybe less." Chelsea said nothing for a few seconds. He caught Carbolo's eye; both understood.

Izzy was the last of the "maybe a hundred."

When Chelsea turned, Gorham touched his sleeve to keep his attention. The old man wasn't about to release his captive audience.

"You think my troubles ended when the war was over? A year later I was back in Poland. My parents and brother and sister were dead, and when I returned to our home I found strangers living there. You know about Poland, Captain? Poland invented pogroms before Hitler was born. I wound up in a refugee camp and finally made it to America." He shook his head in sad reflection. "My father was a tailor and he taught me the trade, but I never liked it. So I joined the U.S. Army and fought in Korea. In the Army I learned not only to fight with guns, but with my fists. I became a boxer after the Army—that's how I met my wife. She was a fight fan, believe it or not. But she didn't like watching me get beat up. To tell the truth, I was too old for the fight game."

Izzy paused to soothe a twitching eyelid and catch his breath. He was visibly tiring, but Chelsea allowed him to unburden himself.

"We had some money saved and opened a dry cleaning

store near"—he hesitated, in recollection, then he named a synagogue in the Bronx. "You maybe know it, Captain?"

Chelsea shook his head, although he did in fact remember the name. He had been on the force a year when vandals painted swastikas on the synagogue's walls.

"A bad neighborhood," Izzy said, slowing down. "And getting worse with each year. The muggings, the junkies . . . Ugh!" He grimaced. "So, I run away to Florida—and what happens?—it starts up again." He caught Chelsea's eye. "So, tell me, Captain. What has this to do with Dachau?"

"Maybe nothing. We like to check all angles, no matter how far out it may seem. Do you ever discuss those terrible days with any of your friends?"

"Discuss Dachau? You must be mad! Whoever was there is trying to forget. If such a thing is possible."

"But you do have friends who have—" Chelsea was interrupted as the door opened.

"Izzy . . ." An old man walked in, tall, thin, his face a leather-lined mask. He was followed by two others. One was short with a potbelly; the other was of medium height and walked with the aid of a cane. Izzy Gorham beamed at his visitors.

"You brought the cards?" he asked.

"You can play?" asked the tall one, examining Izzy's bandaged head in what looked like a professional manner.

"If the nurse didn't see you, we can play." Waving a hand at the tall man, Izzy introduced him. "This is Dr. Feldman, retired, a good physician but a lousy pinochle player." He pointed out his rotund friend. "Dr. Malcolm, a retired orthodontist." The physician nodded; the orthodontist wore a worried smile. "And let's not forget Max Litvinoff, formerly an engineer with GM."

All three were dressed in casual but expensive clothing.

Their short-sleeved shirts bore designer logos. Their shoes were Gucci, or the equivalent. Chelsea caught the tattooed numbers on the wrists of all three men.

The engineer leaned on his cane as he shook hands with Chelsea.

"Captain Chelsea, Lieutenant Carbolo . . . It's nice meeting the detectives working on Izzy's behalf." Litvinoff wore dark glasses; Chelsea couldn't read his eyes. Were they smiling?

Outside, Carbolo walked Chelsea to his Ciera. The heat shimmered above its rooftop. Chelsea said, "How long can you keep security on him?"

"Twenty-four hours, while he's hospitalized. Before he leaves, I'll talk him into having a security alarm installed in his apartment."

"The man have any relatives?"

"Three sons. One very well off, an attorney in Cleveland. He came down and is staying at the Boca Raton Country Club. I think I can get him to foot the cost of an alarm system."

"While I'm thinking of it," Chelsea said, "check out Izzy's friends."

"What's going on?" Carbolo asked.

"Nothing. I like to touch all bases. What about the Resort? How are you going to handle it?"

"I know someone in a Miami brokerage house. Even if the Resort isn't on any exchange, he might be able to tell me something about them.

Chelsea nodded, then asked, "You into stocks?"

Carbolo's face screwed up in mock horror. "Me! You crazy? The stock market is the world's biggest crap shoot. No way. Whatever loose change I collect goes into property.

When I retire, there's going to be a small hacienda waiting for me in Ponce."

Chelsea grinned approval. "Smart boy. You coming back to our office? We have a plotting board set up in a back room."

Carbolo checked his watch. "No, I'm still on duty." He made a move to leave, then held back and scratched his ear. "Tell me, Captain . . . What did you really expect to accomplish on your alleged cruise?"

"We had to learn Hobbs's destination. We played it by ear, with no specific plan in mind."

"So, it's possible it was nothing more than a joyride for you."

Chelsea eyed him, and realized that he liked Carbolo's playing devil's advocate. "I don't think so," he said quietly.

"Okay, accepting it as an educated guess, how do we follow it up?" The lieutenant pulled at his ear lobe. *A warning itch?* "Our small bastard group certainly isn't equipped to take them on. We're working in the dark and without enough manpower."

"We don't have to *take* them on," Chelsea replied, thinking, *Am I convincing him or myself?* "We've got them worried. Sooner or later they'll make the wrong move . . ."

Carbolo's eyes dilated. "Shit! Captain! I hope to hell you know what you're doing. Because I sure as hell don't. You got *me* worried. We're talking about an invisible international cartel controlling an invisible army . . ."

Chelsea chuckled. "That's why we're playing it by ear. The best quarterback on the best team sometimes fumbles. If the opposition is any good, they take advantage."

Finished playing with his ear, Carbolo now scratched his head. "Maybe we should stick to football."

Chelsea laughed and reached for the car door.

"Let me know what you find out about the Resort—and

also Izzy's friends." The lieutenant waved him away good-humoredly.

In the car, some minutes later, driving down Linton Boulevard, Chelsea's expression sobered.

Was he holding a tiger by the tail?

19

The room was large and bordered on the elegant: a sofa, two fan-backed chairs, a coffee table with a bowl of fresh fruit as a centerpiece. Fran Fargo noted the color television, the writing desk with an extension that held a computer. On the opposite wall a king-size bed looked almost lost in the immensity of the room. A wet bar and small refrigerator stood next to the door of a walk-in closet. A marble bathroom with a lighted makeup mirror rounded out the facilities.

Although the daylight was just fading—with the time-zone change, she had arrived in Atlanta a mere five hours after leaving Rome.

She drifted to the window. From the fifth floor she could see the skyscrapers in the downtown district. The bellman, recognizing her as a first-time visitor, had mentioned, among other items of interest, a new shopping mall.

After further examination of the room, she decided it was one reserved for dignitaries. Perplexed, she asked herself: *Why me?* Did they treat all hired help in this manner? She considered her own query. *Since she wasn't even hired as yet, why had they gone to the trouble of falsifying a passport merely for another interview?*

Chelsea stood at a slate blackboard. He had just finished chalking in the latest developments. Dave Ward was at the computer, adding the new information to a disk, keeping it up-to-date. Later it would go into the firm's vault for safekeeping. Josh slouched in a striped deck chair, his face a study in fresh doubt.

"So now we're dealing with maniacs," he remarked dryly. He lit a cigarette, despite Ward's protestations not to smoke near the computer. "An organization that wipes out memory and installs new ones, for whatever purpose." He shifted uncomfortably.

Chelsea smiled condescendingly; he might have been a professor placating a failing student. Ward swiveled around from the keyboard to face him.

"Joey, my boy, have you wondered yet how many hundred—possibly thousands—of these clones have been produced over the years?"

"*Pawns*, Dave. Not *clones*. They're being manipulated as such. The number of pawns isn't as important as their purpose. Regardless of their numbers, I'd like to know how they're controlled." A heartbeat later he said, "Chop off the head of the octopus and the tentacles are useless."

Ward snorted derisively. "Terrific. All we have to do is find the octopus. It can't be the original Dr. Seltzer. He's long gone."

Chelsea screwed up his face, deepening the character lines. "You said 'original.' Who took over after his death, when the government closed up shop? Someone in the government?" A tentative smile appeared. "Are the files still classified?"

Ward got up from his chair. "No, you don't, Joey. Forget it. I don't want to have to keep looking over my shoulder to see if there's a car bearing down upon me." He closed down the computer to underscore his protest.

Josh pushed himself from the deck chair. "And on that note, I think we should call it a day." He gestured wearily. "The Brenners will stop in tomorrow morning. Let's see what they come up with."

Chelsea shrugged. *Can't win 'em all.* "We eating out tonight? It's time I treated the gang to dinner. How about it? Either of you can pick out the restaurant."

Ward beamed. "As Mae would say, 'Splendid idea.' How about Japanese? There's a good sushi restaurant on Federal Highway, not too far from here."

"You think the Brenners would be interested?"

"They have a job tonight." Reminded of his own commitments, Ward added, "Mae and I can't stay out late. I have an early-morning charter. One doesn't live by pension alone." Moving toward the door, he thought of something else. "What about the Brenners' equipment? Is it still on board the *Ark*?"

Josh nodded. "It's safe. No need to worry on that score."

Chelsea waited outside for Josh to lock up the storeroom and say good night to the four men who would work the night shift. From the parking lot, Joe's eyes scanned the street in both directions. There was no traffic whatsoever. It was a warehouse district and most places had closed down for the day. The few cars remaining in other lots were empty, none of them suspicious. He thought it unusual. Either surveillance on them had been dropped or else they had experts on the job.

Chelsea sniffed the air. "What is that odor?" he asked when Josh came out of the office.

"Marsh grass. A small channel runs behind the plants

across the way. We don't smell it unless there's a wind shift." Chelsea pinched his nose, and Josh chided him. "Don't knock it. Even a near-perfect paradise has its flaws."

"Paradise?"

Josh laughed. "You've forgotten the South Bronx and the East River district? Thank God for small favors."

Chelsea drifted off to his car. "As long as we're thanking God, ask Him to back us up." Josh waved him away.

"You know where the restaurant is? We'll meet you there in two hours."

Fran Fargo turned off the water and slid open the glass door of the shower stall. Was the phone ringing? It sounded again, off to her right; there was an extension on the wall, beside the vanity. Puzzled, she found a towel, dried her hands, and then draped the towel about her head.

"Yes?" she inquired, not offering her name.

"Miss Fran Fargo?" She frowned and wiped beads of water that dripped from her hair.

"Who wishes to know?"

"I'm Jason Stoner. I represent Wellington Security. You were recommended to me by Lester Horvath."

She now recalled the card that Horvath had given her.

"My appointment was for tomorrow morning."

"I realize that. But an emergency cropped up. I have an out-of-town conference in the morning. My coming to see you at this time is preferable to delaying your visit."

Coming to see her? The voice was soft, yet demanding. The caller sounded younger than she remembered Horvath. "I've just come out of the shower—"

The caller interrupted. "It's only five past eight. Have you had dinner? We can dine and talk in the Peach Lounge in the hotel where you're staying."

Fran held the towel against her cheek. She felt her

stomach roiling. The man was moving too fast; she didn't like it. "I don't know . . . I have to dress . . ."

"Just casual," came a ready response. "Can I expect you in a half-hour?"

"Would forty-five minutes be satisfactory?"

"Perfectly okay. Just ask the maître' d for my table."

When Fran told the maître' d that Jason Stoner was expecting her, his haughty expression softened. Unescorted attractive women were not especially welcome in the Peach Lounge. He immediately led her to Stoner's table.

Jason Stoner's blue eyes sparkled, and he didn't bother to hide his surprise as he appraised her. His look wasn't lost on her.

"Did I forget to put something on?" she asked.

The blond six-footer stood up, extending his hand in greeting. His grip was firm, but he didn't squeeze. "I don't believe you have a thing missing." A smile came easily to Fran.

"Do you usually conduct an interview in this manner?"

He touched a hand to his forehead, as if reminded. "I truly regret the inconvenience I've caused you. Please sit." He held out Fran's chair. His eyes lingering on her, he couldn't help wondering: *What sort of clandestine assignment have they in mind for her?*

Jason Stoner was a nephew of Elias Stoner, the founder of Wellington Security, and had been in his uncle's employ a mere three years. Although nepotism had brought him into the firm, it was a natural talent that made him head of personnel in the Atlanta office, an office which served the entire Southeast. Wealthy in his own right, he had wasted the years after Harvard in self-indulgence. After four years of idling in jet-set resorts he had had his fill of vacuous, saccharine women and fortune-hunters. In a state of ennui he walked into a U.S. Marine Corps recruiting office one day. The stint in the Marines, with its discipline, wrought a profound change in his character. He had learned how to deal with himself and his fellow man, in any situation. It was then that he had accepted his uncle's offer, and found himself in his element almost from the beginning. Selecting personnel for particular assignments had been a singular challenge, but he had accomplished it with no trouble.

Although Jason was established in a major position in the firm, he knew nothing as yet of Elias Stoner's extracurricular "investments."

Fran Fargo tried to regard Jason Stoner objectively. He was younger—probably no more than thirty—than she had expected, and much too handsome. Although he was businesslike in manner, his eyes sparkled with hidden humor. Were those eyes appraising her for a particular job—or for himself?

Fran felt his penetrating gaze down to her toes. She was uncomfortable, not knowing whether to like or be wary of him. She lifted the menu to escape his eyes. "What would you suggest?"

"Since I have to make an eleven-thirty flight, I took the liberty of ordering earlier. A garden salad, followed by Lobster Fra Diavolo. Does that meet with your approval? If not, it can be changed."

Fran laid the menu aside. "It will do quite nicely." His suit was silk, well-tailored and expensive-looking. She toyed with a fork. "To get back to my earlier question . . . Is this an American custom—conducting an interview in a public place?" His smile was pleasant, and she thought he was appraising her once again.

"The company does not approve of our speaking with a prospective employee of the opposite sex in a hotel room. It is not only frowned upon—it's taboo." He was aware of the beige silk blouse, and the pale-blue cashmere cardigan that matched her skirt. Her bosom heaved a bit, as if she was having a nervous moment.

"Relax, Ms. Fargo." He had noted the absence of a wedding band. Her jewelry consisted of a pearl ring and matching earrings and a locket on a thin gold chain. "Would you like a cocktail?" he asked.

"No. But I would like some wine."

Stoner signaled for the waiter.

It was about ten when Stoner checked his Rolex. They had finished their entrees and he suggested ordering Pineapple Marie, a dessert consisting of crushed pineapple, vanilla, sugar, egg yolks, whipped heavy cream, and tangerines, all blended together and set into the empty core of the pineapple.

Conversation during the meal was confined to polite social discourse, mostly about travel in Europe. Fran was more or less at ease after dessert, yet she couldn't help wondering when Jason Stoner would get to the purpose of their meeting.

Stoner waited for the waiter to depart after pouring coffee. He then said, "Relate your experience with underwater demolition."

His abrupt switch from pleasantries to business caught Fran off guard. She licked her lips; it was time for the half-truths. Clasping her hands in her lap, she began:

"A year ago I worked on a wreck that was sunk during World War Two." *In truth, she was merely an assistant to her cousin Antonio, who was her tutor at the time.* "My task was to retrieve a cargo of silver ingots from a locked hold. The procedure called for extreme caution so as not to scatter the bullion all over the sea bottom."

She held his gaze and considered whether it sounded plausible or not. He wore a half-smile, as if trying to make up his mind. He had suddenly become so formal, a total reversal of his previous easygoing manner. His expression wasn't harsh; he might have been struggling to make an objective assessment.

Fran finished her recitation, then lifted the cup of coffee to her lips. After taking a sip she asked, "Is that it?"

"Your father never discussed his assignments with our firm?" She gave him a sidelong glance. *Where was he leading?* She forced a smile she didn't feel.

"No, he didn't. I believe you already knew that."

Stoner's thoughts clouded. Fran Fargo was an enigma. He didn't know what to make of her enlistment. His own office held no records of Emilio Franco's assignments, other than that the man was hired for a special duty. A frown marred the handsome face. *Something smelled!*

"And you have no idea of what your father accomplished on those particular occasions?"

"All I know is that he was well paid. And that's all I'm interested in." She noted his uncertainty, and vague suspicions surfaced. All that money in a Swiss bank . . . "Are you suggesting my father's assignments were of a clandestine nature?" She was thinking "illegal," but couldn't bring herself to say the word. *Her father!*

Stoner's eyes clouded. He was the head of the Southeast office and the interview was proceeding beyond his knowledge of what to seek in her. So, she had the experience they required. *But for what purpose?*

Fran was puzzled by his manner. "Well, do I get a commendation from you? Or do I simply repack and return home?" His eyebrows lifted.

"You have the commendation. I'm not quite certain it should make you happy." To himself he added: *As a matter of fact I'm not quite certain* I'm *happy with your acceptance.*

Fran leaned forward. "Will you please explain yourself?"

He waved away her question, then pulled out an envelope from the inside pocket of his jacket. This is a ticket for Fort Lauderdale, on a flight leaving tomorrow morning. A taxi will be waiting when you land, to take you to a hotel in Boca Raton. You will be contacted in a day or two with further instructions." Her eyes widened.

"Just like that?" she said. "No more questions?"

Jason glanced at the bill left earlier by the waiter, but ignored it. "Fran . . . May I call you Fran?" He didn't wait for an answer. "I wish you wouldn't take the assignment."

She leaned back and looked up at him. He was taller than she had thought earlier. "And why not?"

"You don't know what the job entails—and admitting that I don't either—I would advise you to consider it carefully before you leave for Florida."

Fran's pulse rate quickened. Was that an implied threat—or simply an admonition to be cautious? Her thoughts confused, she rose from her seat.

"I'm merely following in my father's footsteps," she told him, for want of anything better to say.

"Blindly? Without any knowledge of what the job requires?" Assignment was the proper term, but he hated the word, especially in this instance.

Fran was at a momentary loss. Why did Stoner feel the need to caution her? She said finally, "You know of my father's illness?" He nodded.

"Yes, I'm sorry. But it doesn't alter my position." He signaled for the waiter and handed him a credit card. When the waiter had gone he said, "I have to leave now, but you can expect to see me the day after tomorrow."

She played with the ring on her finger. An inner voice

told her that his visit to Florida wasn't scheduled. She allowed him to take her arm and escort her to the lobby, where they said good night.

Going up in the elevator, Fran could only wonder what was happening to her. First to Washington, D.C., then Atlanta, tomorrow Florida—to a place called Boca Raton. What did it all mean? And why was Jason Stoner cautioning her? What would her father say, if he knew? She needn't guess—she knew. She would be back in the office attending to business, as usual. Out of trouble. Out of the action.

At the hotel entrance Stoner waited for the valet to bring around his Mercedes convertible. Fran Fargo, nee Francesca Franco, occupied his thoughts, prompting questions for which he had no answers. What were her father's assignments? The Wellington Security files merely showed his name and qualifications. For additional information he had turned to the computer, and was told an access code was necessary for a need-to-know file. Jason wasn't privy to the code.

The car arrived and he slid behind the wheel, but his brain struggled for comprehension. Until meeting Fran Fargo he had not given it a second thought, assuming the missing code was an oversight by the previous manager.

He sat in the car, unmoving, latent suspicions surfacing. *The man had been hired for illegal operations!* He hit the gas pedal, greatly disturbed.

Was Wellington Security being used by some government agency? If so, why was foreign talent necessary?

Jason shook his head in disbelief, yet . . . What other explanation was there? He himself, as head of the Southeast section, was not privy to the nature of Franco's commissions. Was someone within the company engaged in subversive activity that even his uncle knew nothing about? The answer was reflected in Jason's eyes and tight lips . . . *Not possible!*

He jammed his foot on the gas pedal and shot into the street; for a second he forgot the airport was his destination.

Apprehension beset him from every direction. Fran Fargo claimed that she didn't know the nature of her father's duties for the firm, and he believed her. Was she tempting fate by blindly following in her father's footsteps?

He parked at the airport, still struggling with his conscience. As head of his division, he was obliged to attend the next day's conference in Chicago. His jaw set, he reminded himself they would have computers available there—and possibly someone who knew the access code for Emilio Franco.

He made a mental note to have someone pick up his car in the morning. A private investigation was in order, and following the Chicago conference he would immediately leave for Florida—whether or not he learned anything further from the computer, and without permission from his uncle.

As he was about to slide out of the car, the car phone chirped. As expected, it was his uncle, Elias Stoner, inquiring about his interview with Fran Fargo. He was then told to forget about her, that she would be answerable to the Miami office.

Jason Stoner frowned. Forget her? *No way!*

20

Joe Chelsea was extremely pleased as he left the maintenance department of the Ford agency on Federal Highway. The three new vehicles he'd ordered—including one unmarked car—would be available in two weeks. A generous bonus always helped, he mused. The sun's glare on the concrete surface was fierce; he tilted his Yankees cap in order to adjust his sunglasses. As he approached his Ciera, he was surprised to see Rudy Carbolo sitting in the passenger seat.

"So much for locked cars," Chelsea said dryly, sliding behind the wheel. "Was this part of your early training?"

Carbolo grinned. "Don't knock it. If I get caught moonlighting on company time, I might have to pursue it for a living."

Chelsea twisted in his seat. "You have trouble with the department?"

"Not yet, but my captain's been asking questions."

"About what?"

"For what it's worth, he seemed unduly interested in Izzy

Gorham. Now, I ask you, why would he be concerned with that old man?"

Chelsea rubbed his nose. The itch was there.

"What was he asking?"

"At first, the usual questions: 'How's the investigation going? Do you have any ideas?' "

"What's wrong with that?"

Carbolo gave him a curious look. "He wants to drop the twenty-four-hour security."

"So? He probably doesn't believe it necessary. Maybe he feels the manpower isn't warranted. Your department strapped at the moment?" Rudy shook his head, then tapped his stomach.

"It's not something I can explain. Sometimes my gut tells me things that aren't obvious."

Chelsea stuck out his lower lip and chewed on it.

"You know the man. I don't. What's your reading on this?"

The lieutenant shrugged. "I don't know. It's not something I want to believe." He knew Chelsea was mulling over his own suspicions. "You tell me . . . Is it possible? *My own precinct captain is one of them?*"

Chelsea rubbed his chin. He had shaved early that morning, and the stubble seemed to flourish in the tropical heat.

Aware of Carbolo's unhappiness he asked, "Did you learn anything more about the Resort—or Izzy's friends?"

"Zip on all accounts. Nothing of any significance other than what we already know. The Resort's not on the exchange. It's a private organization set up to rehabilitate retired executives. That's all I could get without raising eyebrows. Izzy's friends are strictly kosher. Checking on them was a waste of time." Rudy reached for the door handle. "I've gotta go. I can't have the captain getting funny ideas."

"Watch your step," Chelsea said.

"Don't you mean my back?"

Chelsea sniffed. Things were never dull in paradise.

Carbolo tarried a moment longer. "Captain, I think we're chewing on something we can't swallow." He walked away then, not expecting a response.

Chelsea watched him scan the busy thoroughfare before attempting to make it across to his unmarked car. When he finally pulled out into traffic, Chelsea muttered, "Tread softly, amigo. We still have a long way to go."

For the first time in weeks, Chelsea craved a stiff drink. His expression sour, he reached for his tobacco pouch and pipe lying atop the dash. Stuffing the bowl, he was reminded of Ellie's "Liquor is only a temporary substitute for shutting out a problem. It will never solve it."

Dear, wonderful, rarely complaining Ellie. Platitudes never solved anything either. He smiled wanly, capsulizing what he was putting her through, and her stoic acceptance of it. She deserved much better and he well knew it.

His teeth bit into the stem of the briar. *Ellie, you know I can't quit. I've never left a job undone. Let me finish this . . . I promise . . .*

Sweat broke out on his ruddy face, with the direction his thoughts were taking. Can't quit? What nonsense! Was he now becoming his own devil's advocate? He recalled some of the abject faces seen in the adult communities, which in itself had aided him and Ellie in their final selection. The faces displaying an early tiredness were too evident. It was a disease sapping their vitality. How could it happen? Why were they resigned to letting a slow death overtake them?

His morose thoughts brought a scowl. He recognized that he wasn't painting a true overall picture. The old man Izzy

Gorham and his friends were admirable exceptions. Death was a mortal wound and they weren't waiting for it to happen. Izzy, despite his seventy-odd years, and his complaining, was still imbued with life.

Chelsea looked up suddenly, as if he'd just discovered an earthshaking secret. Why did he categorize Izzy and his friends as being old? They were no more than five to ten years older than he was. He never had thought of himself as being old until it was "suggested" he retire.

He snapped on the air conditioner and, puffing heavily, blew out a cloud of gray smoke. He observed it as if seeking absolution.

His eyes caught the digital clock; almost noon. Ellie was at home. He lifted the car phone. Whatever the reason, he had a sudden desire to take her to lunch.

Jason Stoner was on the tenth floor of the Chicago hotel, his room equipped with the computer requested. After the morning session, he had begged off invitations to lunch.

IDENTITY UNKNOWN. MUST HAVE MORE DATA.

This was in reply to Stoner's asking for Emilio Franco's file. Stoner punched in:

EMPLOYEE OF WELLINGTON SECURITY.

The monitor read: SEARCHING. And then came up with:

EMILIO FRANCO IS NOT AN EMPLOYEE OF WELLINGTON SECURITY.

Jason sat back, his face a study in bewilderment. In the Atlanta office the computer had asked for a need-to-know access code. Now it was saying the man was not in their employ.

He leaned forward and punched in an additional query.

THERE IS NO EXISTING FILE ON EMILIO FRANCO.

Stoner gazed at the response for long seconds, uncertain

how to proceed. Reasoning, all he could come up with was: *Franco had been wiped from memory.*

He got to his feet and went to the window. Ten floors below, people resembled ants crawling on ribboned concrete. In the distance Lake Michigan's horizon merged with an overcast sky. Along the shoreline a prewinter wind churned the dark waters into white froth.

He gazed at the dreary scene with unseeing eyes.

Why was Franco's name erased? And by whom?

He stood there, undecided, and noticed his unfinished sandwich. He was no longer hungry. His thoughts drifted to Fran Fargo. Why was she hired? And to do what?

His uncertainty making him uncomfortable, he walked to the phone and called the airport. After reserving a seat on a 7:30 P.M. flight to West Palm Beach, he called the desk to leave a message for the officer chairing the afternoon session, pleading an unexpected emergency.

Replacing the phone, he looked up to observe the monitor mocking him. Glowering, he strode back to the keyboard.

ON WHOSE ORDERS WAS EMILIO FRANCO'S FILE REMOVED?

DATA NOT UNDERSTOOD. PLEASE EXPLAIN.

"Damn!" Angered, frustrated, he balled a fist as if about to strike the machine. Then, calming himself, he switched off the computer.

He sat there, gathering his thoughts, wondering how it was possible he wasn't a party to all company projects. Calculating, he came up with the only possible explanation. Either the company, or someone within it, was involved in subversive activities.

He thought of Fran Fargo, that attractive creature . . . Was her innocence all pretense? Or was she being duped?

He got to his feet and strode to the walk-in closet. Retrieving his overnight bag, he suddenly realized that other than knowing Fran Fargo would be contacted in Boca Raton, he himself was never informed of the contact's identity.

What the hell was going on!

He thought of phoning his uncle Elias, then dismissed the idea peremptorily. The call might precipitate an investigation that would be out of his personal control.

Jason could feel the veins in his temples pulsing. Why did the entire situation cause him to feel apprehensive? He thrust his hands in his pants pockets, thinking, and he had no answer.

No, he decided finally. It was simply that he was suffering a humiliation intolerable for a man in his position. His personal pride had been bruised. And it called for action of some kind.

Jason Stoner's uncle sat behind his desk, straightening some papers. The headquarters of Wellington Security occupied the entire top floor of a twenty-four-story tower overlooking the city of Dallas.

Elias Stoner was short, on the plump side, with wiry gray hair surrounding a balding pate. His cheeks were soft and puffy, and despite the excess weight, he carried himself as a self-styled autocrat. His eyes, dark and opaque behind horn-rimmed spectacles, hinting of a fire within, held the clue to his success. He was a man who controlled an empire, an empire of his own creation, and his subordinates flinched in his presence.

Stoner was preparing to leave for a luncheon appointment when his private phone buzzed. The phone was in a locked drawer on the right-hand side of the immaculate, black-enameled desk. Stoner frowned, creasing his flaccid cheeks.

Using a key attacked to a chain around his neck, he unlocked the drawer.

"Hello, Jon," he said, knowing no one else had the number.

Jon Seltzmann didn't bother with amenities. "Elias, how trustworthy is your nephew?"

Stoner grimaced. How he detested this pompous, overbearing man. "Is there a problem?" he asked calmly.

"He's been searching the computer for classified documents."

Stoner remained composed, despite the tone of Seltzmann's voice.

"So, why should it bother you? Jason's integrity is beyond question. His position permits him leeway."

"Elias, your nephew is digging into Franco's files. You, yourself, apparently didn't see fit to apprise him of those specific files. I ask you again, Is he trustworthy?"

Stoner's brows knitted. *My God! What was Jason looking for? Why couldn't he keep his nose clean?* His voice evenly pitched, he spoke into the phone.

"Jon, I can manage my own house. I don't want interference from you or from any other quarter. Is that understood?"

"Quite. And you must understand I will hold you personally responsible."

Stoner gnashed his teeth and hung up on Jon Seltzmann. "Damn his arrogance!" He punched the intercom and got his secretary in an outer office. "Call Chicago and get me Jason Stoner."

He sat back, fingered his lower lip, and waited.

Five minutes later Stoner learned his nephew had left Chicago, without attending the afternoon session of the conference. Elias Stoner's eyes darkened. "Damn fool!" he muttered. A mere three years in the firm and he was earning eighty thousand per. Why couldn't he behave responsibly?

Stoner tapped his fingers on the desk, a habit that in the presence of other people meant "Don't interrupt." He hit the intercom again.

"Louise, see if you can get Nestor Hobbs at his Palm Beach residence."

Nestor Hobbs wasn't at home.

"Murphy's Law," Stoner grumbled. He rose from behind the desk and went to the window, where he stood unmoving, his mind preoccupied. Instinct suggested that Jason was probably getting involved with that woman, Fran Fargo. No longer hesitant, he turned back to the intercom.

"Louise, call the Miami office."

Calvin Rodgers, presently working out of the Miami office, was Fran Fargo's Boca Raton contact. A former CIA agent, with a law degree, he had been employed by Wellington Security for the past five years. A clever man, with a trigger-quick mind, his skills—both mental and physical—were well-honed.

Rodgers had just passed his thirty-third birthday, and to a casual observer, looked ten years younger. His face was unmarked, but the square jaw hinted of determination. Although he was well-muscled, there wasn't a single ounce of excess fat on his six-foot frame, and even his simplest movement displayed an athletic grace.

Learning it was Elias Stoner calling, he switched on a jammer. Showing no emotion, he listened to Stoner's instructions, and waited a full five minutes before responding; one never interrupted Elias Stoner. Rodgers then spoke his piece and asked for corroboration.

"I'm to judge the woman's conduct before the final hiring. If she's clean, it will be my decision whether to continue with her. And if your nephew attempts to throw a monkey wrench into these plans, I'm permitted to use my own discretion. Is that correct, sir?" He listened intently once more. Then, nodding, he said, "I understand, sir. The Home Office will not abide bad blood in the 'family.' Regarding the woman—if she reneges on the projected mission—it will again be my decision on how to proceed."

21

The airport taxi turned into a street just south of Spanish River Boulevard. Seconds later it entered a curved driveway and stopped at the front entrance of a two-story beige stucco apartment-hotel.

Fran Fargo was relieved to step out of the car. During the almost hour-long ride, few words had passed between her and the taciturn middle-aged driver. She studied the building while waiting for him to retrieve her luggage from the trunk.

The exterior was well-maintained, freshly painted, with flower boxes on every window; a narrow, bordering lawn was hedged with flowering shrubbery. The driver told her to wait while he took her luggage into the lobby. She obeyed dutifully, expectantly.

The man returned and handed her a set of keys. He nodded toward a white Thunderbird at the far end of the parking area. "It's yours for the length of your stay. Please return it to its reserved area when no longer in use. You need only register at the desk for your room key." He handed her a folded road map. "It's a street map for you to study." Finishing his practiced speech, he got into his cab and drove off.

The apartment was an unexpected bonus, an efficiency unit with loveseat, easy chairs, and a coffee table. A television set faced the sofa. At the far end, to the right, was a king-size bed flanked by night tables.

Fran flicked a wall switch opposite the small sitting area, and entered the kitchen. Exploring, she discovered it was equipped with an ice-making refrigerator, sink with garbage disposal, microwave oven, toaster, electric coffeemaker, and all the other equipment needed for complete housekeeping.

She plopped down onto the sofa and kicked off her shoes, a sense of unreal elation overtaking her. She wondered whether her father had been treated in a like manner. Emilio coming to mind, she decided to call Napoli. There was a plug-in phone on a small table beside one of the easy chairs.

Emilio Franco's condition was unchanged.

Her expression morose, Fran went to the window and peered through the curtains. The apartment was at the rear of the building, facing a grass lawn that sloped down to a wide waterway. On the water a cruiser and fishing trawler moved at a leisurely pace. She watched them dispassionately, until her stomach reminded her she had not had lunch yet.

She considered looking for a restaurant—she had seen a number of them as she traveled along Route One. On impulse she took out the street map the taxi driver had given her. It took her five minutes to find her present location. Spanish River Boulevard led onto A1A, a road that paralleled the ocean. She made her decision.

She familiarized herself with the controls of the Thunderbird, then switched on the engine. The street map was spread out on the bucket seat beside her.

On A1A she turned north and followed the signs for Palm Beach. She drove at a leisurely pace, fascinated by the high-rise pastel condominiums and palatial private homes. The architecture varied from new-world contemporary to Spanish Mediterranean.

By the time she reached the outskirts of Palm Beach, she was starving. The first time she'd looked at the map she noted shopping centers clearly marked.

She left the ocean road, got on to the Federal Highway, and pulled into the first market she came to.

Leaving the car, she became aware of a black sedan parking a dozen spaces away. Unobtrusively she gave it a sidelong glance, and wondered if it was the same black car she'd noticed earlier on the ocean road. She shrugged it off and went into the market.

She purchased a number of items, including a bottle of sherry.

When she left the market, the black car was still there, the driver invisible in the growing twilight. It would be dark soon. She consulted the map for the quickest way back and decided on Interstate 95.

In the failing light she couldn't be sure if the black car had followed her. Either her eyes had been playing tricks or else he was hanging back.

Forty-five minutes later she was back in the apartment, and immediately became aware of a red light blinking on the phone. There was a message for her. Lifting the receiver, she got the front desk.

"Ms. Fargo, there's a message for you. Will you come to the desk or would you rather I read it?"

She was immediately concerned about her father, but then remembered that she hadn't left her number. "Please read it."

" 'Will arrive tomorrow morning for a business meeting.' The name given was Calvin Rodgers."

"Thank you," Fran said, although a bit puzzled.

Another contact? Did Jason Stoner change his mind about hiring her?

Unsure of herself, she went to the window. Lights hidden in the palm trees made the lawn appear greener. Hibiscus cast shadows in the corners; the Waterway appeared purple in the dusk, its surface rippling as a late yacht sailed by.

Shrugging off dark feelings, she started to unload her packages. Unwrapping a pasta dish, she read the instructions before placing it in the microwave.

She turned on the radio, searched for soft music, then settled down on the sofa and waited for the microwave to ping.

Except for the music, the room was quiet. It was almost as if the entire place were deserted. She shook her shoulders, her eyes clouding with self-doubt. She wondered about this Calvin Rodgers, sensing the meeting with him would be the point of no return. *Watch yourself, Francesca.*

Joe Chelsea sat in the comfortable lounge chair, but felt uncomfortable. He put aside the paper he was reading after scanning the same line three times. Restless fingers beat a tattoo on the arms of his chair.

After a heavy lunch, he and Ellie had been satisfied with a fish salad for dinner. Dessert was postponed for later in the evening.

Ellie was settled in a fan-backed chair, watching the news on television. Without looking away, she asked, "You still hungry, Joe?"

Chelsea turned his head and leaned forward. "How would you like to take a ride?"

Now she faced him. "At this hour? It's almost nine. Where would we go?"

Chelsea reached for his pipe on the small table beside his chair. "I have to see the area where Izzy Gorham lives."

"Whatever for?"

Chelsea stalled briefly, considering an innocuous reply. To say it was merely idle curiosity—although in a way it was—would seem inane. He told her about a recent phone conversation with Izzy. "The man is impossible, Ellie. He's still enraged by what happened to him."

"Can you blame him?"

"No, of course not. But I tried to explain that, considering his minor injuries, he was extremely fortunate." Chelsea's eyes crinkled with humor. "When I told him he had no right to remain angry, he said—get this, Ellie—the man said, 'I've a right to be angry. That *momzer* could have caught me in a compromising position with a lady friend.'"

"And you find that funny?"

He gave her an oblique glance, realizing he had offended her somehow. "The man will be seventy-five on his next birthday. You don't find that—"

"Where is there a law that says passion dies with age?"

Chelsea suppressed a sigh. The conversation had taken a wrong turn. He held his hands up defensively. "Sorry, El, I just thought—"

"I know what you thought," she interrupted. "And I also know what you have in mind." She used the remote to switch off the TV.

Chelsea looked at her questioningly, waiting for additional comment. She didn't disappoint him. "You want to explore his neck of the woods. His lifestyle intrigues you. Isn't that it, Joe?"

Chelsea got up and planted a kiss on her cheek. "As Ralph Cramden used to say, 'You're the greatest.'"

"So are you, Joe. But you're becoming obvious. You have to see for yourself that people don't sit around waiting for the Grim Reaper to overtake them." From her chair she could see a hanging plant on the terrace swinging in a slight breeze. "The temperature might drop to sixty. If we do any walking, we'll need sweaters."

"Take one if you want, but we won't be getting out of the car. It's strictly observation from a distance."

"And what area are we observing?" she asked, smiling.

"It's not far. Gorham lives near the village of Oriole, off Atlantic Avenue. But the section has other developments. I thought we'd just drive through. Their clubhouses play a big part in the way they live, according to Izzy. Entertainment, exercise and game rooms, and good friends. Izzy said that all those things, plus the weather, are the principal reasons for his continuing to live in Florida."

Driving west on Atlantic Avenue, neither one of them spoke. Grim Reaper indeed, Joe mused, wincing. The woman was clever, but that was hitting below the belt. He puffed on the briar and watched the rearview mirror in the continuing silence.

Ellie lit a cigarette to calm her nerves. Prior to Joe's forced retirement, any discussion of either one of them dying had been taboo. Now, with the risks involved in Joe's "final case," he was taking her to see—*see what? Another life style for widows?* Damn him! She cracked the window. The smoke was clouding her eyes, causing them to mist.

They passed a synagogue, and she realized it was the first one she'd noticed since coming south. It gave her an opening to break the silence. "I was thinking of joining one, Joe," she said quietly.

"Joining what?" Had he missed something?

"A synagogue. We just passed one." He gave her a brief,

sharp glance. "I believe it's time I renewed acquaintance with my heritage."

He paused for a moment before saying, "You've been considering it seriously."

She nodded. "Would you mind?"

"Why would I mind?" He gave it added thought. "Except for not dropping this investigation, have I ever refused you anything?"

She made a face, as if it was an absurd question, then waved a hand to disperse the pipe smoke drifting in her direction. He cracked the driver's window.

Silence overtook them again. Ellie thought his acquiescence, though sincere, was too casual. Was this Joe's applied philosophy for prospective widows? No, he had never refused her anything. Vignettes of happiness came to mind: their honeymoon, summer vacations, evenings at the theatre, the weekly get-togethers with dear friends to play cards or test their skills with intricate word games.

And who could forget the overpowering joy when they purchased their new home. She could recall in precise detail the day that they moved in and Joe carried her across the threshold. Their neighbors had mistaken them for newlyweds.

Joe had always had a certain strength about him, yet she remembered a time that it deserted him, during his first talk on home security before one of the organizations she belonged to. Facing an audience composed entirely of women had been more frightening for him than confronting armed criminals. Oh, they had shared such good times together. She couldn't allow his forced retirement to haunt him.

She placed a hand on his thigh and squeezed gently. "Sorry, Joe, I didn't mean to just throw it at you."

"It's okay. I'll go along with whatever makes you happy.

Out of curiosity, when did you really think of joining a congregation?"

"It was Cindy's suggestion." Ellie smiled her pleasant smile. "It wouldn't do you any harm to attend church once in a while."

His eyebrows lifted. "Whatever for?"

"You do believe in the Almighty. I know that for a fact. I've seen you muttering a silent prayer on occasion. Like the time when I was hospitalized with a ruptured appendix."

He snorted. "Force of habit. A throwback to my youth, when I didn't know better. I never saw God in the stationhouse."

"He was there. You just didn't see Him."

He laughed sardonically. When did they last discuss religion?

"Was He with you in France?" he asked.

She twisted around to confront him. "If He weren't, I wouldn't have lived to meet you."

A ready answer. A superficial reply to all problems. How many times had he observed vicious criminals crossing themselves? Calling for priests to hear their confessions and, when the situation demanded it, grant absolution.

Yielding without agreeing, he said, "I suppose. My agnostic leanings always prevailed over atheism."

When Ellie again squeezed his thigh playfully, he said, "I hope you're not going totally Orthodox on me."

She laughed softly, elated with the change in mood. "Don't worry about that. I won't go overboard. It will be good to get involved again. Like you, I feel stifled in retirement."

She peered through the windshield. They were approaching a shopping center, the first of many in this particular area. A Publix market, clothing stores, movie houses, numerous restaurants on both sides of the avenue.

When he slowed to enter the parking lot Ellie said, "Why are we going in? Except for the supermarket everything's shut down for the night."

"Just for a look-see. We're not stopping." He followed the road around the Publix market.

The parking area here was more spacious, accommodating additional shops, plus a movie theatre and a couple of restaurants. Chelsea nodded toward the people lined up for the late film show. Almost everyone had gray hair or white. "That should give you a good idea of the average resident's age here."

Ellie harrumphed. "So what! Don't knock it. Cindy and Josh admit to taking the senior citizen discount at the movies. Why complain. Take advantage of it and go with the flow. Need I remind you we're in the same category, whether you like it or not."

Chelsea winced. "I'm going to ask one favor of you, Ellie." She eyed him, wondering, What now?

"When we have our get-togethers, I don't mind waxing nostalgic, but let's go easy on the memorabilia. I expect to have memories of events I haven't as yet experienced. Leave that bit for the elderly."

"Ye gods! Do you know what you sound like!" She laughed suddenly, realizing how inane their discussion had become. "Joe, tell me something—If you were asked to address these people, like in the *old days*"—she stressed "old days" facetiously—"What would your subject be?"

Parked with the engine running, he pondered a reply.

"The subject would be on 'keeping busy' and not reproaching yourself for all the things you've never done. Try to stay healthy and make the future a better past."

Ellie applauded silently. "And that's what you're doing? By investigating an international cartel that could wipe out your future?"

He shrugged, disregarding the serious overtone. "Each of us has a particular road to travel. I know mine, others can look at a map for direction." He shrugged again. "For what it's worth, that's my philosophy."

He tapped his pipe out in the ashtray as Ellie lit up a cigarette. "I think we've covered the subject, don't you? Let's change it."

Ellie ignored him, noticing the canes carried by many on the line at the theatre. It could be their own future someday, she acknowledged bleakly. Joe's "stay healthy" lingered in her mind. Good trick. Her mouth set stubbornly. Tomorrow she would join the Sisterhood at Cindy's synagogue.

There were no stars out and a canopy of humidity hung over parked cars. Shrugging her shoulders, Ellie forced a cheerfulness she didn't feel. "Well, youngster . . . Where to next?"

Chelsea sniffed. "Camelot," he said.

"What?"

"It's one of the developments past Jog Road. It's also close to Izzy Gorham's place."

"Joe, I hope you're not planning to visit his apartment." Rain appeared imminent and Ellie wanted to leave and perhaps stop for coffee somewhere.

"I couldn't investigate even if I wanted to. Rudy's chief has been pressing him. If I sniffed around, it could cause problems."

"For him—or you?"

He looked at her, then shifted into gear, drove out of the parking lot and back to the boulevard.

While most roads were through streets, going either north to south, or west to east, the streets of the development were a maze of concentric circles. Stopped by a guard at the gate, Chelsea showed his Novick Security ID and said he was going to the Gorham apartment. The car was passed through.

Chelsea eventually slowed at a four-story building.

"The corner apartment," he volunteered, anticipating Ellie's question. "On the second floor."

"The catwalks again," she remarked. No catwalks was something they had agreed upon when they were apartment-hunting. Neither did they want a property that featured a golf course. Chelsea never had time for the game and had been warned that he would be an outcast in a golf community.

Chelsea spoke as if to himself. "The intruder had to pass each apartment, and without being seen." Opening a locked door was no problem for a professional.

Ellie watched him and shivered. "Joe, I feel like an interloper." The parking space allotted for tenants was almost filled, and the quiet lent an eerie feeling.

A middle-aged couple with grocery bags were the only people about. As they walked past the Ciera, their sneaker-clad feet made scraping sounds. The woman eyed the Chelseas suspiciously. "Let's go," Ellie said wearily.

Chelsea shifted the gear and pulled up by the couple. He leaned out his window. "Do you know if Izzy Gorham is home? His apartment looks dark." He knew the place was empty, but he wasn't about to have two worried people calling the police with his license number. Ellie shook her head.

The man's accent was pure Bronx. "Home! The man is in the hospital. You didn't know?"

"I'd heard, but I thought he might have come home by this time." Sounding disappointed but resigned, he added, "We're old friends. I guess we'll visit him tomorrow. Thanks. Sorry to have troubled you."

The woman tugged at her husband's sleeve impatiently.

"Richie, it's going to rain." With a change in attitude she addressed Chelsea. "Tell Izzy not to worry. We're watching his apartment."

"Thanks. I'll tell him." Chelsea waved good night. He waited for them to leave and decided to circle the building.

Most of the apartments were dark; the condo owners evidently retired early or were at their clubhouse. At the rear, street lamps illuminated a twisting path past small villas and green lawns to a well-lighted swimming pool.

As Chelsea followed the roadway, faint sounds of music drifted into the open windows of the car. "Where's it coming from?" Ellie asked.

"Straight ahead, the other side of the pool. Someone must have left the clubhouse door open." It was a sprawling ranch-type structure, with a single tower breaking the rooftop line.

"Sounds great," she said, waxing sentimental. "Reminds me of the big-band era."

Chelsea glanced at her, barely turning his head. "The entertainment sometimes includes borscht belt comics."

A trace of a smile appeared on her lips. "Joe, the truth . . . Why did you bring me here?"

He lifted his eyes. A pretense of surprise. "To scout Izzy Gorham's neighborhood. The life style he described to me." He shot her a penetrating look. "You've got a suspicious mind, young lady."

Unaccountably Ellie's thoughts took a new direction, shifting inward. The people inside were having a good time. Most were parents, many also grandparents. Many years ago Joe had been told his sperm count was too low to procreate and, even if it wasn't, Ellie knew she could not conceive. She couldn't help wondering: Where was the child she had lost almost four decades ago?

The years go by, and you forget, except for an occasional reminder.

Ellie sighed deeply, with vague regret; she had lived with the acceptance of God's will for too long. "You okay?" intruded.

She turned, as if awakening from a bad dream. She had frightened him. She smiled easily, a habit learned over the years, solely for his benefit.

"Of course. Now, are we going home or stopping for coffee?"

Twenty minutes later, he spied a Denny's on Federal Highway and turned off. As he locked the car he said, "You don't suppose they could make a New York pastrami on rye? All the delis are closed."

Ellie laughed. "You're pressing your luck."

A Chrysler Le Baron roared down the highway, causing a car leaving the restaurant to brake sharply. Cursing, the driver blew his horn in a futile gesture.

"I'm not the only one pressing my luck," Chelsea remarked dryly. "That Chrysler's heading for trouble."

And we're not? Ellie asked herself.

22

It was precisely nine A.M. the following morning—hours before Jason Stoner's expected arrival—when Rodgers presented himself at Fran Fargo's door. He observed her pleasantly as she read his business card. Apparently satisfied, she asked him in.

She was wearing beige slacks; a matching blouse hung over the beltline. Rodgers noted the designer logo above the pocket. Expensive. She lived well. She was even more attractive than he had imagined. The shadowed occasional glimpse of her a previous time had given only a hint of her beauty. What a waste, he mused, his expression offering no clue to his thoughts. He continued to smile pleasantly. Starscope night-glasses did not provide a true picture.

Fran offered him coffee but he declined.

"I would prefer we get down to business," he said.

Viewing him, Fran was reminded of an old paternal warning: Beware of plastic smiles. They are in the same category as crocodile tears.

"Make yourself comfortable," she said. She took the chair

by the window overlooking the rear lawn. Earlier she had drawn the curtains to permit a welcoming sun to enter; it added a much-needed cheerfulness.

Like the others preceding him, he had a file on her.

"Ms. Fargo, how well prepared are you to undertake a task that might be considered somewhat shady?"

"What do you mean by 'somewhat'? Is it, or isn't it?" She thought his plastic smile marred an otherwise attractive face.

"Let me put it this way. There are some people forced into a position not of their own choosing. Unfortunately, the only way they can extricate themselves from this intolerable situation is through means that are not quite legal. Despite the illegality, the results would plainly justify the means." He leveled his eyes with hers. "Do I make myself clear? You should understand I can't reveal more until I'm sure you're in full agreement."

Fran fingered her lower lip with her pinky, a habit her father had long chided her for.

"It depends on what is required of me," she said, choosing words carefully. "I will not agree to do anything that would cause bodily harm. Otherwise . . ."

Rodgers gave a small laugh. "Bodily harm! My dear young lady"—Fran winced inwardly at his expression; she detested being patronized—"my firm doesn't get itself involved in such dealings."

"Then what is it you want of me?" She reminded herself of Jason Stoner's warning.

"First, I must know whether these terms are acceptable to you."

What terms? As yet, there had been no mention of payment. She brought it up.

"What is it worth to your client?"

Rodgers eyed her quizzically. Apparently, she surprised

him. Quickly, he reached into his leather file case, pulled out a thick envelope, and placed it on the cocktail table. "There's five thousand dollars in hundred-dollar bills. There will be an additional five thousand compensation at the completion of your task."

Fran studied the envelope without moving, frozen in her chair, her heart pounding. Was this how they paid Papa?

"I still haven't been told what I must do to earn it."

Rodgers nodded, seemingly satisfied.

"You understand that whatever is discussed here is strictly confidential?" She nodded. "In that case . . ."

The story was that their client was caught in a bind not of his own making. Without going into detail, Rodgers said that the man was land-rich but cash-poor, and couldn't meet a $500,000 loan. Among his possessions was a yacht insured for more than enough to cover his debt. Simply put, the yacht had become expendable and was to be sacrificed for the better good.

Fran was shocked. "You want me to destroy a beautiful yacht?"

Rodgers responded condescendingly. "You should feel for the man and his family, not an inanimate object." He allowed her no time for rejection. "The yacht must be destroyed by fire. And there must be no sign of arson. I trust you can manage that."

Fran gathered together rambling, disturbing thoughts without looking at Rodgers; she could feel his eyes focused on her, probing for some weakness. She licked her upper lip tentatively.

"I must have particulars, type and size of vessel, its location. And there is special equipment to be considered."

"Everything you need will be provided"—he paused for a beat—"in due time." He caught her questioning look.

Anticipating, he reassured her, "There will be no one aboard."

He pulled out a small square object from his pocket and placed it on the table.

"This is a beeper," he explained. "Wear it at all times. When it signals, you call this number." He wrote the number on the money envelope. "All instructions—time, place, and so on—will be given to you."

"How long must I wait?"

Rodgers closed his leather case. "You should hear from us in two, possibly three, days. Your instructions will allow you twenty-four hours to complete the project."

They shook hands and he left. Fran sat down again, her thoughts shifting from Rodgers to her father before settling on Jason Stoner. Acceptance of the assignment battled with guilt feelings. She shook her head. The money in the Swiss account was all the justification she needed.

Jason Stoner was something else. Although he was employed by the same firm, Fran fully realized he wouldn't understand what she was contemplating.

Contemplating?

She got to her feet. She had already accepted the assignment. There was no reneging and, paradoxically, there was no denying the anticipation working in her. The client was in dire straits. Considering his circumstances, was the loss of a yacht so terrible? It had become an unaffordable luxury.

She dredged an importuning thought from the back of her mind. Why couldn't the client have just sold it? And why hadn't she thought of putting the question to Rodgers? Too late now, she supposed, watching the sun sift through the curtains. A slight breeze caused the light to waver on the beige carpet. It was too beautiful a day to stay indoors and wallow in self-doubt.

She unlocked the Thunderbird in bright sunshine. But the uncertainties crept back, refusing to be stifled by the thought of the money awaiting her. Pulling out of the parking lot and heading for the Federal Highway, she wished she had reserved her final decision.

23

Chelsea entered the cost of his business lunch with the new client—$94.50. He closed the account book and returned it to the leather portfolio lying on the bucket seat beside him. The expense was minor, considering what he'd accomplished.

It was a local department store, one of many in a national chain. Chelsea had undercut Wellington Security by two percent, but it was the added guarantees that won the contract. His men were all former police or servicemen—all bonded, and screened for drug use.

Chelsea grinned, enjoying himself. Although it was only one store in the chain, Wellington wouldn't be happy to learn they had lost it to Novick Security. He started the car, switched on the radio, and caught a station that played band music from the thirties and forties. In high spirits, he was reminded that it meant hiring ten additional personnel, including two women, within a space of six weeks. The firm was growing fast. His smile broadened with confidence, and he was forced to admit he was taking to selling as if he'd been doing it for years.

He left the Boca Town Center Shopping Mall and turned onto Glades Road. By the time he connected with I-95 he was humming along with the radio.

Nevertheless, merging into the fast lane, his good mood didn't preclude watching his rearview mirror. He switched off the radio; it had suddenly become an intrusion.

His brain insisted the Benefactor Alliance had shifted gears; no more tails, no more threats. As far as his small group was concerned, to all appearances the Alliance had gone underground. Chelsea knew better. This organization wouldn't sit still long. They had to be concocting a plan. It was in the nature of the beast to do so.

Taking the down ramp to Linton Boulevard, he headed for the office. His thoughts focused on the Resort, sensing it was the key to the entire cartel. If only they could discover its head . . . All Dave could wring from the computer was a list of unidentifiable names.

Heading west, a thought struck him.

Did Dr. Seltzer have any children!

He lifted the car phone to call Ellie at home. Among the books he'd brought to Florida was an encyclopedia of World War Two. He caught her just going out to meet with Cindy, and he asked her to search the volumes for a Dr. Emil Seltzer, a German scientist involved with biological experimentation. If the man had any children, she was to call him at the office.

Novick Security's quarters were undergoing a transformation. Ecru paint, still wet, now covered the drab gray exterior. It made the building stand out in an otherwise nondescript neighborhood. Down the street, one or two other firms were taking the hint. Josh had met with the owners and convinced them property values would rise if the area looked more presentable.

Chelsea walked into a new lobby. Doreen Flowers, the widow of a policeman, sat behind a reception desk. She was a woman in her early sixties, small in stature, with traces of copper-colored hair showing through the gray. Her mild blue eyes radiated warmth as Chelsea came in.

"Good afternoon, Mr. Chelsea." He affected a wince. She smiled tentatively. "*Joe* . . . I'll try to remember. Mr.—er, Josh is waiting for you in his office."

"That's much better, Doreen. Thank you."

Josh sat behind a new desk. Dark as ebony, it gleamed with a mirrorlike finish. Chelsea had the twin in his own office.

Josh looked up from the computer sheets laid out before him. He could make nothing of Chelsea's expression.

"Well, you going to keep me on hold" Breaking into a grin, Chelsea made a circle of his thumb and forefinger.

"Okay, details. What did it cost us?"

"Forgetting the expensive lunch?"

"Joe . . ."

"I had to undercut Wellington by two percent. We have a one-year contract. If they're happy with us, they'll extend it another three.

"Starting date?"

"December."

Josh leaned back and smiled. "You better get crackin' with personnel. The hiring is your domain." He gave his friend a searching look. "You've found your element, Joe. You have to admit this beats fighting department politics."

Chelsea's face sobered. "Not quite. I'm expecting a call from Ellie." He got out of his jacket and loosened his tie.

Josh blew out a deep breath of air. "Now, how did I know you were going to say that? About the call . . ."

Chelsea repeated his instructions to Ellie.

Josh made a face as if something distasteful were on his tongue. "Christ! Talk about a wild goose chase! If Seltzer had any children, what do you expect to make of it?"

"It's a shot in the dark." Chelsea shrugged. "It's better than waiting for the other shoe to drop. If it were up to me . . ." He fell silent.

"Go on. If it were up to you . . . What?" He was almost fearful of the answer.

"The key is on the Resort's island. The cartel is international, but that little island is their home base. I'm willing to bet my life on it."

Josh winced. "How about mine?" He quickly held up his hands, palms out. "Sorry. That was below the belt."

"Okay. Noted. You hear anything from Rudy?"

"Rudy's afraid to move. His chief of detectives worries him. He also thinks he caught a shadow on himself."

"Thinks?"

"Well, he's pretty sure."

"You know the chief?"

"The name's Andrew Magellan. That's the extent of my knowledge. We've never met."

"Is there any way we can do a check on his chief?"

"Hah! Forget it!"

Chelsea moved to the door. "I'll ask Dave. He's the expert." He was through the doorway before Josh could stop him.

Chelsea hung up the phone on his desk. Dave was on a charter. Mae didn't expect him back until after five.

Chelsea sat drumming his fingers on the desktop, waiting for Ellie's call. His tongue played with an annoying particle of food caught in his upper bridge. Unable to dislodge it, he went into his private washroom and was in the middle off cleaning his teeth when the phone rang.

Chelsea detected a click on the line when he lifted the receiver. He said nothing until he heard Ellie's voice. Cutting her off, he told her to go down to the lobby and call him from there. He hung up and punched the intercom for Josh.

"We've got new problems, Josh. Please come into my office."

He opened a drawer in his desk and hit a button on the tape recorder there. Voice-operated, it would record all phone messages.

The wait lasted five minutes; Josh was already seated in the leather chair on the other side of the desk.

"Ellie? Okay. First, I want to know whether you had any visitors in the apartment today." He heard Cindy in the background, but could distinguish nothing she sad.

"Two fire inspectors. The building security said they were okay. They were inspecting all apartments."

"Fire inspectors? They show you IDs? You didn't by any chance get any names?"

"No. If Security wasn't worried, why should I?"

"Ellie, you and Cindy go back to the apartment. I'll be there in less than an hour. Look, it's okay," he added. "I just like to be careful. See you."

Josh leaned forward. "What bothers you about this?"

"Ellie called from the lobby. On her earlier call from the apartment there was an unmistakable click. It's a dead giveaway to a traditional voice-operated machine."

Josh shook his head. "I knew it was too damn quiet." He got to his feet. "You want me along?"

"No. There's too much work here. You stay. I'll borrow Alex for a couple of hours."

Chelsea and Alex entered the apartment. Ellie and Cindy were on the terrace, speaking in whispers.

Alex was wearing faded dungarees and a T-shirt that said

I Lost It In The Virgins. At twenty-eight, he'd already served four years in the Marines. His hair was cut short, military style. A compact man with a rugged face, his demeanor was a bit too serious for someone his age. He greeted the women with an expressionless half-salute. At Chelsea's nod, he went to work.

From a duffle bag he removed a dial meter and held it over the phone on the side table in the living room. The pointer swung as if jolted. Chelsea watched over his shoulder, without interrupting.

The only sound in the room was the swishing of the palm fronds outside the terrace, the eerie whisperings carried in on a windward breeze.

Alex unscrewed the phone and, using plastic tweezers, removed a small flat disk. He handed it to Chelsea, then walked about the room, watching the meter as he continued testing end tables, sofa and chairs, lamps and drapes. They were all clean.

Fifteen minutes later he looked toward the bedroom, and then to Chelsea, from whom he received a nod.

The phone on the night table produced another chip. Two others, of a different type, were discovered in the lamp shades on the night tables. Chelsea's lips were thin lines. More confidences were revealed in the bedroom than anywhere else.

The women had followed them into the bedroom. Ellie's face reddened with full comprehension. Cindy, utterly flabbergasted, started to speak, then thought better of it.

Chelsea took the chips to the kitchen and placed them in a glass of water. He then went to his desk to find a number in the telephone directory. Next he removed a portable phone from a desk drawer. Taking it apart, he found it clean; all phones were now clean.

He called the main number for the fire department,

introduced himself, and asked how often his apartment complex was inspected for fire hazards. A thick voice that sounded as if it belonged to a heavy smoker told him, "Once a year." The next inspection wasn't due until March of the following year. Chelsea thanked him.

For the benefit of his audience he held a finger to his lips; they were to maintain silence. A trace of a smile on Alex's face displayed admiration. The women seemed befuddled. Chelsea had kept one chip. To their astonishment he placed it in the phone. Without pushing any buttons, he spoke into the mouthpiece.

"This is Joe Chelsea. To whom it may concern: I believe it's time to stop the game-playing. I suggest we meet and discuss matters of great concern. I can be reached either here or in my office. Or, if you wish, on my car phone. I assume you have all numbers. Thank you for the devices."

Chelsea removed the chip and handed it to Alex, who had a metal box ready to receive it. "There's an answering machine on the other end," Chelsea said. "I want a voice-activated recorder here, and one for my car phone."

"I've got one for this phone," Alex told him, "but I'll have to dig up another for the car."

Chelsea turned to Ellie. "Can you describe either one of the so-called inspectors?"

"They wore uniforms, Joe, and Security passed them." She saw Chelsea cock his head. "Tall, both of them." She closed her eyes, trying to visualize them again. "They were very polite, and had dark hair cut short—"

Cindy interjected, "Also dark glasses. You couldn't see their eyes."

"You didn't stay with them while they moved around?"

"We didn't want to be in their way. We stayed on the terrace."

Chelsea caught Alex's smile. He took Ellie's hand.

"Okay, El, from now on no one gets into the apartment without Security accompanying them." He released her hand and kissed her on the cheek, something he felt the need to do. "All right, now let's get back to Seltzer. Did you find anything?"

She eyed him obliquely for a moment; he was worried.

"Two children, Jon and Marta." Her features eased into a humorous smile. "Sounds like an old routine. Remember, 'Oh John—Oh Marsha'?" Chelsea nodded, masking impatience. "Marta married some German executive about twenty years ago, and Jon—" She shrugged. "There was nothing on him other than he was older than his sister. It was almost as if the man was too unimportant to write about."

Too unimportant! Horseshit! The omission of information was suspect.

"All right, ladies, let it ride. You're on your own. We're going back to the office."

At the door, he paused. "Didn't the bio even say whether he was married?"

Ellie's eyes flickered with amusement. "No, Lieutenant Columbo. There was no additional information other than he was born after the war."

Chelsea perked up. "Where?"

"In America. So was his sister." She tilted her head and rubbed her forehead with a finger. *I am getting old*, she thought. *How could I have forgotten*?

"Ellie, we have to go. I'll call if I work late."

After inspecting the telephone lines in the basement, Chelsea and Alex stopped in the lobby to speak with the security officer on duty. Chelsea advised him to check with his home office about any so-called inspectors before allowing strangers into the building.

In the car Alex's curiosity got the better of him. Heretofore his job with Novick Security had consisted of office and grounds patrol, at times in a prowl car. But what was happening now smacked of intrigue.

"You know, Mr. Chel—er, Joe, these chips are what military spooks use." His voice was low, almost conspiratorial.

Chelsea nodded. "So?"

"So what gives? Can you let me in on it? I worked intelligence in the service."

Chelsea deliberated a moment. "I can't give you everything, but I can tell you that someone doesn't like us. And this someone could be very bad news."

"You don't know who this someone is."

Chelsea smiled pleasantly. A good man, Alex—and smart. "We're working on it."

Alex nodded, comprehending. "I'm available for undercover work," he said.

"I'll keep it in mind."

Both men were silent until they stopped for a light on the highway. Alex couldn't resist another question. "This Jon Seltzer . . . How will you find him?"

"You said you were in intelligence. How would you go about it?"

The younger man draped an arm outside his window, his mind working. After a long pause he said, "If he's an American—or even a foreigner employed here, he must have a social security number."

Chelsea gave him a pleased glance. "You just passed the test, Alex."

24

From a motel in Delray, Jason called Fran Fargo's apartment. After six fruitless rings he tried the desk. "Did Ms. Fargo leave a number where she can be reached?"

"May I ask who's calling, sir?"

"Jason Stoner." He gave his position with Wellington Security and his ID number. The apartment-hotel was owned by Wellington. The clerk said he wasn't instructed to give out Ms. Fargo's car-phone number. Jason insisted it was urgent that the clerk get in touch with her and have her call him at the motel.

Five minutes later Jason lifted the phone on the second ring. "Yes," he said tersely, waiting. Hearing her tremulous "Jason?" set off an alarm bell.

"Fran, where are you?"

"I'm at a pharmacy at the Royal Palm Plaza. Jason—" He cut her short.

"Relax and just tell me if you met with your contact."

The name Calvin Rodgers rang a bell; the head man out

of the Miami office, someone Jason had never met. He stopped her again.

"Fran, listen to me carefully. I want you to drive north on Federal Highway and make a right on to Route 800. Continue to Ocean Boulevard and make another right. About a hundred yards down, you'll find the entrance to Spanish River Park. Get out of your car and look for the tunnel entrance to the beach. Go through the tunnel and wait for me. It shouldn't take me more than twenty minutes to reach you. Do you understand?" He made her repeat his instructions.

Less than twenty minutes later Jason paid the eight-dollar entry fee to a middle-aged man in a wooden cubicle. He entered a two-lane road that meandered beneath a bower of shade trees. An occasional splash of sunlight penetrated only at the discretion of the ocean breeze tossing the top branches. The park was no more than half-filled; it was still too early in the season for the winter "snowbirds."

Parking, he noted a van pulling into a space alongside a standing barbecue grill. Hesitating, Jason watched a man emerge, then a woman with two small, over-excited children. The man swore at the kids, threatening to leave if they misbehaved. The children looked to their mother, but quieted down.

There were signs with arrows pointing the way to the tunnel that crossed under the road to the beach. Jason strode toward it without looking back. Once there, he turned around. No one was behind him.

He saw Fran on the beach, standing about twenty feet beyond the tunnel. She was holding her sandals in one hand, her purse in the other. Her lips twitched nervously on seeing him, but other than that he couldn't read her expression behind the dark glasses she wore. Walking toward her, he put on his most reassuring smile.

Close up, he knew she was fighting tears. So calm and self-reliant on their previous meeting, she now seemed a lost soul.

What had she discovered since then?

He took her hand. "You're among friends, Fran." He nodded toward a spot about thirty yards from a lifeguard station. It was a broad stretch of white sand but he doubted there were a hundred people present within a quarter-mile. It was extremely warm but a strong breeze kept most swimmers from attempting the heavy surf.

Jason removed his sport shirt and spread it on the sand for Fran to sit on and then, bare-chested, sat down beside her. She seemed a bit taken aback, but said nothing.

"Okay," he said gently. "Now, calmly, tell me what transpired this morning. Take your time and try not to omit anything."

Ten minutes later she asked the question that had nagged at her all morning. "Why the subterfuge? Why couldn't the client simply sell his yacht?"

Jason watched the breeze tugging at her hair. She pushed back an insistent strand falling across her cheek; her eyes searched his beseechingly.

"I had a friend on the Riviera," he said. "It took him two years to sell his boat." He let a fistful of sand run through his fingers. "True, it was a megayacht, but a half-mil cruiser would be just as difficult to sell in a hurry."

"Jason, what should I do?"

"Why did you agree to his proposition?"

"I'm substituting for my father. He always accepted the assignment."

"So, now you follow blindly." He fell silent for a few seconds. "You'll have to keep up the pretense of going through with it. Neither of us can do a thing until you hear from Rodgers. Then, perhaps . . ."

Calvin Rodgers preyed on his mind. Something didn't ring true. He wondered then how much of Rodgers' story was genuine. The doubts were building.

"Did Rodgers ever mention the client's name?" When she shook her head, he said, "Okay, Rodgers said no one would be harmed?" She nodded. "All right, then are you certain he said nothing else?"

Fran lost patience. "I may be upset, but I do have an excellent memory." She shook her head, suddenly contrite. "I'm sorry. I didn't mean to snap at you. It's just—"

"It's okay. Under the circumstances—"

"Jason, what should I do?"

When he reached toward her waist she stiffened, relaxing only when she realized all he wanted was to examine the beeper attached to her belt. "You won't get a call for at least another day. What do you intend doing with yourself in the meantime?"

With his head bent to the beeper, she suddenly became aware of his bare, muscled arms and chest. She looked away, temporarily embarrassed, then said, "I have no plans, but . . . I wish you'd stay with me."

Jason gave her a quick glance, then turned to two small children playing in the sand a few yards away. It was an innocent request, he decided. He shouldn't read anything into it.

"I can stay through lunch only. I have appointments that can't be postponed."

She paused for a moment before saying, "Jason, don't misinterpret my seeking your help."

"I understand. No explanation is necessary." He changed the subject. "Rodgers said nothing about the location of the vessel? Or gave you its make and size?"

"No mention of it. All I could gather was that it might possibly be in this area."

Jason got to his feet and extended a hand to help her up, then picked up his shirt and put it back on. "I'm familiar with this area. There's about five marinas within a mile of where we stand, which is no help at all. There are just too many private docks along the Waterway."

Back at the spot where Jason's car was parked, the family with the van was already eating hamburgers. The husband was still griping. "I had to take off a day to do what I could have done at home at any time." His wife was silent, her lips pressed tightly together.

Jason looked about, casually scanning all the cars in the immediate vicinity. Only one was occupied, and it had just arrived. Fran pointed out her car.

Struck by a sudden thought, he felt under the rear bumper of the Thunderbird. "What are you doing?" Fran asked, puzzled.

He worked a hand along the inside of the bumper, coming to a stop finally where it joined with the fender. His lips tightened and he again surveyed the area. A line of tall trees hid one parking area from another. "A direction-finder," he said. "They're keeping tabs on you."

Fran's lips twisted in distress. They were tracking her like an animal. "What should I do?" she asked almost inaudibly.

Jason thought of removing the tracking device, but decided not to. Why let them know?

"Take the T-bird back to your place. Park it and walk out to the street. Go down a block, and I'll pick you up in my car."

He sat in his own car, watched her pull out, then waited for three minutes before starting the engine. No one had followed Fran.

Twenty minutes later he spotted her on Federal Highway, walking with quick strides.

A middle-aged couple was strolling hand in hand nearby,

oblivious to the heat of the noonday sun. No one else was in sight. He waved his hand and caught Fran's eye.

His rented Ford Taurus was parked in front of a furniture store. As soon as she settled into the car he took off, driving to the rear of the building, to an alley that led to Spanish River Boulevard. From there he headed west to I-95, then swept up the south ramp.

A couple of cars had followed him up the ramp. He slowed, guardedly, allowing them to pass. Reassured, he said, "We'll stop at a mall." He spoke lightly, attempting to ease her anxiety. "Ever eat in an American consortium of foreign fast-food restaurants?" Apparently he succeeded; a puzzled frown replaced her dour expression. "An American custom for shoppers to eat on the run," he added in explanation.

"Whatever it is, I hope I can enjoy it."

So tense, he thought. Why would they even consider her for this job?

He let a few seconds pass, then said, "After lunch I'll take you back to your place. I'll give you a number to call if you should need me. If I'm not in, leave a message on my answering machine. I always carry one when I travel."

Fran nodded, avoiding his brief glance. "Want a cigarette?" he asked, seeing her swallow apprehensively.

He held out a gold cigarette case but she shook her head. Her eyes misting, she turned her gaze to the flat landscape flickering by.

"Where's your confidence?" he said, and then, trying to make her smile, "No one is permitted to frown in the land of sunshine."

Still looking outside the window, she said, "Jason, would you stay with me overnight? I don't think I can manage alone."

Jason felt a tightness in his chest. It was the second time

she had asked. She was like Gretel in the woods, lost, in need of someone she could trust. Was he expected to play Hansel—the boy who looked after his sister? It posed a problem, not fully understanding her request.

"I don't think it would be a good idea, Fran." He told her it was possible that her place was bugged. "It's more prudent we keep our friendship low key." In this instance he was grateful for the bugs. It meant no nonsense, no matter her needs. Or his.

25

Dave Ward glanced at his watch; after ten. He had been at Novick's computer for three hours. He rubbed tired eyes, then looked at Chelsea relaxing in a leather armchair, his teeth clamped on an unlit briar. "Gentlemen, I have to leave. I have an early morning charter. I remind you I still have to make a living." When Chelsea remained silent he added, "Where can you go with this?"

Chelsea tapped the stem of his pipe on his teeth. It had taken Ward a while to discover that Jon Seltzer had indeed legally changed his name to Seltzmann. Seltzmann was married, to a woman who was wealthy in her own right, and they had two teenage children. Jon, among various other pursuits, was the CEO of a Texas oil company. There was, however, no information on any involvement with the Founding Fathers. He owned three homes, located in Dallas, Nassau, and Monaco. The one in Nassau held Chelsea's interest.

Josh, observing his friend dolefully, pushed himself out of his chair. "Let's call it a night, Joe. Let's sleep on what we've learned."

Absorbed in thought, Chelsea nodded as if only half-listening. Instinct warned him of imminent danger. His tiny group had become a troublesome burr, gnawing at the Alliance like an insidious cancer. They would have to remove it.

And they were good at that.

Yawning, he compiled his thoughts. The problem for Chelsea lay in the invisibility of the enemy. It was their substance, their strength, yet could also become their weakness—once that shield was broken.

He felt Josh prodding his shoulder and held up both hands in mock defense. "Okay, so call it a night. What about tomorrow evening? We still going out on the yacht?"

"I thought it was decided. Although the women aren't too happy with our late hours."

Chelsea rubbed cobwebs from his eyes. "All right. What's the schedule?"

"We cruise down to Fort Lauderdale. There's a boatel with a fine restaurant. I made reservations for nine P.M." He turned to Ward. "Dave, please, no shorts." Ward grinned and waved good night.

It was after midnight when Calvin Rodgers returned to his high-rise oceanside condo in Hallandale. He knew that Jason Stoner and Fargo were together. Where they went, what they did, what they confided to each other, he had no idea.

Stoner had obviously warned Fargo of the bugs in her apartment. She made no phone calls, and other than the sounds of her moving about, the radio was the only sound generated. Rodgers had left the listening-post only a half-hour ago.

As soon as he entered his living room, he saw the red

light glowing on his answering machine. He moved quickly to lift the receiver. It was his man in Palm Beach.

"I picked this up at the fisherman's boat." He proceeded to tell Rodgers about the planned cruise to Fort Lauderdale.

Five minutes later Rodgers stood on his terrace, smoking a cigarette behind a glass windscreen. Eight floors down he could see the swimming pool, despite the darkness, all blue and light.

Squashing the butt in a shell ashtray, he returned to the living room. His brain was busy, adapting the latest information; the operation had to be moved up, but that, in itself, wasn't the problem.

The problem was Fran Fargo. He recognized the signs of reneging, something he couldn't permit; it was too late in the game. He had been advised, in no uncertain terms, that the assignment was urgent, to be executed at the first opportunity. It meant she had to be threatened. Her father was in no position to be hurt, but her relatives running the salvage company were expendable.

The snag was Jason Stoner; he wasn't supposed to be involved.

Why was he?

So far the man was impervious to intimidation. The thought reminded Rodgers of his own tenuous position. Elias Stoner never accepted failure from his employees. It would be imprudent to believe otherwise. He had to keep Jason Stoner from fouling up the works.

He lit another cigarette, playing with ideas, trying to solve the dilemma of Jason Stoner's presence. A diversion was needed to keep him and Fran apart. He thought of calling Elias Stoner but pride forbade it. *Use your own discretion* had been more a forewarning than instruction.

He sat thinking for long minutes, his eyes traveling the ceiling as if seeking answers there. Then, slowly, his troubled expression cleared. He glanced at his wristwatch; almost one A.M. He arose from his chair and went to the phone.

It was past midnight when Jason escorted Fran to her door. It had been an instructive evening for both—each, unaccountably, having revealed personal family backgrounds.

With the door to her apartment open, they could hear the rain that had threatened all evening now pounding in sheets against the windows.

"You better come in and wait it out," Fran said. "I'll make some coffee."

"I'm not sure that's wise. Remember, the place is bugged."

Holding her hand, he gently pulled her toward him and kissed her on the lips. Fran let the kiss linger, then leaned back against the wall. "Jason, it's not the reason I'm asking you in."

"I know, but it's something I had to do—and not while someone was listening."

An hour later, the storm gave no sign of letting up. Rolling thunder shook the windowpanes.

It was finally decided that Jason would stay the night, sleeping on the loveseat, which opened into a single bed. There was no real debate; both were too tired to argue.

More than an hour later, Jason still stirred restlessly. On the verge of dropping off, he wasn't certain what was preventing him. A sound, perhaps? He leaned on an elbow to peer over the top of the sofa. All he could make out was a vague shadow. Fran? The room wasn't completely dark; a night light from the kitchen cast a pale glow along the carpeting.

He heard the sound again, a footfall behind him. There was no mistaking it. Holding his breath, he tried to ease off the small sofa-bed.

Too late!

An arm was around his neck, pulling his head back. Another pair of arms grabbed his. A cloth was held to his face, stifling him—and he recognized the odor.

Chloroform!

He struggled in vain; muscular arms held him tightly until he suddenly found the sleep he had been seeking.

At the far end of the room, a third man clapped a hand across Fran's mouth. "Be quiet and listen." His voice was a husky, commanding whisper. "Obey instructions and your friend will not be harmed. Do you understand?"

Her heart pounding, she could only nod. Peering through the darkness she could just make out two formless shadows standing over Jason. An attempted scream was forced into a moan. The figure at her side was dark and his hand smelled of stale tobacco.

"Lady, I will warn you once more. If you make a sound your friend is finished." He paused. "Now, get out of bed and get dressed. You have an appointment." He took his hand from her mouth, but kept it at the ready. "Mind you, no talking and no light except for the bathroom, where you'll dress."

Fran took a jumpsuit with her to the bathroom, closed the door, and turned on the light. She blinked at the sudden glare and caught sight of herself in the mirror. Her face was a white mask, matching the tile.

She leaned on the sink, sick at the thought of Jason lying there helpless. She dry-scrubbed her face, but the vigorous action failed to dissipate the overwhelming dread she felt. The bathroom was warm but she shivered.

She stalled for a moment, and there was a tap on the door. "Another minute," she said tremulously. To clear her brain, she doused her face with cold water. No options were left. To ensure Jason's safety she had to comply with whatever they asked of her. Facing the mirror, she thought she saw her father's image. Was it anger in his face—or hers? Her carelessness had made her a hostage. What would be the cost?

Certainly not money.

Jason stirred; his head felt like an enormous melon. The odor of chloroform still lingered in his nostrils; he fought a wave of nausea. Then, suddenly, with full comprehension, he struggled to his feet and staggered across the room.

The bed was empty.

He moved to the window and drew the curtains aside. In the early morning sun waving palms cast long shadows across the driveway below. He pressed his fingers to his forehead, trying to think clearly.

All he could recall were the strong arms pinning him, and the cloth over his face. Now the men were gone, and Fran with them. He moved about aimlessly, not knowing what to do next. There was a terrible pressure in his chest. He had never felt so powerless.

Take hold, he said to himself. *Think.* How long had he been out? It had been dark when he was attacked, but he recalled hearing birds chirping, and he remembered reading somewhere that they always chirped an hour before dawn. The clock on the night table read 7:10. He had been out for at least two hours. He peered out the window again. The sun slanted across the lawn; the blades of Bermuda grass, beaded with water, looked like a carpet of sequins.

Fists clenched, he spun around. *Think, man*! In seconds he was reminded of Calvin Rodgers, and the operation outlined for Fran Fargo. It struck him then that the timetable had been moved up—and that he had merely been in the way.

Why now?

He went to the sofa and put on his shirt and shoes, at the same time isolating his thoughts from a police siren screeching down the highway a block away.

Where would they be taking her? He shook his head, knowing he hadn't the slightest idea. He stood up and reached for his jacket.

In the lobby a security man was on duty, but Jason didn't dare question him; he could be on Rodgers' payroll. He strode through the lobby and went outside. He was alone, in more ways than one.

Although the highway was hidden from view, he could hear the morning traffic build. He wondered again, *Where have they taken her*?

He went to his car and in frustration banged the car hood with his fist. The effort, besides giving him a jolt of pain, sent rivulets of rainwater down the windshield.

Water! A marina!

He got into his car, then paused before starting the engine. He was assuming a marina; it didn't have to be. Still, as he mulled it over, it was his only lead.

He switched on the engine. As he pulled out of the driveway, his eye was caught by a phone booth across the road, in front of a pharmacy. He gazed at it blindly until an inner void prompted: *Call every harbormaster within five miles. Find out who has yachts matching Rodgers' vague description.*

He fought the traffic to get across A1A to the phone booth. He checked his watch while going through the Yellow Pages. Almost eight.

How many hours did he have?

Chelsea climbed out of the pool; the cool water had done little to relax him. His stomach was in knots and his brain nagged at him relentlessly. "Ease off," he growled to himself. Tension was no stranger to him. How many times had he come up against gut-wrenching situations? The countless police raids ate up a piece of him each time, churning his stomach acids, warning it could be the final time if he didn't play it carefully. Before that, it was the landing at Omaha Beach. He was seasick before hitting the beach while, at the same time, ducking shells and machine-gun fire; he remembered thinking: *Dying is taking the easy way out.*

He toweled himself off, fully recognizing the cause of his apprehension. Heretofore he had always known the identity of the enemy. Now, there was only speculation. He winced, realizing that waiting for the other shoe to drop could be asking for an ulcer.

He ran a comb through his wet hair, then lifted his wristwatch from the deck chair: 8:30 A.M. Josh would be getting ready to leave for the office. Chelsea slipped into his terry-cloth jacket and sandals and headed back to his apartment.

Josh was almost out the door when Cindy called him back. "Someone wants to speak with you, personally." He glanced at his watch and shook his head; business belonged in the office. Despite this, he took the call.

The man introduced himself as Jason Stoner. Josh's eyebrows rose. Stoner was a recognizable name. "How can I help you?" he asked calmly.

"I'm looking for a motor yacht in a price range of five hundred thousand to a million. I believe you have such a craft."

Josh permitted himself a silent whistle. *What was Jason Stoner up to?* He wondered whether Joe had heard anything.

"You believe correctly," Josh replied. "But it's not for sale. Who gave you the idea that it might be?"

"That's unimportant, Mr. Novick. More important, I must ask whether you've ever had any dealings with Wellington Security." Jason had asked the same question of three of the five yacht owners whose names he had collected. He'd obtained the names when inquiring about large boats—not necessarily for sale, but using the marina to gas up.

Dumbstruck at first, Josh asked, "Why do you wish to know?"

"I need to find out whether you had any trouble with them. Can you tell me that much?" Jason was aware of Novick's hesitation and sensed he had found his target. "The information is urgent, Mr. Novick, for both our sakes."

Josh rubbed his forehead, trying to size up the situation. Stoner sounded as if he was under stress. "Where are you calling from?"

"I'd rather not say, but I can be at your home in less than twenty minutes. I can tell from your hesitancy that you're the party I've been seeking. I repeat, it's extremely urgent that we meet to discuss this further."

"Hold on a second—I have a question for you. Are you related to Elias Stoner?" Josh heard a gasp, and then "Oh, Christ!" "Well?"

"Yes, but that's neither here nor there." Jason's mind worked furiously. Novick's boat was to be Fran's target. It had to be. The connection was apparent but the whys and wherefores weren't.

He spoke hurriedly. "Look, Mr. Novick, I'm in trouble, you're in trouble—and most of all, a friend of mine is in trouble. It's too involved to discuss over the phone. Can I—"

"You said twenty minutes. I'll be waiting." Josh rang off, and immediately punched in the number of Chelsea's car phone.

"Joe, come to the house. A Jason Stoner just called me." He quickly recounted the conversation.

Chelsea felt dread overtaking him. "Did he sound genuine? Could you sense an ulterior motive? We can't forget he works for an alleged enemy."

"Joe, I can't tell you anything more. He sounded strained, but in control. I don't want to indulge in wild speculation. Just get here as fast as you can."

Chelsea drove off I-95 and turned into the first shopping plaza. He checked to see whether he had been followed. The plaza was almost empty at this hour; it was too early for shoppers. Satisfied, he left after waiting a minute.

He was only a block away when he saw a white Taurus turning into the Novick driveway.

26

Fran, blindfolded since entering the car, realized that with all the turns and railroad crossings taken by the Mercedes, they might plausibly be no more than a block from the original starting point. There were two men in the car, the driver and a man sitting in the back with her. The third fellow had stayed behind, apparently to cover their tracks.

The car finally stopped; emerging from the vehicle, she felt a gravelly surface beneath her feet. Though she'd been frightened at first, it now dawned on her—it had been a slow process—that these men intended her no harm. She was needed for the operation.

They guided her inside a building, then removed her blindfold. The two men were dressed like twins, dark slacks, lightweight gray sweaters. Their faces were unfamiliar, but had matching expressions—grim, hard. They were in a huge warehouse; crates of all sizes and shapes were piled twenty feet high. The men motioned her toward a corridor formed by the crates, to a glass-walled office at the far end.

Calvin Rodgers sat at a scratched desk, his elbows

propped on top, chin resting in his palms. He observed her for a moment before speaking.

"This method could have been avoided, signorina, if you had kept your nose clean." She remained silent. "Jason Stoner doesn't belong in this operation." Her silence continued. "Do you understand the position you put me in?"

Anger slowly festered in her. "I fully realize the position you put *me* in."

Rodgers' lips curved in a smile. He was satisfied she would obey orders. He waved toward a wooden armchair. "Please be seated. We have to go over details."

Fran folded her arms and remained standing. "Suit yourself," he said calmly. "The craft is a fifty-four-foot Hatteras, twin diesel engines. How would you go about firing it—that is, without arousing any suspicion of arson?"

"You're certain there won't be anyone aboard?" she said quietly, not trusting him.

Rodgers pulled out a cigarette case from his jacket, and offered it to her. She shook her head. He took a cigarette for himself, lighting it with a gold butane lighter.

"There will be no one aboard," he responded, in total control.

"A hot engine might cause a premature explosion, while a cold engine would require the placement of a delayed miniature detonator. I recommend the latter." She stared at him coldly. "If anyone is aboard, I will abort the operation."

"Agreed," he said finally. He pushed his chair back and stood up. "If you will please follow me, we'll go over the equipment." Fran didn't move. He looked at her. "Is there a problem?"

She bit her lip. Rodgers had the look of a fox who owned his own henhouse. "I need details before examining any gear. Location, water depth. Will the yacht be tied up at a public dock? Choice of day or night could be a factor."

"We're working on it. You should have all information within the hour." He gestured impatiently. "Now, if you please, the equipment."

Josh and Stoner were introducing themselves in the foyer when Chelsea strode in. "My partner, Joe Chelsea," Josh said, and then added, "Let's go out to the dock. We can talk in privacy aboard the vessel you assumed was for sale."

Chelsea followed, meanwhile appraising Stoner. Clean-cut, but that meant nothing. Nobody spoke until they'd clambered up the port beam ladder. "Either of you had breakfast yet?" Josh asked. Chelsea nodded, knocking ashes from his pipe before entering the salon.

Jason was reminded that he hadn't eaten since the previous evening. "Just coffee, if it's no trouble," he said.

"No problem," Josh assured him. The galley was behind the forward wall of the salon. "Meanwhile talk to Joe. I can listen from the galley."

Chelsea waited for Stoner to seat himself on the sofa.

"Okay, let's start where you left off in your phone call. We can guess your relationship with Wellington Security. Why do you believe we're all in trouble?"

Jason ran a hand through his hair. Something told him: *Go slow. Be sure of yourself. Don't anger this man.* "I'm not sure I know where to start."

"Why not try at the beginning?"

"Mr. Chelsea, to tell the truth I don't understand what's been happening—or why." He felt Chelsea's eyes boring into his. *Oh, man!* He shifted forward nervously in his seat.

He spoke hastily, omitting nothing. Except for the narrowing of Chelsea's eyes, there was no change in his expression. Big, muscular, perhaps an extra pound or two, but certainly no visible deterioration; the man was middle-aged, but his eyes displayed a deceptive strength. Taking it for concealed anger, Jason didn't wait for an explosion.

"Mr. Chelsea, there wasn't anything I could do to help Fran Fargo. I was out cold for two hours."

"What's your true connection with Wellington? I'm referring to your official position with the firm. Why would you be in trouble working for your uncle?"

"For breaking into private files." Jason waited a beat, then hurried on. "I work for Wellington and haven't the slightest idea why Emilio Franco was hired."

Chelsea frowned, obviously weighing Jason's words. The younger man hoped nervously that he passed muster.

"Stoner, it's confession time. What's your role here?" Chelsea recognized a fellow-sufferer. He waited.

"Well . . ." Chelsea prompted.

Jason expelled a deep breath. "First off, you must understand—despite my position with Wellington—I haven't the slightest idea why the firm should be concerned with you."

Josh took that moment to reenter with a carafe of boiling water, packets of Sanka, and powdered milk. "It's the best I can do," he apologized, then remarked, "Regarding your firm, we can make more than an educated guess of the problem we caused *them*."

Jason felt he was finally on track. The odds had been against a long shot.

"About Fran Fargo . . ." Chelsea prompted.

Jason nodded, as if reassuring himself. For the next twenty minutes he held their attention. There were no interruptions except for the occasional exchange of glances between Chelsea and Novick.

Chelsea sipped black coffee, his eyes never leaving their unexpected guest. Josh sat in an easy chair, tapping his fingers on the arms.

When Jason had finished his story, Chelsea asked, "Why weren't you taken hostage?"

A frown. "I don't know. It puzzled me also. I assumed it was orders from a higher-up."

Chelsea's fingers played with an empty pipe. "They wanted to shadow you, to see what you would do."

"No way. I kept an eye out for a tail all the way here. I would have known."

"Your uncle is Elias Stoner." It was more statement than query. "Why would he want to . . . to harm any of us?" Chelsea watched the probe elicit a look of disbelief.

"My uncle—involved?" Jason registered total astonishment. "I can't believe it. It must be Calvin Rodgers—working a rogue position within the firm." He leaned forward. "Or do you know something you're not sharing?"

When neither man responded, Jason stood up. "I don't understand you guys. So calm, so collected—no reaction. What gives? I'm exposing a plot to blow up your boat. Doesn't it bother you?" He flopped back onto the sofa, fighting despair. He had told them everything he'd done with the computers. They knew something, but it was like butting one's head against a stone wall to get anything from them.

Chelsea asked, "You and Fargo just met. What does she mean to you?"

Jason rubbed his forehead; a headache was forming behind his eyes. "We're just friends in need." He had avoided Chelsea's eyes, but now looked up at him. "What are we going to do about it?"

Chelsea took a deep breath, then exhaled slowly. "At this moment, our sole lead could be Fran Fargo. You hinted she was doing this against her will."

"No doubt. She's in over her head."

"The woman, Fran Fargo, will no doubt be killed after

completing her mission—whether successful in the commission of it or not." Jason started up from the sofa at these words.

"Drink your coffee. I have to think on it," Chelsea pulled out his tobacco pouch and filled his pipe. Turning his back on both men, he walked out onto the rear deck.

Jason began to sweat. He turned to Josh. "I don't understand either of you. What's going on? What did you do to start this mess?"

Josh set his cup down. "You're in a need-to-know situation. All I can say is, your uncle is just one member of an illegal cartel. And it was by pure chance we made the discovery." He noted the knotted eyebrows. "What would you expect us to do about it?"

It took a few seconds for Jason to digest "one member of an illegal cartel."

"Who are you two?" he asked Josh. "Military?" It brought a gentle smile.

"Novick Security. Nothing else. Joe and I are former cops. Joe's been retired for some months from the NYPD."

Jason was somewhat appeased by this statement, but it didn't reduce his anxiety. "So, what's to be done about the present situation? We can't simply sit around twiddling our thumbs."

"Joe's working on it. Be patient."

A 40-foot ketch, its mainsail unfurled, cast a moving shadow that drifted across the starboard beam of the *Ark*. Jason flinched, startled as the salon darkened briefly. He prayed that it wasn't an omen. Intermittent shadows increased as the Waterway traffic built up. Catching Novick observing him, Jason felt as if he were in a fishbowl.

"You're not going to tell me what this is all about, are you?"

"It will be Joe Chelsea's decision."

"Why him?"

Josh took a cigarette from a pack on the coffee table. "We're not the only ones involved. Chelsea is the one most qualified to head our so-called investigation." He held a lighter to the cigarette. "You've just entered the fray; we've been at it for a while." He noted Stoner's jaw working. "Waiting can be difficult, but there's no other way. To go off half-cocked, unprepared, without knowing the options . . ." He shrugged.

Jason got to his feet and looked toward the open door to the afterdeck. Chelsea was leaning on the railing, his pipe sending wisps of smoke into the air. It was almost as if he was not concerned. *Others involved*, Jason thought. Who were they?

Chelsea watched a 60-foot sloop slide out from a slip thirty yards off his stern. There were six people on deck, two unfurling sails. An innocent, happy time for some.

His mind searching, he knew Fran Fargo would, unknowing, have to lead them. According to Stoner, she wasn't to have been called for a couple of days. What was the reason for abducting her? Did it mean the schedule was being pushed forward?

Knitting his brows, he thought, *If the bastards knew we were using the yacht tonight* . . . His eyes clouded. Josh only mentioned the cruise to Fort Lauderdale the previous evening, and yet they knew of it almost instantly. *Where did I screw up!*

He pulled on the pipe. Stoner said "arson." How could it be accomplished? And where? He pulled on the briar again, this time sucking air. Emptying the pipe was a distraction. He returned to his configurations. Fort Lauderdale was out; the yacht would remain here, on home base, with all aboard. The bait would be irresistible. The Brenners would be needed. And now Ward had two more names to play with on his IBM: Elias Stoner and Calvin Rodgers. As for Jason Stoner . . .

"Call Fran Fargo," Chelsea ordered Jason. "See if she has really checked out."

It didn't take long to discover Fran Fargo had checked out of the suite.

After the useless call Chelsea asked Jason to sit. "I need to know more from you," he said. "For instance, you hold an important position at Wellington. I can't help wondering where your loyalty lies. You haven't told us anything of your uncle. Do you really believe him to be a dupe in his own firm?"

Jason held a palm to his forehead, as if reminded of a terrible dream. He had told them of his computer search. "At first, I refused to believe it, but since . . ." he spoke hurriedly, recounting in greater detail his queries about Emilio Franco and the erased records. "As for loyalty to either my uncle or the firm, you can forget it. As of yesterday, I've been on their shit list."

Chelsea's ability to judge character had never failed him. He sensed truth in Jason Stoner. "All right, putting it all aside, I'd like to know your background."

"Whatever for?"

"Until today I never heard of you."

Jason's face reddened. "That makes us even. I never heard of you either." He held up his hands defensively. "Oh shit! You might as well hear it from me rather than from someone else. You won't like it." He told Chelsea about the early, misspent years, but stressed his later service with the Marines and the change it had wrought in him. "There, you have it. How does it alter anything?"

Chelsea smiled gently, approvingly. "It adds confidence, if nothing else."

Jason tilted his chin. "So, does that confidence admit me to your private circle?"

Chelsea deflected the question with one of his own. "Stoner, have you ever heard of the Benefactor Alliance?"

Jason frowned. "Is the name synonymous with the illegal cartel you mentioned?"

"Explanations will follow later. Right now, just listen. We have work to do—and time is a factor."

27

The windowless eight-by-eight room was nothing more than a cell. Arms folded across her chest, Fran paced back and forth like a hungry animal. There was a chair, a folding cot, and a table with a small radio on it. Playing softly, it announced the time was eight-thirty, just as Calvin Rodgers entered. Unsmiling, he said, “It is time. Please follow me.”

Her pulse racing, she took a deep breath. They went through a long corridor of unmarked crates. At one side of the building a forklift was removing a stack of heavy wooden cases; it exposed a metal door. Except for the machine, the warehouse was eerily silent.

Unlocking the metal door, Rodgers waved her through.

Rubber suits, air tanks, compressors, and other diving paraphernalia lined the walls.

“Everything you asked for is in the van,” Rodgers told her. “You need only get into a suit.” He smiled his humorless, obnoxious smile. “You have ten minutes.” He left her alone.

Rodgers was a punctual individual; he returned in exactly

ten minutes to see that she was zipped into the close-fitting black rubber suit. "There're flippers in the van," he said, then used a black scarf to blindfold her.

Fran heard metal doors sliding open. Rodgers took her elbow and steered her across a concrete floor; their footsteps echoed hollowly. He guided her up a few steps into the back of the van.

"Must I wear this blindfold?" she asked. "I'm feeling sick." A Thermos was thrust into her hands. "Take a drink. It's only black coffee," he said when she hesitated.

Fran took a sip, and strained her ears for recognizable sounds. The van rode straight down whatever road it was taking, then made a right onto a gravelly surface. The van was a four-wheel drive, and the slippage was unmistakable as it threshed the gritty surface. There was a pervasive odor of seawater, a tang familiar to her from childhood. The van eventually came to a stop.

Her blindfold was removed, and Rodgers said, "Now, Ms. Fargo, I caution you to follow all prescribed instructions. You've already been told of the consequences—" He gripped her elbow. "You do your job, and we can all go home happy."

In seconds she knew where she was. The east side of the Waterway. Jason and she had gone there. Across the water, to her right, she recognized the Royal Palm Yacht Club. Farther along was the hotel with its pink towers.

Rodgers pointed out a group of islands to her left, across a narrow expanse of dark water; she judged them to be no more than a half-kilometer distant. He handed her a pair of high-powered binoculars. "The canals flowing around the islands . . . Follow the flow until you find *Novick's Ark*. That's your target," he said simply. The driver of the van clipped a waterproof bag to her belt.

A tremor shot through her. There were people aboard; she

could see at least four on the afterdeck. She spun on him angrily, "You gave me your word no one would be harmed!"

"Ms. Fargo, you have the remote. You can set it off at any time you think proper. They won't be partying all night."

The remote! It was ludicrous to believe he would allow any delay. She understood now. He had no interest in the yacht. It was the people he wanted to destroy.

The driver had returned with an air tank. "Lift your arms, please," he said politely but firmly.

Rodgers tilted her chin when she resisted. "Haven't I made myself clear, Ms. Fargo?" His tone was ominous. "Now, pay attention. You're to drop those pellets in the filler cap, as you yourself suggested. The remote will be in your hands, to control as you wish." His free hand felt for the twin remote in his jacket pocket. "If I have to send someone else to complete your job . . ."

The threat to replace her was merely a bluff. She knew very well that no one else was available on such short notice.

She forced a shrug. *Fool!* she thought. *Keep your head! Stop antagonizing him!* "All right," she said aloud. "I'm ready."

Rodgers scanned the area they had chosen. They were in a copse of overgrown Australian pines that hid them from the mansions fronting the Waterway. Overhead, the sky was clear, with little cloud cover. He turned to watch Fargo tie the harness. "The pellets . . ." he said gruffly. "How long will it take the coating to dissolve?" The coating covered miniature detonators.

"Thirty minutes, forty at most. Until it does, the remote will have no effect. I need the infrared glasses also."

"They're in your kit."

She stood on the concrete edge of the sea wall and peered down at the dark water. "What is the depth here?"

Rodgers muttered a curse under his breath. "Quit stalling. You're in a rubber suit. Get into your flippers."

Fran had reached the point of no return. She pulled on the flippers, stood with her back to the water, and flopped over.

Once she disappeared, Rodgers ordered the deflated Zodiac in the van to be filled with air. "Follow discreetly," he told his men. "If she gives any sign of a double-cross, you have your orders. Keep at a distance. Should anyone be curious, you're crossing to the yacht club."

It took Rodgers' man twenty minutes to row a hundred yards out, principally because of the strong pull of the tide.

Fighting the current, his craft was suddenly jolted, as if it had hit a reef, and there was no mistaking the hissing sound of escaping air above a five-knot breeze. He muttered a curse and leaned over, seeking its source.

Seconds later, he heard more hissing, at the prow. "Damn!" His usual cool was fast deserting him as his imagination took over. *Sharks?* He had heard they sometimes entered the Waterway. The look on his face was one of stark terror. The rubber craft was deflating fast. The woman be damned! He'd rather face Rodgers. His arms worked like pistons, racing against time.

A head bobbed up on the water. A greased face wearing a nightscope watched the fleeing oarsman. Unconcerned, Noah Brenner turned to look back at the yacht. Neither Aaron nor the woman was in sight. Aaron had to have taken her aboard. Without conjecturing further, Noah dove beneath the surface. Navigating at a lower depth was easier than fighting the current above.

Fran took a sip of the brandy offered by one of the women. It did little to still her trembling. Events had moved rapidly since she entered the water.

She had been no more than ten yards from the yacht's

starboard beam when she halted, beset by indecision. Her infrared glasses had caught a dark shape swooping toward her.

A large fish? A shark! Madre mia! No!

Spinning around, she made a desperate effort to reach open space between two yachts. At the sea wall, she turned and discovered the suspected shark to be a man. A man in a suit matching her own; he had a spear gun aimed at her. Frozen in position, she saw him point his weapon to a wooden ladder spiked to the wall. There was no escaping him; the man was wearing a nightscope and was watching her every movement.

Who was he? Why was he here?

Backed against the wall, she suddenly felt her shoulder caught in a viselike grip. Terror-stricken, she twisted around to discover another diver. He pointed to her flippers. He wanted her to take them off.

As the second diver ascended the moss-covered rungs she noted the sheathed dagger strapped to his thigh.

My God! Who were these men? Coast Guard frogmen?

Topside, the diver helped her to the dock. Unmasked, he displayed a hard, unsmiling face. He nodded to her kit. "Let me have it," he said flatly. She unclipped it without argument. The dock area was quiet, private.

By this time the spear gun carrier had reappeared. His face, unlike his partner's, bore a slight smile–which ironically was unnerving. It was as if she had been expected.

The harsh face waved her to the *Ark*'s portside beam.

Smiley spoke gently. "You needn't be frightened. Regardless of how it seems, you're in good hands."

She was now thoroughly befuddled. None of what was happening made sense.

Approaching the ramp-ladder, she stiffened. Jason was

aboard, extending a hand to help her. She moved forward, too stunned to speak.

There were two other men standing at the railing, one a large gray-haired fellow, the other almost as tall but leaner. Both wore grim expressions.

"How could you have known?" she asked Jason, her eyes searching the other men guardedly.

"We're not alone, Fran. We have allies, and they know everything."

"I don't understand. How would they . . ."

Chelsea intervened. "Take her below, Jason." He turned to Josh. "She's about Cindy's size. Would she have anything to fit her?"

"No problem. I'll speak to her."

Her face ashen, Fran took another sip of the brandy. Her sense of relief was short-lived as Chelsea, masking his impatience, started to debrief her.

Ellie, accompanied by Cindy and Mae, had come up from below. Chelsea avoided her eyes. From time to time the women exchanged disbelieving looks as they listened to Fran's narrative. The men seemed to accept it matter-of-factly.

Ellie, outwardly calm, but with emotions roiling beneath the surface, asked Fran tentatively, "You do this for a living?" It was hard to understand how this young woman had been hired for such a job.

Fran looked up. The woman was a stranger, as were the others, but seemed so caring. "No. I am merely an employee in my father's compa—" Suddenly reminded, she started to push forward from her seat. "I must call my cousin Antonio. He has to be warned. Rodgers threatened—"

Chelsea's hand stayed her. "Does your cousin have a telex or fax machine?" "Both," she answered. Chelsea prodded her, "You know the codes?" She nodded and he gave her his notebook so she could write them down.

"Your job, Dave," he said, handing him the notebook.

"What message should I send?" he asked, pulling at his beard.

Chelsea looked to Fran. "It's your message. We'll edit whatever is necessary."

She pondered briefly. " 'Put extra guards on the barges. Will explain later.' Sign it 'Francesca.' "

"Short but sweet," Chelsea remarked. "Now, one more question. What were you instructed to do after completion of your mission?"

"I was to leave for Italy via Alitalia in the morning."

Chelsea's expression did not reflect his thoughts.

Never in a million years would they have allowed her to return to her home.

"I would suggest all the women accompany Ms. Fargo to the house. We have unfinished business to discuss with the Brenners." He caught Ellie's are-you-hiding-something-else-from-me look, and shook his head slightly.

"I'm in on whatever you're planning," Jason stated resolutely.

Chelsea noted the look, the stance, the attitude. Musing, he was reminded of the eternal questions: When does one fall in love? What is the signal that produces that special chemistry? Fran and Jason barely knew each other. There was no explaining it. And yet, Chelsea could pinpoint when it happened to him and Ellie. She had been ascending a stairway from the U.N. lobby. He had been right behind her when the heel of her shoe broke off. Stumbling, she fell back into his arms. Her face had reddened with embarrassment, but then a smile broke through. He thought she was the most beautiful woman he had ever met.

* * *

Within a few minutes the Brenner brothers, fully dressed, joined them. All scuba gear had been stowed away in their van.

"Her captors are long gone," Noah remarked dryly. "What did you learn from the woman?" The query brought Chelsea back to the present.

"We have a name—Calvin Rodgers. We also have a place, of sorts." He described Fran's blindfolded trip to the warehouse. "They crossed railroad tracks, at least four times, stopping finally on a graveled surface seconds after the final crossing." He paused briefly. "It was a large warehouse, most likely on an Amtrak siding. The crisscrossing of rails was probably to throw Fargo off."

Jason had waited for him to finish. His face solemn, he said, "Don't underestimate Rodgers. He's former CIA."

Chelsea looked at Ward without saying anything.

Ward blew out a deep breath. "Yeah, I'll check into it, Joey."

Josh said, "We're going to need Carbolo's help in finding that warehouse. No one knows the area better."

"Yes, and we do that quietly. We can't have him in hot water with his own department." Chelsea fell silent for a moment. "Any undue publicity will lead to a lot of action we can't handle."

Noah Brenner shook his head. "And you believe we can handle this by ourselves?"

Chelsea, seated, looked up at him. "Don't mistake me for one of those retirees whose sole occupation is waiting for the daily mail. If you want to call it quits, you can do so. No ill feelings."

Aaron's cough broke the tension. He nudged Noah's elbow. "We'll be back in the morning. We'll be ready if you need us earlier." He paused for a moment. "If you'd like me to, I'll stay aboard the *Ark* tonight."

Jason stepped forward. "No need, I'll stay. I'd like to pull my own weight. I'm as much involved as anyone."

No one gave him an argument, least of all Chelsea. He was beginning to feel his age, no matter his protestations, to himself or others.

"What about Fran?" Jason asked. "Can she stay here temporarily? She was checked out of her apartment, and I feel responsible for her."

Chelsea was chewing on the stem of his pipe.

"Joe . . ." Josh prodded.

"Yes, she can stay," Chelsea said. "Until we find a safer place. If we leave her on her own, she's finished." He stood up, as if terminating any discussion, but looked disturbed.

"What is it?" Jason asked.

His expression became more animated. "No one's life should be in danger. The Alliance doesn't have to kill anymore. For whatever the reason, we know that Gorham was supposed to have been the final termination."

"Joe, what are you talking about?" Josh asked.

Jason looked bewildered. *Alliance? What is this alliance they keep referring to*?

Chelsea seemed to read his mind. "The assassins protected the Alliance by killing off any remaining witnesses who could identify the original members of the cartel."

"So, why is the cartel worried about us?" Josh argued. "We have nothing but allegations, and can't prove a thing. We don't even know yet who they are."

"Correction, Josh. We can make an educated guess. We have the names Seltzmann, Nestor Hobbs, and now Jason's uncle Elias, the head of Wellington Security."

Chelsea noted Jason's consternation. "Anything to add, Jason?"

"My uncle Elias? I find it a bit difficult to see him in the light you do. This alliance you keep mentioning. What is their purpose? And I don't know why you disassociate the yacht incident from assassination. 'A rose by any other name . . .' "

"Conceded. But we're not in the same category as the original victims. We're dangerous to the *present* members of the Alliance cartel."

Jason squinted in frustration. "I have no idea what you're talking about. What is this alleged cartel supposed to be doing? And the names you mentioned, when you added my uncle to them . . . What would be their function? And where does it all lead?"

It was warm but Chelsea felt an icy chill, and only a strong will prevented a sick feeling from overcoming him. He removed his sunglasses to wipe his face, trying to suppress a growing dread. Thirty years on the force and never once had his family or circle of friends been threatened by his work.

That is, not until he had decided retirement wasn't for him. *Damned fool!*

He stared through the open porthole, his eyes angry pinpoints. A showy bush of flowering hibiscus stirred, seemingly mocking him. The "land of paradise," he recalled Ellie saying. Some paradise! Because of his own blind obstinacy he had made it into a private hell for all. He didn't know how Ellie could hold back a flood of tears. But there were no remonstrations, only a pleading in her eyes.

Chelsea felt a tap on his forearm.

"Mr. Chelsea," Jason said, "I want to help. I have to know where Fran is. But I also have to know what we're up against."

"The Founding Fathers Resort," Chelsea said, his jawline rigid. "I believe your uncle Elias to be a member there in good standing."

28

Elias Stoner lifted the phone from the locked drawer of his desk, his puffy features rigid with displeasure. Calvin Rodgers' maneuver the previous evening had been a fiasco, leading to this phone call from Headquarters.

"Yes?" he said, his voice restrained.

The caller's voice barely suppressed his anger. "Stoner," Seltzmann began ominously, "can you tell me how a mere handful of men can cause so much trouble for a ten-billion-dollar foolproof investment?"

"The mere handful of men you refer to are very clever. Clever enough to discover your system is not foolproof."

"Don't be a smartass, Stoner. You know very well you didn't handle your nephew properly."

Stoner gritted his teeth. "I'll take care of it."

"Not so fast. It's no longer in your hands. We can't have the Stoner name in headlines. What I want is to have Jason Stoner in the laboratory. Do I make myself clear?"

"Very." Stoner displayed no feelings for his nephew. "What about the others?"

"You're to contact Rodgers. Instruct him to find your nephew and, under the guise of revealing the truth, have him offer to take Jason to our more expedient Florida base. A trail should be left for the others to follow. The Base security will take it from there."

As much as Stoner detested Seltzmann, he had to admit it would be the perfect solution. Wholesale assassinations were unwise. Instead, all those involved would become Factors.

The idea was clever, but . . . "You really believe those men would fall for it? I repeat, they're men of intelligence, not easily deceived."

"These so-called clever men couldn't possibly resist the chance to trail Jason." Seltzmann's voice took on a threatening tone. "Rodgers has forty-eight hours, no more. Be sure he understands. This has already played too long."

Chelsea drove his own car, with Alex in the passenger seat. They were following Jason Stoner's Taurus back to Fran Fargo's former apartment. When Jason had called his answering machine for messages, there was one from Calvin Rodgers, asking him to come to the Spanish River apartment-hotel, where he would explain why the Fargo woman had been hired by the firm.

Chelsea sensed some sort of a trap, but he was willing to explore further. Chewing on the unlit briar in his mouth, he said to Alex, "Give me your opinion of the woman."

"Scared, but stubborn."

"That's it?"

Alex shrugged. "You want more? At first, I thought she and Stoner had a thing going. But then I changed my mind. The woman wants to go back to Italy, but not until she's free of all threats. She's afraid to stay and she's afraid to leave."

He fell silent a moment. "Overall, after what's happened, I'd say they both had guts."

"Would you trust them to follow my orders?"

Alex shrugged again. "I would say so. They'd be lost without your direction."

Chelsea took the pipe from his mouth. "Let's hope you're right." Above all else, Chelsea knew they had to stay together.

Pulling into the parking lot, he said, "Stay here, Alex, and keep an eye on the entrance. I'm going in after Stoner."

Entering the lobby, Chelsea caught Jason at the front desk asking for Calvin Rodgers. "A message was left for you, Mr. Stoner," the clerk said. He handed Jason a sealed envelope, then looked over at Chelsea. "Can I help you, sir?"

Chelsea gave him a cheery smile. "No, thanks. I'm with Mr. Stoner."

Chelsea told Jason to hold off opening the envelope. Upstairs, on the floor where Fran had stayed, the blue-carpeted corridor was empty. When Jason turned the key in the lock, Chelsea directed him to step aside.

Pushing the door open, he could see the entire length of the efficiency apartment. The drapes were open and the afternoon sun slanted across a chair near the window. The room was silent, meticulously clean, the bed made. Chelsea nodded; the place was as he expected it to be.

He held a finger to his lips. The wiretap Jason had mentioned could still be in place. He motioned for Jason to open the message.

"What gall!" Jason muttered when he had read it. He handed the single sheet of paper to Chelsea.

Jason, I apologize for the unfortunate events that involved you unnecessarily. I had intended taking you into my confidence at a later date, when you had proved yourself. I realize now it was an egregious oversight not to have done so earlier. I now ask for your trust, and that you call Calvin Rodgers at his Miami office. There will be no intimidation of either you or Ms. Fargo. Rodgers will accompany both of you to our headquarters, where everything will be explained to your satisfaction. Please follow orders. This will lead to a better understanding and a brighter future for you on the horizon.

The signature was "Uncle Elias." Chelsea noticed that the message had been sent by fax, most likely to Rodgers, who had relayed it to Fargo's apartment and then left the telephone message for Jason asking him to go there.

Headquarters? For what? Certainly not a promotion.

Chelsea swore softly. "Call Rodgers."

Jason delayed. "Why do I need Rodgers to take me to Dallas?"

"Dallas? Forget it. Their so-called headquarters I would guess is on a small island fortress near Nassau. Make the call."

Jason hesitated, unable to grasp Chelsea's meaning. "Nassau?"

Chelsea prodded him. "Make the call. I'll explain in the car. It's possible we can make this work for us."

Chelsea lifted the kitchen wall phone and waited for Jason to use the one beside the bed. It was apparent that Jason knew Rodgers' number in Miami.

Chelsea's mind wandered briefly, reflecting that he had reached a new dimension—no, a new plateau—in his self-appointed sleuthing. The technique called for, and employed, was a far cry from local police work. And it was being accomplished with a small force of retired lawmen. So far, it had stood him in good stead. There was a sudden churning in his stomach, balancing his effulgent thoughts. He heard a voice respond to Jason:

"Stoner, is Ms. Fargo with you?"

Jason saw Chelsea nod. "Yes. No thanks to you."

Rodgers disregarded the sarcasm. "Is someone there with you?"

"No, I'm quite alone. What's on your mind?"

"You read your uncle's instructions. Stay where you are and wait for pickup. I caution you not to do anything that would antagonize your uncle."

"Where will we be going?" Jason questioned coolly.

"Be patient. You'll know in a few minutes." The phone went dead. Jason turned toward Chelsea—and then suddenly froze.

Chelsea caught the look, directed over his shoulder. Spinning around, he discovered two men walking in, both holding pistols. "Shit!" he muttered. *Careless old fool!*

Both men were tall, one thin, the other stocky; both wore sneakers, faded dungarees, T-shirts, and dark glasses. The thickset one was apparently in command. "Good afternoon, we're your private escort." His eyes swept the room, then rested on Chelsea, noting his balled fists. He nodded to his companion, who immediately moved to Chelsea and patted him down.

"Enlighten me," Chelsea said. "Why the artillery?"

Stocky's expression remained impassive. "Just following orders. You've acquired a reputation." He glanced at his partner, who had just finished with Jason.

Chelsea seemed somewhat phlegmatic. He seated himself at the kitchen counter. "We have to wait for Rodgers," he said nonchalantly.

The thickset one snickered. "Pay attention. I'm following the man's orders. We're going to calmly walk out to a van parked at the entrance. Behave and no one will get hurt."

Chelsea realized he and Jason had been set up. The two men had been ready, most likely listening with a stethoscope on the wall abutting the next apartment.

The desk clerk smiled as they walked past. "Have a good day," he said. "Come back again, sometime."

"We will," Chelsea mumbled. He wondered how observant Alex had been. There had to be another man outside with the van.

Alex was aware of the van that had parked at the entrance. The driver didn't budge, but his eyes probed the parking lot. Alex, unseen, about thirty feet away, leaned forward to open the glove compartment. He knew Chelsea kept a Smith & Wesson police special there. His eyes lifted, seeing the silencer; he screwed it into place. He had a gut feeling that trouble was brewing.

As Chelsea and Jason were escorted through the lobby, sandwiched between the gunmen, Chelsea was doing some thinking. During his last ten years on the police force he had, more or less, been a desk man—one in a chain of command, planning strategy, delegating orders, rarely entering the field. Now he wondered, for the first time, whether his aging faculties could hold up to the younger men. These particular thugs were a different breed from the criminal element generally encountered by local police departments. They were trained professionals, accomplishing their jobs coolly, dispassionately, and with complete confidence. Chelsea had created a situation from which there was no backing off.

Feeling a gun prod his back, he stiffened angrily, his old sense of professional pride reemerging. "Don't try anything foolish," came a whispered threat in his ear. Age or no, the sibilant tone annoyed him thoroughly.

When the driver got out of the van to slide open a side door, Alex slipped out of Chelsea's car. His nerve ends tingled; now he felt sure his employer was in trouble. In a crouch he made his way to the front of the car, where he caught Chelsea's almost imperceptible nod in his direction.

Holding the S & W in both hands, Alex stretched his arms across the top of the hood and drew a bead on the nearest man at the side of the van. His voice knifed across the deserted lot.

"Don't move! Just hold your positions."

The unexpected intervention caught the Alliance men off guard. The man behind Chelsea ran into his heels. Taking instant advantage, Chelsea lifted his right foot and brought it down hard on Stocky's instep. Simultaneously, in a fluid movement he swung around, his balled fist uppercutting the man's jaw. The single punch drove Stocky back into a hibiscus bush. Chelsea retrieved his dropped weapon and waved him to his feet.

Jason took the other man's weapon as Alex ran forward with the police special trained on the driver.

In less than two minutes the three would-be abductors had been herded into the back of the van. Fortunately, there had been no witnesses. Alex, behind the wheel, switched on the van's air-conditioner, then trained his gun on the three captives. Chelsea was already looking over the business cards taken from their wallets. Although all were ID'd employees of Wellington Security, each man had come from a different state office. Chelsea handed the cards to Jason, who sat near the side door. "The names mean anything to you?" he asked.

"Never heard of them. I would have to go through personnel files, but I doubt—"

Chelsea interrupted. "Mark down this date, Jason, to check on later." Chelsea handed him the men's driver's licenses. All three men were born on the same day, of the same year, yet no one name or facial feature matched the other.

Chelsea studied the faces of the three men, all impassive, strangely devoid of expression. On impulse he addressed the stocky one. "When was the surgery performed?" The man's eyes narrowed in thought, the first outward sign of emotion.

"What surgery?"

"The scar at the nape of your neck suggests surgery."

The man's hand explored the back of his neck. "This? I was born with it. It's a birth defect."

Jason looked puzzled, as did Alex. Where was this line of questioning leading? Surgery? Birth defect?

When Chelsea directed Jason to let the air out of the van's tires, Alex gave his boss a curious look. "You're not going to have them charged with anything," he said.

"No. I don't want our names on a formal complaint. At least, not at this time." To Jason he said, "You're certain their names ring no bells."

"No, they're new."

Chelsea nodded, ruminating. *Birth defect!* How many were there walking around with a like defect? These men were generations apart from the death camp refugees. What was their purpose? A complement of young assassins worldwide made no sense. The international members of the cartel were too important to bother with simply backing an assassination bureau.

An icy finger ran down Chelsea's spine. Stiffening, he told Alex and Jason to stay put while he made a phone call. Something nagged at him, telling him the surgery wasn't performed exclusively to create assassins. He recalled Izzy Gorham's account of a tailor suddenly becoming an expert at mathematics . . .

The surgery was performed for some kind of mind-bending!

His stomach churning, he strode purposefully across the parking lot. Tall hedges muted the sounds of street traffic. He lifted the car phone in the Ciera and called Carbolo.

"Can we talk, Rudy?" He waited. "Okay. If I give you three men, all caught in an attempted mugging, could you come up with some pretext to order a physical examination?" Chelsea listened for a few seconds. "Sure. Good idea. Check them for HIV positive and, at the same time, examine the scar tissue each man has at the nape of his neck."

A squad car would pick up the prisoners. Carbolo would take care of the charges.

Chelsea pulled out the empty briar from his shirt pocket and clamped it between his lips, the gesture initiating resolve. He would have to explain his abrupt change of plan to Alex and Jason.

He sucked on the empty pipe, got out of the car, and cleared his mind of distracting thoughts. From Jason he needed Calvin Rodgers' Miami phone number.

29

There was no shock or surprise in Calvin Rodgers' voice when Chelsea, calling from his car phone, identified himself. *The man was good*, Chelsea decided.

"How can I help you?" Rodgers asked.

Chelsea played down an urge to shout into the mouthpiece. He delayed two seconds only. "No beating around the bush. My friends and I want to get off the hot seat. Can we make a deal?"

"You're using a car phone. Call me back from a phone booth."

"You're stalling."

"If you want to talk business with me, do as you're told." Chelsea ground his teeth as Rodgers continued. "When you've complied with my instructions, we can set up a meeting." The phone went dead.

Jason was at the side of the car. "What happened?"

"The man doesn't like car phones. Too public for him. I have to call him back on another phone."

"And then what? Rodgers can't be trusted."

"I know. But for the moment he's holding the reins."

Jason didn't press him.

The younger man caught Chelsea's contemplative look as he slid out of the car. *He's wondering about me.*

"Are you prepared to follow my orders?" Chelsea asked bluntly. "Without question?"

"All the way. I meant everything I said earlier."

Chelsea nodded. "All right. Let's find a phone booth."

The windows of the storefront were shuttered; a sign on the door read "Boutique Closed For Alterations." Inside, the shop was empty except for a single wooden folding chair and an empty milk crate standing vertically. A phone rested atop the crate.

The store was located in a shopping center on Federal Highway, no more than a quarter-mile away from the Spanish River apartment-hotel.

Calvin Rodgers, his face drawn, sat in the chair, waiting for his private Miami number to be relayed. Since Chelsea knew the number, Jason must have joined forces with him.

Rodgers twisted uncomfortably. He had heard everything go down successfully in the apartment. *What had happened to the three-man crew to change the situation?* And where was Chelsea hiding Fargo?

The phone rang; he flipped a switch to scramble his end of the conversation. "You're on," he said simply.

Chelsea's voice was calm. "We have three of your men in custody. I'll exchange them for a deal of your choosing." He heard a snicker from Rodgers.

"You can keep them, Chelsea. They are of no further use to either of us. You will learn nothing from them other than what they tried to accomplish."

"So, what are you dealing? Keep in mind that I can start a tidal wave with the little I do know."

"Don't talk nonsense, Chelsea. You want your wife and the rest of your entourage to stay alive. Do you have any idea of what you're attempting to take on? Even if you were a David, you'd be a total fool to challenge a race of Goliaths. Wake up. You're a joke to my crew—a pesky fly. Their only reason for playing along with you was to find out how you learned of their existence."

Chelsea raised a balled fist, ready to punch the phone in the open booth. Jason, recognizing the frustration behind the action, clapped his hand over Chelsea's wrist. He shook his head to indicate that flaring up wasn't the answer, no matter how Rodgers provoked him.

Chelsea turned away to hide his chagrin. He had broken his own cardinal rule: Never, under any circumstances, blow your top in front of a squad member.

He nodded and, regaining control, spoke into the mouthpiece. "What do you want?"

"Stay close. You'll be contacted within twenty-four hours."

"If anyone in my group is harmed in any way . . ."

"I don't make the final decisions."

"Then you better speak to your control, because if anything—"

"Get something straight, Chelsea. I'm just a cog in a wheel of massive proportions. To my superiors you are of even less importance. If the organization was so disposed, your whole little group would disappear. That they haven't done so as yet only means they have other plans for you—and most likely for your friends."

Chelsea frowned, looking past Jason. His eyes scanned the parking lot of the shopping plaza, catching a Lincoln Continental whose driver was blowing his horn impatiently at a Buick blocking his way.

Before Jason could tell what he was looking at, Chelsea leaned close to his ear. "I can hear the Continental's horn over the phone. The bastard's in one of the shops here."

Jason was astonished. "A relay phone here? From Miami?"

Chelsea spoke into the phone. "Where should I expect the call?"

"If your friend doesn't already have one, put an answering machine on *Novick's Ark.* If no one stays aboard, have someone check it every hour. And, also, when you receive the call, have Novick, the Fargo woman, Jason Stoner, Ward, and his woman stand by with you."

The omission of Cindy and Ellie and the Brenner brothers bewildered Chelsea for only a moment. The parties Rodgers wanted to stand by weren't meant to disappear; they were candidates for surgery.

The phone went dead, and Chelsea hung up. He urged Jason toward the doorway of a Walgreen drugstore. "You know how the relay setup works. Which shop would he most likely use?"

The thirty shops of the plaza formed a giant U, with the entrance to a parking lot at the open end. Jason's eyes skimmed along each storefront.

"He could have heard the horn blasting over his phone also," Chelsea remarked. "He cut off too quickly."

Jason nodded. "It has to be one of the three empty stores. A relay phone is a temporary connection and almost never used as an adjunct to a legitimate business." He turned to look at Chelsea and noted a subtle hardness in his eyes. Physical evidence of Chelsea's authority may have diminished with the years, but it hadn't affected his ability to command. For a man of his . . .

God! How his father had detested the expression "Man of your age." He had once switched doctors because of his physician's constant use of it.

"We wait . . ." Chelsea said, "and keep a watchful eye. He has to appear sooner or later."

He gave Jason, hovering in the doorway, a probing glance. There was no hostility behind the look, merely a questioning. *Jason Stoner was a Wellington executive*. How far could he really trust him?

Jason tilted his chin and sniffed. "You're smelling the Japanese restaurant next door," Chelsea said. People were coming out, having finished lunch. "If you're hungry, curb your appetite. Stay alert. I'm relying on you to identify Rodgers."

Jason frowned. All his business with Rodgers over a couple of years had been conducted by phone. Saying nothing to Chelsea, he adjusted his sunglasses and swung his head from one empty store to another.

"I say something wrong?" Chelsea asked, not missing a thing. His eyes followed Jason's search. "You can't identify him, can you?"

"I think we may have met once—I'd guess it could be two years back." His gaze stayed on a storefront some fifty yards away, on the opposite side of the parking lot; its front door was opening. "Maybe," he said, squinting in the glare of the midday sun. "It could be the guy coming out. He's the right build, as I remember." He moved out onto the sidewalk. "It's him!" he exclaimed. "I'm sure of it."

Chelsea was on Jason's heels, both men taking long strides without actually running. "Watch for his car, Stoner. I want the bastard tailed, not apprehended as yet. You follow on foot. I'm going for my car. I'll keep an eye on you and watch for your signal." He laid a delaying hand on his shoulder. "Are you certain it's Rodgers?"

Halting suddenly and kneeling behind a parked car, Jason pointed toward the store. "You have any doubts now?"

* * *

Rodgers stood on the sidewalk directly in front of the empty store, his attention drawn to the parking lot, and then to some passers-by. He planted dark glasses on his face and didn't move for perhaps half a minute or so. Apparently satisfied that no one was unduly interested in him, he moved out on the walk and pulled a remote control from his shirt pocket. As he pressed it, the sound of a car door unlocking could be heard.

"It's the white Jaguar," Chelsea said. "Let's head back to our car. Under no circumstances can we lose him."

They walked slowly, unobtrusively, between the cars, the pervasive humidity enveloping their faces like a wet towel.

"I'll drive," Jason said, avoiding the older man's eyes. "A few years back I spent an entire summer stock-car racing. I can handle it." It got him a stare and then the car keys.

In the car Chelsea said, "Give him a few seconds before pulling out. If he was aware of the Lincoln's horn, he'll be watching for us."

"What about your man Alex? And the three men we left him with?"

"He'll go back with Carbolo—or the arresting officers—to make a formal complaint."

Heading north on the Federal Highway they followed the Jaguar past Boca's and Delray's new-car showrooms. There was little traffic; in the midday heat people stayed on the beach or around their pools. At Lincoln Boulevard, the Ciera followed the Jaguar into a left turn and then into the right-hand lane.

Chelsea waited until Rodgers found I-95 and entered the north lane. "No closer than a hundred feet," he said, lifting the car phone. He got Josh at the office.

"We're tailing Rodgers on 95. I have a hunch he's

heading for a marina in West Palm. Whether he is or not, call Mae and have her contact Ward. It's getting close to showdown time."

Rodgers kept his speed at 55 m.p.h., the legal limit, allowing just about everyone else to pass him. No one abided by the speed limit but Rodgers and a single car behind him. It was only a few minutes before he became aware of the Ciera.

Chelsea!

Rogers waited until two 18-wheelers in the middle lane came up broadside. He then accelerated, passed the lead trailer and cut in front and across him. The truck driver gave Rodgers the horn and simultaneously applied his brakes. The second semi, riding his tail, jammed his own brakes, causing him to fishtail into the outside lane.

The Ciera, about to be hit broadside, swung onto the shoulder, and onto an unexpected off-ramp.

"Damn!"

Grim-lipped, Jason raced down the Lake Worth exit, but instead of following the lane east, shot across six lanes, causing the two-way traffic to come to a screeching halt. Irate drivers could be heard screaming and cursing above a three-car crash.

The Ciera, untouched, tore into the north lane of I-95 again, its speedometer reaching 85 m.p.h. in seconds. Another two minutes at that speed and they knew they had lost Rodgers.

"Slow it down," Chelsea yelled. "He's long gone. He could have got off anywhere."

Jason banged the steering wheel with his fist. "Shit!" he muttered. "I blew it!"

"Stop flogging yourself. It could have been worse."

"Yeah! How? We've not only lost Rodgers, we've lost any chance of getting real information."

Chelsea winced. "We could have been in that mess you left back there. Rodgers orchestrated his move cleverly, waiting for the semis to come alongside, forcing us to exit 95. Forget it. Take the next off-ramp and get onto Federal Highway. Maybe we'll luck out at Ward's marina."

The air-conditioner was on full blast but Chelsea cracked his side window. What breeze there was worked the humidity into his pores. Nevertheless he took a deep breath, trying to calm a pounding heart and a growing anxiety. It's time, he thought, for Ward to come up with some outside help.

Help we can all trust.

A gradual sense of defeat cloaked his shoulders. The case had become too big.

Yet, sniffing, in seconds he quickly roused himself. Self-pity was something he had encountered in a hundred faces over the years while still a member of the police force. It wasn't a state of mind confined to the aged, or any one group. But he refused to become one of its victims.

Jason noticed the change in his manner. "You okay?" he asked.

"Yeah, just great." Chelsea sighed, closing his window. "For a man in retirement, I've really screwed up." Thoughts of Ellie suffering in silence fostered an anguish he couldn't quite mask. "Just finish it" was all she had said.

"Mr. Chel . . ."

"It's okay. Forget it." Unaccountably, the words began to spill out. "In South Florida you reach a certain age, you're allowed the privilege, albeit an abused privilege, of escaping into the past. While most people down here appear to enjoy their present situation, there are some—men, at least—who are still focused on their World War Two experiences as the only important moments in their lives. I don't say they should forget those times—just don't keep reliving them as if that's all there was to life."

He caught himself for a moment, knowing he was merely indulging his own philosophic platitudes. Yet he was unable to stop himself.

"Barring chronic disabilities, these men, no matter their ages, should still be forging ahead, seeking a brighter, possibly more productive, future. There are plenty of outlets, clubs for example, available to test their mettle."

"Why should it bother you? You seem to have escaped dwelling in the past."

Chelsea rubbed his forehead. It brought a slight easement. "Perhaps. But had I learned my place in the scheme of things earlier, this mess wouldn't exist. I should have been smarter, and joined one of those clubs I mentioned."

Jason passed a sanitation truck; a sign on its side advertised free snow removal.

"That makes it paradise," Chelsea snorted.

"How can you spurn paradise?" Jason asked, trying to lighten Chelsea's mood.

There was no immediate reply. Finally Chelsea said, "How much you earn in a year? Approximate." Jason looked bewildered by the abrupt change of subject, and the new topic.

"Is it important?"

"Just curiosity. I'll explain in a moment."

"Eighty grand—with bonus, another twenty." Jason gave his interrogator an oblique glance.

"If you're on the up-and-up with us, and I believe you are, you've already lost your position with Wellington."

Jason swallowed with an uneasy relief. "Mr. Chelsea, I never *had* to work for my uncle. My personal income and portfolio make me financially independent. That's not my problem." He turned the subject aside. "Which marina do we want?"

"A quarter-mile ahead, take a right. Port of Palm Beach."

"Then what?"

"We drive through the parking lot. If Rodgers is in this marina, a white Jag shouldn't be too hard to spot. I've got his plate number."

"Why this particular marina?"

"Just chancing it. It's where Ward docks his boat."

There was one white Jaguar; wrong plates.

Chelsea nodded toward the far end of the parking lot, an area abutting an extended dock. "Ward has a small office at the rear of the building adjacent to the yacht club. Pull up behind it. He won't be in yet, but Mae should be waiting for us."

The office wasn't much more than a cubbyhole; a desk, one chair behind it, and two cane chairs for prospective clients in front. Two four-foot metal files stood against one wall. On the opposite wall Ward's computer had a special setup on another desk.

Finding the door behind the screen door slightly ajar alerted both men. A closed door and a small window air-conditioner were a must for the computer equipment; Ward was fanatic on the subject.

Chelsea motioned Jason to the hinge side of the screen door, then positioned himself at the other side. Jason obeyed silently, seeing the man was back in his element, in control, his S&W .38 drawn from his belt.

"Mae," Chelsea called out. "I need a hand with a package."

A flock of sea gulls screeched by, patrolling the dock, startling the two men momentarily. From within the office, the only sound was the humming of the air-conditioner.

Random explanations flew through Chelsea's mind. Something was definitely wrong; Mae should have been waiting. Josh must have spoken with her on the phone not ten minutes ago—he hadn't called back to say otherwise—and they weren't five minutes behind Rodgers. If someone had gotten to her it couldn't possibly have been Rodgers.

There was no point in waiting. Chelsea yanked open the screen door and shoved the inner door wide open. One stride took him into the room, the S&W police special held upright in both hands. Jason at his heels almost ran into him.

No Mae—harmed or unharmed.

Ward's filing cabinets were open, computer disks strewn on the floor, paper files scattered on top of the desk and behind it.

Jason recalled meeting Mae, on Novick's boat, the night they rescued Fran. "You think they took her?" he asked. "What for? What would they gain?"

Chelsea shook his head, attempting to stem the anger building within him, thinking, *Ward will want to throttle him.* He returned the weapon to his belt.

"A hostage." He nodded at the files. "They didn't get what they were looking for. All our disks on the Alliance are locked up in our office safe."

"On the phone with Novick you said 'showdown time.' Do you—or don't you—have backup to handle this so-called alliance?"

"Not so-called. It's Alliance with a capital A—as in Benefactor Alliance. Your uncle is a board member, but not the star." He tossed a look at the computer. "It's a multibillion-dollar combine, but you won't find them on any stock exchange. I'm only amazed that you never knew of your uncle's role in this."

Jason winced. "*You're* amazed! I'm stunned! I still find it difficult to believe my uncle has a hand in this, and that he's as ruthless as you seem to think." Catching the probing, deprecating glance—at least Chelsea was in charge again, he decided, as he was at the Spanish River hotel, and no longer the moody ex–police captain of just minutes ago in the car Jason said, "All right, so what's our next move? How do we get Mae Warren back?"

There was no reply. Chelsea searched under the loose files on the desk for the phone, then got Josh again at the office. "You get Mae or Dave yet?" he barked into the mouthpiece. He waited a moment, his lips tightening as he heard neither could be contacted at either his home or his boat. Chelsea continued, his voice compressed, "I think they've taken Mae—and possibly Dave also." He noted Jason's mouth agape. "I'm going to check out Dave's boat. Meanwhile, get in touch with the Brenners. We have to work out these complications. And, Josh, keep the women at your home with double the security."

Ward's 45-foot Viking was not in its usual slip. The harbormaster told them Ward had gone out early. He recalled that there were four men with the fishing charter and, no matter his concentration, couldn't recall what they looked like, or how they had arrived.

Jason was trying to digest what was happening. In one week his whole life had been altered. It had started with the Fargo woman—and the cryptic background of her father. The information that his own computer-prying had produced further changed what had been familiar landscape, and meeting Chelsea—and then his "retired" crew—had finished the process.

Watching the former policeman deep in thought—*or was it indecision*?—Jason's restlessness increased.

"How are we going to fight an invisible army of unknown proportions?" he asked.

Chelsea's gaze turned upon him, his look blank for a moment. A shrug followed. "I don't really know."

"Earlier you were certain you knew where you were heading. What happened to change your mind?"

"It's too apparent. They know we know about their private island. We told them that we were willing to back off, but they're unwilling to trust us to stand aside and await instructions. So, now they have Mae Warren, and probably Ward. All protective measures on their part. We're forced to wait, to let them play their hand without obstructing them." A heavy sign escaped. "And we don't have any choice."

"Jesus Christ!" Jason sputtered. "They've got your friends."

"Yes, I know that—only too well." Chelsea took Jason's arm and gently steered him from the dock area and then fished out a notebook from his shirt pocket. Wondering what the hell the man was up to, Jason read as Chelsea wrote, "Don't look now—but there's an eighty-foot yawl across the Waterway, in a private dock. Unless I'm becoming paranoid, I would guess the mainmast has a microphonic ear turned in our direction."

"Jesus! What next?" Jason muttered disgustedly.

Chelsea prodded him to the car. "What next is finding out who owns the boat, the dock, and the private estate where it's tied up. For what it's worth, it's our only lead."

Jason waited for Chelsea to switch on the ignition before speaking. "With your friend Ward out of reach, just how are you going to pick up any information? He's your computer expert."

"Correction. From what you've told me previously, I understood you to be as knowledgeable. We're going back to my office in Boca. Between you and Josh we should get what we want."

"And then what?" Jason retorted facetiously. "We surround that property with about four or five of your men?"

Chelsea ignored the flippancy. "We get in touch with the Brenners and then decide what we can accomplish."

"What about Carbolo, your detective friend?"

"He's strictly an information man. We don't dare use him in the field. The Alliance is like an octopus with countless tentacles; they could have a man planted in the sheriff's office. Nothing would surprise me anymore." He gave Jason a direct look. "They've been in existence for more than four decades. For all I know your uncle could be a charter member."

"You still don't fully trust me," Jason said with a trace of anger. "If not, why are you asking me to work with you?"

"Because of the Fargo woman—I feel sorry for her."

"And it's because of Fran I'm here. What more do you want? Where would you be if I hadn't given you all the dope on her?"

Chelsea held up a soothing hand. *Stoner didn't know it but he was in love with Fargo.* "Okay, you've made your point. I'll accept it." He lifted the car phone and punched in Josh's number again and then parried the questions coming over the line.

"When Alex calls in, have him go straight to your estate. I want him to guard the women *in* the house, regardless of the men you have prowling the grounds. That's all for now. I'm coming in with Jason, and will bring you up to date.

30

Within three hours of leaving Ward's cubbyhole office Chelsea's suspicions were confirmed. Josh had put in a call to the Coast Guard, explaining he couldn't reach Ward's Viking by ship-to-shore, and he was worried that it might not be a radio problem.

The Coast Guard called back two and a half hours later, with the news that a 45-foot Viking was docked in the Lantana marina. Its captain, a David Ward, had prepaid a month's docking fee.

Josh had contacted the Lantana harbormaster and immediately learned that the Viking had docked early in the morning and that its captain's description didn't fit Ward.

Josh grunted disgustedly. "Now what! Joe? This is blowing up in our faces. It's time to call in the troops."

"Troops . . ." Chelsea muttered. "What troops? Without Dave we have no contact. We can't use Carbolo—we can't even get him involved." He fell silent a moment and then, reminded, asked, "Did Carbolo come up with a location for the warehouse Fran was taken to?"

"Zilch. He had a possible. While it tallied with Fargo's description the warehouse was empty and the place had been up for sale for more than a year."

"The owner?"

"A shipping company—staving off a Chapter Eleven; the owners are a foreign outfit, with a name that doesn't resemble Dave's printouts."

Jason could no longer keep silent. "What about the three men taken out at Spanish River Park? Nothing more was learned from them?"

Josh shook his head. "All three men developed amnesia. Whether self-induced or controlled by others, nobody knows."

"And the yacht in the Intracoastal—nothing?"

"The yacht was stolen ten days ago, and apparently tied up at that particular dock to keep an eye—or ear—on Ward. The owners of the Palm Beach estate haven't as yet opened their winter home and, on being contacted, knew nothing of the boat. They have their own, a hundred-foot megayacht, still anchored in New England." He looked at Chelsea. "What you guessed to be a microphonic ear was not on the boat."

"So, where do we go from here?" Jason asked.

Chelsea asked Josh, "What about the Brenners? Have you brought them up to date?" Josh shook his head, scowling.

"What can they do? Talk about a 'tiger by the tail,' we're trying to swing an elephant. And now we've got almost everyone in deep shit."

Chelsea's jaw twitched. *I got them in deep shit—Josh had nothing to do with it.* He fumbled in his shirt pocket for his tobacco pouch. "Check to see if Alex is at your house," he said, with some resignation.

Josh reached for his desk phone—and froze.

The light on the phone had gone out—and the security

monitor on the wall went blank. Shouts from other rooms reached his office an instant later.

It was the twilight hour, and without electricity, every room in the building was thrown into gloomy shadow. Chelsea was out the door in seconds, heading for the main monitor room, Josh and Jason at his heels.

A shout greeted them from Tony Ossilena, an ex-cop, seated at a console commanding a set of four screens. "Hey, Joe, you forget to put a quarter in the meter?"

Josh immediately went to the circuit-breaker box, and removed the magnetized flashlight attached to its cover.

The main breaker had shorted out, but more ominously the emergency backup generator had failed to take over.

Ossilena was the only employee on duty; all the others were nine-to-fivers and had left for the day about two hours ago. Ossilena's relief wasn't due for another six hours. Chelsea barked orders. "Tony, check the front lot from the windows. If we're the only building that's lost power it could mean trouble. Josh—take the side windows. Jason and I will take the rear door to find out why the generator didn't kick in."

He grasped Jason's elbow before Josh could protest.

It didn't matter.

From the monitor room everyone heard the rear door of the building cave in with a resounding crash. Chelsea realized that the loss of power was total; no alarms went off. He also knew that no one outside the building would be aware of the raid; the plants in the immediate area had shut down for the day.

Chelsea's grip on Jason's elbow prevented the younger man from darting into the corridor that led to the rear door.

Jason tried to break loose, muttering indignantly, "Why are you holding back? We've lost any advantage we might have had."

"We're not armed—they are. They blew that door in." The smell of cordite drifted to their nostrils.

Chelsea felt Ossilena at his shoulder. "I'm armed, Joe. A police special .38. You want me to—"

"Forget it. You've already done your bit. Let me have your weapon. It's my call." He heard Josh mutter, "Shit!" Chelsea spun around and spoke softly but quickly. "Everyone get down, lie flat on your stomach, two on each side of the doorway. They, whoever they are, will be charging in any second. Don't make a move unless I order you to." Sweating, he stared across the darkened room. "I mean it, Josh. You know the drill. We've done it before." Josh and Ossilena were already stretched out on the right side of the open doorway. Chelsea put his ear to the wall, then glanced over his shoulder. "You okay, Stoner?" he whispered. He got a nod.

It was then that Jason decided that Chelsea was addicted to action. What he had thought, earlier, to be indecision was merely frustration wrought by inactivity. Now Chelsea was in his element, completely confident, making decisions, expecting obedience from his "squad" without question.

Chelsea speculated in a low whisper that it was a team, rather than a one-man operation, bursting into their plant. They would come charging or tumbling into the room intending to capture, not kill. Killing meant publicity; the Alliance couldn't afford headlines or investigations. Low-key was their style; the method employed to murder death camp survivors proved the point. All deaths had to appear as coming from natural causes. In this instance Chelsea was almost certain he and his companions were to be taken for "alteration," by whatever means the Alliance deemed necessary, to protect their organization.

In the short time the power had been out, the heat and humidity in the room had built up unbearably; sweat glands were pushed into overtime. Chelsea, stretched out on the floor tile, leaned on his elbows, with Jason at his side and slightly behind him. Their faces were barely visible in the dusk.

Jason felt a tug at his sleeve and heard whispered instructions. "Go to the window side, behind the desk, stand and shout, 'Where the hell's the fuse box!' Then drop down behind the desk." He was shoved. "Go! You've got only ten seconds and it's counting down." Jason could only assume that he was being used as bait.

Obeying instructions, he dropped behind the desk on the final word. An instant later a *whoosh* followed; not a gunshot, but something hit the wall behind him, just missing his right ear.

Hell broke loose a moment later as two black-clad figures, one behind the other, and all but invisible, stormed into the room. Josh and Ossilena dove for the backs of their legs. The surprise attack drove them to their knees and caused them to fall backward. Chelsea, with the flashlight in one hand, spotlighted the closest one and put his gun to the man's head.

"Both of you, drop your weapons."

Josh and Ossilena had both men pinned down on their backs.

Chelsea, his eyes riveted on the two black-clad assailants, barked orders. "Josh, get their weapons—Tony, go out back and check on the generator." He looked up for a second. "Jason, reach into my shirt pocket for my car keys. Bring back the cellular phone. The lines here can't be trusted yet. We need Carbolo and then Florida Power and Light."

He studied the man with the weapon stuck in his face; curiously, despite the excessive humidity, he wasn't sweating. His eyes showed no emotion. Chelsea wondered how far along the Alliance had progressed in their technique. He waited for Josh to finish frisking both men.

Josh grunted, "You were right, Joe. Pellet and dart guns, like the kind that are used to sedate animals. We were meant to be taken alive."

Chelsa had guessed correctly. But it gave him little satisfaction; many more questions needed to be answered. His thoughts were cut short as the lights came back on, along with the air-conditioning. All the computer screens lit up at once as Jason returned.

"Take the phone, Josh. Jason, you recognize these faces?"

"Never saw them before. If they're Wellington I'd have to go into the computer."

"I lay you odds that you won't find them there. Check out their wallets."

Josh, in the middle of punching in Carbolo's private number, said, "It's a waste of time. They have no IDs on them."

"So, what else is new?" Chelsea remarked dryly, then told Jason, "Get them to their feet."

"Two more for your collection, Rudy," Josh said when Carbolo picked up. He listened for a moment. "Yeah, I know. At this rate we'll all be re-retired before we can even dent their defenses." He was silent, then responded. "Breaking and entering, and attempted armed robbery—whatever."

Ossilena returned. "They didn't touch the generator. It was only a loose wire. You'll need FPL for regular service though. These guys cut the power on the pole."

Chelsea asked Ossilena to search for a pellet or dart in the wall.

Jason was acutely aware of the talents of these so-called retirees. If their ages slowed them down, they didn't show it, going about their business zealously. It was quite a contrast to the impassivity of their two, much younger, captives, whose faces wore the blank expressions of programmed robots.

The Alliance—how had Joe Chelsea described them? *An invisible cartel except for its deeds.* Now what? Jason wondered. How would Chelsea and his men proceed? He doubted they would learn anything from the two men captured. *And if by some miracle they did, how could they possibly handle it?* He heard Chelsea barking new orders at Josh, who was about to put down the cellular phone. "Get the house. Be sure the women are okay. We've angered the octopus and its tentacles are reaching for all of us."

Josh lost control for a moment. "Dammit, Joe! You knew this could happen." He then punched in his house number.

Chelsea waited to hear that all was quiet at the Novick estate, and the guards had been put on alert. Then he continued giving orders, outwardly unperturbed. "Tony, stay with Josh and wait for Carbolo's men. Jason, let's go. We have work to do."

Josh stared at him. "Joe, what the hell are you up to now!" Chelsea retrieved his car phone. "Make sure all the phones here are clean; then alert the Brenners. I'll call back as soon as I can."

"Goddammit! Joe!" Josh sputtered, but with Jason at his heels his partner had disappeared down the corridor.

31

Dave Ward came to in a small, cell-like room. "Came to" was the only way to describe it. His head was foggy, heavy, as if he'd been drugged.

Damn! The coffee on the boat!

He sat up and held his head, then swung his legs from the narrow bed. Although the effort left him dizzy, he saw that he was sitting on the edge of a hospital bed.

As he squeezed his temples, Mae leaped into memory, but she was nowhere in sight. *Damn!*

Except for the bed, the room offered only an unbroken expanse of white on white—the floor, walls, and ceiling. Fluorescent tubes behind translucent glass on the ceiling produced an uncomfortable glare.

Getting to his feet, he became aware of the white jumpsuit he was wearing. *When? When did it happen?*

And what did happen!

He pulled up a sleeve, searching for his watch; his Rolex was gone. *Part of the treatment. Disorientation. Loss of time and place.*

Ward shook his head; he couldn't let this happen. He had to stay calm, search; there must be a door. One hand scratched at his beard, the other slid along the wall, feeling for a hidden panel. He sensed unseen eyes following his every movement; human or mechanical, he was sure of it. Unable to subdue a steadily growing uneasiness, he began to sweat.

He stopped suddenly—and grabbed for the back of his neck.

There was nothing. The relief was slight; it didn't slow his heavy breathing. Anxiety for Mae increased his rage. He banged the wall with a fist.

"Dammit! Whoever you are I know you're there. Talk to me!"

Chelsea was at the wheel of his car, driving north on I-95. Jason waited a full five minutes before breaking the silence between them. "Where are we going?"

"The Lantana marina—to check out the Viking. I know Dave. No matter what happened on his boat, he would manage to leave something for us."

"And if he did, what then? What can you do against an organization that's global?"

Chelsea gave him a brief glance. "We can speculate with a few names, but we do have two identities we're sure of. Your uncle and Nestor Hobbs."

"So?" Jason retorted mockingly. "And how will that help us? You have a matching secret organization behind you?"

Chelsea lifted an eyebrow. Jason was losing his cool, using cynicism to hide a sense of futility.

He didn't speak again until they'd parked in the marina lot.

"Don't disappoint me, Stoner," he said, pointing a finger at him. "Because of Fargo, I've accepted you as a member of our so-called organization. What we're engaged in needs cool, rational heads." He made a move to open the car door, then stopped. "Don't think me a cold-hearted, insensitive man. Fargo's predicament has never left my thoughts. Just keep in mind we're doing our best for everyone involved." He shoved his door open, the abrupt movement startling a strolling sea gull into flight. "Now, let's get on with it. We have work to do."

The lounge was large, windowless, and apparently deserted; a wall of mirrors at one end magnified its size. The pastel colors of sofas and chairs enhanced the sense of quiet.

Jon Seltzmann waved Mae Warren toward a beige leather sofa. "I have to leave for a few minutes. Make yourself comfortable. If you require anything, just press the button on one of the sofa tables."

Mae gazed at him arrogantly. "Cigarettes—are they permitted here?"

He tolerated her gaze. "Sorry, there are none on the premises. Anything else . . ." There was the hint of a smile at the corner of his mouth. "Be patient, you'll be receiving familiar visitors shortly."

Familiar visitors! Now what! Dave? Others?

She caught his appraising look. Was he wondering what price she would bring on the slave market?

He left the room then, and as soon as he'd done so, Mae punched a button set into a glass-topped table behind the nearest sofa. She needed a drink.

A minute later, a statuesque blonde appeared with her order, a straight vodka. Standing, Mae sipped at the drink, going over everything that had happened.

There were no answers to the questions that crowded her mind. Four men had come aboard the Viking and forced her and Dave to go with them out to sea. She remembered having a cup of coffee on board, and the next thing she knew she was in a room, a desensitizing all-white room. Her own clothes were gone, replaced by a white jumpsuit. She had no idea of what they had done with Dave—or where he was.

Mae shook herself, attempting to stem her growing anxiety. "Damn them!" she muttered. "Men can be such bloody fools at times. You would think they'd had enough of the game-playing."

"Who brought you here?"

She spun around at the sound of the voice. It was Dave, striding into the lounge from an arched doorway. He held a finger to his lips as he approached her. Unsmiling, he placed a reassuring arm around her shoulder and whispered conspiratorially, "The place is rigged with bugs. Speak softly from now on." His eyes took her in. "Other than altering your dress code, is that all they've done to you?"

"I'm not hurting. I already did a body check; thighs, legs, arms, and even my backside." She stepped back. "I see you're in style. How come we're wearing matching outfits?"

"And why jumpsuits?" he wondered.

"Maybe they don't like to look at our legs."

The attempt at humor didn't help. Ward held up a quieting palm. "Okay. Did you meet anyone?"

"The big man himself, Jon Seltzmann."

This silenced Ward for a second. "Did our 'host' mention his plans for us?" He didn't wait for an answer. "Have you used the head here?"

Perplexed, she said, "I did. Sometime ago. Why? What are you getting at, Dave?"

"Mae, think. Was it an electric toilet?"

"Yes . . ." A light dawned in her eyes. "Electric toilets

and no windows—*We're below sea level.* We have to be on the Alliance's private island."

Ward shook his head. "Wrong. Unlike you I have to use the john every four or five hours. I've gone once and don't feel the urge right now. Which means we're not more than eight—nine hours from the mainland. My Viking couldn't make Nassau in less than twelve hours."

"Then where are we?" Mae asked. "If we don't know, how will Chelsea find us?"

Ward pondered a reply. "Our host . . . He told you nothing? Showed you nothing?"

"I was invited to lunch with him and then was promised a tour of the premises." She made a face. "Said tour, however, never took place. Instead, we descended a level to this lounge, and he told me I would be seeing familiar faces." She pouted. "So, Dave, where does this get us?"

Ward played with his beard. "Describe our host."

After she'd done so, Dave nodded. "Just checking. It was Jon Seltzmann himself."

Mae was restless. "Dave, let's cut the chatter. How do we get out of here?"

"There's an elevator in the corridor—let's try it."

It was a waste. A key was needed to open the doors.

Dave looked at her vodka. "Mae, who brought the drink?"

"A waitress. Tall, blond, and totally silent.

Ward smiled and winked. "It's time *I* met someone on the staff. Suddenly, I'm very thirsty."

"Where are we headed?" Jason asked, after ten minutes of Chelsea's driving in silence.

"Back to the Novicks' house. I want to personally check out the women's security. The way things are movin—"

The car phone interrupted. It was Carbolo, greatly disturbed.

"Hey, Captain, listen good. I'm telling you this is beginning to escalate beyond our capabilities. I just got off the phone with Novick, and he warned me not to talk. *Your* security office is bugged. How about that!

"I was trying to tell Novick that Izzy Gorham has disappeared—Don't interrupt; I'm not finished. His three friends also have disappeared. And, if that doesn't grab you, how about this. I had his three friends rechecked, and while the names and backgrounds of all three men ring true, they don't belong to Gorham's friends. I have no idea who his three friends really are."

"How about Gorham? Are you telling me he's living a lie also?"

"No. Izzy's all right. But he's the only one that checks out completely."

Jason was bewildered. He was getting only a part of the conversation. *Why all the fuss? Who was Izzy Gorham?*

"Was Gorham ever discharged from the hospital?"

"No."

"Where you calling from, Lieutenant?"

"From Gorham's apartment."

An exasperated sigh came from Chelsea. "You check for fingerprints in the apartments of his so-called friends?"

"Captain—please . . . Officially, they're not missing yet. The wait, you know, is forty-eight hours. I have a man in one apartment now—doing a favor for me. Anything else?"

The hurt tone wasn't lost on Chelsea. He sighed, but his manner wasn't contrite. "Forget the forty-eight hours; you're now looking for alleged kidnappers. You have to check out airlines, ships—"

"How do I do that without notifying my office? This whole damn venture has been going on . . . Shit! How do I explain all this undercover work to my chief? Where the hell is your friend Ward? It's time he called on his government friends."

Chelsea hesitated, wondering how to tell Carbolo that Dave was beyond offering any assistance. "Forget Ward. Do you personally know anyone in the fed? Someone you can trust—either FBI or CIA? Set up a meet. I'll do the talking."

Silence greeted the request. Then, Carbolo, almost hissing, said, "Something's happened to Ward."

Chelsea didn't get a chance to reply. They were on Federal Highway, no more than five minutes from Josh's estate when two motor bikers from the sheriff's office pulled alongside the Ciera. One of them motioned Chelsea to the curb.

Chelsea nodded, but left the car phone open. "Rudy, something's going down. Two of your bikers are stopping me on Federal for no apparent reason. I'm keeping the line open. Keep your mouth shut, and your ears tuned." To Jason he said, "I'll do all the talking. Got it?"

Jason could only nod. He had no idea what confrontation Chelsea was expecting—or contemplating.

Both bikers wore helmets, their eyes hidden behind dark glasses. Chelsea slowed the car but didn't stop until he pulled into a shopping plaza.

As soon as the car was parked one of the bikers dropped to the rear; the other opened the back door and slid inside. Chelsea felt a gun at his neck. The movement was well hidden from prying eyes but the caution was unnecessary. The shopping center was new, with only half of its stores rented.

A command from the biker kept Jason from making any move. "Eyes front, lock your hands behind your head. You—" His revolver nudged Chelsea. "You follow behind the officer up front when he gets through tying my bike to your rear bumper."

"Can I see some ID?" Chelsea asked.

"My ID is pressing against your neck. Just follow orders."

Jason almost smiled, his private anxieties put on hold for a moment. The entire routine was like watching a bit of theatre. Even Chelsea, who had stiffened under the insistent weapon, seemed to be taking it in stride. Was it something preternatural—an atavistic trait—or something born of being a policeman? He wondered what was drifting through Chelsea's mind—and whether he was still carrying his police special.

As if reading Jason's mind, the gunman pressed harder with his silencer-equipped revolver, and with his other hand reached over Chelsea's shoulder to check for a hidden weapon.

The shoulder holster was empty.

To Jason he muttered menacingly, "Open the dash compartment slowly. Using two fingers, remove the stashed weapon and, without turning around, hand it to me over your shoulder."

Jason caught Chelsea's eye movement, then noted his hand on the gear shift. The engine was still running, on idle. Obeying the biker's command, Jason removed the S&W .38 and held it up, above his right shoulder.

"Smart—smart. Forget any tricks. Just hand it back."

Jason twisted slightly to reach back—and that was the moment Chelsea wanted.

Within a single heartbeat he had the shift in first gear and jammed his foot on the gas pedal. The car shot forward, propelling the gunman backward; his weapon fired wildly, the shot puncturing the ceiling. Chelsea took that moment to jam the brakes, then shoved the car into reverse, pitching the man forward, totally out of control, along with the biker trying to tie up to their rear bumper. There was no mistaking the tortured cry from behind the car.

Chelsea halted the car, shouting at Jason. "Get this joker's weapon. I'm going for the other guy."

Jason's response was instant. Twisting in his seat, he got on his knees and leaned over the backrest. His right hand jammed the S&W into the chest of the dazed but uninjured biker. Then, using his left hand, he tore the man's weapon from his grip in a single motion. A 9mm Beretta with a new type of silencer—no more than an inch and a half in length. Definitely not standard issue for law enforcement officers.

The uniformed man, still wearing dark glasses, compressed his lips but, curiously, showed no anger. Like the three men at Spanish River Park, he was docile, accepting defeat without a struggle.

A flaw in the creating of the—the—The what?

Jason peered through the rear window, saw Chelsea kneeling, assessing the damage caused by the car's abrupt shift into reverse. He wondered whether the biker had been killed or merely hurt. He was also aware that it didn't faze him one way or the other.

His train of thought was interrupted by agitated sounds coming from the phone on the console beside him. *Carbolo.* With his eyes on the subdued biker, Jason lifted the phone.

"It's Jason, Lieutenant. Jason Stoner."

"Where's the captain? What the hell's going on there?"

"You heard?"

"Yeah, I heard. The screeching of rubber tires and—I don't know what else. Where are you?"

"Hold on. Chelsea's back."

The parking lot was dark and almost totally deserted. The incident had gone unnoticed. Either that, or no one wanted to get involved. Chelsea's gaze focused on their captive in the rear seat.

"Dammit! Remove your helmet and dark glasses." The "officer" complied with a mechanical gesture. Chelsea took the phone from Jason without entering the car.

Jason stared at the biker, then took the glasses from him. It was dark out. Why the dark glasses? Infrared?"

The man remained silent, and it was too dark to read his expression. If he was worried about his cohort, he gave no indication of it.

"There's two of them," Chelsea said. "One dead. No ID on the victim. The live one won't have any either. Get someone down here in a hurry to clean up. I'm taking off as soon as your men show. Give them instructions to that effect. I'll bring you up to date when we meet."

He got behind the wheel and punched in Novick's house number, waiting out fifteen rings before slamming the phone down in anger. There had been two men on house security, besides Alex, who had been expected there.

Without dwelling on the implications, Chelsea punched in Noah Brenner's home number. It was answered on the fourth ring.

"It's Chelsea, Noah. I need a big favor. Novick's home phone doesn't answer. You and Aaron are in position to beat me there. Go in slow. We've been assaulted three times today already. Be on the alert for anything out of the ordinary. I'll see you and clarify all the complications cropping up. Take care and—thanks."

Jason waited long seconds of silence, the S&W still trained on their captive. He said finally, "We wait—without questioning this man?"

"We wait for the lieutenant's men. Questioning the culprit"—Chelsea made a face; he detested the overworked "culprit" and "alleged," and wished someone would come up with a new choice of words—"would be a waste of time.

Look at him. He's become a zombie. Close examination will likely reveal an injury at the nape of the neck."

Whether to satisfy Jason or himself, he got out of the car to climb into the rear seat. Without protest the prisoner allowed him to tilt his head forward for examination.

Chelsea held up two fingers for Jason to observe. *Blood.* He extracted a tissue from a pack stashed in the netting clipped to the back of the front seat.

"I doubt interrogation will accomplish anything. The same neck surgery as the others—and my shenanigans probably ruined him. Perhaps for life."

"You can't blame yourself for this man's condition."

Chelsea waved a palm in front of the man's eyes. There was no response other than a blink. He cocked his head, as if struggling to remember something.

"His condition!" Chelsea remarked tartly. "No. Merely the failure to counteract it."

"You can't be expected to—"

"Expected? I was warned it was a can of worms in the very beginning. But I was the smart one, the man of indomitable will, the man who refused to retire from the ranks, the man who—" Approaching police sirens silenced him.

32

Ward had ordered a Scotch and water from the attendant. In less than three minutes the woman returned with his drink on a sterling silver salver and set it down on the glass-topped coffee table. Her face expressionless, she asked, "Will that be all, sir?"

"No," Ward said, instantly getting behind her and twisting her arm in a hammerlock. "What we'd like is some information from you. Simply put: Where are we—and how do we leave these premises?"

The woman's bland expression didn't change. She made no effort to break Ward's hold on her. "I'm sorry, sir. It's not possible for me to honor your request."

Ward yanked her arm up farther behind her back. If she felt any pain she gave no hint of it; her expression remained constant, her eyes distinct, as if nothing were happening to her.

Ward's left arm was around her neck, his right was shoving her arm up higher. "Christ!" he exploded, "Don't you give a damn? I'm ready to break off your arm."

"Sorry, sir," the blonde said calmly, without feeling. "If you must, you must. I cannot prevent you."

"Dave . . ." Mae muttered protestingly. "You can't . . ."

"Mae, stay out of it. Can't you see she doesn't feel a thing? I've got her arm up to her shoulderblade and she's still standing flat-footed." He released his hold and waved a dismissal. As she left, Ward took note of the archway she used.

Ward left his drink untouched. Mae folded her arms across her chest. "What now, Dave? How do we combat such people? No feeling, no pain. What are they? What's been done to them? How is it possible? I thought we were just dealing with memory alteration. What did we just witness?"

Ward, ruminating, merely waved a hand.

After a full minute had elapsed, he said, "I'm not an expert, but Joe and I have been doing some reading on memory control. What we came up with doesn't have anything to do with what just took place—but I can speculate on it.

"A hippocampus is one of the two curved ridges on each lateral ventricle of the brain." He noted Mae's frown. "Please bear with me. The subject is as new to me as it is to you.

"The hippocampus is crucial to memory, because the brain cells within it are rich in a particular molecule called the NMDA Receptor. Don't ask me to explain how it works. All we learned was that this receptor accepts memories and encodes them for recall. Should anything interfere with the receptor, the memories already within the brain cannot be accessed."

"And they've found a way to put in new memories that possibly have no reference to the past," Mae remarked.

"It's not as simple as that. Based on what we just saw, I

now believe they've progressed beyond that. I think they've discovered how to erase any memory of pain, in effect deleting the ability to feel."

"My God! You're implying that woman could have been in pain, but couldn't be aware of it."

"That's about it. You saw her. She made no struggle."

Mae regarded Ward closely. "You think we could be on their agenda of victims."

He made a face. "Don't think evil thoughts. Think instead of getting out of here. That passage the woman took—was that how you came in?"

"I came down from the floor above, and—" Ward had an ear cocked. "What are you listening to?"

"The silence. I find it strange. A big room—in a seemingly large building—and we meet or hear no one outside of Seltzmann and the woman who served our drinks. It's as if the place were deserted, which I doubt. More likely, we're being watched and studied to see how we perform."

"So, why are we waiting?" Mae whispered impatiently.

"Right. For what it's worth let's try the first archway on your left. It's the one used by our barmaid."

Despite the air-conditioning in the car, both Chelsea and Jason had removed their jackets. For the past ten minutes they had shared an oppressive silence. Chelsea, absorbed in thought, did not invite conversation.

The Ciera approached Novick's driveway in a circuitous manner. If the Brenners had arrived, their van was well concealed. Their former occupations had served them in good stead.

Chelsea turned off his headlamps and, at almost an idling pace, pulled off the driveway to ease through a stand of eucalyptus and palm trees. He parked adjacent to the sea wall on a dark edge of the property. The rear of the mansion was about fifty yards distant, the screened terrace visible under a dim light.

Jason, about to open his door, was stayed by Chelsea.

"First, observe—then listen. "*Novick's Ark* is not in its mooring."

A silent ten seconds elapsed, then two shadowy figures were seen moving stealthily across the terrace. The door slowly opened; a gun in the classic two-handed grip pointed outward, swinging from left to right, seeking.

Chelsea had his .38 out, but he didn't stir.

Both he and Jason relaxed when they saw Noah Brenner behind the gun. But the relief was short-lived.

"Damn!" Chelsea exploded. "It means we're all too late. The house must be empty." He shouted to Noah, alerting him to their presence before opening the car door. Noah, his face grim, waved recognition.

"No one?" he asked Noah as Aaron Brenner joined them.

Aaron answered. "There're two dead men inside. I think they were part of your security detail. We found one body on the terrace, the other just off the front foyer." His eyes cast down, he added, "Sorry, Chelsea. We've been through the house and can't find a clue to what has happened."

"Jesus!" Jason muttered. "It's never-ending. How do we beat these odds?" He caught Chelsea glaring at him and was taken momentarily aback. "Well, how do we! They always have something waiting, whittling us down one by one."

Chelsea's eyes blazed. "The first thing you do is get Novick on the phone and have him contact the Coast Guard. The *Ark* can't be more than an hour on the water. Get moving. Use the car phone."

Chelsea spun on the Brenners. "There were three women, my wife, Ellen, Josh's Cindy, and the Fargo woman. Did you check the IDs on the men? Or did you just assume they're my security people?"

Noah eyed him carefully. The man had the right to feel angry. "We didn't take the time to check. It was obvious that they were dead." Chelsea said nothing, thinking, *Alex should have been here, beside the two other men. Was he taken also?* And then with added distress, he remembered that one of the men had a family.

"You have to notify the authorities," Aaron said. "With the body count growing, there's no way we can handle it by ourselves."

Seconds of silence passed before Chelsea said, "Let's check out the dock before calling Carbolo."

Aaron glanced at Noah, who shrugged. It was obvious that both thought it a waste of time. Their opponents had survived for decades; they weren't in the habit of making errors. Chelsea's two—supposedly experienced—security men had been taken out with little trouble; there had been no sign of a struggle elsewhere in the house.

The dock was clean; not a scrap of paper. Even the canal was free of detritus. Chelsea turned to a phone box attached to a wooden post. He punched in Carbolo's car phone.

There was no answer. The lieutenant was either at the parking lot with the bogus officers—or with Josh at the office. With a heavy heart, Chelsea punched in the office number. Neither of the Brenners said anything, but their eyes never stopped scanning the grounds. Standing on the dock, under lights at five-foot intervals, they were in plain sight of anyone who might be watching.

At the sound of Chelsea's voice, Josh burst forth venomously. "What the hell have you done, Joe! Now, what do we do? Jesus! I told you I was too old for this shit!"

Chelsea mopped his sweaty brow with a large handkerchief extracted from his back pocket. A swarm of mosquitoes buzzed about his head. He took in Josh's anger and waited for the tirade to subside. He couldn't debate the issue; he, Chelsea, hadn't foreseen the particular dangers associated with the "case of his retirement."

"Josh, this is no time for spreading blame. In any case I accept the responsibility."

"Big deal! So what! How does that get our women back? God Almighty! It's my own damn fault for letting you talk me into following your drummer."

Carbolo's voice cut in, apparently having grabbed an extension. "We call in the FeeBees, Chelsea. There's no other recourse now. We don't have the capacity to handle this situation. It's gotten too messy."

Chelsea's eyes were closed beneath the handkerchief. He stifled a choking sensation in his throat, then forced himself to take a deep breath.

"Rudy, before calling in the feds, let's recheck that warehouse you looked into; the one where Fargo might have been detained."

"What for? It's a waste of time. There was nothing there of any consequence."

Chelsea blew air from between his teeth. "Humor me. Call it a hunch—or whatever. I feel we missed something. If it's a fool's errand—okay, I'll go along with calling in the troops. I have more at stake than you do." He held his breath a second. "Josh, you still on? Did you get the Coast Guard?"

Joe heard nothing for a couple of beats.

"Yeah. For what it's worth. They'll be looking."

"Josh . . ." Chelsea fell silent, unable to speak.

"Forget it, Joe. I said my piece. I understand you—I just don't understand myself for listening. Now, what have you got in mind? What are you really expecting to get out of that warehouse?"

"I don't know. But we must have missed something. No one can completely cover up an operation that's been going on for who knows how long. That includes Rodgers—he's no superbrain. We do know the place has had only a single owner for years; therefore it can't be a new base for him."

"The place is foreign-owned—nothing matching anything on our computer sheets. You talking gut hunch?"

"Humor me. Wait a bit before pulling in outside help?"

Jason stood at the edge of the sea wall, close to the dock where the *Ark* usually tied up. He observed Chelsea in the shadowy light cast by the ground lamps. He was thinking the man was again invulnerable, unable to concede defeat, no matter the odds against him. Was it a benign character trait—or a perverse obstinacy?

A power boat started up across the canal, its engine drowning out Chelsea's conversation with Carbolo. He was ready to hang up, but took additional seconds to mention that two more victims had to be taken care of. He held the phone away from his ear, then hung up, obviously to escape Carbolo's vociferous response.

All eyes followed the small cruiser until it left the area, its ever-widening wake slapping against the sea wall. Satisfied it posed no additional problem, Noah said, "We go to the warehouse?"

"First we look at the men inside."

Two hours earlier Alex had sensed something wrong as soon as his Ford entered the Novicks' driveway. There should have been a security man at the entrance gate. Switching his headlamps off, he pulled over just beyond the open gate and got out of the car. From his trunk he took out a small sack and withdrew his gun. The 9mm Beretta, with silencer attached, already had a full clip in it. He held the weapon, facing up, as he moved stealthily across the damp grass, toward the house.

A light was on over the front door; the door ajar sent

danger signals. He stood without moving, behind a tall palm, his ears straining for alien sounds.

He waited out a full minute, then heard a roaring from the rear of the estate—a power boat starting its engines. Without further thought, he shot out the lamp over the door and plunged forward.

He came through the doorway, crouching, and then tumbling across the foyer floor and coming to his feet with his gun hand outstretched, prepared for whatever awaited him.

He froze in position, spying a figure lying on the floor, unmoving. The foyer lights were out but a dim glow from an adjoining room offered enough illumination to see it was a body sprawled in a pool of blood. Alex's nose twitched with the familiar, malodorous smell of death. He had seen enough bodies to recognize a lifeless one. Nonetheless he bent over, feeling for the carotid artery. He turned the body over and recognized Owens, a man who'd come on the job only three weeks before himself. Owens' chest was a bloody mess. Alex swore under his breath; *Owens had left Nam for this.*

As Alex straightened, holding a handkerchief to his nose, he could see another body, in the living room. "Damn!" he muttered sourly. It took only seconds to verify that it was Brent, his throat slashed. He had been hired along with Owens. Both had spent a tour in Nam, and were experienced at responding to sudden deadly assaults.

For all the good it did them.

Alex stared at the pool of blood staining the carpet, mesmerized by the memories it recalled. *So much blood—why was it spilled?*

He shook himself, breaking out of his stupor, and stepped back into the foyer. Moving in a half-crouch, with his gun ready for instant targeting, he inspected each downstairs room before trying the staircase.

Nothing but white noise—an empty house. Empty at least, of living beings, he thought somberly.

He took the stairs, went through each of the seven rooms—and found nothing. There were no signs of struggle. The women were gone, taken, abducted. There had to have been at least three men to do the job. Fewer than three, Owens and Brent could have handled.

He found a hall phone and covered it with a sleeve before dialing. Chelsea's car phone refused to answer. He tried the Novick Security office—and was told by a taped voice the number was temporarily out of order.

Speculating on his next move, he heard a boat rev its engines and come to a full roar. He took off for the rear of the house and from the screened terrace saw *Novick's Ark* steaming out of the canal.

He muttered a curse, realizing they had been there all the time. He had his gun out, but the target was vanishing, most likely heading for the Boca inlet. Once out to sea . . .

He raced through the house, got into his car, and shot out the driveway. He could still make the marina on the Intracoastal and charter a speedboat by the time the *Ark* reached the inlet.

The motor yacht was through the inlet, heading into open water when he got to the marina. He could see none of its crew or "guests."

Ten minutes were wasted in argument because of the late hour for rental. His ID and credit card from Novick Security finally did the convincing. A 31-foot Tiara, an open power boat with twin 350 Crusaders was available. There was a delay while its tank was topped.

Alex carried his bag from the car, most of its contents supplied days earlier by the Brenner brothers. By the time he hit the swells in the channel, the lights on the *Ark* were barely visible. Reaching into his bag of tricks, he pulled out a pair of odd-shaped binoculars; the lenses protruded and above the nosepiece a stem leaned forward. The lenses were nightscopes and the protruding nose guard was a microphonic ear, capable of picking up sound from a distance of 150 yards.

Doing better than thirty knots, the Tiara crept to within 500 yards of the *Ark,* at which point Alex turned off running lights and cut down on his speed. He made no attempt to overtake them; his purpose was merely to follow and discover their course. *Unless they were heading for the Caribbean.*

They were about ten miles out to sea when his quarry slowed their speed. Alex followed suit, searching with his glasses for the reason. Turning his head and aiming the microphonic ear, he caught the sound of another boat. In minutes a cruiser, at least an eighty-footer, pulled alongside the port beam of the *Ark*, which had come to almost a dead halt.

The Tiara crept forward until Alex was in range to hear voices. "Get the women out, we . . ." The voices faded in and out as the Tiara was shunted out of position by the swells of the sea.

Alex got the drift of their conversation: All on board the *Ark* were switching boats. He watched helplessly as the three women were helped across a swaying rope gangplank. Three men followed after them and pulled the gangplank aboard. Running abeam at about five knots, the eighty-footer suddenly swung to starboard and deserted the *Ark*.

Bewildered only briefly, Alex understood what was happening. In moments the *Ark*, its bilge plugs removed, would list. It would sink without a trace, its cushions and all floatables tied down or locked away. It was the preferable solution; demolition would have left debris.

Alex was left no choice; the eighty-footer's destination had become the first priority. He now had to follow the motor yacht as best he could, hoping the ship's crew was overconfident enough to be neglectful of their detection equipment.

Caribbean? He wondered, checking his gas; he would lose them. He was hoping for something closer.

He lay farther back, not tempting fate, keeping them in sight with his nightscope. The yacht's swing to starboard continued into a 180-degree turn, then went another 90 degrees. *West? Palm Beach?*

Trailing five hundred yards astern, his running lights off, Alex looked back. The *Ark*, all lights out, was already listing to port. Without his glasses, the doomed cruiser would be invisible. He had no trouble keeping the eighty-footer in sight.

Despite the heavy swells, the Tiara handled well and Alex had time to contemplate the meaning of his surveillance. When he had been taken on by Novick's firm, he'd assumed the job would be simple security, watchman or something similar. Engaged now in covert action, he wondered why he was doing it.

With mixed emotions he thought of Chelsea. The older man was like a shining knight with a cause to follow. Nam hadn't had any causes—if any existed, they'd been well disguised. It was now time to follow the shining knight. And, of course, there was now just cause, despite the uneven odds.

Ruminating, he wondered why Chelsea hadn't asked for outside help. It would be nice to know there was backup somewhere.

* * *

Chelsea stood up after examining both bodies. "Someone was here—" he said, "after they were killed."

The Brenners made no comment. "How do you know that?" Jason asked, holding a handkerchief to his nose.

"The blood coagulated there. Brent's body's here and there's no blood . . ." He paused. "Alex must have been here."

Chelsea got Josh on his cellular phone. "Did Alex call in?"

"No—he might have tried, when the phone lines were down. They only just came back on. You got something, Joe?"

"No, but Alex might be onto something. I see signs of his having been here. We're going to the warehouse. I'll have the cellular with me. Let me know when Alex calls in."

Chelsea hung up and turned to Jason. "Stay here until the police arrive."

Jason stiffened. "Like hell! I'm not a watchdog. I'm not a puppet on a string to dangle as you please. If I'm in your way, just say so. I'll go in alone." He skirted the body and headed for the front door.

Chelsea looked at the Brenners. The brothers shrugged; this was Chelsea's problem. He shouted across the foyer. "Where do you think you're going?"

Jason turned at the door. "Back to my motel, to pick up my car. Then I'm going to do what I should have done earlier: confront Nestor Hobbs. I have to know the truth about my uncle's alleged connection with the Alliance."

"And you expect that to bring you closer to Fargo?"

"If my uncle is part of the conspiracy—as you insist he is—it might be possible for me to deal with him."

Chelsea sighed audibly. "Jason, you can bet on your motel room being under surveillance. Don't play into their hands." He waited as Jason stood, undecided. "In due time we'll get to Nestor Hobbs. Just hang in with us."

Jason appeared confused. "How can you be so calm? Your wife, your partner's wife—not to mention your friends—all taken, and you move at a snail's pace."

Chelsea strode across the foyer and confronted Jason. "You listen to me, young man. I thought I had made my position clear earlier. My family's welfare has always been foremost in my mind, but I will not be spooked into doing something rash. Nestor Hobbs can wait. We're going to fine-comb that warehouse again."

Jason winced. "Why bother, when they're probably all at the Founding Fathers Resort."

"We don't know that. And I don't believe it. That place is just too convenient to accept. Especially now, when they know it's suspect."

Jason weakened visibly. "So, what's the purpose of the fortified island?"

"Speculating, I'd say privacy. For the meetings of their clientele, their invisible cartel. Where better in the world could they be so protected?"

"So we go to the warehouse—then what?" Jason continued sardonically. "You search for missed clues, and should we find one, we then surround the Alliance and their invisible army with our—what is it? The four of us—plus perhaps a dozen of your security men, if you have that many."

Chelsea's eyes narrowed. "I'm not trying to conquer an army. Let's get that straight. I want to know who their leader is." He turned toward the Brenners. "Are we agreed on that?"

"As far as we can take it," Noah said. Aaron merely nodded, abstractedly studying the pool of blood, and thinking: They'll never get the stain out of the limestone floor.

"Jason?"

Jason nodded, grudgingly. "Yeah, at least until we can apprehend their so-called leader."

Chelsea didn't respond. What had he achieved with his rah-rah oratory? Was he only fooling himself?

He shook his head. "Carbolo will be annoyed when he finds no one here, but let's go." To Noah he said, "Jason will be with me. You follow in your van. You know where it is if you lose us."

They drove east to the Old Dixie Highway, then turned left. Chelsea had retrieved his Dunhill briar from the car's ashtray and had clamped it in his mouth. He let it remain unfilled. Traffic was light, fortunately.

Chelsea swung in toward the railroad tracks and then crossed over. The Brenner brothers' van was seconds behind him, but the gravel-surfaced driveway prevented a silent approach. Except for the halogen lamps brightening the walls of the warehouse, the parking lot was dark. Both vehicles found spaces away from the building.

By the time Noah had unlocked the office door Aaron had supplied each man with a flashlight. No one drew a weapon until after entering.

It only took ten minutes to determine that the place, as described by Carbolo, had been abandoned. Several empty, dust-laden packing cases were scattered about haphazardly.

After another unfruitful ten minutes, Noah remarked, "There's nothing here but an empty office and a warehouse full of empty crates. What did you expect to find?"

"How about the room where the Fargo woman was detained?" Chelsea swung his flash along a row of cases piled to the ceiling.

Jason's eyes strayed to the forklift he had noticed when he'd entered the warehouse. "Let's see if this baby starts."

The machine burped twice, causing a flurry of dust before

settling into a steady run. So much for the warehouse being abandoned, he thought. He carefully tested different handles to learn its operation, then moved the heavy equipment toward the cases now illuminated by everyone's flashlights. It took some minutes for the row of crates to be moved away from the wall. Clouds of dust forced everyone to cover their faces with handkerchiefs and the lack of air conditioning added to their discomfort. The dust also made them wonder whether they had the correct building.

The top fifteen feet of piled crates had been removed with another fifteen to go when Chelsea turned to Noah.

"Could I be wrong about this place? With all this dust the Fargo woman couldn't have been confined here less than a week ago."

"Dust can be created. It's a bit far-out, but I knew a film-maker in Israel who produced clouds of dust for a movie scene."

Chelsea didn't bother responding. Nothing was beyond imagining when dealing with their invisible adversary. The physical discomfort of dust stirring stale air added a growing feeling of hopelessness.

Where could he go from here? He had taken on the leadership, had forced an endorsement of it from all. Now where was he to take them? *Those that were left!*

Aaron suddenly gave a shout, and aimed his flashlight at a section of exposed wall.

"There's the top of a door showing!"

Chelsea's diminished resolve was forgotten. He barked at Jason. "Get that contraption moving. We don't have all night."

Jason, sweating, absorbed in maneuvering the lumbering machine, grunted an affirmative. The forklift's motor drowned out all sound from outside.

*   *   *

Outside the building, aware of the two vehicles parked there, two Dodge Caravans slowly entered the lot, their headlamps out. From the lead van Calvin Rodgers recognized Chelsea's Ciera. His lips twisted in an admiring smile. "I'll give him that much. The man is either a step behind or one ahead of us at all times. Our technicians will love to have the retired cop in the laboratory."

The driver's face was devoid of expression. "What's our next step?" He asked solemnly, studying the van adjacent to the Ciera. "We don't know their strength."

Rodgers spoke without hesitation. "Drive slowly around to the back, to the extension. The sleeping gas is still in operation. Our intruders need only to break into the hidden room to activate it. Now let's be sure the rear is clean."

One block over, where the Old Dixie Highway crossed over the road leading east and west, the area was a breeding ground for drug dealers. No matter the arrests, new dealers were always in the background ready to take up any slack. Almost all of the retail shops in the neighborhood had iron-barred windows and doors. In the late-night hours buyers could drive by and pick up a bag of coke without getting out of their car.

Rodgers, satisfied that no cokeheads were in the vicinity, withdrew a set of keys to open a graffiti-scarred steel door. A number of scratches gave evidence of attempted, unsuccessful break-ins. The door was a two-inch-thick steel barrier requiring three separate keys to unlock it.

He pushed open the door to a twelve-by-twelve windowless room. Except for a vague hum from an air vent the room was silent and dark. Entering alone, he shoved the door closed behind him, automatically signaling all equipment disturbed in the room to resume operation. Metal cylinders resembling scuba tanks lined part of one wall; electronic equipment crowded the rest.

Rodgers was aware that no sound was coming from the cylinders. He sat down before what looked like a hi-fi amplifier and lifted a pair of headphones to his ears. The grinding sound of the forklift was unmistakable. Rodgers could almost visualize them trying to break into the inner office. His eyes went to the cylinders; their sudden operation would tell him they had succeeded. He waited; time was on his side.

Noah tried unsuccessfully to unlock the door until Chelsea pulled at his arm. "We're wasting time. Let Jason ram the door." He signaled Jason. "Ram the fork end into the lock—the door opens in." He got a nod.

When one of the huge tines broke through, Chelsea didn't realize they'd walked into a trap until seconds later. The hissing sound suggested leaking air pressure for some unknown reason, but . . . He was sinking to his knees, unable to help himself or warn the others. "Damn!" he growled. "The room was rigged . . . Jas . . ."

33

Chelsea coughed, and his eyelids flickered. Someone had forced him into a sitting position on a cordovan sofa. He had trouble keeping his eyes open, and when he tried focusing he couldn't believe what he was seeing.

Behind an enormous oaken desk, seated in a high-backed leather-upholstered chair, was Izzy Gorham. A lazy smile met Chelsea's incredulous stare.

Chelsea spoke falteringly. "You? Izzy?" He tried shaking the cobwebs from his brain. "No," he managed. "I'm hallucinating."

Gorham's finger smoothed one unruly gray eyebrow. "No, Captain, there's nothing wrong with your vision. If you're up to it, explanations are in order. I leave it to you."

Looking around the office, Chelsea became aware of Gorham's three associates, supposedly missing: the two doctors, Feldman and Malcolm, and Max Litvinoff. All three stood just behind Gorham, as if waiting in attendance. Two heavily muscled white-jacketed men—one at each of the two entrances into the office—stood guard.

"Where are my friends?" Chelsea managed, gathering his thoughts.

"The Brenner brothers were released two hours ago on the mainland—with a warning to forget about going to the police. Both men have families to consider; it would be foolish to believe they could be protected."

"What about Jason Stoner? He's one of you—also?"

"Unfortunately, no." Gorham waved an impatient hand. "Young Stoner is unimportant now. He will be with the rest of your associates—and taken care of properly. In due time . . ."

Chelsea's eyes glared. "My family and friends—what have you done to them?" He started to push himself to his feet but was instantly restrained by someone behind him he hadn't been aware of.

"Patience, my dear captain. I said explanations would be in order when you were ready to listen."

Chelsea wiped his face with his hand. *Izzy Gorham!* It was beyond imagining. "Okay," he said. "Let's have it." Gorham seemed only too eager to talk. Why, Chelsea couldn't even begin to guess. It wasn't gloating; that seemed out of character. Chelsea gave his Rolex an imperceptible glance. Only three hours had passed since the break-in. *Which meant what? He was—or had been—on a boat?* With two fingers he rubbed his forehead, as if trying to soothe a headache. No, he decided, he wasn't on a boat. The room was too businesslike, too silent—and had no portholes. He looked up to catch Izzy Gorham observing him. Chelsea kept silent, forcing Gorham to take the initiative.

"Captain Chelsea, it's obvious you're trying to unravel the enigma of Izzy Gorham. Yet you ask no questions."

Chelsea leaned back, playing it cool, working an old routine. "Very well. I see a perfect double for Izzy Gorham.

But you forgot his head injury. Who are you really?" The man's eyes blinked.

"Very astute of you to believe so, but you are wrong in your assumption. Forgive me for not standing to take a bow, but I am the real Izzy Gorham."

Chelsea's eyes narrowed. It didn't make sense. "Are you telling me the attack on your person and the hospital layup was all an extraordinary scam?"

"Not quite." The man behind the desk chuckled. Not a habit of the Gorham that Chelsea had met. "My own staff attended my needs. What you fail to comprehend as yet is that I simply adopted Izzy Gorham's body for my temporary use."

"Who is *I?*"

This brought another unfamiliar chuckle. "Come, come, Captain. Surely you've figured it out. *I'm Dr. Emil Seltzer.*"

Chelsea was stunned. It took a few seconds for him to gather his thoughts. "Seltzer died in . . . in 1953, I believe."

"You've done your homework. But not completely. My body perished—but not before my memory banks with all their knowledge were installed in a new host."

Chelsea's mind was reeling. "Are you telling me Seltzer's brain was transferred to another person successfully?"

"No, I am not. That skill has not yet been acquired. In due time, perhaps. Pay attention, Captain. My work has always been in the field of retaining, restoring, and fostering new memory banks."

Chelsea looked incredulous. This was science fiction, not reality. "You're confessing to me that Izzy Gorham's body and brain now hold both Seltzer's and Gorham's memories and knowledge, to direct in whatever manner you choose?"

"Quite correct, Captain."

"If Seltzer . . . Your body expired in 1953—where

were you until now?" This brought a smile. The pupil was asking the right question. Chelsea's expression gave nothing back.

"I have had a previous host. Sadly, his body aged rapidly under the strain. I will have to update more often to avoid that."

"Gorham's body is already seventy-odd years old. Why was he chosen over a younger man?"

Seltzer-Gorham sighed deeply. "An unavoidable step. I was deteriorating too rapidly. My technicians, after an emergency search, selected Gorham for temporary abode. He had been under observation for more than two months. We couldn't wait any longer. Although elderly, he was in good physical shape."

Chelsea still found it difficult to accept. "With whom am I dealing now? I see Gorham—I hear Gorham's voice. Why isn't Izzy in control as himself instead of you as Seltzer?"

Gorham's eyebrows lifted. "A matter of will power. I as Seltzer will always be the controller of the host pod." He sat back, visibly tiring. "If that is all . . ."

Chelsea chewed on his lip. "If, as you stated, the use of Gorham's body is merely a temporary measure—" He left it unfinished, sorry he'd voiced his suspicions.

"Yes, my dear captain, I believe you now understand me fully." He lifted a finger to signal one of the white-jacketed attendants.

Chelsea took that moment to try breaking through to the real Gorham.

"IZZY!" he shouted, leaping to his feet before he could be stopped. One of the orderlies instantly darted in front of him. The man behind Chelsea gripped his arms in a viselike hold.

Chelsea continued to shout. "Izzy, don't accept Seltzer! He was a Nazi!"

The seated figure, attempting to rise, froze, then fell back. His eyes stared wildly and a grunt escaped him, angry and belligerent. A noise that came from Izzy, not Seltzer.

The three men known to Chelsea as Gorham's friends leaped to his side, visibly concerned; one took his pulse; another peered into his eyes. The man's anger faded abruptly, but the face had become ugly, vicious, totally out of character for Izzy Gorham. Seltzer-Gorham fell back into the chair while his friends attended him. The white-jacketed muscle man forced Chelsea back onto the sofa. Cooperative, he smiled affably, satisfied he had discovered a weak link in an old chain, and also that Izzy's three friends, by their actions, were in truth Seltzer's physicians.

The doctors stepped back. The one Chelsea remembered as Dr. Feldman whispered in Gorham's ear. He got a reluctant nod in return. Gorham-Seltzer signaled to his orderlies.

It was then that Chelsea noted the wheelchair in the far corner of the room. One of the orderlies retrieved it and brought it to the side of the desk. His twin lifted Gorham's figure from the high-backed chair and sat him gently into the wheelchair.

Chelsea's eyes narrowed. Yet another weakness. There was a sudden urge to taunt the egotistical scientist, pierce his vanity. He considered his next words carefully.

"Seltzer, you're a fraud. Izzy Gorham had perfect use of his limbs."

Seltzer-Gorham grunted, then snarled. "In the body of my previous host I was an arthritic cripple for five years. And because of that host's knowledge I had lost the memory of walking. In time the new host will rectify that handicap. Until such time I can't allow Gorham's memory to be the stronger influence. Now—"

He was interrupted by a door opening. A younger man

entered, and Chelsea immediately recognized that the leading intelligence of the illicit cartel had appeared. The man eyed the doctors, and one, Malcolm, nodded toward Seltzer.

Somehow, Chelsea speculated, Malcolm had summoned the younger man. It was either that or the room had a hidden camera. It was likely the room was monitored: Seltzer was talking too much to be trusted. *A trait or failing—inherited from Gorham?*

The latest entry must be Jon Seltzmann, Seltzer's son. With his thatch of wavy, sand-colored hair and blue eyes set in an oval face, he bore no resemblance to Gorham, but that was to be expected.

Seltzmann glared at his father's host. *The transference had been too hasty.* But for the emergency, the two-month surveillance of Gorham would have been extended to six. He was unable to summon the tenderness he usually felt only for his father. He couldn't yet accept his new body. He pursed his lips; then, suppressing all emotion, he turned to Chelsea. He observed him a few seconds without belligerency.

"You've been quite an adversary, Captain Chelsea."

Chelsea met his gaze. "Is that meant to be flattery?"

The blue eyes glinted. "You should consider it so. You and your cohorts are the first ever to intrude on our privacy."

Like father, like son—egomaniacs, Chelsea thought, and was suddenly tired of the verbal game-playing. "Where is my wife?"

"Safe, I assure you. In a few minutes you will all meet." He lifted a hand, indicating that Seltzer-Gorham be removed. Malcolm, Feldman, and Litvinoff followed the wheelchair out of the room. One orderly remained behind with Seltzmann and Chelsea.

Chelsea fought to suppress a gnawing impatience. No sounds could be heard from outside the room when the door was opened.

Where was he? The Founding Fathers fortress? Three hours was more than adequate for making the trip by air.

Totally in command, Seltzmann settled behind the desk, pulled open a drawer, and took out a miniature television set. Closed-circuit, Chelsea guessed. He watched Seltzmann play with some buttons, wondering what he was up to.

To all appearances, Jon Seltzmann was normal. Some women might even find him attractive, Chelsea decided begrudgingly. There was no outward sign by which one could judge him an evil man.

Chelsea rose from the sofa, waving back the orderly who had started forward. "Am I permitted to stretch my legs?"

Seltzmann pointed a finger admonishingly. "As long as you behave."

Chelsea snorted derisively, muttering silently: *The young snot!*

The room was roughly fifteen feet square, its walnut-paneled walls bare of bookshelves or pictures, offering no clue to its location or why it existed. Chelsea could find no evidence of a camera. The furnishings consisted of the desk, sofa, and two straight chairs set against one wall, all on a thick carpet. The room was set up for interviews—or better put, interrogations.

"Ah!" he heard Seltzmann exclaim. Chelsea turned to see him watching his handset television receiver, smiling, and then looking expectantly toward the door.

In brief seconds the door opened, and standing there, looking in, was Dave Ward with Mae peering over his shoulder. Stunned expressions became eager smiles as they pushed past the door. Then, Ward, spying Seltzmann, glanced morosely at Chelsea. "Joe—Christ, Joe—not you too!"

Ignoring Dave's comment, Chelsea asked, "Did any of

you see Ellie or Cindy?" He got looks of befuddlement. "Or Jason and the Fargo woman?"

"You mean they've been taken also?" Ward said. "Jesus, Joe, who's left? Josh and . . ." He halted in mid-sentence. Seltzmann was observing them with obvious interest.

"Yes, Mr. Ward, who is left to help? The Brenner brothers are unharmed, but they're out of it. As for Josh Novick, his hands are bound with frustration, unable to continue the operation as long as you remain my guests."

"Guests?" Mae remarked derisively.

Seltzmann seemed to be enjoying himself. "A mere forty-eight hours and . . ." He paused, then continued abruptly, sternly. "I caution you, Captain Chelsea, not to attempt anything foolish. Even if you should manage to overpower a guard, it's not possible for any of you to leave the premises."

He slid a hand beneath a corner of the desk, and the paneled wall behind him slid open, revealing four armed men standing guard, awaiting instructions.

Seltzmann stood up. "These men will escort you to a suite that will accommodate you quite comfortably. It is not my desire to mistreat you. These men are simply here to protect you from doing yourself harm." He checked a gold wrist-watch. "It is past the dinner hour, but I expect you haven't eaten. A private dining room will be ready within the hour. Your personal attendants will escort you wherever necessary." He nodded to the orderly at the door to take over as he left the room.

Ward moved to Chelsea's side. "Joe, he may be the kingpin of this organization, but I'm not taking this crap lying down. I don't have to tell you what he's lining up for us."

"Patience," Chelsea replied. "Both of you. They've already

killed two of our security guards. Ellie, Cindy, and the Fargo woman were taken and I suspect they are here also."

Dave's eyes were dark with misgivings. "Joe—" He was interrupted.

Chelsea's response was a shade above a whisper. "Not now, Dave. Take it for granted that every room is bugged. We can't do anything until we learn more about our surroundings."

Ward waited a moment, then whispered, "Can we expect any outside help?"

"I don't know. Despite Seltzmann's arrogance, I can't rule out the Brenners as yet. Jason—I don't where he is—or even if he's been taken prisoner." He glanced at the four so-called attendants. Silent, they appeared to be biding their time, awaiting the wishes of their guests.

"That leaves Alex and Josh," Chelsea continued. "I can't even begin to guess what either will be doing."

Ward's forehead ridged into a deep frown. "So, we're on our own, and damned if I can see a way out."

Chelsea eyed the guards again, then bent to Ward's ear. "If we can find a computer . . . one unattended . . . Or better yet, a fax machine . . ."

Mae Warren gaped at him. Unless she read the signs wrong, the man was actually thriving on the crisis they were undergoing. Planning, submitting ideas . . . What next? She became aware of Dave's attempting a smile. *Damn! The two of them!*

Mae tossed Chelsea an indignant glance. "I can see the germ of an idea forming. If it's what I'm thinking, you can forget it. I'm no longer the siren of my corrupted youth. And I don't think you should ask or expect it of me."

Chelsea feigned befuddlement, and looked to Ward for support. He received a grin. "Right. Forget it. Now, were we promised a suite where we could freshen up before dinner?"

"Right," Chelsea agreed. "I believe the extra calories might be needed." He turned to confront the one guard who was attired in a three-piece suit; the others wore black cotton sweaters over black slacks. "Our suite, please," Chelsea said. He might have been speaking with the bellman at the Ritz.

Two men led them out; the other two trailed behind. Chelsea blinked. The situation was like something out of an exploitation movie, the bad guys dressed in black, cast as ninja clones of the Japanese Yakuza.

"Something strike you as humorous, Joe?" Dave remarked, aware of Chelsea's half-smile.

"No, I was just reflecting on old movies. No matter how dire the circumstances, the conflict between good and evil, there would always be a happy ending."

Two steps behind the men, Mae leaned in to Dave. "This a new side of your friend? What's with him? For a while I thought I saw something of merit, but now . . ."

"Hold it, Mae. Wait until we get into our so-called quarters before having any discussions. I trust Joey to come up with something. If you're having trouble with that, then allow me to keep the faith for both of us."

"I was reminding myself that the boat's final payment will be this year. We didn't need this, Dave. We wouldn't be here if it weren't for Chelsea."

Ward gripped her hand. "I owed him, Mae. If it wasn't for Joe Chelsea, my life would have ended ten years ago. All you need to know is that I wouldn't have been around for us to eventually meet. What he did on that one day made it all possible."

Mae squeezed his hand. Her lips trembling, she said, "I'll never bring it up again."

He gave her a brief glance. "Someday, we'll discuss it."

The blank-walled corridor was coming to an end, to a double-doored entrance. The three captives became quiet.

Alex was in a quandary. The big cruiser had slowed to pull alongside and tie up at a private dock on the Intracoastal, somewhere north of Palm Beach.

With his own lights out, Alex piloted the Tiara to the opposite side of the Waterway and tied up at an abandoned dock. Red mangrove crumbled the flanking sea wall unimpeded. Three hundred yards off his quarry's portside beam, Alex watched through his nightscope.

Since all passengers were disembarking starboard—the blind side—Alex could distinguish nothing of any consequence. Just beyond the boat, inland, the nightscope picked up young buttonwoods, gumbo-limbo, seagrape . . . a cultivated jungle. Raising the lenses, he caught a sprawling red-tiled rooftop slightly higher than the royal palms. By its width he judged it to be a building of immense proportions; its size, even for Florida, was not that of your average private domicile.

Undecided as to his next move, he put his thoughts on hold as another, smaller cruiser silently and cautiously crept along the Waterway, apparently to tie up alongside the eighty-footer.

Alex could see hurried movements aboard the newly arrived boat. Focusing his nightscope, he picked out two men carrying a stretcher. Less than a minute later another two men carried out another stretcher. The green pictures produced by the nightscope obscured the identity of the victims, although one was large enough to have been Joe Chelsea. The thought brought a shiver.

Alex tried turning the microphonic ear, but small gusts of wind, rustling the branches of the trees behind him and scudding across the water, carried all sound away from him.

He could do nothing but wait while his apprehension mounted.

If they had Joe Chelsea, most likely the other victim was Jason Stoner. Alex started to blow out air noisily, then caught himself. He sat down on a boat cushion, biding his time while he deliberated on what he could accomplish.

He had to get to a phone—the Tiara wasn't equipped with ship-to-shore communications—and try Josh Novick again; if he failed to contact him, he'd try the Brenners. There was no one else.

He remembered the cellular, grabbed for his duffle bag, and pulled out the phone, then waited for all movement from across the Waterway to cease.

Without warning, the wind shifted abruptly, bringing with it a few drops of rain. An acerbic odor emanating from the surrounding rotting undergrowth wrinkled Alex's nose. But the shifting wind also carried voices—undulating, they were difficult to decipher. The smaller boat was about to depart, and from what Alex could gather, the eighty-footer would soon follow.

He waited, watched, and listened for another five minutes, then made his call to Novick Security.

Josh took the call at his desk, alone in the building but for two men working at the monitors, which were operating again. Carbolo's men had left with the black-clad intruders, who were charged with breaking and entering. Carbolo himself was at the Novick homestead, taking personal charge of the fiasco.

Rubbing his forehead, Josh felt his world spinning away from him. Every turn brought another tragedy. The body count was building and he still didn't know where Cindy and Ellie were. And there was also Dave and his Mae Warren . . .

A spasm of pain shot across his forehead, lingering above

his right eye. *Good Lord! Now Joe, along with Jason Stoner . . .*

He struggled against the distress threatening to consume him. *Who was left to help*?

Alex's voice reached him as from a tunnel, hollow-sounding and somewhat breathless. "Mr. Novick, what instructions do you have for me? I've got the place pinpointed, but I definitely can't go it alone. They could have a small army inside."

Josh stared beyond the phone, trying to think. "What about the Brenners?" he asked. "You saw no sign of them? Are you certain they weren't taken also?"

"I'm sure there were only two figures carried from the second yacht, and I know three women were taken off the *Ark* before it was scuttled. As for the Brenners . . . I know nothing of their whereabouts."

"But they were with Chelsea and Stoner."

"Maybe so, but I can't add anything to what I've told you."

Josh lifted his splitting head, his eyes burning. "Okay," he managed. "Give me an exact fix on your location."

Alex gave him his position on the Waterway.

"Get off the boat and locate the place landside; then call me back. Meanwhile I'll try to find the Brenners. And for God's sake, Alex, don't try anything on your own."

"I'm not that foolish, Mr. Novick. You'd need commandos to take this place.

"Good! All I want from you is reconnaissance. I'm assuming you have the experience"

"Yes, sir, it's been a while, but it's like riding a bike."

The Brenner brothers had been arguing for the past ten minutes, ever since discovering they had been in a deep sleep for over three hours. The disagreement was triggered by a hand-printed note inside a blank envelope attached to Noah's shirt pocket. In very clear language it said they'd be risking the lives of their families if they persisted in any further investigation. The note shriveled into ash three minutes after exposure to the air.

They had regained consciousness in their van, discovering they were parked in an empty lot behind a furniture factory. The quarrel started immediately after Noah's reading of the message.

"We can't abandon them because of that note," Aaron argued.

Noah spun on him. "We didn't come to America to fight terrorists. We were finished with that life ten years ago. And now, with our families involved . . . Their organization could be larger than any of the Arab factions. And this one is invisible. We don't even know who we're up against."

"Chelsea and the others don't know either. But it didn't faze them. He and Novick—not to mention their FBI friend—could be living very comfortably in retirement. They don't even need to earn a living."

Noah's eyes became pinpoints. "Are you *meshuga!* How do we protect our family from all this? There's no place to hide from this organization. Just tell me one place where they would be safe."

Aaron had an answer ready. "Israel!"

Noah took a few seconds to absorb that, then said, finally, "And how do we convince our wives?"

"Tell them the truth—or at least a part-truth, that our present assignment involves working undercover for a government agency. And that our work would be much simpler knowing our families were safe in the homeland."

Noah snorted. "You believe Yetta will go for that? Safer in Israel than here?"

"Don't argue with me. Tell her we were conscripted

because of our talents and past experience, and had no choice of refusal. Convince her. And quickly. We could have them all on a flight within twenty-four hours."

Noah shook his head, knowing he had lost the argument. "Convince her? You are a *meshugeneh.*" He started to put the van in gear, but halted. "So, what's our next move after all the *tummel* we're going to have at home?"

Aaron reached for his pipe in the dashboard ashtray. "We could call in some of our old friends. What do you think?"

"Who? We've been away for a long time. We're not in the mother country. Forget it. We'll call Novick. He has to know about Chelsea and Stoner. It's their theatre of operation; we're still only part of the troops."

Aaron had other ideas. He was thinking of his wife's cousin Aaron Ritter, a member of the Knesset—and a former head of the Israeli Mossad.

34

Once inside the "private suite," Chelsea sought the bathroom and motioned Ward to follow. After a thorough examination of the room he turned on the faucets in the shower and washbasin and proceeded to bring him up to date on all events.

Ward, glum, said, "So, Joey, where do we go from here? And more to the point, Where *can* we go?" He fingered his beard despondently. "And if we did get out, where would we run? These guys are everywhere, coming out of the woodwork."

"Can you venture an opinion on our location?"

Ward screwed up his face, as if in pain. "For what it's worth, I don't think it's their island 'resort.' "

"Well, at least we agree on that. But that makes me ask: For what purpose were we brought here? A holding station?" From habit Chelsea dug into his shirt pocket for his Dunhill pipe, then realized it was missing, along with his other personal effects. No wallet, no ID. He muttered a curse under his breath. He had never felt so naked, so beaten. He put his hand under the faucet and splashed water on his face and neck. His capacity to wear well was stretching thin. Grabbing a thick towel, he scrubbed himself dry, then cursed aloud. "Okay, we've got work to do but, first, fill me in. You and Mae are wearing some sort of uniform. Why?"

Ward said he had no explanation, but didn't believe they'd been used, or abused, in any way. There was however a servant who seemingly had no sensation of pain. He recounted the curious incident with the waitress. Chelsea didn't appear shocked.

Reminded of the Seltzer–Izzy Gorham episode, Chelsea said, "Apparently they've learned how to apply different systems to each individual. Adding memory to some, aborting old memories from others. In the case of the waitress, they've created a derelict mind—she can't remember where she's been and knows no direction other than what is dictated to her."

"Good Lord!" Ward exclaimed, his voice rising. "How far have they gone with all this? They've been at it for years." He shook his head, his eyes darkening. "Jesus, Joey, we could also be at the end of the line." He fell silent, feeling Chelsea's glare of suppressed anger. He held up his hands defensively. "Look, Joey, don't eyeball me like that. Before you turned up at our door, Mae and I had a tacit agreement, that we would live together, share our boat and our small dreams, and when our time was up, for whatever reason, we would take our boat and sail into a final sunset together. If that sounds melodramatic, so be it. But, dammit, Joey, this isn't the place we selected for our final sunset."

Chelsea gripped Ward's shoulders. "Now, you listen to me. I was forced into retirement. I wasn't ready for—or even contemplating—a final sunset. In Florida or anywhere else. If nothing else, I've finally learned to look at the past without hankering for it. I'm now only concerned with the future." He gave Ward's cheek a friendly pat. "So, listen to the old philosopher—cut the crap, and put your 'sailing into the sunset' on hold. We've got work to do. So let's get out of here before your girl gets any funny ideas about us."

As soon as they reentered the sitting room, Mae asked, "Can we talk?" Chelsea nodded and waved her and Dave to a beige leather sofa. All the furniture was functional and nondescript. There was a matching sofa opposite, separated by a glass-topped table. "Forget the bugs," he said. "I want them to hear all of our discussion."

Chelsea, sitting opposite Ward, leaned forward and whispered. "Take your cues from me." He waited a moment, then spoke aloud. "I believe the old Dr. Seltzer, with his so-called memory supposedly installed in Izzy Gorham, is a washout. Seltzer is—or was—an old man, with an old man's memory. A new host doesn't stop the continuous aging process of the original mind. Seltzer's memory diminishes with each new transmission. He can't remember how to walk, even though he's using Gorham's memory bank—not to mention his physical body."

Ward stared at him. What was Chelsea stirring up?

"At this point I find it ironic that Izzy Gorham, a Jew and former inmate of Seltzer's concentration camp, was selected for the host body. I was told it was an emergency, and temporary. But it was never explained why Seltzer's personal doctors also chose Jewish identities for themselves." He paused for effect. "Guilt complex? Possibly. Who knows how the egomanical mind works.

"Which brings me to Jon Seltzmann, who we can assume is at present the principal leader of the Alliance. You've both met the man—I'd like your personal opinions of him."

Although Mae was following his every word, her eyes lifted toward the wall opposite, high up near the ceiling.

Chelsea's eyes crinkled with understanding. There was a video camera behind the air duct.

Mae grimaced. "You can add 'weird,' among other choice adjectives."

Ward said, "So where does this leave us?"

Chelsea pushed himself from the sofa. "Hungry. We were offered dinner. I say we take Mr. Seltzmann up on it. Our escort is outside the door waiting for us." He leaned over to whisper, "Don't be surprised if Ellie, Cindy, and the Fargo woman are there."

"How can you be so sure?"

"The Seltzer family loves lording it over others. Bringing us together, for them, would be considered a *coup d'état*."

"You didn't mention Jason," Dave reminded him.

Chelsea squinted. "You like him—I like him. But he's still a question mark. Don't forget he's a Stoner."

It had taken the Brenner brothers a good hour to convince their wives that their immediate departure for Israel was necessary. It took pleading and cajoling to make them understand that any delay was out of the question. The children would be only too happy to leave school and spend two weeks in Israel visiting relatives they had never met. Through friends in a travel agency they were booked on an early morning flight going from Miami to New York. There they would connect with an El Al flight in early afternoon.

Now, three hours later, with midnight approaching, Noah and Aaron Brenner were at Novick Security with Josh. From the van phone Noah and Josh had brought each other up to date, terse and unemotional. Josh had moved past self-flagellation, and was working up a full gut of anger to displace the fear.

Josh squeezed into the van behind Aaron, who was already in the driver's seat. "Take 95 to West Palm; then take any bridge across the Intracoastal to Palm Beach, then north on A1A. Within thirty minutes from now Alex will call us on his cellular. He's on foot, but it's safe. The adjacent properties on both sides of the estate are cultivated jungles, inhabited by only one caretaker, who makes an hourly walking patrol that could miss an army, if we only had one."

Noah, up front beside Aaron, said, "What do you really expect we can do? We can't just blast our way in with Uzis."

Josh sniffed. "Christ! I have no plan. All I know is we have to do something. Like Joe always says, 'one step at a time.'" He noted raindrops splashing the windshield, and the wipers starting. He wondered if it was an advantage. Then, reminded, he said, "You mentioned Uzis—all I have is a .38 special with reloads. You have Uzis?"

"Four," Aaron said. "With ten cartridges. Also two Colt .45s with extra clips, and three Berettas."

Josh couldn't resist. "What! No grenade launchers?"

Soberly, Aaron said, "No launchers, but we do have about a dozen grenades. Along with some tear-gas bombs."

"Christ!" Josh exploded. "What were you guys? An extermination squad?"

Noah twisted in his seat; his face was beaded with sweat, despite the air-conditioning. "Should we have brought kid gloves?"

Josh held his face in his hands. Like the French, they were going to storm the Bastille. It was all insanity, he thought despondently. He looked up, felt the tilt of the van as it crossed over the hump bridging the Intracoastal waters. Nearing their objective appeared to rouse the cellular phone. Josh lifted it to his ear and let the caller speak and deliver all instructions.

Alex had docked his boat in a marina two miles north of his original surveillance area, then had taken a cab back to

A1A, where he was dropped off at a hotel half a mile from the "fortress." He would wait for them in the hotel parking lot.

Fifteen minutes later everyone was in the van, and riding down A1A. Alex directed Aaron into a thicket, a hundred yards short of the so-called cultivated jungle. There they took time to study Alex's information.

The patrolling guard never varied his walking gait or path, which suggested the jungle might have trip wires setting off alarms within the huge building. Alex hadn't found any at the outer edge, but the hour and a half spent in learning the guard's routine had made it impossible to investigate further.

"Did you bring the nightscopes?" Alex asked. "We're dead without them. It's not only trip wires—we have to watch for cameras also. These guys wouldn't miss a trick."

All four men had sacks on their backs. Five minutes earlier each man had blackened his face and hands, as much to dissuade clouds of disturbed mosquitoes and other insects as to hide themselves. The earlier light rain had stopped, but the foliage steamed with the heat and humidity. On signal, all slipped on glasses. Josh and the Brenners wore infrareds; Alex had his nightscope. Although Josh had been on the police force for almost two decades, he knew his three companions were more experienced on night recons such as this. He gave Alex the lead because of his Vietnam background. He wondered whether the Brenners would be resentful. To his relief he felt nothing of the sort from either man.

Alex held up a finger. "We have five minutes for the guard to arrive and then we wait another five for him to disappear. I'll lead, looking ahead, up, and down. Noah and Aaron, scan our right and left. Mr. Nov—"

"Jesus!" Josh muttered hoarsely. "Stop with the damn

mister—it's Josh. And while we have another minute, are you certain the women looked okay? You couldn't have missed something?"

"The only damage I witnessed was to your boat. Sorry, Josh. Now keep your eyes peeled for those remote cameras. Anywhere from ten to fifteen feet off the ground. Most likely hidden in among the palm fronds."

They knelt down, hidden behind scrub palms. It was past midnight and only an occasional car traveled along A1A. The southern lane was only fifteen feet behind them but the men were no more than shadows in the blackness.

Five minutes after the guard went by Alex gave the signal to move. The rain started again, in small droplets, thickening the humidity and dampening their clothing.

Ellen Chelsea was seated at a dinner table with Cindy and Fran Fargo. She spun around at the sound of a door opening. Seeing Chelsea, her face turned ashen and she forced herself to her feet. Her lips twisted, repressing a rush of emotion. Chelsea was suddenly at her side, embracing her. "Thank God, you're safe," he mumbled, trembling.

Unable to speak, Ellie closed her eyes for a brief moment in silent prayer; then, stepping back, she glanced over his shoulder. Her lips quivered on seeing Ward and Mae Warren.

A lump in Chelsea's throat made him unable to speak; despite all that had occurred, there were no remonstrations from Ellie. Her eyes displayed a trace of diminishing anxiety, replaced by hope with his appearance. Not a hair out of place; she was always a lady—a lovely lady—more than he deserved. He took her hand in his.

Suddenly Cindy decided she'd had all she could take. "What are you doing here without Josh and the rest of the troops?" she burst out. The bluster immediately turned to concern. "And where *is* Josh? Is . . . Is he safe?"

Chelsea, taken aback briefly, reassured her as best he could. He noticed that their guide had disappeared and also that Fran Fargo was sitting at the table, her hands clasped together; there was no mistaking the misery in her eyes.

He continued to hold his wife's hand. "Sorry, El, I really messed up our retirement."

"You might say that," she returned, with a small glint of humor. "I should have known better. I had expected Florida to be a place where everything under the sun existed for a perfect retirement. No cold weather, no snow . . . golf courses galore. And above all, no crimes to involve you. I was wrong. It's not enough for a man like you, for a man who indulges in sports merely as a spectator."

Chelsea tried a small smile. "You weren't wrong. But 'everything under the sun' includes both good and evil. The Garden of Eden was never perfect." His eyes held her. "Unfortunately, you married a man who's been fighting evil most of his life and is unable to stop. They had no right to retire me—at least not for the reasons they gave me." His eyes saddened. "I'm sorry, El. I'm sounding macho—it's not what I intended."

He tore his gaze away from her to scan the room. Like the previous room it was windowless, its walls bare of adornment. *Was that a conceit? Or did it have a purpose?*

The dining table was as long as a conference table, with place settings for more than a dozen people. Chelsea gripped Ellie's hand. "Let's eat. We'll talk after dinner."

"And then what?" Ward said, unhappily. "We all take a nap like good boys?"

Chelsea knew they were being observed. "Stay cool, Dave. You know we have to do what I suggested earlier. Let's eat. We're all too hungry to think clearly."

* * *

Jon Seltzmann was seated at an immaculate walnut desk, his eyes on a color monitor several feet away. Jason sat on the edge of a heavy leather lounge chair, also focused on the monitor. From stereo speakers all conversation but whispers could be heard. Chelsea had just embraced his wife.

"How touching," Seltzmann remarked dryly. From his desk he switched off the set.

"Why have I been separated from the others?" Jason demanded angrily, his nerve ends bristling. The lone bright spot was that Fran was safe, and to some degree he was relieved to see the others also looked unharmed.

"We have to talk," Seltzmann replied. "I must know for certain where your allegiance lies. I must also consider the fact that you are the nephew of Elias Stoner, one of our directors. Because of my own father, some small measure of nepotism is allowed."

Jason snorted derisively. "That policy should have been made known to Calvin Rodgers."

"Don't be a fool, Stoner. He was given certain directives because of your behavior. You should have recognized one particular fact when you weren't taken along with the others—that you were being offered a second chance. A chance which you blew." Seltzmann leaned forward on his elbows, exhibiting an air of high authority, his manner mocking. "Did you know that your uncle Elias was ready to sacrifice you for the good of the organization?"

Jason fell silent, finding the statement too incredible to accept. Yet . . . under the circumstances it couldn't be refuted. Calvin Rodgers had warned him. His mind spun, seeking exits—and he discovered a role he thought he could play. His face eased into a forced smile. Leaning back he folded his arms across his chest.

"So, what is it you're expecting from me?"

Seltzmann's eyes narrowed. "Don't fool with me, Stoner. It simply won't work. We'll always be a step ahead. Every move you make will be a test."

"Get to the point."

Seltzmann nodded, his eyes suspicious.

"A group, or organization, goes undetected for almost four decades, without a problem or dilemma that cannot be resolved. Then one day an individual—practically a non-entity—stumbles upon its existence. I would like—no, not like—I *must know* how ex-Captain Chelsea accomplished this penetration, a penetration no state or federal intelligence agency in the entire world has been able to achieve. And for this knowledge, your collaboration—there are no two ways about it—is compulsory."

"So you want me to spy for you."

Seltzmann regarded him dolefully. It had been too much to expect understanding. He tilted his head. "You're being offered—against my will, by the way—an opportunity to redeem yourself. But, no, instead of being grateful, you give me that smartass attitude so prevalent among Chelsea's entourage."

Jason struggled to lean forward from the deep lounge chair. The chair was too deep, too relaxing. It was the type of seating that discouraged argument from its occupant.

"Damn!" he exploded, getting to his feet finally. "So, I'm a lousy actor. Did you expect me to succumb to your threats?"

Seltzmann, wary, his gaze fixed, steeled himself for any attack on his person. His finger hovered above a button on a console at the edge of the desk. "You'll play along, Stoner, or suffer the consequences."

Jason lifted his head. "What consequences? Will I be dealt with like the two men you left in Novick's home?"

"Hardly. We have no permanent disposal plans for any of

you. Regarding Captain Chelsea—his life will be reserved for a new future. Your own life and the lives of the others will hinge on your actions." He paused a moment, and as Jason edged forward, he issued an additional warning. "Don't try anything foolish. Follow orders as instructed."

"And should I agree to follow such orders, do I get to learn the purpose of this organization—and each one's function in it? As, for example, my uncle—what is his role?"

Seltzmann's gaze remained fixed, mistrustful. "Nothing can be revealed until you've proven yourself. Until that time . . ." He hit a button on the desk console.

A door at one side of the room opened, letting in two black-suited men, both armed with pistols. "You may go, Stoner, to dine with your friends. How you conduct yourself will determine the direction of your future."

Seltzmann nodded to the two strongmen, who waved their weapons, motioning Jason out of the room.

Jason entered the corridor sandwiched between his escorts, wondering what Seltzmann had in mind for Chelsea. The long corridor was empty, blinding white under strong fluorescents, bare of any human touch. Like the two rooms he'd been in, it seemed to have been designed by someone with a totally joyless outlook.

The walkway was of limestone, echoing back the sound of his footsteps and competing with his thoughts of Fran. He wondered how they should greet each other.

The four men pushed through the hummock, the light rain helping to mask any inadvertent noise. No one spoke, each trailing after Alex, and obeying his hand signals. Twice within thirty yards he pointed out trip wires. He also alerted them to animal nests, cautioning the men to leave them undisturbed.

They had been walking for thirty minutes when Josh began to have misgivings. His bad leg was tiring, and stiffening more than usual. What the hell were they trying to do!

"Playing it by ear" was for the birds. Literally. They couldn't even speculate on a plan. It was only by pure dumb luck they had discovered the existence of the cartel.

"Damn!" he muttered, almost stumbling into Noah, who had halted. He wiped his wet infrared lenses to better see what Noah was pointing out.

It was a clearing, a grass lawn twenty feet wide, broken only by a colored slate walk extending from a metal door and hemming the side of a ten-foot-high brick wall. That brick barricade paralleled the contour of the huge mansion until it was out of sight. There was no foliage to conceal trespassers.

The four men stood abreast at the edge of the lawn, still hidden. "What now?" Josh muttered. "Any ideas? I'm fresh out."

Noah addressed himself to Alex. "You know your jungle very well. We've now entered my area of expertise." He touched Josh. "I go alone to that door. If and when I'm ready, I'll signal for all of you to follow me. Is that understood?" Everyone nodded.

Noah was on his stomach, frog-crawling across the grass. He stopped once, about halfway, to swipe at insects buzzing furiously about his head and glasses.

At the door, he stood up to study the entire framing, then dropped to his knees to examine the lock. Seconds later he pulled something from his knapsack.

Another minute passed and he gave them a come-ahead signal.

All eyes turned to Jason as soon as he entered the room. Fran started to rise, but then sank back self-consciously.

"Have a seat," Chelsea said. "We were wondering when you would join us. We're all ears to learn how you fared."

Jason cocked his head. "All ears?" Odd thing for him to say. Then, suddenly he understood. *The place was bugged.*

He nodded, seating himself next to Ward. "I see we're all okay—so far." He fixed his gaze upon Fran. *God! She gets more beautiful each time I see her.* Aloud he said, "What are we being served at this late hour? If your favorite dish isn't available, I know another place in Palm Beach—" He stopped speaking suddenly. Chelsea was staring at him silently, questioningly, *Another place in Palm Beach*?

It took a few seconds for the meaning of Chelsea's unspoken query to register. *Good Lord!* Jason thought. *How could I know we were in Palm Beach?* He looked again at Chelsea, and saw suspicion in his eyes. Jason held his palms up plaintively, and shrugged, silently pleading innocence. Chelsea nodded to Ward, obviously handing him the ball, then said, "As long as we're guests, I'm ordering steak, medium rare. As for the others . . ." He waved a careless hand.

Fran Fargo, on the edge too long, sighed heavily. She brought a linen napkin to her face, fighting tears. "I don't know how you people stand it. You joke as if you were all on holiday." She started to slide her chair back, but Chelsea was instantly at her side, preventing her. She looked at him pleadingly. "My father is terminally ill. I can't stay here and have him worrying about my absence."

Chelsea lifted his head, seeking assistance from Ellie and Cindy. Cindy had only to lean toward Fran, but Ellie came around the table to join her. It was then that Chelsea remembered Fran had faxed a message to her father's firm. He whispered to Ellie, "Get Fargo's fax number in Italy from her. I have to speak with Jason and Dave."

He tugged Jason's arm, then prodded Ward away from the

table. "Okay, Jason, tell us how you decided we're in Palm Beach." His voice was a mere whisper, but demanding.

"Okay," Jason replied. "Believe it or not, it's only just come to me. I was here, three years ago, with my uncle Elias. The first room I was in didn't ring any bells. But Seltzmann's office, the walnut desk matching the paneled walls—Even the deep, leather lounge chair I sat in was the same one. I don't know why I didn't recognize it instantly. Then the blazing-white, polished-tile corridor—all it needed was a hospital odor. I remember asking my uncle if the architect and designer were misanthropes."

"So, dammit!" Ward exploded, "where the hell are we?"

Jason reflected. "I'd guess we're about two or three miles north of your marina."

"That's the best you can do?" Chelsea said dryly. "What was the purpose of your visit?"

"I was new to the firm. My uncle was introducing me to a prospective client. At least that was what I assumed."

"You're privy to the security here?"

"No. That's another department. My job was personnel. Except for this venture, I wasn't ready as yet."

"Who is the owner?" Chelsea pressed.

Jason rubbed his forehead, wringing memories. "A German company, no personal name comes to mind." He kept stealing glances at Fran; she was watching him. "From what I've learned in the past three weeks, my guess is that it's a dummy company. One that doesn't exist anywhere except on paper. Speculating, I would say it could belong to Wellington Security."

"Just another piece of innocuous property shuffled somewhere in the long list of properties owned by the Benefactor Alliance," Ward said dourly.

Chelsea said, "Dave, if you sent a fax from here, would it tell us our location?"

"Not necessarily. Like all the other names we tried, it could be relayed to any number of stations, thereby protecting its point of origin. What did you have in mind?"

"I thought they might be willing to fax a message to Italy. One that they could censor themselves."

Before anyone could come up with a follow-through, Ellie was at Chelsea's side. "Joe, it's after midnight. I don't think food is on anyone's mind—" She stopped, recognizing the signs; he wasn't ready to call it a night. "If you insist, we could just ask for some coffee or tea."

Chelsea deliberated. "Okay, coffee or tea, but in our suite, if our host agrees. I take it the suite can accommodate all of us—I'm pretty sure it has four bedrooms."

Ward scratched his cheek. "Joey, what are you planning?"

Chelsea shouted to the ceiling. "How does one get any service here?" A servant appeared in seconds, apparently awaiting their wishes. "How can I help you?" she said.

"We would like coffee and tea served in our suite. And some other, harder drinks."

"Your suite has a fully stocked bar as well as coffee and tea service. If you are ready to leave, your escort will be here momentarily."

By the time the servant reached the archway, the two strongmen—unarmed this time—had appeared from another doorway. They gestured for everyone to follow them.

Jason went to Fran. Neither said anything immediately. Fran finally tested the waters. "I see you weren't harmed in any way. Care to tell me how you accomplished that?"

Jason weighed a reply. He had yet to earn their full trust. And yet her eyes sought him, as if hoping for more than trust. He ran nervous fingers through his hair.

Her attitude upset him deeply. Couldn't she see it? Weren't his feelings for her obvious? She started to turn away, but he gripped her elbow.

"Fran, don't do this. I'm on your side. Should I have given up my life to prove it?"

She glanced at her elbow; he released it and held his palms up, facing her. "Okay, you win. So, if in a weak moment I should happen to confess I love you, don't be persuaded to believe me. After all—I am a Stoner and all Stoners are the enemy. No question about that. Right?"

Fran's thoughts were swimming. *Love?* When did love enter their relat—Someone called them.

"Jason . . ." she managed. "We have to go. I have to think. We'll talk again."

Ellie took Mae's arm and said, "Those two are in love and don't know it."

"Yes. Sure. Just like Dave and I are."

Ellie gave her a sidelong glance. "Was that a joke?"

Mae sighed wearily and rubbed her eyes. "Not intentionally." She tossed her head. "Forget it. I don't always say what I actually mean. Men are such bloody fools at times."

As the women walked off, joined by Fran, Chelsea went to Jason's side. "Jason, a question. I suspect we are below sea level here. Can you tell me why?"

"I've no idea. I was never privy to Wellington's outside activities. Or interests, if you will." He paused. "You still don't believe me?" Chelsea didn't answer; his face was expressionless. "Okay. All I can say is that these corridors resemble the level above us; bleached, sanitized, antiseptic."

"Hospital- or laboratory-clean," Chelsea remarked dully, yawning despite his dire thoughts. "What about the private island near Nassau? You have no idea what it's used for? The place is guarded like Fort Knox."

Jason sighed tiredly. "Obviously you find this difficult to believe, but I never even knew of its existence. I'm taking your word that it does exist."

"Okay," Chelsea said, relenting. He placed an avuncular hand on Jason's shoulder. "Let's continue this in our suite. Running water in the bathroom will discourage any eavesdroppers."

Jason held back. "What about Mr. Novick? Right now he's our only outside help." He quickly added, "Unless you're holding something back."

Chelsea held a finger to his lips, then whispered, "Our friends won't be sleeping." He took Jason's elbow, steering him toward the others, who had gone ahead. "Keep an ear open and an alert eye. Watch for cameras, and as we pass each doorway in the corridor listen for any sound you can pick up in this soundless prison."

Josh hesitated, despite Noah's come-ahead signal. "This is too easy," he said to Aaron. "No guards, no cameras? I feel like that door is a mousetrap."

Aaron prodded him. "Let's go. Noah knows what he's doing." He looked to Alex for his okay.

"Can you signal Noah not to push the door open until I check it? I've come across booby traps and alarms you can't possibly imagine."

"Maybe so," Aaron remarked dryly, "but this isn't Vietnam."

Josh snorted. "What a time for disagreement. Aaron, signal your brother to hold up at the door until we get there."

There was no sound other than night insects. Aaron snapped his fingers and caught Noah's attention. Aaron held his arms forward, open palms toward himself, directing Noah to keep his hands from the door.

When all four men were crowded around the unlocked but closed metal door, Alex stepped back and asked for a boost up the ten-foot wall.

Feeling along the edge of the top he found what he

expected: broken glass embedded in the brick-and-concrete surface. *No wonder there were no guards.* "You better be wearing combat boots for this," he warned those below. They were.

In a crouch he held his precarious position and used the nightscope to study the inside of the door and then the building itself, another ten feet away.

There was no one, not a light, not a sound other than insects, mostly cicadas and, surprisingly, the occasional croaking of a frog. His nightscope scanned the side of the four-story limestone building and in seconds discovered it had no windows. Other than that lack, it could have been the vacation retreat of any multimillionaire. There was no camera in sight either, he quickly noted. "I'm dropping down to check the door," he said.

The extreme care was unnecessary. No wires, no alarms, no exotic security. All four men thought it strange—and suspicious.

Alex leading, they followed the contour of the mansion toward the rear, toward the Intracoastal. This side of the building faced north and had no means of entry. There was no foliage around the area, and it struck Josh that it was like following the base of a huge crypt. The thought brought a cold shiver, and relief came only with the sighting of the yacht tied up at the dock leading away from the mansion. Alex nodded, confirming it was the cruiser that brought the hostages.

Moonlight filtered through stately palms screening the rear of the mansion, planted there apparently to discourage rubbernecking sailors on the Waterway.

"It's your move, Noah," Josh said. "There should be an entrance here."

"One second," Alex warned. He pointed to flowering hibiscus hedges flanking a concrete walk that led straight to double doors beneath a canvas canopy. With his glasses he could see infrared lines crossing the walk. They hadn't been visible until they'd reached the pier.

"Okay, we do as before," Josh instructed. "Two on each side of the hedges, and watch for cameras above or beside the doorway."

Aaron was the one to catch the almost-hidden rotating camera stuck into the corner beside the door, beneath a limestone overhang. He warned them to stay in position without moving while he waited for the camera to face away. He then moved quickly beneath it and, rummaging in his backpack, fished out an aerosol can. In seconds the camera lens disappeared behind thick soaplike suds.

Next he pointed to a box on the door with a dim red light blinking above it. A digital computer door alarm.

Noah was ready as soon as he saw the light. The inoperative camera wouldn't trouble anyone monitoring. One camera down among many had to be a mechanical failure. A door alarm coupled with a camera failure, however, would garner attention.

Noah held something resembling a meter against the box. With each turn of the knob on the meter a red number was displayed on a green screen. After five numbers showed, the lock on the door clicked. Noah turned the brass handle, and the door opened without a sound.

35

Chelsea was the last to enter their suite of rooms. At that point their two escorts departed. He had thought it odd there were no cameras in the corridor; no guards patrolling, no house servants other than the two men accompanying them. Stranger yet was the eerie stillness, here and behind the closed doors they passed. Somehow ominous, although he wondered if it could be attributed to nothing more than the late hour.

The thought brought a frown. It wasn't possible they weren't under constant surveillance. There had to be other guards—in other rooms, watching them on monitors.

Ward had found the bar by opening a wall cupboard. Everyone watched as he lathered his hand with soap, then stood on tiptoe to smooth the lather over the lens of a camera placed behind a wire screen just above the cupboard. Ward turned to catch Chelsea motioning for him to check out the bathroom as well.

Understanding what the men were up to, the women

watched without saying a word. Spotting a Thermos of coffee on the bar, Ellie began filling some mugs.

In the bathroom the camera lens was located just behind an air duct screen. Ward repeated his earlier routine. The bathroom was above average size, about twelve by twelve, with all conveniences, including a whirlpool and a bidet. Chelsea immediately turned on all the faucets.

"Okay," he said, turning to Jason. "Do you have any idea of the security setup in this place?"

Jason shrugged. "I don't know anything more than I've already told you. I was here only that one time."

"What about the corridors?" Ward asked. "You telling us the hallways on all the floors are alike, with no surveillance cameras? I didn't catch a single one in the entire length of the corridor."

Jason ran a finger over his lip, trying to dredge up an old memory. "The wall . . ." he said. "It was warm to the touch—you didn't notice?" He snapped his fingers suddenly. "The wall has heat sensors, sensitive to body temperatures. Anyone walking the corridors would be monitored. Somewhere in the building there has to be a control room where a schematic of the corridors depicts anyone walking in any hall as a red or blue dot. One man can track anyone moving past a heat-sensored wall. I now remember Wellington installing a similar system in a federal government project."

"Why a red or blue dot? Is there a purpose?"

"A blue dot signifies an employee. They'd have to have something on their person to register as such on the sensors." Jason winced with another observation. "Must be one of the perks Wellington gets from being associated with the Alliance."

Chelsea thought about the wearing apparel of everyone

they'd encountered and could remember nothing significant. Ward and Jason weren't any help when questioned.

"Perhaps the women were more observant," Chelsea said, leading them back into the sitting room.

Fran Fargo was the one to offer a clue. "The two maids we saw wore identical necklaces, silver or some silver-like metal. A single ball dangled from it."

Jason said, "I noticed a necklace on one of the men also, but assumed it was nothing more than jewelry."

Ward and Chelsea exchanged glances. Acquiring the necklaces had become a high priority.

And yet, seconds later, observing the women sipping coffee, seemingly more relaxed now, Chelsea couldn't stop thinking about the possible cost of what he and Ward were contemplating. Sudden doubts produced a bead of sweat on his brow. Had he finally reached the age of lost confidence? Were his mental and physical abilities going downhill?

The bead of perspiration now had company. Chelsea wiped at his forehead with the back of his hand and was surprised to see how wet it was. He muttered a curse under his breath. *Damn! Was he becoming like all those people he had spoken about so disparagingly?*

He headed for the bathroom, to wash his face—to wipe away the nagging inner fears. *Face it, you're an old man playing macho games.*

"Damn!" he muttered, feeling a towel thrust at him. Ellie was there, her lips a grim line, her eyes dark but reflecting an indomitable spirit.

Chelsea rubbed his face and wet hair with the thick towel, his eyes on his wife. "What's the problem, Ellie?"

"I was about to ask you the very same question."

He finger-combed his hair and remained silent. Finally, he said, "I've somehow lost my comb. You wouldn't by any chance have one on you?"

"No. But I have no complaints as long as it's only a comb you're missing." She touched his cheek. "Joe, no matter what happens . . ."

He took her hands in his. "Ellie, I'm all right. It's just a little touch of age catching up. I'm okay now. As long as my back holds out, I can handle it." He peered over her shoulder and caught Mae in the open doorway, trying to catch his attention. "Dave wants you. Something's happening outside the sitting room. We can hear people running through the corridor."

In an instant Chelsea was at the door. Ward said, "My first thought was they were coming to check the monitors we blocked out." He took his ear from the door. "But they passed us. I'd guess four men at least. What do you think, Joey? Time for us to move?"

Chelsea looked askance at his companion. Was Ward going macho on him?

"I got all my marbles, Joey. I think our hosts have goofed. They left our door unlocked." He turned the knob and pulled the door ajar.

"Hold it, Dave. Something's not kosher. This is too easy. It's got to be a test. I can't believe . . ."

The sound of running footsteps was heard again—a single person this time. Whoever it was passed their door without a glance. Chelsea pulled the door open just enough to peer out and glimpse a black-clad figure racing down the long white hallway with a weapon in his upraised hand. Chelsea couldn't be sure, but he thought it was a .380-caliber Beretta automatic with a silencer.

"Someone's in trouble," he muttered to Ward.

Ward snickered. "Yeah, it's us." He jerked the door open all the way. "Let's go, Joey. We've all got itchy—"

A robotic voice interrupted, blaring from hidden speakers.

"ATTENTION ALL GUESTS, VISITORS, AND EM-

PLOYEES. THIS IS AN UNSCHEDULED TEST. EVERYONE MUST RETURN TO THEIR QUARTERS IMMEDIATELY. WE REPEAT—IMMEDIATELY."

"They must have opened all doors for the so-called emergency," Chelsea said. "That's why ours is open."

"Then it's time for a move. Anything's better than hanging around." When Chelsea hesitated, Ward glared at him defiantly. "What is it? Why the delay?"

Without further hesitation, Chelsea called the women together. The plan was to follow the corridor, the opposite way of the runners. He and Jason would lead. Ward was to bring up the rear.

Just before heading out, Chelsea whispered, "I don't believe this is a test. It's a real emergency—and it could be our guys."

Ward grunted. "Perhaps. In any case, let's get going. I don't believe in miracles."

Ten minutes earlier, somewhere central in the building, in a circular room thirty feet in diameter, five men sat at computer stations, watching huge monitors that lined the walls. Beneath the monitors was a schematic of the building showing all its rooms and corridors. Like on a checkerboard, blue and red dots moved back and forth in different directions.

The room was silent except for the clicking of computer boards. One crew-cut blond man broke the silence. "The west screen has blanked out." Without looking around, he spoke to one of six men sitting at a table laden with phones. "It has to be checked out bef—" He pursed thick lips. "Hold one moment. The rear doors have opened; the proper key code was used." His eyes sparked suddenly. "We have intruders. Red dots—four of them."

The crew-cut blond hit a button; it opened a panel at his

right. He pulled a red-handled switch, which brought instant response from somewhere in the area breached. "We see it. We're on our way."

Three blue dots raced down the corridor, joining two others descending from a floor above. A dark-haired man at the telephone table lifted a microphone and gave the warning that was heard by everyone in the building.

Josh, Alex, and the Brenner brothers had taken no more than four steps into the small foyer when they heard the warning. All notions of entering the building undetected were swept away.

"Crap! Now what!" Josh muttered, breathing heavily.

Noah Brenner took command. "Your backpacks are equipped with gas masks. Get them on. Don't do anything else. Aaron and I have tear gas canisters in readiness. We'll each use one as someone shows. Josh, you and Alex hold yours in reserve." He looked back. "Are you ready?"

The gruesome masks in place, they nodded to each other, then moved forward in pairs, the Brenners leading.

Josh's breathing was labored. In addition to everything else, he was wondering about the Brenners. Were they still working for the Mossad? Undercover? Their equipment wasn't your everyday gear for private security men.

Beginning to feel dizzy, he made an effort to slow his breathing. It was almost fifteen years since he'd done any field work with the police department. *Fifteen years!* It felt like fifty, dragging his handicapped leg—which was beginning to feel like a dead weight.

He felt a nudge at his elbow and caught Alex's look of concern. Sweating under the mask, Josh took a deep breath and exhaled slowly. Staunchly he held up a hand, forming a circle with his thumb and forefinger.

Before Alex could respond, the Brenners had halted all

forward movement. Two black-clad armed men had appeared at the far end of the long corridor, three others at their heels. Noah and Aaron pulled at the canisters and tossed them thirty feet ahead, no more than twenty feet in front of the charging men.

Two of them, coughing violently, made it through to the Brenners. Noah, prepared, karate-chopped the lead man on the back of the neck, knocking him out. Aaron followed suit with the other. There wasn't a wasted movement between the brothers, Josh noted. Their Mossad training showed.

It became more apparent a moment later when the two brothers shoved Alex and Josh to the floor, where the four of them lay prone behind the two unconscious figures. In seconds a volley of bullets swept through the corridor, raking the ceiling, the walls, and floors. The two fallen men, bulwarking the Brenners, took the brunt of the barrage.

The long hall was filled with smoke; bullets ricocheting off the walls found the entry doors. The confined area reeked of cordite, but there was no advance by the gunners.

A lull followed the twenty-second barrage, and it was another ten seconds before anyone dared peek above the two lifeless figures. There was no sound or sign of movement coming from the far end, but a sudden whooshing of air came from above. A sucking sound.

"They're pulling the gas out," Josh muttered through clenched teeth.

Alex pushed at Noah's shoulder. "I'll take the point if it's okay with you. Offense is still the best defense, but we have to go now."

Noah glanced at Aaron, got a nod, then turned to Josh. "Are you ready for more of this?"

"Damn!" he sputtered. "Stop mothering me."

"Keep your masks on," Noah said, getting to his feet. In a half-crouch Alex moved forward, stepping over the two bloody figures. He stopped at each door to test the knob. Every door was locked.

Alex stayed them just before the T-head of the corridor. He fell to his stomach and rolled beyond the corner, his gun swinging in both directions. No one was there.

"This way," he said, going left, taking the opposite direction from where the attackers had appeared. The corridor to the left was wider, its floor carpeted rather than tiled, and more promising, with staircases leading both up and down at the far end. They covered the distance without incident.

The four of them stood before the winding staircases, checking in all directions. It was another world, at odds with the unexplainably Spartan corridor they had left. Rich, red plush carpeting covered ascending staircases that flanked a wide descending one.

They sensed they were being watched, or observed on some monitor. TV cameras occupied all corners.

With the first sigh of hesitation Josh said, "We take the down stairs. I would guess they're more likely to hold hostages below."

Aaron raised an eyebrow. "Did you ever hear of the Tower of London?"

"Okay, then you decide. Let's not just stand here." Beneath the gas mask sweat was running into Josh's eyes, and his stubble of beard was itching like mad. He couldn't remember when he had last been so tired.

Noah scanned both directions. Either their attackers were regrouping or they were simply biding their time, waiting for the flies to be caught in a prepared web. Noah pointed a thumb down. They followed him down the staircase.

It led them into a large lounge, windowless, but with a number of archways leading elsewhere. Massive sofas, tables, and chairs were spaced about the room; small lamps on end tables provided pleasant lighting. It was a room designed for comfort and welcome guests.

Josh dropped into a straight leather chair, catering to a body which—because of age or overactivity—had become a sullen servant. He pulled off his mask and wiped a hand across his face, with a look that dared anyone to censure him.

No one said anything, but Noah had walked to the nearest archway, twenty feet away. He peered down its unadorned length, and studied the wall abutting the lounge. His hand groped along the surface, feeling the texture, then reached into his backpack and fished out a stethoscope. Removing his mask, he inserted the earpieces and planted the metal cone against the wall.

Josh continued to marvel at the equipment the Brenners were carrying—their bag of tricks seemed to hold something for any situation. He watched Noah slide the instrument along the wall, trying to isolate any telltale sound.

Aaron waited only briefly before producing another stethoscope from his own knapsack, and working the opposite wall.

Josh got Alex's attention with a cough. "What are they expecting to find?" he asked.

"From what can be seen, there's no break in the entire length of the wall. So, something must be going on behind it." He nodded toward the Brenners. "It's possible they can pick up a clue."

Aaron Brenner leaned back suddenly, startled, his features a blend of surprise and confusion. He spun around to face his brother. "The one called Stoner—Jason . . . I heard his voice. For just a second."

Josh pushed himself to his feet. "What was he saying?"

Noah was instantly at the wall, running his own stethoscope across its surface. He shook his head; he was getting nothing but white noise.

Josh tugged at Aaron's shoulder. "What do you think you heard?"

"'This way,' was all I got. But it was definitely Stoner." He looked down the remaining length of the wall—fifteen feet. Noah was already there. It met another wall, angling to the right. The place was a maze, with a few stopping-off points. They had no choice but to follow.

The corridor was deeply carpeted, muffling their footsteps, the space otherwise silent and empty. Josh glanced at his wristwatch: two A.M. He was breathing heavy again, and for a moment had to fight off a wave of dizziness. The backpack had become a load of iron weights draining his strength. His sweat glands had dried up; he no longer perspired.

Alex, alerted, called out to Aaron Brenner in a hushed tone. "Either of you think to bring a canteen of water? It's needed back here."

Aaron took in Josh's condition at a glance. Reaching into a zippered pocket on his sleeve, he pulled out a pillbox and handed him two pills, then unhooked the canteen attached to his belt. "They're salt pills. Three swallows from the flask should help it down."

Seconds later Josh said, "Sorry for the holdup. Forge ahead. If you heard Stoner speaking, the others must be with him." He held out the canteen, but Aaron told him to keep it.

A brief resentment took hold of Josh. "Don't treat me like a fifth wheel, Aaron. Take back your canteen. I can hold up my end."

Aaron gazed at him. "If we thought you were a fifth wheel, we wouldn't have let you come along with us. You were dehydrated. When was the last time you carried a forty-pound backpack?"

Josh nodded, quiescent, but pointing a finger to indicate that they move along without further comment.

Noah had found a door, the first in the corridor, and had the stethoscope on it. Apparently hearing only white noise, he reached for the door handle.

In the next instant he startled the others by leaping to one side. Flattening himself against the wall, he signaled them to follow suite. They flanked the door, their weapons held upright. The door handle was already turning.

The door opened inward, away from the corridor.

The door was ajar, silence beyond it. Chelsea and the others had heard the gunshots minutes before, but they had come from a distance. All was quiet now except for the rush of air being sucked into vents. They had no idea what it meant. Chelsea caught Ward's eye; he pointed a finger at himself and then the others, indicating he would go first. He widened the door opening and took one step over the threshold—

—and instantly froze.

A handgun was jammed against his right temple, another at his left.

"Shit!" he growled, unable to move, but staring at two black-faced figures.

A laugh from one greeted his expletive. "Yeah—and you sure stepped in it."

"Josh!" Chelsea exploded. "What the hell—?"

A squeal came from behind him, from Cindy. "Damn you, Josh!"

"Yeah, right," Josh returned. "Save it for later, hon. We gotta keep movin'."

Chelsea moved into the corridor. "No, we have to end it. Once and for all." He took in the blackened faces at a glance, and noted their backpacks. "Has anyone got a match, anything that could start a fire?"

He didn't see any smoke alarms in the hall, but had noted two in their suite.

Jason spoke up from behind him. "It won't work. They won't be tied to the city fire department. Most likely they have their own fire brigade. The last thing they would want is an invasion of this property."

"How about their computer room, their laboratories? You're the expert. How would it be protected from water damage?"

"There's no sprinkler system in those rooms. They're protected by state-of-the-art equipment. At any sign of fire or danger, a thirty-second warning goes into effect for everyone to leave the area. A computerized device seals all doors and sets off a vacuum system pulling out all oxygen. Without oxygen, the fire goes out and—God help anyone caught in there."

Noah signaled Chelsea. "We can't delay. Our immediate concern is to get out. Anything else should be postponed for other troops."

Chelsea gave him an odd look. *What troops?* Were the Brenners working on something they hadn't mentioned? He could read nothing in the blackened face. Whatever thoughts he toyed with were shunted aside by Ellie.

"Why the discussion, Joe? Why are we standing here?"

He nodded, only half-listening. "Noah, you have any spare armament in those bags?"

Noah turned his back to Chelsea and said, "Reach into my pack. There's a Walther PPK on the left side pocket."

Chelsea found it—a semiautomatic with seven bullets plus one in hold; it was small enough to fit in a woman's handbag.

He looked back and took in the grim faces. Dave Ward and Fran Fargo were hanging back, checking the smoke alarm in the sitting room. Ward said, "Joey, there's no sprinkler system in here."

Noah tossed a butane lighter through the doorway to Ward. "Light something and hold it under the alarm. Whatever confusion we cause will work to our benefit."

Fran handed him a couple of tissues. Ward held the lighter to them.

Chelsea said, "Whoever's taking the point, I want Stoner right behind him." He caught Jason's eye. "He might just direct us to an exit."

Josh started slipping out of his backpack. "Take it, Jason, I know when I'm beat."

Noah said, "If everything else is settled, I'll lead."

Jon Seltzmann was in the computer room, watching the red dots move along the schematic on the wall beneath the monitors. A larger, square red marker was blinking furiously in what was designated as their "guests" suite.

"Damn them!" he muttered, curiously more annoyed than angered. He couldn't understand the security breach.

A door opened, and an orderly wheeled in a scowling Izzy Gorham. His face, however, bore the thoughts of Emil Seltzer. When he spoke his speech was guarded. As Jon had observed before, the transfer to the new host had been too hasty; Izzy Gorham was fighting him.

He was wheeled to the console desk, beside his son. Emil Seltzer had always been a man slow to anger, but now he sounded peevish. "Why are you delaying my new transition? My present host is too overpowering to control. Before it's too late . . ." He looked up at the electronic board. "Is that them?"

"Yes, but you needn't concern yourself. They're not going anywhere except where I want them to."

Izzy Gorham's face contorted in a painful frown. "Isn't

that the fire alarm on the board?" His lips formed a wry grin. "It's the captain, Chelsea, isn't it?" And, immediately, the scowl returned.

Emil Seltzer tugged at his son's arm. "Jon, you must do something . . . And quickly. I shall be lost . . . I can't remain in Gorham's brain. He is getting stronger and you don't know what's in his mind."

His son looked apprehensive for the first time.

"Can you return to surgery, to complete the takeover?"

The scientist's lips twisted in anguish. "Yes—and no. I can go into surgery, but only to switch to a new host. My time is running out. It is imperative that Joseph Chelsea be brought to the laboratory as soon as possible—for total preparation, not the halfway measures taken with Gorham."

The younger man watched the red dots moving on the electronic board, sensing that he and his father had reached a climactic moment in their lives. Could his father go on forever, for all eternity, as he truly believed? Going from one host body to another—to be immortal. And with each additional changeover becoming physically and—more important—mentally stronger?

For one moment an importuning thought—a dormant one, lingering for months—shook loose. *What if my mind were to take over my father's . . .* ?

"What are you thinking, Jon? Why are you waiting?"

"Patience, Father. I have to keep an eye on your projected new host. He's one of those red dots, now numbering eleven, creeping through the guest corridor."

The older man writhed. "Patience," he grunted. "It's something I can no longer indulge. My host doesn't allow it. The use of Gorham was an atrocious error. Litvinoff should have recognized that the man was too aggressive, too much of a fighter. He should have been dealt with four decades ago in the camp."

He squirmed suddenly, holding his hands to his stomach as if suffering severe cramps. His lips looked misshapen, then just as quickly adjusted to some semblance of normalcy. His voice hissed, "Jon, do something before it's too late! I can't go on this way. If this continues, he will become master of *my* will."

Jon turned to stare at his father, incredulous. "Are you telling me his uneducated brain is stronger than your own?"

"He's younger, more physically fit than I was. My will has aged; it has memory, but not the mental strength of my youth. My memory bank did not replace Gorham's; it was an addition to his mind before I could absorb his. Because of the emergency Litvinoff and his crew did not allow for a proper linkup with synaptic—"

"Okay, Father. It's enough. You've made your point."

Others, working the phones and monitors, were listening, with astonishment and some embarrassment. It was a rare occasion—if indeed it ever happened—when father and son had a disagreement.

Jon turned to a wide-eyed young man at a phone console. "Notify the team of Doctors Feldman, Malcolm, and Max Litvinoff to convene in the operating room and prepare for emergency surgery."

He spun around to the orderly attending his father. "You know where to take Dr. Seltzer." To his father he said, "Remember, you always cautioned 'no hysterics.' "

Gorham's head nodded, wearing an enigmatic smile.

Chelsea searched each face. "It's important that I know how you found us. And does anyone else know where you are?"

No one spoke immediately. Moving forward stealthily was difficult enough without carrying on a whispered conversation.

Noah finally said, "I suggest we discuss this later. And no one knows we're here. Credit Alex for finding you."

Chelsea respected the ensuing silence only until they encountered a stairwell at a turn in the corridor. There he tapped Noah's shoulder.

"I think you should know that if and when you see Izzy Gorham, it won't be him—entirely. Dr. Emil Seltzer had his own memory linked with Gorham's." The statement brought incredulous stares from those who heard him. "I met with Seltzer and was tacitly warned I was to be the next so-called receptor for his memory bank. Principally because Seltzer's surgeons botched the job with Gorham. Izzy has been fighting Seltzer—not physically, but with brain waves. Something to do with linking the memory to a particular section of the brain. Emil Seltzer doesn't have complete control of Izzy. So, bear it in mind should we meet him again."

Ward whispered to Mae in front of him, "So that's how the bugger got listed as dead. The body was physically dead, but the memory or will, or whatever, was attached to a new host. And when that host ran down . . ."

"Yes," Chelsea said, overhearing, and scanning the staircase, "and that about sums it up. On which level did you guys enter the building?"

"One floor above," Josh said. "It's street level."

Noah broke in. "We can't retrack. They must have deployed a cleanup crew by now and closed the exit."

"You have no idea how many men are quartered in this building? You must have counted cars in the parking area."

Alex, moving up from the rear, said, "Not actual count, but about ten. There's no way we could have checked the entire property."

Chelsea scanned the carpeted staircase again. Deserted

and silent. "There's no way they can't know where we are. I feel like we're walking into an ambush. Any ideas?"

"Mind if I butt in?" Ward said. "I remind you we have women here. Are you thinking escape or attack?"

"The first step is to get the women out," Chelsea stated firmly. "Then we . . ."

"Christ!" Josh exploded. "Then what? They have a cab waiting for us while we're working on doomsday?"

"And while we're on the subject," Ward added sarcastically, "how do we achieve a safe exit from here for *anyone?* You going to beam us out, Joey?"

"We storm the Bastille."

"What are you talking about, Joey?"

Chelsea ran a hand through his hair. "Okay, the women go back to the suite, a temporary refuge. It's clean by now and they'd never expect anyone to return. The men forge ahead, searching for the computer room—or the laboratory; regardless of what's on the foundation island, I'm certain there's one here. Seltzer is in need of it. ASAP."

There were skeptical looks from everyone. He spoke hurriedly. "We have no options. We get caught again, our lives, as we know them, are over." He finished up softly. "It has to end now. Once and for all."

His short speech did nothing to erase their skepticism. Ward muttered an oath. "Jesus, Joey, such dedication. Why couldn't you have accepted a quiet retirement?"

Josh could only wonder where Chelsea got the energy. Joe was right: He wasn't ready for retirement. His maneuvering of the group here reminded Josh of earlier days in the squad room.

Josh studied the women—and then Alex. He made his decision. "Alex, you go with the men. You'll be of more use up front. I'll escort the women back to the suite." He caught

Chelsea's rueful expression. "It's okay, Joe. It's better this way." Cindy took his hand.

"Ellie . . ." Chelsea began.

"Just go, Joe," she said. "Finish it—and come back for us." She gave him a wink, and he returned it. Nothing more was said, but he noted a teardrop on her cheek. Ward nodded at Mae; her lips were clamped shut. Jason squeezed Fran Fargo's hand; she squeezed back, but neither said a word.

It was a depressing moment for all, but Noah waited until they were almost out of sight. "Now what! Chelsea, why are we standing around? Do you really have something in mind?"

"Alex, go down one landing on the staircase. If you see any signs of activity, let us know." Chelsea faced Noah. "I said before that I feel we're walking into an ambush. Do you realize no one's come after us? Why haven't they?"

Noah let out a deep breath. "I'm not stupid, Chelsea. At a guess I'd say they're expecting us, knowing the direction we're headed. More than likely they have us under surveillance on computer screens somewhere.

Ward leaned forward. "Joey, what the hell are we doing here? Why don't we head for where the Brenners came in and storm our way out." He scanned the backpacks. "I'm assuming they have enough fire power."

"And Josh and the women—" Chelsea snorted. "We simply abandon them?"

Ward's expression was pained. "Of course not! Once we got out, I would call in friends from the Bureau. We've already waited too long."

Aaron nudged his brother and whispered in his ear. "Noah, if you don't speak, I will."

Chelsea was instantly suspicious; the Brenners were keeping secrets. "You mentioned troops before," he said. "You mean literally?"

Noah's cheek twitched. He replied in a very low voice, fearful of hidden mikes. "If we can take out this place—or at least cause substantial damage—it will be all over for the Alliance. We have friends working on the elimination of the Founding Fathers Resort."

Chelsea ground his teeth. "You call this working as a team? We trusted you not to call in outsiders."

"Don't be a fool," Aaron spit out. "This is too big an operation. It's been too big from the start. The body count has grown in the past two days, and is still growing. It's about ready to blow up in our faces. It amazes me that you don't feel threatened by all this. Your family, friends, all involved . . . Did you really believe you could bring down the Alliance on your own? You're good, Chelsea, but you're not Rambo. The situation calls for outside help. Help that is qual . . ."

Noah jumped in. "And we did just that—called for help. As of two days ago. We tried contacting you, but for the past forty-eight hours you were not available. You were either in trouble or escaping from it." He rubbed sweat from his cheeks. "Now, if it weren't for your man Alex . . ."

Chelsea didn't reply. There was a sag in his shoulders, a heavy weight pressing his large physique down onto weak knees. He was suddenly thrust past middle age, into the twilight of advanced age. *In so many words he had been told he couldn't hack it.*

Jason, a few feet away from Chelsea, sensed what was happening. Chelsea's most conspicuous feature was his bright eyes; they now appeared washed-out. He was reminded of an aging athlete, the body no longer rugged, and the spirit gone. "Chelsea . . ." he called out.

Chelsea heard his name. He lifted his head wearily. "Yes, you were saying . . ."

Aaron stayed Noah, who was about to speak. "Captain Chelsea, we're awaiting your orders."

Chelsea brought a hand to his face, covering his mouth and chin. He squeezed and rubbed his lips, mulling over confused thoughts, then shook his shoulders. His voice exploded.

"Damn! You called in Mossad? You're still members." His eyes were bright again, glaring at Noah. "And what is their plan—and timetable?"

Aaron said, "We know nothing of their plan, but we were told not to interfere. And that in three or four weeks all will come to fruition."

"That's it? We forget about it—and wait for an announcement telling us the Alliance has been . . . What? Dissolved?"

"We still have a job here," Jason interjected.

Ward said, "I know what you want, Joey. It's the lab. You want to wreck it." Ward's comment got a nod from Chelsea.

"Yes. It must be on a lower level, protected from unexpected visitors." He almost smiled. "The lower level—that's where it belongs." He peered into Noah's blackened face. "It also means we make an effort to get Izzy Gorham out, with or without Seltzer's consent. We take Gorham-Seltzer hostage, no one will dare touch us." He stared from one sooty face to the other. "You guys are dressed as commandos—does that mean you're capable?"

Aaron said with a tight grin, "We're capable—but we wouldn't refuse help from the Almighty."

Chelsea moved to the staircase; he could see Alex on the landing below, crouching, listening. Alex looked up, shrugged, and shook his head. The silence was ominous.

Chelsea said, "Noah, you and Aaron lead. You have the equipment. You have gas bombs? I don't like killing unless it can't be avoided."

"Tear gas—and sleeping gas," Noah replied. "We don't like unnecessary killing either." Chelsea glanced at the Beretta.

"That's for the 'can't be avoided.' "

"Jason, I want you at my side," Chelsea ordered imperiously, and waved a hand. "Let's move."

Ward snorted. "It's about time. I have a charter to get back to." The bravado was forced, drawing grim smiles.

"The final stage, Dave," Chelsea said.

Ward snickered. "Yeah—but for whom?"

"You think the girls will be okay, Dave? I've really messed up with all of you."

"You did what you felt you had to do. This isn't the time for backlash—or whipping yourself. The girls will hold out as long as we do." He gave Chelsea a sharp glance. "Don't go morbid on me now. Just tell me what you expect us to accomplish. They could have a hundred-man platoon waiting for us."

"However it's done, we have to get inside the lab—or surgery—whatever it's called."

Jason, listening to the discussion, wondered also where Chelsea was leading. It was only minutes ago that he seemed to have "lost" it.

"Why the lab?" Ward asked. "Because of Gorham?"

"The lab is the center of their universe. It must be destroyed."

"How?" Jason interjected, quietly sliding down another step. His thoughts swinging between Chelsea and Fran, he didn't know which group he preferred to be with. *Had it been smart to leave the women there?*

"The lower floors must be below sea level. A single crack in a wall . . ."

"We're below sea level now—why not try cracking the

wall right here? Anywhere below sea level in the building will serve the same purpose."

"No, the lab likely has its own safety features that seal it off from the rest of the building. We have to destroy the room itself."

Ward's lips compressed. "Man, you're not asking much, are you?"

Chelsea scratched a stubbled chin. "Yes, I know. But I admit the Brenners made it easier. I don't like the way they went about it, but calling in their 'friends' was a master stroke. I must have been whistling in the dark to believe we could handle Operation Sunset by ourselves." Ward grimaced; Chelsea must have been nursing this name for the mission from the outset. "Your friends in the Bureau could commandeer this place when and if we get out."

"Jesus! Operation Sunset! Good God! I should have known it. Felt it. I should have been warned."

Another landing and the staircase ended, with still no sound or sign of anyone. A wide, white-walled corridor stretched before them, as inviting as a spider's web. The white tile floor was hospital-clean.

Alex looked back at Chelsea, awaiting instructions.

"Alex, get on your hands and knees. Check . . ." He hesitated and asked Aaron, "You wouldn't happen to have a metal detector on you?"

"Whatever for?"

Chelsea told him of the meeting with Seltzmann, and the armed men appearing from behind sliding wall panels.

Without further question, the Brenners brought out their stethoscopes again. No one moved while they "listened" to the walls in the tunnel-like corridor, which was at least thirty feet long.

At the end of the tunnel were two closed doors spanning the width of the corridor.

Nothing but white noise was heard behind the walls. Ten minutes later they stood at the pair of wood doors, which bore metal handles rather than knobs. Aaron turned and looked back, with a now-what expression. The gauntlet had been run and nothing had occurred.

Chelsea hand-signaled the Brenners to put away the stethoscopes, then motioned for the three "commandos" to don their gas masks again. He directed Alex to the door, cautioning, "Be sure the handle isn't electrified."

Before Alex could make a move Noah stayed him, and pulled another meter from his bag of tricks. It took only seconds for him to mouth "Safe."

Chelsea pointed out the absence of hinges; it meant the doors opened inward. Alex was to lead but, along with Noah and Aaron, was to have a hand weapon ready.

Chelsea moved back a few feet, pulling Jason and Ward with him. His shirt was sweat-soaked, his face beaded, despite the air-conditioning. Everyone watched as he wiped at his eyes with a handkerchief.

They were now on the threshold of their personal destinies—and he was leading them. *God help us!*

He licked at the salt on his lips and waved them on.

36

Josh looked up from the bathroom mirror, the black makeup almost cleaned off. He felt an utter fool being here; his place was with the men. He leaned heavily on his game leg, trying to salve his conscience. The self-recriminations continued. He felt like an old man, trying to right youthful mistakes.

Cindy stood in the doorway. "You need help? There's still some of that gook behind your ears."

"Cindy, please, I don't need mothering."

She moved to his side. "What do you need? More soldiering? We wouldn't be here if—" She bit her lip, and her eyes started to mist.

He took her hand compassionately. "You know the word *bershaert?* Your mother used it quite often. It was her rationale for everything that had ever happened to her. If it was meant to happen, it will happen. What will be, will be."

His words brought a small smile. "If she was here now, she would probably get us out safely."

Josh took a towel from Cindy, wiped his face, then the

back of his neck. Avoiding her eyes, he said, "About getting out, I don't think we can afford to wait for Joe."

"What are you saying? You were involved in a shooting earlier. How are we supposed to . . ."

He tossed the towel away and took her hands. "Cindy, we can't wait for Joe and Ward. Do you understand?"

Her eyes shadowed. She shook her head, refusing to acknowledge what Josh was saying. "No, no, I don't want to hear it. Why would Joe tell us to wait if . . ."

Josh squeezed her hands. "That's what he said aloud; it's not what he meant. Remember, this place is lousy with bugs. It's the reason we have to keep whispering."

Cindy's eyes darted from one place to another, as if seeking escape from reality. "We can't leave. What would you tell Ellie?"

"I think Ellie will be more understanding than you imagine. I know Joe gave her some sort of signal." He took Cindy's arm, steering her toward the bathroom door. "Send in the others. Ward told me this is the only safe room he could vouch for."

Besides the whirlpool bath at one end and a shower stall at the other, the big bathroom was furnished with a dressing table and bench. Ellie, studying Cindy's face, insisted on standing. She told—no, ordered—Fran and Mae to share the bench, then listened to Josh explain the situation.

"No questions?" Josh said.

Fran Fargo, hesitant, raised her hand. "Yes, what are you expecting from us?"

"Agreement," Ellie replied.

"To what?" Mae asked.

Josh held up a silencing hand. "We retrace the path I took to get in." He shushed them as protests started. "No one followed us back here and there's no one guarding our door.

That tells me they feel safe at this end, and that they judge Joe and the others to be a greater threat to them."

Ellie listened with half an ear, her thoughts elsewhere. A single tear formed at the corner of her eye; she dabbed at it before it could fall.

"I might add, Ellie, that Joe is not expecting us to hang around."

She was in agreement, though her expression remained solemn, but it was too much for Mae. She erupted from the bench. "You can't possibly leave without . . ."

Surprisingly, Fran Fargo took Mae's hand. "Why don't we listen to Mr. Novick before arguing about anything."

Grateful for Fargo's aid, Josh pointed toward the sitting room. "Follow me," he said.

After scanning the bleached-look hallway, he turned back to the anxious group and observed them briefly before proposing his plan. Except for Mae, they were waiting, eager, ready to follow just about any instruction.

"Okay," he said quickly. "We're about to cause confusion by blowing some fuses."

"And that gets us out?" Mae asked sharply.

"And how does it help Joe and the others?" Ellie queried.

Before he could reply, Fran interjected, "You apparently want to blow out the lights. How do you expect to accomplish that?" She pointed beyond the door to the concealed lighting in the ceiling.

Still on the obstinate side, Mae complained. "And how do we find our way in the dark?"

Josh held up his hands defensively. "Okay, one at a time. Short-circuiting the system could possibly help Joe more than us. It's simply a diversion—anything to cause confusion." He pulled off the nightscope attached to his belt and briefly explained its use. "Once I crack that light and cause it to short out, each of you has to grab on to the other's coattail to follow me out. Now, how do you want to line up? Make your own decisions."

The lineup decided on was Cindy, Ellie, Mae, and Fran.

Satisfied, Josh examined the lighting with a practiced eye. It was the usual system of translucent light South Florida engendered in most apartment-condo complexes, fluorescent tubes above plastic shields making for soft light. Where ceilings met walls, the shields were usually curved, conveying the sense of living under a dome.

All Josh had to do was bring out a straight chair from the sitting room, stand on it, reach up, and push a clear plastic panel aside. Once the four-foot, 40-watt tubes were exposed, it was a simple task to twist two tubes from their sockets. He handed both down to Cindy, then stepped off the chair and retrieved one of them. "Hold the other until I need it," he said. From a pocket in his sweater he fished out a package of rubber gloves. Carrying them around was an old habit, left over from his days on the police force. "You really never know," he mused.

Josh studied the women's faces, then sent them back to the doorway to wait for his signal. He gripped the four-foot tube like a baseball bat. "Everybody ready?" He asked quietly, and received affirmative nods.

He set his night-vision glasses in place, and then grasping the glass tube, swung it across the remaining two tubes in the ceiling.

There was a gasp from the women as broken glass spattered the hallway. Intermittent sparks flew from the fixture before all the lights in the hallway flickered and then went out. Inside the doorway the suite remained illuminated.

It wasn't unexpected. Josh was only interested in the hallways they would have to walk through. "Hold on to that other tube," he reminded Cindy. "We're going to need it in another hallway."

Enough light came from the suite that they could see halfway down the corridor. "Let's go. We're on our way out," he said confidently.

Cindy, unable to contain her misgivings, whispered anxiously, "You don't really expect us to just walk out of this place, do you?"

Josh attempted a smile. "I'm banking on a crazy idea that keeps running through my brain, that no one will be watching the door I entered originally. Why would they even suspect we would try it? With all that's happening now, they've probably got a lot more to worry about than us." The scope made the dark end of the corridor appear green, though clearly visible. "Any questions?" he asked before getting underway.

"What can we expect ahead?" Ellie murmured.

"We go up the staircase at the end of the hall. One flight only. Then, as instructed, follow me.

"Everyone understand?" he asked, again searching their faces. *A squad of four women following him blindly. God help him to find the way.*

Jon Seltzman, wearing a surgical gown and mask, stood beside the prone but conscious figure of Izzy Gorham.

Gorham twisted his head; he spoke slowly, with an effort, his speech that of Emil Seltzer. "You realize nothing dare go amiss." His son nodded, although his inner thoughts seethed with doubts. The old man's memory bank had displayed wear and tear despite engaging a new host. Apparently there were limits of endurance and age that his father couldn't eliminate or overcome. Jon's suspicions had been confirmed by the surgical crew of Feldman, Malcolm, and Litvinoff. His father's personal surgeons for the past thirty years, they had joined with him permanently after his reported "death." Seltzer's memory from his own brain had been stored in a microchip. The chip would last almost forever, but the brain matter had weakened. The next host would be the final one for Emil Seltzer.

"The new host, is it ready?" Gorham asked wearily. The anesthetic was taking effect.

"Soon, Father." Jon looked toward the see-through glass walls of the operating room. Two of those walls permitted one to look into an adjoining glass-walled room. A red light glowed above the double doors that opened into that room from the corridor. Seltzmann smiled. The glowing red light was notification of an unclassified, if not unexpected, presence outside the doors.

He looked toward the team of gowned doctors and the three male nurses in attendance. They were ready. His attention was drawn back to the red light, and the door handle which was moving downward. "Yes, Father," he murmured. "At any moment."

Alex pushed down on the handle of the left-hand door. Noah, Aaron, Jason, Chelsea, and Ward had their backs to the wall abutting the right-hand door.

With the door open mere inches, Alex held his revolver in his right hand, pointing upward. With his left hand he pulled a grenade from his kit. Prepared, he kicked the door open but held his position.

Chelsea and the others saw a look of astonishment creep into Alex's features. "Well," Chelsea muttered impatiently. "What is it?"

Alex sounded puzzled. "It's a glass room. No—gotta be Plexiglas. I can't see any seam from here."

"How about people?"

"I can't tell." He didn't move. "I have a feeling something—or someone—is waiting for us inside."

"You're quite correct," a voice boomed through a speaker. "I suggest you all enter. We've been expecting you."

Chelsea motioned for Noah and Aaron to follow Alex into the room. He then gestured toward Alex's grenade, whispering, "Only as a last resort."

Alex pulled the pin on the grenade, and raised his gun hand again before kicking the door completely open.

It was like entering a drained twenty-foot-square fish tank; except for one small area straight ahead, translucent Plexiglas walls on three sides permitted no more than moving shadowy images to be seen.

Seltzmann was standing dead ahead, visible behind the center wall. His voice echoed hollowly through hidden speakers. "Welcome, gentlemen. Captain Chelsea, please join your cohorts." He motioned casually toward the grenade in Alex's hand. "I highly advise against aggression; the ricochet in your room would wound or kill all of you."

Chelsea, followed by Ward and Jason, stepped over the threshold. He said nothing, but his eyes swept the area. His calm exterior belied his thoughts. They had been searching for the enemy, and the enemy had found them. The door behind them banged shut.

Trapped.

Damn! Damn! Damn! Thirty years on the force and he had been taken like a rank amateur.

He felt Ward nudging him. "You remember that old TV show—*The Life of Reilly*? And William Bendix with his famous line, 'What a revoltin' development!' Well, Joey, this is one hell of a *revoltin'* development!"

Jason almost smiled despite his stomach knotting. Their situation didn't quality for humor and yet it didn't stop . . . His eyes had caught a rainbow of color—a glass prism twisting with the slightest movement of his head. He centered his vision on an almost invisible joining of glass dead center in the wall.

It must be a door into the surgery.

He leaned toward Chelsea and whispered in his ear. As Chelsea tipped his head, Seltzmann's voice reached them again. "Before we continue, you must place all your weapons on the floor, and kick them aside, toward the wall on your left. Please obey. We do not wish any of you harm, only a better future—an improvement for both you and our organization. If that sounds a bit cryptic, it will be—Never mind." He gestured dismissively, as if explanations were of little importance at the moment.

When no one made a move to obey the order, Seltzmann spoke angrily. "Look around you. You don't have a choice. Disarming means the gas masks too. They serve no purpose here. You are about to enter a sterilized area and the less you carry, the better. Please don't make me repeat my request." The voice was flat, uncompromising.

Jason had a grenade in his hand. Partially shielded behind Chelsea and Ward, he jammed it into a back pocket of his slacks. He then turned around and asked Chelsea to help him off with his backpack. With their backs to Seltzmann, Jason pressed a hunter's knife into Chelsea's hand. Chelsea stuck it under his shirt, securing it with his belt against his waist. He wondered briefly what he would do with it. A knife was new to him. Not since combat in World War Two France had he used one, and then only on one occasion. He blinked his eyes, refusing to dredge up an old memory.

Two men in surgical masks and gowns, incongruously armed with Uzis, suddenly flanked Jon Seltzmann. They had emerged from doors behind him. Before the doors slammed shut, there was a brief glimpse of cement-block walls. It was an outside wall, Chelsea was certain, just what he was seeking. But now . . .

The Plexiglas door in front of Seltzmann slid aside, creating a six-foot-wide entry. The gowned men armed with Uzis entered and kicked aside the backpacks released by Chelsea's group, then returned to stand guard at the open doors. Chelsea fumed inwardly, helpless to react. Outwitted at every turn by the egomaniac. They should have held on to their weapons; it could have been a standoff. He leaned forward on his toes, as if prepared to charge the enemy.

"Don't try it, Captain." Seltzmann responded by snapping his fingers at someone out of sight. Izzy Gorham was brought into view, handcuffed, two unarmed gowned men holding him erect. He seemed drugged; his lips moved, saying nothing. He bore no resemblance to the figure that Emil Seltzer had controlled.

"What have you done with him?"

"He's been, what we call, cleaned. Himself again." His snicker reminded Chelsea of the days of silent film, when the audience would respond with hisses and boos.

"You can have him," Seltzmann continued. "You're to be honored, Captain, as the new host for my father. Please step forward for the exchange."

Jason started forward, but Chelsea grabbed his arm. Jason spun on him. "Christ! You're not going for this! This man is bonkers—out of his mind!"

"Cool it. I'll handle it," Chelsea barked authoritatively, then faced Seltzmann fifteen feet away. The two armed guards lifted their weapons threateningly.

"It won't work," Chelsea stated vigorously. "I witnessed the problem with the previous host. He will never control me."

"The previous surgery was an emergency." Jon spoke

with assurance, but his eyes were worried. "Don't stall, Captain. You have to be prepped."

Chelsea stood his ground. "You don't know when to call it quits, do you?" he said tauntingly. "Your cartel is no longer invisible. I am, that is *we* are your first stumbling blocks." It was all bluster, a delaying action until something came to mind. He could only hope Josh could remember the way out.

At that point a figure in mask and gown appeared at Seltzmann's side to whisper in his ear. Focusing on him Chelsea recognized Dr. Malcolm behind the mask, the missing alleged retired orthodontist, supposedly a friend of Izzy Gorham.

"Problems, Doctor?" Chelsea said provokingly.

Seltzmann's lips distorted angrily. "Stop this foolish talk. It will accomplish you nothing." He gestured to the two men holding Gorham erect by his elbows. Izzy's eyes were glazed, unseeing. They started forward, through the open Plexiglas door.

Chelsea whispered to Ward and Jason, "The two guys aren't armed, but won't be expecting or creating trouble at this end. They need me alive. Dave, Jason, if it bothers you to kick at their nuts, aim for their shins. And, Jason, we have about five seconds. Get that grenade ready to toss into the other room immediately following the initial assault." He turned his head slightly. "Jason, are you up to it?" His eyes caught Alex and the Brenners. A slight nod toward the men with the Uzzis was understood.

There was no time for a verbal response. Jason and Ward responded to Chelsea's command in unison, their right legs swinging as if punting a football. Ward caught one man in the shin; Jason got the other in the knee. As both gowned men bent over in pain, Chelsea grabbed Gorham before he could follow his two captors to the floor.

Alex and the Brenners had been watching Chelsea with rapt expressions, following his stalling action. Now, with perfect timing, they went into action. Alex, standing beside Noah, pointed to the armed man left of the doorway. "I'll take him. You get the other. They don't dare fire their Uzis now."

Noah delayed until Alex made his move. Alex dropped to the floor and slid feet-first into the man he had targeted; his legs lashing out tripped the late charging man and then caught him in a body-crushing leg scissors. The Uzi was dropped and slid away. Noah, in motion an instant after him, dove headfirst for his designated target, toppling the stunned man from his feet. Aaron seemingly coming out of a daze quickly reacted to take control of all weapons.

Seltzmann was livid with rage. The seemingly orchestrated action had required mere seconds to perform and had totally wiped out his control. Dr. Malcolm tugged at his arm, trying to get his attention. Failing, he signaled to a shadow behind a wall of Plexiglas.

Chelsea saw the Plexiglas doors starting to slide closed. "Jason—the grenade! Now! The door behind Seltzmann! Aaron, Noah . . . Block the door from closing!"

All dropped to the floor as the grenade soared through the air, over Seltzmann's shoulder. The Brenners ensured its entry with two of the Uzis shoved into the doortrack. The doors stopped, blocked, within inches of shutting completely. Seltzmann and Dr. Malcolm froze in position, too stunned to react; their guards incapacitated just lay on the floor of the anteroom.

The noise was deafening in the enclosed room. Shrapnel fragmented into the shape of metal balls splattered the walls, some ricocheting into hidden areas. A cloud of smoke brought a pervading smell of cordite before erupting into a ball of fire. Tortured cries drifted from the unseen area of the operating room.

Chelsea lifted his head, saw Seltzmann and Malcolm lying on the floor, both men torn and bleeding and still as death. Just briefly he was torn between remorse and elation. He checked Izzy Gorham beside him; the man was in another world, talking to himself, aware of nothing going on, but otherwise uninjured.

Chelsea looked around. "Everyone okay?" he asked fearfully. There were thumbs up from all before they got to their feet. Chelsea motioned for Alex to take the point. He and the others, now all armed, would follow.

Once inside, Chelsea knelt beside the two prone figures and directed the Brenners to check out others in the surgery. He indicated the target door for Alex's inspection. Jason and Ward stood beside Chelsea as he examined Seltzmann's bloody face. He found no pulse at the carotid artery and the body already exuded the smell of death. Malcolm's figure stirred, his face a bloody smear. A moan escaped from tortured lips.

Chelsea called to the Brenners. "This one's alive and needs attention. Anyone there to help?"

A concerned shout burst from Aaron Brenner. "We have to vacate. The fire down at this end will soon be out of control and there are cabinets of chemicals I can't vouch for."

Noah Brenner held his Beretta aimed at one of the guards sitting on the tile floor with his back against the Plexiglas wall. He was holding his head in his hands. If he was injured, it wasn't immediately apparent. Noah waved his weapon at the remaining men, not including the doctors Feldman and Litvinoff. When he ordered them to pick up the wounded, Litvinoff disobeyed by going to a humidity-controlled glass case.

"Stop him!" Chelsea yelled to Noah. Noah took two strides and roughly bumped Litvinoff off his feet.

Litvinoff was close to hysteria. "It's Dr. Seltzer's memory bank," he screamed. "We can't desert him."

Chelsea ignored the man. He lifted one of the weapons from the floor and coolly took aim at the glass case. "Maybe you can't desert him. Mankind can."

Three quick shots exploded the case and its contents. Litvinoff held his hands to his head and openly wept. It was the end of his world. The flames were spreading behind him, casting wavering orange images along the Plexiglas wall. Noah prodded Litvinoff. "On your way."

"So much for Humpty Dumpty," Jason remarked dully. He turned to Chelsea. "Alex has the lab door open. Will that be our exit or do we backtrack?"

Chelsea gazed at Jon Seltzmann's body. He wrinkled his nose against the malodor pervading the area, blew out a deep breath of air, and, grunting, got to his feet. "Our mission here is still unfinished. Herd the sus— Shit! Suspects! Get them through that door. Dave, give Jason a hand with them."

Ward hung back. "What's with you, Joey? What are you attempting? What about the women?"

"Josh should be almost out of this place by now, or at least at a safe distance. I want this room empty—now!"

Alone, Chelsea stood watching the fire consume an entire wall of cabinets. The spotlights above the operating table had been shattered, all instruments scattered. His mind considered an important question: Would the deaths of the Seltzer governing bodies and the destruction of this laboratory have any effect on the Alliance? He certainly hoped so.

Holding a handkerchief to his nose, he gazed once more at the corpse of Jon Seltzmann, who, along with his father, the eminent Dr. Emil Seltzer, formerly headed the world's most powerful and yet most invisible cartel. Dr. Seltzer's brain-memory had finally met its destiny, burning in a crematory, like so many of his victims in the death camps.

Chelsea coughed; gray smoke filled the room. As a final gesture he removed one of the Uzis wedged between the sliding doors and sprayed all the walls until the magazine ran dry. Then, without looking back, he walked past the wrecked door. Explosions from the abandoned room brought a feeling of elation, of a job well done.

Jason was waiting for him, but didn't share his elation. "We've got to get out of here and check on the others before the whole place comes down. It's two flights up to street level."

The smoke was streaking through the corridor, the fire torching the carpeting and trailing them up the staircase. Lights went out, forcing them to use their nightscopes. Whatever fire doors existed failed to work because of the power failure.

"Chelsea . . ." Jason urged. Getting to Fran preyed on his mind.

"Hold on. Will the computer room continue to operate? And the fire brigade . . . Can they function without power?" He didn't wait for a response, expected none.

"I want this place destroyed, so it's utterly impossible to rebuild. We have to go back down a flight. The outer wall of the foundation must be breached. The place has to be under water."

Jason grasped Chelsea's arm. "It isn't necessary. The explosion and fire will accomplish all that."

Chelsea shook his hand off. "No way. The Alliance has billions to play with. They can repair all damage, rebuild everything. The lower floors must be flooded and made unsafe for reconstruction."

Jason rubbed the grime from his face, realizing there was

no turning Chelsea back. The man was driven, and probably correct in his assumption.

Christ! Jason thought. *Why am I doing this? I have to find Fran!*

Chelsea started back down the staircase, then hesitated. "You coming or not? If not, I need a couple of grenades from your pack. More if you have them."

"Shit! Yes! I'm coming! I'm right behind you."

Chelsea grunted, but smiled.

They should have had the gas masks. Choking smoke filled the corridors with a heavy stench that clogged their nostrils and made their eyes water even through the handkerchiefs they clasped to their faces. The carpet had burned out, producing acrid smoke that made it more difficult to breathe.

They were almost back to the surgery when Chelsea called a halt. He felt along the cement-block wall, which he had guessed earlier to be an outside retaining wall. The blocks felt cold despite the high temperatures caused by the laboratory fire.

Pulling the knife from his belt, he felt for a joining seam in the concrete blocks. He gouged an inch-deep hole into the stubborn cement joint, then another, and another, until Jason urged him aside to relieve him. He reamed them out deeper.

Finally, Jason stopped and said, "There're four grenades left in my pack." Chelsea fished them out and said, "I'll handle it from here. You can take off now."

"Like hell you will. This is one time I'm more knowledgeable than you. I also need the roll of tape." Chelsea was too tired to argue. He handed over the grenades one at a time, and then the tape.

The holes had been reamed about an inch wide and two inches deep. The grenades were forced in as far as they could go with the pins on the outside. The tape prevented them from coming loose.

"You know the timing?" Chelsea asked.

Jason nodded, wiping the sweat from his face with his sleeve. "You take off first," he said. "I can run faster than you. When you get to the staircase, give a shout and head up. That's my signal to pull the pins. They're set for ten seconds. Don't wait for me. I'll be on your heels."

Chelsea was too spent to resist. His will was strong but the events of the past twenty-four sleepless hours had whittled down his almost inexhaustible reserves.

The last grenade in place, Jason turned from the wall. Chelsea's cheeks were grimy with gray ash and sweat. His eyes were tearing, squinting with fatigue. "What are you waiting for?" Jason rasped. "To criticize my contribution?"

Chelsea snorted, ran a hand through his disheveled hair, then spun away and ran off.

The plastic ceiling shields were fireproof, but were warping and creating an odor that made him nauseous. He took deep swallows, awaiting Chelsea's shout.

When Chelsea reached the staircase, Ward was coming down toward him. "I sent the others ahead to look for Josh. Why the hell are you holding back? Where's Stoner?"

Chelsea waved him to silence, then looked down the dark smoke-filled corridor. An orange glow undulated far down its length. He cupped his hands to his lips and roared, "NOW, JASON!"

"What the hell—!" Ward sputtered as he was roughly shoved back up the steps. "Jason will be right behind us," Chelsea yelled. "The octopus is dead; we just have to worry about the tentacles."

On the first landing he stopped, stared back, and listened for footsteps. Jason was on top of him almost before he heard him. "Go ahead," Jason cried out. "I'll check it before leaving."

The sound of the explosion roared through the corridor, delivering angry clouds of choking smoke and cement dust.

"Let's go!" Ward yelled above the noise. He tugged at Chelsea's elbow.

"Not yet. I have to be sure it worked."

"Stay here," Jason ordered. He held a small penlight, which was of little use in the circumstances but was all he had in his pack; he hadn't been left a nightscope. Before Chelsea could stop him, he retraced his steps down the corridor.

Twenty feet from the broken wall the flames were eating the smoke. The stench emanating from melting tile and linoleum was almost unendurable, but he had to know the extent of the damage—if for no other reason than to prevent Chelsea from doing his own investigation.

The blaze made the miniature flashlight useless. The break was visible: a two-foot hole, with globs of mud oozing from it, piling up on the hot tiles, and leveeing the corridor from the flames. Jason muttered a silent curse. They had assumed wrongly; the water they had expected hadn't materialized.

He wondered what his next move should be. Chelsea would insist on returning to make what could only be a futile attempt to—

The wall suddenly bulged; a weakened cement block moved and slid out onto the pile of mud. A surge of water and muck followed, leaping across the mired area. In seconds it was a torrent, splattering mud and debris against the opposite wall with a vengeance.

Jason raised a fist triumphantly. He tore down the hall, racing the river that threatened to engulf him. By the time he reached the staircase the water was a foot deep. He waved

Ward and Chelsea ahead. "Let's find the others," he shouted at them.

The women followed Josh through the door he had originally entered with Alex and the Brenners. Everything he had guessed and hoped for had miraculously worked out. No one had accosted them in the hallways. He could only speculate that the building had been evacuated for some unknown reason. Or that Chelsea had been responsible in some way. Everyone had heard the explosion earlier and wondered what it meant, assuming it wouldn't have been caused by their captors.

It was dark except for one light at the end of the dock. Josh could see no one in the area facing the Intracoastal. *Strange. What would cause the tenants to desert?*

"There's a boat on the next property," Fran Fargo said. It was about fifty yards to their left. "I'm sure I could start it up."

"Good idea," Josh responded eagerly, torn between departing and going back to search for Chelsea. "All of you go. Pull in at the first dock and call Lieutenant Carbolo at his home if he's not on duty."

Cindy pulled at his arm. "Why can't you take care of it yourself?" She caught him avoiding her gaze. Her eyes widened. "You're not going back!"

"Damn right he isn't." A flashlight focused on Josh and a voice shot out from behind a hedge of hibiscus. "None of you are."

A dark figure stood up and walked toward them. Two armed backup men followed menacingly. "Calvin Rodgers," Fran muttered disgustedly, recognizing the voice.

"Quite right. Did you believe for one moment we dispensed with your services?"

"Damn!" Josh burst out. "What next?"

"We're about to take a sail—out to sea again, to complete what should have been done at the outset."

"What for?" Josh said. "Your house is crumbling. It's merely a matter of time before . . ."

"Novick, you've won a battle, not a war. You're a thorn that should have been plucked at an earlier date. A cruiser will be tying up in five minutes. You're all to board. Quietly, I hope, for your sakes."

Fran stepped forward brazenly. "Or what? You kill us here?"

"Yes, if you resist." He lifted his head. The twin engines of a boat could be heard.

"What about Jason?" Fran asked. "Is he with you on this?"

"Jason?" Rodgers sniffed. "Jason's a rebel, to be reckoned with later, at a more convenient—"

Rodgers suddenly gasped, fell forward to his knees, and then collapsed. His two henchmen also dropped in their tracks. Josh and the women stood dumbfounded as Alex and the Brenner brothers suddenly appeared.

Ellie pushed past Josh and searched their blackened faces. "Where's my husband? Why isn't he with—"

"Coming up, Ellie," Chelsea said. He strode into view with Jason and Ward. He leaned toward Alex, whispering, "Check their necks to see whether the karate chops damaged the implants." He moved quickly to take Ellie's hand, and then embraced her.

Neither said anything for a few seconds. Ellie spoke first. "We heard explosions. Does that mean it's over?" She waved a hand toward the three fallen men being examined by Alex. "Or will there be more of this?" Her voice quivered. "Joe, there's a limit to what I can take. You have to find a way of walking away from this. I'm retired—I want you to join me."

He silenced her by kissing her on the lips, then said, "We've accomplished more this day than we dreamed of. It's at least the beginning of an end."

Josh and Cindy, overhearing, moved to join them. "What end, Joe?" Josh asked. "What's our position now?"

Ward and Mae Warren took no notice of them. Dave had pulled her aside, so that they stood apart from the others. He was acutely aware of her attitude, one of abandonment, of giving him up. "Mae, don't do it. Don't think it. If you're going to continually be fretting about me, then I say, marry me."

She said nothing. Once before he had proposed—sort of. She hadn't taken him seriously then—and now? "Are you truly finished with these witless games?"

"Yes, after the cleanup it will be just you and me and our boat."

"Cleanup?"

He nodded soberly. "Yes, it can't be left in limbo." He looked toward the Brenners. "They have friends—talented friends, I might add—who will try to accomplish what's beyond our own capabilities. Chelsea's finally reached that conclusion and is accepting it."

Mae gave him a long look. "Are you certain you're leaving it for others to complete?"

He crossed his heart. "After the cleanup here—yes."

Out of the corner of his eye he saw Alex interrupt Chelsea and Ellie. "Both men," Alex said, "have been successfully incapacitated. In the manner you suggested. And as you predicted, like the others injured in a similar way, omitting Rodgers, they will have lost past memory and will take orders from the closest source."

Chelsea nodded. "Well done, Alex." The younger man's eyes glittered.

As Alex left, Ellie said, "What was he talking about?

What others?" Chelsea told her about the men who had been captured and tied to the outer fence of the grounds. Rudy Carbolo had been notified of their location, via Noah Brenner's cellular phone. He made light of it by adding, "The Brenners seem to carry equipment for any and all occasions."

Ellie searched his face, noted the grime, the weariness, the eyes dark, the spark missing. "What is it, Joe? What haven't you told me? What incapacitation?"

Chelsea couldn't halt the sigh. "The memory bank they surgically implant at the nape of the neck has a flaw, an Achilles' heel. Hit it at the right angle and it loses all contact with the brain. The injured party then becomes acquiescent, a lost soul, taking orders from anyone."

Ellie was horrified. "What happens to the individual? Can't anything be done to reverse the process?"

Chelsea shrugged. "What little I know, and with some added speculation, I would think the microchip implant could be removed and old memory bridges reconnected if they haven't been destroyed. In speaking with Seltzer, I got the impression he had various ways of working with memory. He could add to the old—as he did with Izzy Gorham—or remove it entirely for replacement. It has something to do with synaptic bridges. Don't ask for detailed explanations. I don't know enough."

"How is it possible? Memory is an illusion. You can daydream and upon wakening insist you remember it happening. How can you capture a life's memories from a brain and transfer them to a microchip?"

"You're asking me? Ask Seltzer." *Uh-oh . . .*

Ellie knew he was not telling her the whole story, holding back the details of what actually took place. "And the gunfire—the explosions? No one got hurt?"

Chelsea wiped his face again, a mechanical response to

offset the pain of reliving the killings. In his years on the force he had never once given orders to kill a suspected felon without first attempting to take him alive.

Finally he said, “Jon Seltzmann is dead; so is his father’s brain—or memory bank—whatever.” He caught her questioning look, wanting to know if he had pulled the trigger.

He turned his head, avoiding Ellie for a moment, then said, “I gave the orders. I’m responsible for any deaths. Seltzmann threatened, but had no intention of killing us unless we failed to comply with his demands.” He touched her cheek. “Ellie, the man was evil, as evil as his father ever was. Given a like circumstance, would you have spared Hitler?”

She shuddered. “What about Izzy Gorham?” Chelsea took her in his arms. “He’s okay. He still has his original memories. One of the doctors—one more friendly and concerned with Gorham—is watching over him.” His eyes peered over her shoulder and glimpsed Jason and Fran standing about three feet apart, facing each other.

Jason hesitated, unsure of himself, feeling tongue-tied. He licked parched lips, finally blurting out, “I love you, Fran.” His heart in his throat, he could say no more.

Fran looked at him coolly. “Really? What happened to your affiliation with Wellington?”

Jason took a step closer to her. “Dammit, Fran—why are you being so difficult? I almost gave my life for you.”

“For me?” she said, unable to stop riding him, for reasons she herself didn’t understand.

“It’s not me,” Jason said, struck by a sudden revelation. “It’s yourself you’re not sure of.” He moved closer to her so that their faces were only inches apart. He held her face in his hands and drew her lips to his.

Her arms went around him and he felt a teardrop on his cheek.

Pulling back abruptly, he gazed into her face. "So, it's settled then. Sealed with a kiss. I've wanted to hold you for such a long time . . ."

Moans from the other side of the path made them turn from each other.

Calvin Rodgers was struggling to his feet, rubbing the back of his head. Noah Brenner stood over him, ready for any sudden moves. Aaron Brenner stood guard over the other two men, who were still unconscious.

Chelsea moved to confront Rodgers. He helped him to stand on his own, then held his index finger a foot from Rodger's face. "Can you focus on my finger?" He received a grunt in reply.

"Okay. Then let's get something understood. It's all over. This building and its lab will soon be a total ruin. There's no one here; the rats have deserted the sinking sh—"

Everyone flinched at the sound of muffled explosions. The north wall of the building, unseen from where they stood, blew out seconds later. Amidst a great cloud of dust, spears of flame shot across the bordering tropical gardens, torching everything in their path. The stately regal palms would be giant candles in minutes.

"Everyone to the dock," Chelsea shouted above the din. As the heat from the blaze grew more intense, everyone's hands went up to protect their faces.

"Alex, give Aaron a hand with the two other prisoners," Chelsea directed. "Move," he ordered Rodgers, who was holding a hand to his mouth and nose. Rodgers smiled grimly, but not with any sense of loss, despite the growing devastation.

Turning, he caught Chelsea observing him. "It's merely a setback, Chelsea, nothing more. An impressive effort, but . . ."

Chelsea shoved him, extremely irritated. *How could the*

man insist the destruction of this place was merely a setback?

Chelsea made certain everyone was accounted for on the wooden dock. They would be safe as long as the dock didn't take fire. Fire engine sirens could already be heard in the distance. On the Waterway the lone sound was that of a retreating boat. For the moment their worst enemy was the hordes of insects escaping the jungle inferno, buzzing about the dock like a low-hanging cloud.

More annoying to Chelsea were the words "merely a setback," uttered by Rodgers. *Was the Founding Fathers Resort the key to it all?*

He swatted at his face before confronting Rodgers once again. "You said, 'setback.' Are you aware that Seltzmann is dead and that his father no longer exists in any form?"

It was slow to register on Rodgers. Initial disbelief was followed by smugness. "There are more than fifty thousand Factors in existence, worldwide. That's something that can't be altered. Others will assume leadership of them."

Factors? So that's what they called them. Rodgers interrupted Chelsea's ruminations.

"What do you think you'll do with me? What charges will you file? I'm in the employ of Wellington Security. You mention the existence of Factors, you'll be laughed out of court. All evidence of the Benefactor Alliance—an entity no one's ever heard of on American soil—will have vanished with the destruction of this base." He cocked his head arrogantly toward the blazing building. "Do you honestly believe this is all there is?"

Chelsea whipped out the Beretta and held it to Rodgers' temple. "Who said you would be charged with anything but piracy and kidnapping?" Chelsea's hand trembled; he fought the urge to squeeze the trigger, to end it once and for all.

"Joe, don't do it!" he heard Ellie cry out and then felt her hand on his shoulder.

Rodgers stood his ground, unflinching. Chelsea had to admit the man was correct in his assumption. *How could anyone prove the existence of an invisible cartel that no longer existed? At least not in any computer.*

The Brenners "friends" had to complete the job he'd started with his self-appointed squad.

Chelsea lowered the weapon. He spoke quietly. "Your Factors—so called—will be without direction from now on. Whatever their assignments, they will be carried out at their own dis—"

Josh tugged at Chelsea's elbow. "Joe, there's nothing left for us to do but get out of here. The heat and smoke are getting a bit much for all of us. What about those guys you left at the front gate? What's going to happen with them?"

Chelsea waited for Alex to take charge of Rodgers. "I gave Carbolo a condensed version of what happened and also a plausible story for him to hand the press.

"Your yacht was commandeered by pirates, who then decided to hold the passengers for ransom. Plausible enough? With help from Lieutenant Rudy Carbolo, we discovered the pirates' home base. Right here, surprisingly, in Palm Beach. The rest is history. I left it for Rudy to embellish it any way he wants."

Ward, listening, spoke impatiently. "Terrific tale. Wish I'd thought of it a couple of days earlier. It's over, Joey. What are we waiting for? There're two motor yachts, neighbors from across the Waterway, pulling up at the dock."

Chelsea turned to look back at the flames shooting out of the north side of the building, casting a wavering light over the dock and all those who stood there; an orange glow danced a jig on the Intracoastal. That's it, he thought somberly, a letdown taking hold. The beginning of the end. As Ward had said, "It's over." He had—they had—completed their part. They were not equipped to do more.

It was now up to the Brenner brothers' friends to finalize it all. Would the Alliance board members remain stranded? If not, then what?

He felt Ellie's arm take his to lead him toward the end of the dock, then pull him aside to let Jason and Fran pass. They had an arm around each other's waists.

Ellie smiled, yet Chelsea could see the worry lines bracketing her mouth as she turned to face him.

"They're settled," she said. "Are we? Is this the result you hoped for?"

"Yes—and no. In any case my role is finished. It's up to others to do what remains."

Ellie shivered despite the intense heat. "You're worried that a phoenix may rise from these ashes, aren't you?"

"Not exactly. The thought is there, but I don't believe it possible without the head—so to speak—of the bird.

"Granted there may be some people capable of carrying on with contingency plans, but only with that base in the Caribbean left untouched."

"And that's being left for some other party to take care of?" Chelsea nodded.

Shouts urged them forward to the waiting boats. Ellie tightened her grip on his arm. "In that case, Joe, your role in this is truly over—finished." He nodded once more, not without a slight reluctance.

"Then, Joe, can we go home and start our retirement again?"

EPILOGUE

THREE WEEKS LATER

Chelsea sat at his desk at Novick Security, reading a card from Fran. She and Jason were in Napoli, enjoying a pre-honeymoon, as they chose to call it. Her father's illness didn't allow for a precise wedding date.

Chelsea leaned back and placed his hands behind his head. It was odd the way things turned out. Jason and Fran; Ward and Mae Warren. Chelsea and Josh had presented Alex with a more than generous bonus, and he had agreed to stay on with the added promise of a quick promotion. As for Izzy Gorham, that irrepressible, feisty old man had returned to his former self, except for lost memories of a particular three-day span. He was still wondering why his friends were missing.

Daily calls had been made to the Brenners since the eventful night, but nothing of any consequence had happened. Chelsea sighed deeply and picked up a pencil to check out the résumés of three new applicants to replace lost employees. He studied the second of the three, and sighed again. When Josh came charging into his office, he welcomed the distraction.

Josh, grinning, threw a fax onto the desk. "Read it. It just came in from Noah Brenner. It'll probably make the early news tonight."

MYSTERIOUS EXPLOSIONS ROCK THE ISLAND PARADISE OF THE FOUNDING FATHERS ORGANIZATION IN THE CARIBBEAN. BUILDING TOTALLY DESTROYED. FORTUNATELY NO ONE IN THE BUILDING. ARSON SUSPECTED AND BEING INVESTIGATED.

"How about that!" Josh exclaimed, ecstatically pounding the desk.

His elation was short-lived. "What's the matter with you, Joe? Why are you sitting there with an unhappy face? It's what you wanted ever since you suspected that Emma Mosel was murdered."

Chelsea didn't say anything. What could he say? He took out a briar from a drawer and chewed on the stem without attempting to fill the bowl.

"It's a normal letdown. Nothing more. Winding down just takes time. It's no different from the old days when we finished with an unusually tough case.

"When are you and Cindy going shopping for a new boat? Your insurance will more than cover the cost. You need help? Ellie and I will gladly go with you."

Josh's grin was now a tentative smile. "Joe, you're something else. You knew the FBI couldn't treat the Resort problem because foreign territory is not their beat. So it bothers you that Ward had to call in some old friends from the CIA and that possibly the CIA went in with the Mossad on this latest operation."

Chelsea grimaced. Ward's government friends had taken over the case from Carbolo's office and had quietly put it on the back burner. Ward's intelligent speculation had hit home. Chelsea had been left out, dismissed as the catalyst for the whole operation. It wasn't the credit he missed. His pride was injured, having been passed over for the final action.

Josh rolled his eyes. "You're never going to grow up. Still wanting to play games. Look at the calendar. There comes a time when—"

The phone rang. Chelsea waved a quieting hand and lifted the phone. A vaguely familiar voice answered his.

It was a retired New York district attorney, formerly of Manhattan, and now living on Hutchinson Island. After some reminiscing about an old case in which both were involved, the former D.A. said, "I need your help, Chelsea. My granddaughter is missing, has been for a week."

Chelsea motioned Josh to pick up an extension. "How can I help you?"

"I need you to find her before the police or the press get onto it."

Josh shook his head negatively.

Chelsea said, "You should be calling the police. Missing Persons. I can't help you; I'm not a PI."

"Chelsea, let's not play games. I have friends down here, notably Rudy Carbolo. I know what you've accomplished. I realize I'm taking advantage of your retirement, but—"

The voice drifted off, emotionally stricken. Chelsea looked up to see Josh shaking his head vigorously. He wanted no part of it.

Chelsea spoke into the phone. "Where and when can we meet for a private talk?" Josh put down the extension and waved his hands in a futile gesture.

Chelsea merely smiled. "It's only a gumshoe job," he said.